THE TWILIGHT ZONE

REVISITED AND REVIEWED
VOLUME ONE

ANALYSIS AND CRITIQUE OF
ALL 36 EPISODES OF SEASON ONE

BOB NEARENBERG * K.J. BATTEN * LINN CARPENTER * KEN ARDIZZONE

Wasteland Press
Shelbyville, KY USA
www.wastelandpress.net

The Twilight Zone: Revisited and Reviewed (Volume I)
Analysis and Critique of All 36 Episodes of Season One
Reviews by Bob Nearenberg, K.J. Batten, Linn Carpenter
and Ken Ardizzone
Compiled by Ken Ardizzone

Copyright © 2010 Bob Nearenberg, K.J. Batten, Linn Carpenter
and Ken Ardizzone
ALL RIGHTS RESERVED

First Printing—January 2010
ISBN: 978-1-60047-396-8

Printed in the U.S.A.

TABLE OF CONTENTS

INTRODUCTIONS

By the fall of 1959, I was just a few months away from becoming a teen-ager. But I had been watching television since the early fifties when we purchased our very first tv. Kids back then were not quite as privileged to have their own tv's, music centers, and computers, the way many are today. So I basically had to watch whatever my parents chose to watch during prime time hours. Other than a few westerns, the Mickey Mouse Club and Superman, my daily tv diet had been no different than theirs throughout the fifties.

But on the dawn of a new decade, late on a Friday evening where I lived at the time, when a new science fiction series was about to debut, I was immediately interested. That my parents showed little or no interest in it and actually left the room for awhile, made it even better. For the first time ever, I was about to find an adult drama series I could call my own.

By the time a rather thin, unusual looking, slightly nervous and uncomfortable man holding a lighted cigarette in one hand came on the screen to tell me what the story that was about to unfold before my very eyes was about, well the deal was already pretty much sealed. I would never look away again.

That man was Rod Serling, a brilliant and visionary writer whose name was not totally unfamiliar to me. Serling was already famous in tv circles. He had won many awards for writing a drama for one of tv's most famous early series, "Playhouse 90" That drama was "Requiem For A Heavyweight" and would later go on to become a feature film. I had seen it in its original form since my parents encouraged me to watch adult dramas. I liked it, at least what I could understand of it at the tender age of nine. But...Rod Serling as a science fiction writer? That was news to me.

The Twilight Zone from its very inception was unusual in every way. From its eerie theme music, unusual screen graphics and especially its chain smoking creator who appeared onscreen each week to introduce individual stories, this series looked like nothing else that had come before. But it was the stories and their ability to put average everyday people in out of this world situations that made it most compelling. Combined with an uncanny ability to fool viewers time and time again with endings that clearly anyone could see coming....yet did not, The Twilight Zone, even now on the 50th anniversary of the program, stands alone at the very top of tv history.

As a young boy sitting in front of a small flickering tv screen on a Friday night in the late fifties, with my parents out of the room, when Rod Serling reached out of that screen, grabbed me and pulled me into his new creation, The Twilight Zone, I was a willing victim and I never managed to escape. Nothing has changed. I never wanted to escape and I still don't.

Bobbynear - Seattle, Wa.
January 2010

What does The Twilight Zone mean to me? I first stumbled on The Twilight Zone by sheer accident one day many years ago when I was at my father's house on a Saturday afternoon when I was in junior high. I was channel surfing and I came across a show that had a very young Robert Redford playing a policeman who just got shot and needed assistance from an elderly lady who was afraid to leave her house. This show intrigued me for two reasons, one being that I liked Robert Redford and had only known him as a movie star and not some nobody actor appearing on an old black and white TV show and two, the story got my attention immediately in getting an introduction to the story I was about to watch from Rod Serling who I had never heard much about before.

The story had me hooked and I was delighted to get a second story as well as a follow up. Back in the seventies, we had a local station here that aired a full hour of The Twilight Zone on Saturday afternoons at four o'clock and I tuned in as often as I could remember that it was on. I only had to watch it one time though to realize that this was a fabulous show and I got to see many people on there before they were stars which made it all the more fun to watch.

Before my wonderful husband gave me the entire series for Christmas, I used to watch the marathons that the Sci Fi Channel would do as often as I could and looking at it from the perspective of an adult versus a young teenager, I enjoy it every bit as much as I did back then but I also have more appreciation for the show. Rod Serling made that show when television as a medium was in its infancy and special effects were few and far between without the benefit of computers as producers have now.

Back then the story alone had to carry the show and Rod Serling delivered in my opinion almost every time. I have not seen all of the episodes but I have seen at least three quarters of them and I look forward to reviewing them all and getting to see many for the first time.

It's a pity that Rod Serling died as young as he was because he was truly a brilliant story teller and with the technology that is available in today's world it is a loss to think what we might have seen from Rod Serling had he not left us so soon. I have many times said that if I were to pick a show where television was at its finest hour, then my vote would go to The Twilight Zone.

However I will reserve my opinion on whether it's the best show ever to hit the airwaves after we finish reviewing all of the episodes. As I said I have not seen all of them and it may very well be that the Sci Fi Channel has only shown the good ones.

We shall see. The Twilight Zone has been resurrected in a successful movie back in the eighties and it's been resuscitated as a weekly series twice since then as well. In all cases they presented good stories but since Rod Serling wasn't there for any of them, that special charm that he had in introducing the episodes was gone.   However, they do say imitation in the sincerest form of flattery, so to Rod Serling I say well done and your show has left its mark on many people for the past five decades and it will for generations to come. Let the reviews begin!

Kitty - Seattle, Wa.
January 2010

I was born on January 2, 1959. That was the year when the greatest event, in my opinion, dawned on the world of television - The Twilight Zone. Well, too bad for me. I was just a baby. However, my brother was six years old with a passion for comic books and sci-fi TV shows. He remembers watching The Twilight Zone when it first aired. He may not have understood every tale being told, but my brother was and is a pretty smart guy to this day. I only remember watching the last season when I was about five years old. I know that's young, but somehow, I managed to be captivated by the shows and sort of knew what they were about. Yes, even at the age of five. None of that matters, though. What matters is that I never forgot the series, and throughout my life I have watched these episodes over and over and over again almost as if I were watching them from the first broadcasts. It always seems that way. It seems like the series never ended every time I watch a Twilight Zone marathon or watch my Twilight Zone DVDs. I can't really explain the impact that this television show and the genius known as Rod Serling have made on my life other than to say that I relate many things in my every day life to Twilight Zone episodes. I can honestly say I've watched many of these episodes over 70 times.

When I'm having a particularly bad day, I think of the man in the episode called "Willoughby" and how he just wanted to throw away his rat race life and live a more simple and uncomplicated life in a small, quaint town.

Then there is the unforgettable episode called "Time Enough At Last" which makes me realize that everyone has a passion in life and you have to accept people for who they are or you have no human compassion.

There is also the episode called "What You Need" in which a man who was given gifts by a peddler was not satisfied enough and wanted so much more until he brought his own death upon himself. That moral. Be thankful for what you have. If you get more, just be grateful because you may not live to see tomorrow.

There were so many morals and underlying messages in The Twilight Zone episodes. Yet, some were just meant to amuse, confuse and enthuse us. That they did. To this day, no other television series compares to Rod Serling's Twilight Zone, and I doubt anything ever will. I have no problem with that. I'll never get tired of watching them. Just make sure the next time you get onto a plane, check what's on the menu and make certain you're not the main course as happened in "To Serve Man". However, these days, you're lucky to get a beverage on a flight so I suppose none of us have to really worry about that...unless, we're flying first class...but then, don't look out the window...you never know what or who you'll see on the wing. Long live Rod Serling and the Zone.

Linn - Norristown, Pa.
January 2010

As a little boy coming home from school in 1960's, I could not wait to turn on the television and watch my favorite programs. One show was a must see. It was 'The Twilight Zone.' I am a big science fiction fan. But there is something unique and distinctive about this series. It is downright eerie.

Not only are many episodes fearful and frightening, they are ominous, inspiring, spooky, weird, bizarre, and odd. After watching you feel uneasy. But most of all they are filled with a mystery which most of the time cannot be solved.

Rod Serling and the executive producers did an outstanding job of screenwriting to almost bring this show to real life. Quite frankly, as a little kid I thought these strange events would happen to me. The series also did remarkable and memorable casting of prominent actors to play their roles. William Shanter, Telly Savalas, Burgess Meredith, Billy Mumy, Roddy McDowall, Susan Oliver, Vera Miles, Elizabeth Montgomery, Agnes Moorhead, just to name a few.

I have many 'best-liked' which I have seen over and over again. Anytime there is a Twilight Zone marathon on tv I tune in to watch. I feel the need to re-visit and re-enter the 'Zone.' One of the all-time classics in my viewing has to be 'Mirror Image.' A parallel world has slipped into our world. As a result there is a duplicate that resembles you. Brilliant writing and creepy on every level.

'Time Enough at Last.' A man who loves books survives a nuclear blast. 'The Hitch-Hiker.' I love that passing line-"Going My Way."

Anybody for a plane ride. How about 'Nightmare at 20,000 Feet.' Lookout for monsters on the wing.

'To Serve Man.' Want a free ride to another planet?

And of course who can forget 'Living Doll.' Better be nice to Tina. I could go on and on with stories in this series that are etched into my memory. No doubt my ratings will be favorable to say the least. I look forward to a complete and thorough review of every episode in this new Yahoo discussion group. It will be my pleasure to explore this element again. Be sure to check the Sign Posts ahead.

Ken - Vista, Ca.
January 2010

"The Twilight Zone" Episode 1: "Where is Everybody?"

Original Air Date- October 2,1959
Guest Star: Earl Holliman
Written by Rod Serling
Directed by Robert Stevens

Review by Kitty

It's so exciting to start this new group about one of the best TV shows ever! The year is 1959. Baby Boomers are starting to enter their teens, television classic comedies like I Love Lucy are in their prime, Communism is feared by a lot of people as the USSR now has the bomb, people are building bomb shelters but, on a new frontier the space age is beginning, the Mercury Astronaut program is in its infancy and....America likes Ike!

And one night in 1959, a quirky new show debuts on CBS that's quite different. There is no sitcom family here. In the first scene we see a lonely man whose name will later be revealed as Mike, walking towards a diner. He walks in and tells whoever that there is a customer. He gets no response. He pours himself a cup of coffee and announces he has $2.85 in American money and wants eggs over easy with hash browns. What a concept, breakfast for less than $2.85. Oh those were the days! We also see something of significance as well which is a clock that's broken and shows that time stopped at a quarter after six. Mike concludes that he's got amnesia as he's not sure who he is but he realizes with the money that he's American.

He gets no response and begins to wonder if he's dreaming and why doesn't he wake up? We then see him later walk towards the town. The town by all appearances seems to be like any small town of that era. There's just one problem, nobody is walking around. He hears church bells. Yet, there is nobody it seems to be had. He walks down the street and looks in a bookstore and bakery. The doors are open but nobody is there.

He finally appears to see someone sitting in a truck. It's a lady. The camera work here is very good as we initially only see the lady from afar and then as Mike gets closer we only see his back. He begins to ask her questions but there is no response. He's trying to explain that he can't remember who he is and he needs help.

As he walks to the truck and opens the door a woman does not fall out but a mannequin who looks like a woman falls to the ground. Mike makes a bit of a joke of it but then resumes his search. We see him look in the building and see yet other mannequins.

He hears a phone ringing in a phone booth but when he answers it, nobody is there. He then attempts to call the operator and gets nothing but a recording. He realizes about this time that perhaps he's being watched. The camera work here is also very good as we see the town panned from the inside of the phone booth which is clearly giving us Mike's viewpoint.

He then attempts to exit the phone booth and has a good deal of trouble as he appears to have forgotten how to exit a phone booth. He finally exits and makes his way to the drugstore.

He enters the drugstore and we see something that's obsolete for the most part in this day and age. We see a drugstore with an ice cream parlor in it. He walks up to counter and gets himself a dish of ice cream with sprinkles on it and begins to talk to himself. I found this a very interesting conversation. He quotes Ebenezer Scrooge in a Christmas Carol which is truly one of my all time favorite stories and subsequent movies that have been made but he tells himself that there's more of gravy than of grave about you and that he's just last nights dinner and he's ready to wake up. I found the scene so well done that I wondered if when Earl Holliman filmed this if he actually was looking at a mirror talking to himself or if Rod Serling simply filmed it to make it look like he was talking to a mirror as the image talking back to himself seemed very real.

Mike then walks over and looks at books and concludes that if he's dreaming this is truly the most detailed dream he's ever had. The pinnacle of this scene is when he comes to a rack of books that are all the same. The books all say, The Last Man on Earth. Interestingly enough there was eventually a movie made by that same title in 1964, starring Vincent Price, I wonder if Rod Serling knew something was in the works?

The title is very poignant though as by all accounts he seems to be the last man on earth although as he ponders whether or not we've been bombed he realizes that can't be possible because the town is still there.

He then runs to the movie theater and sees that it's a movie about the Air Force and he realizes that he's in the Air Force. He runs and sees nobody. He runs up to the projection booth and he sees nobody there. We then see another interesting pan of the projection booth to give us yet another view from Mike's perspective. Mike proceeds to run out of the movie theater only to run in to himself in a mirror. That was a very chilling effect. It symbolized I think the total helplessness and confusion that Mike was experiencing.

We then see him as night is falling and he is playing tic tac toe in the sand. As the lights to the town automatically come on he finally loses it completely and hits the street button for the cross signal and screams for help.

We finally see a man who is not actually in a deserted town but in a simulator being observed by several military men. He's pushing a button and the clock in the simulator is stopped at a quarter after six. The Col orders him to be let out and he then explains to everybody that he was in a simulator for over 400 hours to see if a human being could be alone for that long because that's how long they predicted it would take to go to the moon and back and make some orbits around it.

The press comes in and they ask if this test was a failure and he tells them no. He'd like to see how long anyone would last in that box with no human companionship.

He walks to Mike and asks him how he is. Mike asks if he failed and he's told no. The doctor tells him that while they can pump in air and supply food they haven't yet been able to come up with a substitution for someone to talk to. Mike asks the Col if next time it will be real and he's told yes.

The last thing we see is Mike telling the moon to stay right there because we're coming.

Since I was not around in 1959, I can't speak for how prominently it was being discussed for a man to go to the moon.

The Mercury program was just getting started so it was more on the minds of people to get someone in to space I think but, Rod Serling who wrote this story was a visionary. I don't know if he read anything about the training that the astronauts were subjected to but, if anyone has seen the movie The Right Stuff, you know that being in a dark small room in isolation was part of the test to see if they could handle flying solo in a rocket for any length of time.

We all know that when we finally went to the moon it was in teams of three so the loneliness factor wasn't an issue, not even for Michael Collins who had to stay orbiting the moon while Neil Armstrong and Buzz Alderin went to the surface. I recently saw an interview with him and he said he had no time to be lonely when he was orbiting by himself. He said that when he didn't take a sleep break he had Houston in his ear practically all the time and he had a lot things to do so loneliness was not really ever an issue.

However, Rod Serling had no way of knowing that and I would imagine that most people probably would imagine that space flight would be a lonely expedition, but the fact that Rod Serling tackled an idea like this was I think very visionary on his part.

I think this episode is inspiring simply because Serling tackles a subject that we were just delving in to as a nation which is space exploration and when people looked up at the moon in 1959 how many people realistically thought that just ten years from then we would be there walking on it?

Earl Holliman's last line is priceless when he tells the moon to just stay there because we're coming. Many of the Twilight Zone episodes end with sad endings or dark endings but I find this ending positive and uplifting because if I were watching this show for the first time in 1959, I'd find myself saying that maybe someday we really will get there and it won't be in the Twilight Zone, it will be for real.

My rating on this episode is 5 for classic because Rod Serling for his pilot episode chose a subject that truly was real at that time and it was a subject that looks to the future in a positive way.

Review by Bobbynear

The Twilight Zone gets a fast start out of the box with a cautionary tale of being careful what you ask for. In an increasingly crowded and noisy world, who among us has not wanted just a moment of privacy, a chance to be alone with our thoughts, an escape from the cacophony of everyday living?

As the very first Twilight Zone begins, with "Where Is Everybody", we get a first glimpse of a theme that will be repeated many times over the next five years. We have a very ordinary looking man in what appears to be a very ordinary situation, except that something is not quite normal.

The man, wearing what appears to be some sort of military jumpsuit wanders out of the woods and slowly walks towards a town square. Something is odd alright. No people, no noise, no kids in the street, no business being conducted. Where is everybody indeed. Is everyone dead? There are no bodies anywhere......... Has the place been evacuated? Why?

As he wanders around, the first place he goes to is a cafe where he ends up serving himself. The coffee is hot but the atmosphere is cold with no living thing in sight. He's got around three dollars but no waitress to take it from him. From there he wanders the streets and continues to find nobody in any store conducting business of any kind. Suddenly he spots a woman sitting in a car and runs towards her. Wouldn't you know it? She's not terribly responsive or friendly either, for good reason, she's a department store mannequin.

They do have a rather brief but one-sided conversation that also gains the man nothing. And then suddenly, a ringing sound coming from a phone booth, the kind of phone booth you can't even find these days, much less get a call on it. He runs over to it and there is a voice on the other end. Only it turns out just to be the operator who quickly informs him that this is just a recording.

There is a special visual moment at this point that I really enjoyed. The camera, acting as the man's eyes begins to revolve slowly taking in the entire landscape, the utter desolation of a place with no life. Everywhere he looks, we look and the effect is downright creepy. Then as if things aren't bad enough, the man gets trapped briefly in the booth Apparently nobody ever told him you need to pull on the door not push on it......

Eventually he does escape and his next stop is the local police station where this time there is a lighted cigar in an ashtray but nobody to smoke it, and oh yes....no prisoners in the cells either. From there to a local drugstore where the man finally gets to have a conversation with a living being....himself as he talks to his own image in a mirror. He does however get to have what appears to be a very appealing ice cream sundae. And then there is that circular rack of paperback books in a corner of the store. They seem to believe in stocking only one title and it doesn't make him feel any more secure when he sees the titles, "The Last Man On Earth......"

Eventually the day descends into darkness and the lights in the town come on, including a movie marquee which indicates a feature film titled, "Battle Hymn" with Rock Hudson. It's at this point that the man at last remembers something....that he's in the Air Force. A little optimistic at last, he runs into the theatre but nothing changes. Lots of seats but no bodies in them....the movie is running somehow but there is no projectionist to run the show.

Eventually he cracks under the strain as anyone would. Running wildly through the town, he eventually stops at a street light where he repeatedly pushes the button that changes the light while begging for help, "Please somebody help me! Help me, help me, help me!!! Somebody's looking at me. Somebody's watching me!"

As he continues to push the button at the crosswalk, the scene dissolves finally into some actual living persons. We see a group of what appear to be military officers sitting calmly while watching a man completely lose his mind. Are they some sort of sadists? Is this entertainment of some kind for them? Nobody seems too concerned.

Eventually we learn that this has all been an endurance test. An Air Force pilot taking part in an experiment to see if a human can tolerate the loneliness he will experience on a long space flight to the moon and back. The final explanation of all this is given by an Air Force officer and fiction instantly turns into fact at the dawn of the space age in America.

There is much to recommend about this pilot episode. Earl Holliman turns in a terrific performance. Forced to act alone with nobody to play off of, he is always convincing. Four decades later, Tom Hanks would find himself in similar circumstances in "Cast Away" as he gets stranded on a deserted island after a plane crash. The difference though is that at least Hanks knew who he was and where he was and what he needed to do. Plus unlike this poor man, Hanks had the company of a volleyball that he could paint a face on and talk to in moments of extreme loneliness.

Science fiction often turns later into science fact, but not in this instance. Writer Rod Serling had no way of knowing that when we did eventually get to the moon, it would be a crew of men, not just one and there would be so much to do, being lonely would never be an issue. Still though at this point in time, during the early days of the space program, single solitary men were being launched into space in tiny space capsules that could barely hold one person. The difference was however that the flights were extremely short in duration.

This initial episode sets the stage for what is to come. There is always a sense of fear and creepiness that seeps right through the tv screen whenever The Twilight Zone is on. As I stated back in my introduction earlier on this board, I did indeed see this episode the very first time it aired back in 1959. I was twelve years old at the time, and on that Friday night at 10 P.M. Eastern time, both my mother and father, neither having any interest in science fiction left me alone for one of those rare times in our living room sitting in front of an early black and white version of tv.

The flickering images coming off of that tv for thirty minutes would literally change my life and how I would perceive the world around me, when I became a teenager just six months later. This would quickly become my tv series. I discovered it....... As far as I was concerned I was the only person in the world, and at least I had this to keep me company.

Like any child so young, I often wanted my parents to just go away and leave me alone. After sitting through this harrowing episode, for the first time ever, I was actually glad when they came back into the room after it was over.

Up until this point, I had no idea what this place called The Twilight Zone was.

It would be the last time I would ever say that.
My rating on a scale of 5 to 0
5 ~~~ CLASSIC

Review by Linn

This episode is intriguing and disturbing at the same time. Wow. It really gets to you. Imagine walking into a town and not seeing a single person or hearing a single sound other than your own voice. When he served himself food and drink and nobody spoke to him or even came out from anywhere to serve him or take his money, it was chilling. Who made that coffee? Who kept the ice cream cold? Who drove that car that the mannequin was in?

The car with the mannequin was probably the most chilling scene of all. He finally thought he had found a real person......and then.... nothing. Just a piece of plastic. Can you imagine? I sure can't. A nightmare? For sure. Who would want to live through it?

Earl Holliman was phenomenal in that role. He was virtually a nobody back then who rose to a somebody later on.

This Zone is definitely a keeper and a classic.

Review by Ken

The pilot episode of any series is crucial and significant. Can you hook the viewing audience with your show?

A lonely man walking on a dirt road and enters a deserted town. He is strolling along with no worries. He checks out the cafe and pours himself a cup of coffee. He hears the church bells. He surveys the town. But there is a problem. 'Where is everybody?' Are people hiding?

I can't think of a better way to begin a new series. A clean-cut average typical guy walking around town looking for someone to talk too. But he can't find anybody.

This opening story immediately stirred my curiosity. I imagined myself in this guy's shoes. What would I do? Excellent casting by the producers having Earl Holliman in the lead role. His facial expressions were calm one minute and filled with anxiety the next.

As the story unfolded I had no idea what to expect next. I liked that scene where he runs into the mirror and shatters it. The creepy music score also set the tone. Night time comes and this guy is completely baffled and perplexed. Brilliant writing.

The end scenes explains that this guy is a test case for a mission to the moon. We are all relieved that he is okay now. A little letdown for me but hey this is the first episode. I like the show.

As far as rating this story? Was it well written? Yes. Did they cast the right actor to play the character? Yes. The production and directing were superb. I will go with my feeling the first time I saw this episode. It made me feel lonely. Solitary is a nightmare. Isolation is depressing. How would I react to being the last man on earth? I have no idea.

The series is off to a great start. My rating: 5 ~~ Classic

"The Twilight Zone"   Episode 2: "One For The Angels"

Original Air Date- October 9, 1959
Guest Stars- Ed Wynn   Murray Hamilton
Written by Rod Serling
Directed by Robert Parrish

Review by Kitty

This second episode is called One for the Angels. It starts out innocently enough. You see an older man by the name of Louis Bookman standing in front of a building giving a sales pitch on things he has to sell in his very over-sized suitcase.

In the background we see a man in a dark suit taking careful notes. Rod Serling comes on and gives a narration that Louis Bookman a man who is in his sixties will be pursued by death. The camera zooms in on the man in black and he looks at the camera in a foreboding way.

We then see Lou start to walk away but he does notice the man in black as he walks back to his home. On his way, he is greeted by a young girl named Maggie who is obviously a favorite of his. All of the kids surround him and it's apparent that he's popular with them. He gives toys to a couple of them and invites them all for ice cream later.

When he gets in to his apartment he sees the man in black who proceeds to give him the details of his life such as when he was born, who is parents were and his current occupation as a pitchman.

The little girl Maggie comes in to see him to tell him the toy he gave her isn't working right. Lou shows her what she's doing wrong and he continues to talk to the man in black. Maggie asks him who he's talking to and Lou asks her if she sees the man in the corner. She tells him no.

The man tells Lou that she can't see him and that only people who have an appointment with him can. Maggie leaves thinking that Lou is playing a game with her.

The man finally explains to Lou that he's Death and that Lou is scheduled to die in his sleep at midnight. Lou doesn't want to go. Death tells him he doesn't have much choice. They can only grant an extension due to extenuating circumstances. Besides he's lucky because he's got warning. People who get in unexpected accidents get no warning.

Lou asks what the extenuating circumstances are. Death tells him that the first being that there would be undue financial hardship on the family. Lou doesn't have a family. The second being that a person has to be on the brink of an amazing discovery that will help mankind. Looking at the table of toys, Lou doesn't fall in that category either. The third one is unfinished business.

Lou tells him that he fits that category. He tells him first that he's never flown in a helicopter and Death tells him that's not acceptable. He then tells him that he's always wanted to make a big sales pitch. He wants to make a pitch where everybody will want to buy what he's got. It would be a like a pitch for the angels.

Death thinks it over and he decides that Lou has a good point. So he grants him the extension but then realizes Lou has no intention of making a sales pitch any time soon. Death tells him that he's made a mistake and that there will be terrible consequences.

Lou doesn't believe him until he hears a car hitting someone outside and everybody is screaming. Lou runs out and it's little Maggie on the street. She's been hit by a car. Lou tells the driver to call a doctor.

Maggie briefly comes to and then a dark shadow passes over her and she asks Lou who the man standing on the steps is. He walks to the man and tells him not to take Maggie. He tells him that it's too late. He has to take someone at midnight.

The doctor comes by and tells Lou that they don't know if she'll pull through or not. He tells him that they'll know by midnight.

It's quarter to twelve and Death arrives. He tells Lou that he has to go in to Maggie's room at midnight. Lou sets up his suitcase and tells him he's going to make a pitch. Death asks him why there's nobody around. Lou tells him you're here, you never know what might appeal to you.

Lou begins his pitch and while Death is initially uninterested, Lou manages to make everything he's got look interesting enough to make Death want to buy his goods. It's a few minutes before midnight now and Lou makes his final pitch that he'll offer himself for services to Death and be his right hand man and it's at quite a bargain.

At that moment, the clock strikes midnight and Death realizes that he's been distracted by Lou so he missed his appointment and little Maggie is now going to be all right.

Death is rather disappointed but he realizes that Lou made his one pitch for the angels and he's now ready to go. Death tells him after you. They start to walk but then Lou stops and says wait a minute. He walks back to get his suitcase. He tells him that you never know, somebody up there might need something. He then says it is up there isn't it?

Death tells him that yes it is up there and yes he made it. They walk down the street together like a couple of good friends.

Lou in this story was played by Ed Wynn and I've always found him a likable guy. Who couldn't like Lou in this story. He's truly an every guy and everybody appears to like him. Who can't relate to a person who doesn't want to cash in their chips particularly if he doesn't even feel sick?

Death is an interesting guy here. I liked how he appeared in a suit. He clearly is supposed to be the Grim Reaper but he certainly doesn't look like the way we normally see the Grim Reaper. He's portrayed more like simply a businessman doing his job.

I actually felt empathy for both Lou and Death. The story also brings up another interesting point. In this case Lou doesn't have a family but it's evident he's seen kind as a surrogate grandfather to the kids around him and it's obvious that he and Maggie have a special relationship. She's the only child who approaches him and gives him a hug.

This story goes in to a real basic feeling that many older people might feel when they lose say a child or grandchild. The feeling is always why couldn't it have been me instead of my child or grandchild? In this case Lou actually gets to make that change.

Overall, I found the story very endearing and sweet. We don't see a lot of Lou with Maggie but what little we see, it's clearly a genuine friendship that runs deep especially on the part of Lou. Ed

Wynn who's probably one of the most non-threatening looking people in Hollywood, plays the part to perfection.

While I would not rate this episode as a classic. I will give it a four rating for excellent. As I said I felt empathy for all of the characters involved and in the end I was glad to see that Lou had done the right thing in distracting Death long enough so that Maggie could live and hopefully have a long, happy life and Lou got rewarded for his sacrifice by going to Heaven.

Review by Ken

Very odd, strange, and unusual story at no. 2 in this show. I feel the placement of episodes is key to developing your television series and promoting it. Come out the gate(so to speak) with the best of what you have. Ep. 1 hit a home run out of the park. The following episodes should continue with unforgettable classics. Hook the audience and reel them in from the start. 'One For The Angels' is badly misplaced and should be used later in season one. I almost fell asleep watching this unconventional drama.

The Grim Reaper dressed in a clean suit and tie? What? I thought he is a mean Skelton. He has come to inform Mr. Bookman that his time is up. He is scheduled to die and if he comes along peacefully everything will be all right. Bookman wants one last 'Pitch' for the ages. He refuses to go. The Reaper decides to take Maggie. Why?? Does he not want Bookman. Anyway the Reaper is tricked by Bookman and Maggie is saved. Reaper and Bookman walk off into the night. Sorry Guys, dull, boring, and humdrum for me.

First of all this show should be careful about having stories about people being saved in life and death situations. Bookman is a hero for saving the little girl's life. Okay he trades his life for Maggie's. We all feel good as he walks away with Reaper in the end. But excuse me. This show is about another dimension away from time and space. I tune into this show for the unusual, extraordinary, and unfamiliar. If I want to see someone save a girl's life I can tune in and watch 'Superman.'

I first saw this episode back in the early 1990's while on vacation in a motel room. There was a Thanksgiving marathon on and our family watched together late into the rainy night. We had seen many frightful and scary episodes that night and had to keep watching. When 'One For The Angels' came on we were all disappointed. My young kids wanted the scary episodes to come on. I told my kids to look at the main premise of each story and try to figure out the main points. Ed Wynn kept reminding me of that character he played in the movie 'Mary Poppins'. He was that comic professor who kept rising to the ceiling every time he told a joke.

I told my family that The Twilight Zone has many themes and topics which are out of the ordinary. I believe Rod Serling wanted to cover many subject matters in a twisted way. Here in Ep. 2 he wanted to portray and depict death as a casual thing. Sorry Rod I am not buying it. Even my kids complained and whined about this one.

It is watch able but barely.

My rating - 1 POOR

Review by Bobbynear

There certainly was an opportunity here to make a touching story about a kindly old man and the neighborhood children who adored him and his efforts to stay alive as long as possible. Too bad it never quite came together the way I was hoping it would.

This story just doesn't make a whole lot of sense. For one thing, I have to agree with Ken that Mr. Death trying to take the life of the little girl doesn't add up. At first he tells Lou that he's got to go because it simply is his time. Then when Lou refuses.... Death decides to take the life of a small child. Why? To teach Lou a lesson? Is it really Lou's time or does Death just need to fill his quota for the day?

I generally do not like when fictional characters are set up to act one way and then out of nowhere they change for no reason. This is a good example. At first Mr. Death is all business....he tells Lou it's time....no excuses....that's it....unless there is some extenuating circumstance. So magically Lou comes up with one and Death buys into it. Lou has to make one more pitch for the angels? He's had an entire lifetime and he waits till now? So he can sell more of those incredibly ugly ties and wind up robots?

And then there is the scene where Death is totally fooled while sitting on the steps and buying every piece of junk that Lou sells him and forgetting it's almost midnight. I mean....if Death is this much of a pushover....then it's a miracle everybody ever born isn't still alive. At first he's coldly efficient and now he's this easy to fool? I don't think so.

And lastly....Lou ends up being a hero by saving the little girls' life. Well excuse me....but if Lou had agreed to go at the beginning... she never would have been hit by that car....her life would never have been on the line in the first place and Lou wouldn't need to give up his own to save her... In the end it all proves nothing. Lou gets to go to Heaven for saving the life of a child that he put in jeopardy in the first place.

The whole thing is just too weak to appear this early in this series. And I agree with Ken that you really need to start with your very best...not this. However...this is just the beginning of a multi-episode arc that nearly sinks the series before it even is seen by most of the country. Compared to the next two episodes, this is practically a classic. What's coming up is just about the worst tv has ever offered.

Two boring and pointless stories that give not a clue at the tv history that is to come. Thankfully a couple of all time classics are just down the road. You would never know it, but Rod Serling is about to make tv history in spite of what is coming. Thank goodness CBS let him get there.

I don't dislike 'Angels" nearly as much as Ken does. In fact I think it is still a gentle and sweet story in many ways. It just could have been and should have been better.

My rating on a scale of 0 to 5   3 ~~ Good

Review by Linn

I love this episode for it's acting and storyline as well as the various aspects of it such as a caring old man who loves children, especially one child so much, that even though he doesn't want to die he would gladly give his life for that little girl. He had one plan that started with him agreeing to give his "pitch for the angels" to Mr. Death in exchange for a longer life, and then cleverly planned to put that pitch off for a long time. He then changed his plan because his heart was too big and too kind to let a little girl die in his place. He knew he was an old man even though he was healthy, but he also knew that the little girl, Maggie, had her whole life ahead of her. She was only eight years old.

Mr. Death knew that Lou was going to try to get around their deal so he decided to take Maggie in order to make his quota of lives taken. If Lou had known this was going to happen, I'm sure he would have gladly gone.

Watching Mr. Death sitting so smugly on the steps before midnight ready to take Maggie's life in Lou's place made you think that this guy could not be swayed or distracted, but Lou was so convincing and so determined to make that pitch that he blew Mr. Death away. I remember Lou telling him about the special silk spools of thread that were specially made from some sort of birds and were very rare. Mr. Death had beads of sweat on his head as he listened intently to Lou's pitches, and when he talked about the thread, Death said excitedly, "I'll take all you've got!"

When the clock struck midnight, Death knew he had been taken over. That's when the little girl's life was spared and Lou made his biggest sacrifice. However, he was going to go to heaven. A classic, well, maybe not, but a really good one that I also enjoy watching over and over again prompts me to give it a rating of 4. Very good episode and very touching in my opinion. It may not be as scary as most others, but you are on edge till the very end waiting to see if Death or Lou wins the battle. Lou won. I really love this episode.

"The Twilight Zone" Episode 3: "Mr. Denton on Doomsday"

Original Air Date-October 16, 1959
Guest Star- Dan Duryea
Written by Rod Serling
Directed by Allen Reisner

Review by Kitty

This next episode is called Mr. Denton on Doomsday. One of the more endearing aspects of The Twilight Zone that I can think of is that Rod Serling wrote his stories all over the map. Some times they were present day. Some times they were in the future and some times they were in the past as this episode takes us back to the old west.

In this episode we see a drunk coming out of a saloon in probably Anywhere USA in the 1800's and a town bully by the name of Hotaling, played by a very young Martin Landau is demanding that this man whom he calls Rummy to sing and they'll give him something to drink.

The drunken man staggers to his feet and he gives them what they want and he proceeds to sing a song called How Dry I Am. In the background we see a peddler arriving in to town observing all of it. We also see inside the saloon and a saloon woman by the name of Liz is asking Charlie to make them stop bothering Al.

Charlie concurs that he can't do anything about it. Al finishes singing and Hotaling breaks the bottle and throws it to the ground making Al gravel for the last bit of booze that's in there. He then proceeds to pass out. The peddler looks on and smiles slightly.

We then see a gun materialize next to Al. Al wakes up and sees the gun and picks it up. Liz comes out and asks him if he's packing a gun again and Al explains that he simply found the gun. Al then explains that he used to be a very good gunslinger in his younger days. Liz asks what happened and he tells her he can't remember.

At this point Hotaling comes out again and tells him he'll buy him a drink inside if he sings again. Liz tells him not to do it, she can give him a drink and he doesn't have to sing. Al complies anyway and sings. Hotaling tells him to go inside and as Al walks in, he notices that Al has a gun.

Hotaling wants to challenge him to a simple contest of who can draw faster. Al doesn't want to do it. Hotaling tells him he'll even do it left handed. Al is waving the gun and says he doesn't want to do it but then he accidentally shoots Hotaling in the hand. The peddler smiles.

Everybody is impressed with Al at this point and the bartender Charlie offers to buy him a drink. They go inside and Hotaling challenges him in the bar. Al doesn't want any part of it but when he takes out his gun, he inadvertently shoots the light in the bar and it falls on Hotaling and knocks him down. The peddler looking in the saloon smiles again.

Another man approaches Al and asks him if he can buy him a drink and he addresses him as Mr. Denton. Al tells him he's had enough to drink and as he walks away, he tells Hotaling that he is to stop calling him Rummy.

Al goes out to get a shave and Liz follows him. Al tells her it will start all over again. She asks him what will start over. He tells her that he was the fastest gunman in these parts and every day someone would ride in to town to challenge him and he'd kill them all. The last time it happened the challenger was only sixteen and he shot him. He started drinking more and more and gave up his gun.

He goes in to get a shave and that night some men come to see him and tell him that the next day a man by the name of Pete Grant will be in town to challenge him. Al wants no part of it but agrees. He tries to shoot but can't hit anything. As he's packing his things to leave, he sees the peddler again.

He goes down to see him and tells the peddler that he doesn't need anything. The peddler introduces himself as Henry J. Fate. He tells him he peddles pretty much everything including potions. He gives Al the potion and tells him one drink will guaranty a clean shot for ten seconds. He tells him to try it. He does and he's able to shoot a lantern out.

He asks Henry what he owes him and Henry tells him nothing but, to just consider it a time when Fate stepped in.

The next day, Pete Grant shows up in the saloon and as they get on with it, both men realize they've each taken a drink from the same magic potion... They shoot and they both shoot each other in the hand and they both realize they'll never be able to shoot like that again.

Pete walks out and tells his buddies that he gave Al the same as he gave him so it's a draw.

The last thing we see is Al and Liz walking out of the saloon together and the peddler smiles and moves on. The implication being that Al and Liz will ultimately end up together.

Now I know that my co-reviewers don't think a lot of this episode but I rather like it. I thought the final words of Rod Serling said it all that Fate stepped in and helped one man climb out of a pit while helping another man from falling in to one.

The lesson being here that one's life can change radically with one simple decision. I also enjoyed the actors in this. It was fun to see Martin Landau before he was a star and there was also a very young Doug McClure playing Pete Grant so that was fun to see.

I also wanted to make a special note of the actress Jeanne Cooper who played Liz. I watched her for many years as a middle aged lady on the soap opera The Young and the Restless and it was a rare treat to see her in her youth looking extremely pretty. She was a gutsy actress who after several years on the soap opera underwent a face lift right on television for the whole world to see as they wrote her face lift in to her character's storyline.

She's just as good of an actress here in the Twilight Zone in her youth as she was in her later years that I observed.

This episode is not excellent or a classic but I think it is worth watching and the message was a sound one.

When you get right to heart of it, it's about an alcoholic. Alcoholism was not something that was talked much about in the fifties and Rod Serling addressed an issue of what makes people drink and how many people took it so flippantly as illustrated by the Martin Landau character Hotaly. Granted Al probably had good reason to drown his sorrows and many people have started drinking for far less reasons but it was a clear sign to me that when you got right down to it, Al was filled with a lot of self loathing, which is why a lot of people drink because they want to forget as Al said to Liz in the beginning when he said he couldn't remember why he started.

The ending is probably a little too fairy tale as most alcoholics don't quit drinking that fast although there are always the rare people, but since they didn't have Alcoholics Anonymous in the Old West, Rod Serling ended the episode the best way possible by simply showing that there are always other choices that can be made. Overall, I'm going to rank this episode a three rating for good. I don't think it's an episode I'd want to watch over and over again but it is worth taking a look at, at least once.

Review by Bobbynear

You would think that Rod Serling, having begun his legendary writing career in the 50's at a time when western dramas were the main staple of tv, would be able to come up with something other than the clichéd idea of a shoot out between gunslingers as the third episode of his series.

All over tv, by the late 50's, endless tales of famous gunmen facing each other down in the streets of some dusty western town, have been done far too many times. The Twilight Zone hardly needed to add to them.

Featuring another street peddler, the second in a row and the second out of three stories, with a magic potion to change history, there is nothing much new here. The story is mundane, boring and pointless, the acting is either over the top, Martin Landau, or too understated, Doug McClure. Both Landau and McClure were in their mid to late twenties and near the beginning of their acting careers. How they managed to survive this fiasco is beyond me.

I generally appreciate stories that give me someone to like or someone to pull for. But that doesn't happen here. Denton reveals himself to be a hopeless alcoholic when he grovels on the ground for what is left in a broken bottle of whiskey. The two young gunmen are instantly disposable and seem to have limited lifespan in front of them. So I don't much care about anyone.

The ending is pretty obvious and it's tedious getting there. Plus there is just no real tension leading up to the final showdown. If you want to see how it looks when it is done right, get the dvd of one of the most famous western showdown dramas in movie history, High Noon and watch just how tense it can be when it's done correctly.

There is a little humor here however, when the town doctor uses his x-ray eyes to declare the showdown to be a draw and both gunmen to be incapable of engaging in such behavior in the future. This just by taking a five second glance at the hands of both. Then he tends to them medically by loosely and I do mean loosely wrapping a rather dirty looking cloth bandage around their hands. What? Both men have been shot and there is no blood, no broken bones, nothing? Who would have guessed that you could treat a gunshot wound so easily?

It's just another day in the Twilight Zone wit another street peddler coming up with an instant answer to a deadly situation. His magic potion manages to take two gunfighters out of commission leaving only hundreds of others in the old West that he still has to visit.

I don't know, his magic potion works but I think it would have been better used to treat Denton's rampant alcoholism at the beginning of this episode. That way I would not have had to sit through it even once....and certainly never again.

My rating on a scale of 0 to 5....

0 - Lousy, Totally Without Merit

Review by Ken

Okay The Twilight Zone veers off into a Western saga about a drunk. He exits the bar and falls on the ground hopeless. A pretty woman follows him and has compassion. A bad guy mocks him and get's the whole town laughing....

The casting of Dan Duryea in the lead role was terrible. He cannot act and I was immediately disgusted with his dialogue. Jeanne Cooper adds nothing to this contrived story which falls flat on it's face.

The story get's worse. Martin Landau as the bad guy? My grandma would not be afraid of him. He can't even fire a gun correctly.

The final scene makes no sense whatsoever. Doug Mclure shows up as bad guy no.2 and he looks like a good guy. Where did he come from? What relevance does he have? He and the drunk have a shootout which is senseless. They both have a potion which saves them. WOW!

The story ends and we have no clue. The scene fades to a lonely dusty road.

This is the old West? Hey Rod Serling you need to rent two classic movies about what real Westerns are all about. "Shane" and "High Noon."

Rod I know this is your rookie season but try better next episode. I know you can do it. My rating-0 Lousy.

Review by Linn

First off, I agree with Ken that Dan Duryea was not and never was the greatest of actors. Secondly, I agree with Kitty that it was great to see Martin Landau and Doug McClure before anyone even knew who they were. Lastly, I totally agree with Bobby that this was not one of the better episodes. Watch able one, maybe twice, but not more than that. Rod definitely should have done better for his third episode because this one (and thank God it didn't), could have blown the whole series out of the water, in my opinion. Never have two characters who are peddlers within the first three episodes of any series. Redundant.

The premise of the show was silly in many ways because he was offered free drinks from people over and over, yet he chose to sing that stupid song "How Dry I Am" thereby making a fool of himself instead of taking the free drinks offered and keeping his dignity. Who would do that?

Also, as Bobby mentioned, the final scene showing the gunshot draw was silly because both guys took the potion and you knew neither one would bite the dust. No blood, no serious injuries to either of their hands, yet a dirty rag wrapped around each one by a doctor supposedly made everything okay, but they could never shoot again? I don't remember if a bullet was shot into each hand, but if it was, wouldn't that have to be removed. Maybe it was just a brush wound, but if so, why couldn't they ever shoot again. Wounds heal unless they are serious.

As far as Al and the Jeanne Cooper's character, it reminded me of Miss Kitty from Gunsmoke, but she had a much more sober Matt Dillon.

Definitely a bad one. Will watch it on a Marathon but might get something to eat while it's on. I have to give it zero in the polls.

"The Twilight Zone" Episode 4: "The Sixteen-Millimeter Shrine"

Original Air Date- October 23, 1959
Guest Star: Ida Lupino
Written by Rod Serling
Directed by Mitchell Leisen

Review by Kitty

This latest episode called The Sixteen Millimeter Shrine is one of those episodes that reminds me a little too much of another story, namely Sunset Boulevard. Now I have never seen the movie but I did see the musical stage version when it toured with Petula Clark. Petula was great but the play about Norma Desmond was just awful.

Like Norma Desmond, this character that we are introduced to at the beginning by the name of Barbara Jean Trenton is every bit as unsympathetic. She's an aging movie star who has nothing but her past glory days to look at as she spends all of her days in her study watching her old movies and wishing she could be back in the 1930's with all of her friends of that era.

Her housekeeper Sally comes in to bring her food and is very worried about her. A knock at the door occurs and it's Barbara's agent Danny Weiss who is there to tell her about a part at a movie studio. She tells him that she never got along with the studio executive Marty Sall but Danny assures her he's softened up with old age.

Barbara agrees to go and when they get there she is informed that her part is a small but important part. Barbara is told that she's going to be playing a mother. Barbara gets enraged and tells Marty that she doesn't play mothers. Marty tells her to wise up and take what's offered to her because it's all she's going to get as she's nothing more than an aging actress past her prime.

Barbara storms out and Danny is furious that Marty could be so horrible to Barbara. Danny and Barbara go back to her place and Barbara has decided to create her own world without T-shirts and rock stars. Her house is now a place of the 1930's. She wants to throw a party and invite all of her old friends. She mentions three names and Danny reminds her that one is dead, one lives in Chicago now and one, nobody has heard from in quite some time.

Barbara is even more upset and orders Danny out and she locks the door behind him. Two weeks go by and Danny comes back and Sally tells him that Barbara won't leave her study anymore because all she wants to do is watch her old movies.

Danny goes in to tell her that her old co-star Jerry Herndon is in town and is coming over to visit her. She gets excited and goes upstairs to get dressed. When she comes down she sees a much older man and Jerry tells her he gave up acting twenty years ago when he got older. He now owns a supermarket chain in the Chicago area.

Barbara is horrified to hear all of this. She wants them all to leave. Jerry says his goodbyes to her and he and Danny both leave.

She runs back in to her study and sees the younger Jerry on the screen and that's the Jerry that she wanted to see not an old man. She then just begins to wish very hard.

Later, Sally comes to bring her food, there is no answer at the door. Sally walks in and looks around. She then looks at the screen and she screams. We then see Danny show up and Sally tells him she saw Barbara on the screen.

Danny turns on the projector and he sees the entry way to Barbara's house and all of her friends from the 1930's are coming in to the place. Barbara comes down the stairs and greets the Jerry of the past.

Danny calls to her to tell her to come back. Barbara comes to the forefront of the scene. She smiles, blows Danny a kiss and throws him her scarf. The picture is over. Danny walks out and finds her scarf right where she threw it to him. He picks it up and sniffs it and realizes it's the actual scarf and he smiles as he's happy that Barbara found some peace.

My question here though is did she really? One question that I had at the end was that if she was obsessing so much over being old why wasn't she looking younger at the end with all of her friends?

As I said, I really had no sympathy for Barbara. She's the kind of person you just want to grab and shake some sense in to and to tell her to grow up at the same time. It's called people get older and how you deal with it is entirely up to you. She was a superficial person as she had nobody of substance in her life. She had no family, and it was evident that she only liked Jerry for his looks not for him as a person because of how she treated him when he came to see her.

While this episode has a few good moments in it, one being at the beginning when Sally comes in to give her food and Barbara steps out from behind the screen and she mimics herself on the screen with the same pose, that's kind of an interesting moment but otherwise, it's just about an embittered old woman who couldn't deal with getting older. Yes there are people in the world like that but unlike Danny I wouldn't go out of my way to rescue them. If they want to be like Barbara, let them be.

The actors are fine. Ida Lupino plays the part well but again I have no sympathy with her character. Martin Balsam was good but I really didn't understand why he didn't write Barbara off a long time ago. If he's her agent why is he wasting time with her when he could be getting more deserving people work in a competitive business.

My rating for this is a one rating. I think it's a poor episode.

Review by Ken

Okay I know it will be hard for this series to stay clear of a soap opera story because in the 1960's they became popular. Serling must have decided let me tell a sappy tale about a woman who watches her old films. She tries to relive the past and gushes over former love scenes. Her housekeeper tries to persuade her to live a normal life. A friend comes by and tries to uplift her spirit. The woman refuses.

So 'As the World(Zone)Turns' in 1959 the audience can only suffer as the story unfolds. Almost the entire audience knows what is going to happen. She leaves the real world and enters the fantasy world on her projection screen. She is happy and invites her old friends for a good time.

A second grade student could write a better script. Where is the beef?

Ida Lupino played the character of a zombie just fine. Martin Balsam was a drag. But the highlight of the episode was that scream by Alice Frost.

I guess it would be nice to relive old memories again. What would I like? I would go back to my old high school baseball team and hit a grand slam home run in the bottom of the ninth inning.

The series is off to a slow start. I will stay with the show however. My rating for Millimeter 0 - Lousy

Review by Bobbynear

I have little to add to the discussion of this disaster other than this.... Two hopelessly bad episodes in a row at the beginning of this series. Had this been today rather than 1959, none of us would be discussing this series or even have any idea what a Twilight Zone is supposed to be.

Today, a series is given one or two weeks at the most to make an impact. If it does not, it is gone. Bad episodes sink a new series in no time flat. Sometimes even promising episodes are no help if there is no interest out there. It is astonishing that this series survived after this kind of a start.

Two episodes that are so derivative they don't even belong here. First the wretched gunslinger story that was worse than even the worst episode of Gunsmoke. Now this copy of the already bizarre feature film "Sunset Boulevard" makes me feel like I'm the only one in the Twilight Zone....not the fictional characters.

Ida Lupino was a decent actress in her day. If you want to see her in something good, try the 1941 feature film, "High Sierra" in which she plays opposite Humphrey Bogart. An excellent film. She also would go on to become one of Hollywood's first successful female directors. In fact, she returns to The Twilight Zone later, to direct the episode, "The Masks." Here she is just trashing her career.

The story offers nothing and no one to care about. Who gives a crap if this woman wants to sit all day and watch herself in old movies? But I do have a solution if it's that important. Make sure this particular episode is in her projector. One look at this and I guarantee she will run screaming out of the room and never ever sit and watch her old performances again. Case closed.

My rating on a scale of 0 to 5

0 - Lousy ~ Totally Without Merit

Review by Linn

This episode is definitely not a favorite of mine, but I do think that Ida Lupino was very good in her "Norma Desmond" type role. She plays an aging, washed-up actress who longs for her former life and career. She cannot come to grips with the fact that her life as she knew it is no more. She spends her days watching the old movies in which she played the leading lady. In the meantime, her housekeeper and agent are very concerned about her reclusiveness and the fact that she is in denial about aging.

She turns down the first movie role that she's been offered in quite some time because it calls for her to play someone's mother. She becomes indignant and refuses to even consider the part. She even believes that a former leading man who was coming to visit her would look exactly as he did when they appeared in their movies together. When she finds him to be an aging businessman who had retired from acting many years ago, she rudely dismisses him and storms away.

She proceeds to bury herself in the solitude of her study with her old movies and a boatload of self-pity. Finally after a couple of weeks, all of her hoping and wishing and longing for her previous life again comes to fruition when she manages to transport herself back there again. Her housekeeper and agent see her on the projector screen and when her agent yells to her, she blows him a kiss and throws a scarf in his direction which he finds on the floor of the entryway upon leaving the study. She got what she wanted, but for how long we'll never know.

Let's face it. Does anybody really want to grow old? Of course not. However, aging is a part of life as we know it and there is no way to change that. Oh sure, there are hundreds of ways to delay the outward appearance of age such as plastic surgery, nips, tucks, all sort of suctions as well as every type of cream, lotion, pill and injection you can think of, but what about the mental and inward aging. There's not much you can do to prevent the aches, pains and deterioration of the inner body, no matter how well you take care of yourself. Even the outward procedures that people have done are only a temporary fix and in some cases make them look worse in the long run than they would have if they had simply aged naturally. I will admit that I get my hair colored once a month, but that's a relatively minor anti-aging procedure that doesn't involve knives, needles, pills....or a movie star's money.

This is not a great episode and was so much like watching "Sunset Boulevard", but I thought Ida Lupino played her part well. I give this one a 2 (average) rating because there was nothing very special about it.

"The Twilight Zone" Episode: 5 "Walking Distance"

Original Air Date- October 30, 1959
Guest Star: Gig Young
Written by Rod Serling
Directed by Robert Stevens

Review by Kitty

This latest episode is called Walking Distance and I must admit I have mixed feelings about it. On the one hand I did like certain things but on the other hand some of it seemed a little too implausible.

We start by seeing a man we are introduced to as Martin Sloan. His car has broken down at a gas station just a little over a mile from the small town he grew up in called Homewood. It's kind of a catchy name for a person's hometown.

He is very impatient with the man at the gas station as it's going to take a little bit of time for him to fix his car. Martin sees that the town is only a mile and a half away and decides to walk there.

He arrives at the old ice cream parlor and orders his favorite which is a triple chocolate scoop soda. He asks the man if he knows him and the man tells him he's got one of those faces. He tells the man behind the counter that he used to be able to get these for a dime and he's truly amazed how much the place hasn't changed. The man looks at him funny and tells him the price of the soda is a dime. Martin tells him that nobody charges that anymore. The man asks him where he's from and he tells him New York. The man has a look about him that he feels that explains it.

Martin also says he remembers old Mr. Wilson sleeping up in the stock room during the day. The man looks at him funny and Martin leaves. The man then walks up the stairs and wakes up Mr. Wilson to tell him that they need more chocolate syrup and Mr. Wilson replies that he'll order some later that day.

Martin walks up the street and finds a very small boy playing with marbles. The boy is an extremely young Ron Howard! Martin sees him playing with marbles and asks him if he has names for the marbles. He tells him that when he was a child he used to call steel marbles steelies and clear marbles clearies. The boy tells him that he names his marbles too. Martin then tells him that he used to live in that house across the street and his name is Martin Sloan. The boy tells him that he knows Marty Sloan and he's not him. He then runs away.

Martin walks to the park. He sees people eating ice cream and cotton candy and there is music playing. There's a boy climbing a tree and his mother wants him to come down. Martin runs over and helps the boy get down from the tree. He tells the mother that he used to love summers and he'd climb trees all the time when he lived there. He tells her he hasn't lived there in twenty years. He also tells her that he one time carved his name in the bandstand area.

He then looks and he sees a boy doing just that. He approaches him and sees the boy carving Martin Sloan and he realizes he's looking at himself as a child of eleven. He asks the boy if he's carving his name and young Martin tells him yes, but that everybody does it. The boy gets scared and runs away.

Martin goes back to his house and knocks on his door and is surprised to see his father answer the door. He asks him if he can help him and Martin starts railing that he's Martin and calls him Pop. Martin's mother then shows up at the door and he calls her Mom and Martin's father has had enough and shuts the door on him.

Later Martin comes back and he wants to stay. His father comes out and he tells him he doesn't want any trouble but there will be if he doesn't leave. The mother comes out and Martin wants to show her his wallet so that he can prove that he's Martin Sloan their son. The mother throws the wallet on the ground and runs inside.

Martin then runs away because he realizes the person he wants to see is young Martin and he says that as he's running away. He gets to the park area and sees his younger self riding the carousel and eating cotton candy.... Martin jump son the carousel to try to talk to young Martin but he only succeeds in scaring the poor kid and young Martin runs from him and falls off the carousel and breaks his leg in the process. Martin feels it as well.

A man picks up young Martin to get him medical attention. Martin says that all he wanted to do was to tell the boy that he should enjoy summer and everything with it while he can.

Martin is then sitting on the carousel after it has closed and his father approaches him and gives him back his wallet. He tells him that he believes him because he looked at his driver's license and saw that it doesn't expire until 1960 which is twenty-five years in the future and the money in his wallet also has dates on it that have not happened yet either. He also tells him that young Martin will be fine, but he will walk with a slight limp.

He then sits down with Martin and tells him that there is no room for him here and that he has to go back to where he came from because everybody only gets one summer. He also asks him if things are really so bad where he came from. Martin explains that he just wanted to relive the bands, the carousel and the cotton candy. His father asks him if they have things like that where he's from and Martin tells him probably he just never looked for them before. His father tells him to look for them and look to the future.

His father smiles at him and walks away. The carousel starts to turn again and Martin goes back to the ice cream parlor and walks in and hears a juke box playing rock and roll and sees many teenagers hanging out there. A young man from behind the counter asks him what he'd like and Martin asks him if he can do a triple scoop ice cream soda. The soda jerk tells him sure but with three scoops it will cost extra. It will be thirty five cents.

He then asks him if he got that limp in the war. He tells him no, he got it falling off a carousel in the park when he was a kid. The soda jerk tells him that they took that out a few years ago as it needed to be condemned but it wasn't soon enough to help him out.

Martin also asks him about Mr. Wilson. The soda jerk tells him that the old owner Mr. Wilson died many years ago. He then asks him what kind of ice cream he wants for the soda. Martin decides to pass on the soda and leaves.

He limps back to his car, pays the attendant for fixing it and he drives off.

Now, I have to admit that this is one of those episodes for me where I enjoyed the beginning and the end but I have reservations about the middle of it. I think this had a very good premise as I think there are many people who have fantasized about going back in time to either experience something from their youth that they enjoyed or to maybe go back and change something. This episode really touches on both.

You have Martin Sloan who initially just wants to experience his home town as he remembered it from when he was a child and then he wants to make a change. However, I find the change that he wants to make to be a little silly. In the end the reason he chases down his younger self is to tell him to enjoy the summer. Well, call me crazy but the young Martin Sloan appeared to be a happy well adjusted kid who was enjoying his summer until the older Martin caused him to break his leg. That poor kid's summer is pretty well shot for this year.

In the two instances we see them interacting, the boy is carving his name in the grandstand area like other kids have done and then when we have the climax of the story, young Martin appears to having the time of his life riding the carousel, eating cotton candy and listening to the music. What exactly does Martin need to counsel him about?

The person who needs the counseling is obviously the older Martin. He's so burned out from his job that by all accounts he has shut himself off from everybody as there is no mention of a family of his own. He doesn't even indicate that he's dating anyone. He's obviously in severe need of a vacation and what better place than one's childhood where there is no responsibility other than to enjoy your summer.

Now on the subject of Martin's parents I have to admit that I was disappointed. Young Martin is only supposed to be eleven years old and yet his parents especially the actress, Irene Tedrow who was cast as his mother looks like she could be his grandmother. Were there no actresses in their mid to late thirties available for this shoot? The casting of his father Frank Overton was a little more convincing but I still would have preferred to see some younger people playing his parents.

I know what my parents looked like when I was eleven and they did not look like they could be grandparents! That stated, I found the father initially a little too passive. For a small town like that you'd think that after the first encounter he might have called the local sheriff to tell him that there was a weird guy who showed up at their door and was calling them Mom and Pop and to be on the lookout for him.

You would also especially think that his father would have phoned the police when Martin ran off calling for young Martin. I know that child rapists didn't get a lot of press attention back then but, you would think something like that might be going through the father's mind.

However, you can kind of cut him a little bit of slack as we later find out that he found the wallet and looked inside of it although I still would have expected the father to show up at the park on the heels of older Martin though. I have no doubt that if I showed up at my parents door as an adult and then ran off like a lunatic screaming my name for my younger self my father would chase me, tackle me and scream for my mother to call the police.

That stated with the final scene between father and his grown up son, I rather liked it for the most part. I might have liked to have seen the father be a little more inquisitive as to ask his son if there are any grandchildren and if not why?

However, I thought the message was a sound one when the father tells Martin that everybody only gets one summer and had he left it at that it might have sounded a little cold but the fatherly advice comes through when he asks him if they have carousels, cotton candy and bands in the future and perhaps Martin just needs to look for them.

Martin got the advice that's good for everybody which is basically remember the past and the good times fondly but enjoy the present and savor what you have around you because as Martin was reminded you only get one summer and one could also say you only get one spring, autumn and winter as well so, enjoy the ride all the way.

My rating for this is a two. As I said I was disappointed with the middle and I was also surprised that Martin didn't recognize the Ron Howard boy since he was so insistent that he knew Marty Sloan. One would think that Martin might have remembered some of those other kids that he saw and that would have tipped him off a little sooner that things were not quite what they were appearing to be.

Because of the problems that I have with it, I can only rate this an average episode. It's not one I would watch over and over.

It's got a good message to it though, and unlike the last episode where Barbara Jean Trenton willed herself in to La La Land to never return, Martin did face reality and he returned to the present and dealt with the consequences of his return to the past by fessing up to how he got the limp in his walk. You also get the impression that instead of dreaming about cotton candy he may actually go somewhere where he can buy some.

My rating -- 2 (Average)

Review by Bobbynear

Well here we go again. Another episode that is all potential and little pay off. So you can go home again huh? But you just can't stay there. Wow, what a surprise that is.

I didn't get too much out of this. I can only say that it's pretty far fetched, although the reality is that you actually could go back through the last fifty plus years and still see Ron Howard somewhere around. He'll never have to go back and see what it was like when he was a child. He just needs to turn on the tv.

Lots of famous actors in this one. Most notably Gig Young. However this episode might have been a lot more interesting if they had told his story instead of Martin Sloan's. On September 27, 1978, at age 64, Young married his fifth wife, a 31 year-old German art gallery employee named Kim Schmidt. He had met Schmidt on the set of his final film, Game of Death.

On October 19, 1978, three weeks after his marriage to Schmidt, the couple was found dead at home in their Manhattan apartment. Police theorized that Young first shot his wife and then turned the gun on himself in a murder-suicide. After an investigation police stated Young had acted on the spur of the moment and his actions were not planned. The motive of the murder-suicide remains unclear to this day.

Young's will which covered a $200,000 estate, left his Academy Award for "They Shoot Horses, Don't They?" to his agent, Martin Baum and Baum's wife. Young left his only child, daughter, Jennifer, just $10.

Young had married fourth wife Elaine Williams nine months after his divorce from his third wife. Williams was pregnant with Young's child at the time and gave birth to his only child, Jennifer, on April 21, 1964. After three years of marriage, the couple divorced. Young publicly denied Jennifer as being his biological child, saying he felt he had been tricked into marriage.

Perhaps had Gig Young been able to go back and see his childhood like Martin Sloan did, he would have felt better about the way things turned out.

My rating on a scale of 0 to 10

2 - Average

Review by Ken

Another fantasy story. This time a weary man goes back to his home town to mope around on a Sunday afternoon wearing a suit and tie. He strolls around the park and chats with kids about old times. He tosses around a couple of marbles and enjoys the sunny day. But soon he finds out that he has gone back in time to his childhood. For a moment this story had the makings of being a curious dilemma. Questions arise. How did this happen? Is that really him as a child again?

As I kept watching this story I got more confused with each moment. How could Martin Sloan see himself as a child? He goes to his old house and sees his parents. Mom is terrified. Dad is dumbfounded. All reactions are typical but I am perplexed. Were Martin's parents alive before or are they deceased? His father later realizes that this is Martin Sloan as a grown man. Yet his reactions are bizarre.

Whenever a story brings up questions and does not answer them I am furious. This story fizzled out and came to a complete dud. In the end Sloan goes back to his car and drives away. So what is the point? A man goes back in time and sees his childhood, parents, and old house. Nothing happens at all. What is the lesson here?

Gig Young in the lead role was plastic. Even worse was the performance of Frank Overton. He is downright boring. I suggest casting him in the lead role for a Wax Museum. Irene Tedrow added nothing to the story.

The only part I liked in this episode was that ice cream soda. I wish I could buy one of those for 10 cents.

My rating-1 Poor

Review by Linn

This was one of the Twilight Zone's best. I often wish I could go back in time to my childhood and relive it. I've often thought about how many things I would change but, then again, I've also wondered if that would affect my life later on in a good way or a bad way. Some things are better left alone, Yet it still makes me wonder sometimes.

However, only in the Twilight Zone can that happen. I liked this episode because it was well acted, well written, and I'm not ashamed to say the final scene brought tears to my eyes. The older Martin went back to his childhood days, but still he couldn't change certain things such as his limp from the broken leg he brought on his younger self by scaring him off the carousel.

When his father finally came to grips with the fact that this man was in fact his son all grown up, he had to let him know that he was not meant be there and needed to go back to his own life and time. You could also sense the love he felt for him and how it hurt his father to tell him that.

The only complaint I have is with the casting of Irene Tedrow as Martin's mother. She not only looked more like the grandmother of the 10 or 11 year old Martin Sloane, but she also looked much older than Frank Overton who played his father. Other than that, I truly enjoyed Walking Distance and gave it a Good rating.

"The Twilight Zone" Episode: 6 "Escape Clause"

Original Air Date- November 6,1959
Guest Star: David Wayne
Written by Rod Serling
Directed by Mitchell Leisen

Review by Kitty

This latest episode is called Escape Clause and I will start my review by quoting two old sayings. One is that sometimes God punishes you and gives you exactly what you want and the other is that if you make a bargain with the devil you better expect to get burned.

Our story starts off with a man who is in his bed and is being looked at by a doctor. His name is Walter Bedeker. The doctor informs him that he's fine. Walter asks what about his back pain and his inability to sleep.... The doctor tells him that it's in his mind and is most likely caused by nerves.

Walter's wife Ethel comes in and is very concerned and the doctor tells her that here is nothing wrong with Walter. She tells him that he's been sick all week but the doctor insists that he's fine. She sees him to the door and he tells her she looks a little peaked and he writes her a prescription for vitamins.

Walter is yelling to her that he's cold and that there's a draft. She shows the doctor the door and she comes in and closes the window. She told him that it was warm in there and that the doctor thought he should have some fresh air. He accuses her and the doctor of conspiring against him because he finds the prescription and is convinced he's going to die.

Ethel tells him that it's for vitamins and it's for her. He then accuses them all of not caring about him and to just let him alone and die in peace. She tells him all right then. As she walks out the door she explains she was just letting him be to get some sleep.

After Ethel walks out the door, Walter gets a visit from a very large pudgy man who just materializes in front of him and tells him that his name is Mr. Cadwallader. He tells him that he can grant his wish of living as long as he likes and can make sure that no harm will come to his body for a small price that he won't even miss.

Walter asks what that would be and Cadwallader tells him his soul. Walter realizes he's talking to the devil and Cadwallader confirms it. Walter doesn't think his soul is a big deal since he's not going to die. He accepts the offer. Cadwallader does tell him that there is an escape clause. At any time if he wants to check out, he will make sure he dies instantly and without pain. Walter signs on the dotted line with no problem as he believes that living five thousand more years would be amazing.

After Cadwallader leaves, Walter walks over to a very hot radiator and puts both his hands on it and realizes that nothing will hurt him. He walks to the window and throws all of his medicines out the window. Ethel walks in and wants to know what he's doing. Walter informs her that he's a new man.

We then see Walter go to the subway and jump on the tracks as a subway is coming. Everybody on the platform screams thinking this man has committed suicide. After the train goes by, Walter gets up off the tracks and while very dirty from the train, he's no worse for the wear.

We then see Walter at home filling out forms for a claim adjuster and he will get one thousand dollars for the accident. As the one adjuster leaves another one arrives because Walter threw himself in front of a bus and the adjuster is there with a check for fifteen hundred dollars.

Not only is Walter unimpressed with the money but he's very rude to the adjusters. The second one leaves and he tells Ethel that he's now been in fourteen accidents and none of them are thrilling. Ethel doesn't understand why he's so upset. She tells him he should be grateful that he wasn't seriously injured.

Walter is not impressed. He walks in to the bathroom and asks Ethel to get him some ammonia. He fixes himself a lethal cocktail and drinks it. Ethel is horrified and Walter is not impressed. He tells her he just drank enough poison to easily kill someone and yet it tastes like lemonade to him.

Walter then decides to go up to the top of the building and throw himself off because he wants to see how that feels. Ethel runs after him begging him not to do it. She gets in front of him and she accidentally falls off the building to her death.

Walter who's not the least bit concerned that his wife is dead simply states that he wonders what that felt like. He then gets a smile on his face and he goes back to his apartment. As he lights up a cigarette, he calls the police and tells them to come over and arrest him because he just killed his wife.

After he hangs up, he wonders what the electric chair feels like. We then see him in jail with a defense attorney who wants to help him but Walter clearly does not want to be helped.

We then see the judge sentencing him and instead of death by the electric chair, Walter is given life in prison without parole. The defense attorney is thrilled that he saved his client but Walter is devastated.

Walter is sitting in his jail cell and is being given his last meal before going to the penitentiary. The guard jokes with him that life is only forty to forty five years tops for him.

Cadwallader then appears before Walter and is laughing. He asks Walter if he wants to exercise his escape clause and Walter tells him yes. Cadwallader tells him that he looks like a man having a heart attack about now.... Walter falls to the floor dead and Cadwallader disappears. The guard comes running in and discovers Walter dead.

Rod Serling says at the end that each man on this earth is condemned to die, time and method of execution is unknown and that's as it should be.

There were certainly interesting aspects of this episode to like. The first and foremost being the main question which is, if you could live forever would you really want to?

In the case of Walter Bedeker, while I found the performance by David Wayne enjoyable, I had no real sympathy for his character. I think his character is probably the most self centered character we've seen so far but then again if one is going to make a bargain with the devil that's more than likely the kind of person who would do it.

I did feel sorry for his wife Ethel played by Virginia Christine who in later years copped a fake accent and pitched mountain grown Folgers's coffee as the richest blend out there. Nobody had heard of Starbuck's yet.

Ethel was just a concerned wife who ended up giving her life for her husband and he's not even the slightest bit upset that she's dead. On that basis alone, I think he certainly got what he deserved in the end.

The portrayal of the devil AKA Cadwallader I found interesting. This is not the only time we will see a story of the devil or a minion of the devil approaching a person whose soul is ripe for the taking but the one thing that I find consistent with Rod Serling's portrayal of the devil is that in all of the scenarios the devil is portrayed initially as a harmless unassuming person who simply wants to help someone out or wants help from that person.

This is right out of basic Judeo Christian teachings when we are told from the time we are children to beware of wolves in sheep clothing or to always remember that the devil is very devious and will think nothing of trickery.

I think one of the brilliant things about Rod Serling's episodes are that in so many of them there are life lessons to be learned. In this episode, the obvious one being that there are no quick fixes and if something sounds too good to be true then it probably is, particularly if you are gambling with your soul.

Overall, I'm going to give this episode a four rating. I liked the irony at the end. I have seen this episode in the past but I have to admit I did not remember Walter being given a heart attack at the end. I was thinking he was condemned to live out eternity in a jail cell.

The irony being that had he not taken Cadwallader's bargain he would have lived probably a good long time if he had just gotten over his hypochondriac tendencies. His wife would have lived as well. His poor judgment cost not only himself but his wife, again a life lesson that everything you do clearly affects the people around you whether you want it to or not.

Review by Bobbynear

The Twilight Zone returns to familiar territory. Well at least it will be mighty familiar by the time we get later in the series. Time and time again, characters fail to learn the lesson. Don't make deals with death or the devil. They are losing propositions no matter how good they look at the start.

As a lifetime fan of Superman since I was a child, I find this episode both interesting and amusing. It's a look at what Superman might have been like had he turned out to care about nobody but himself. Certainly Walter is about as self centered as a human can be. At first he's worried to death that something will do him in before his time. Later he quickly becomes bored because nothing will do him even when it is his time.

Walter truly is amazing. At first he's afraid that any errant germ may kill him and yet later he doesn't seem the least bit concerned that a jolly fat man just showed up in his bedroom without even coming in the door or down the chimney and he doesn't have any gifts in his hands. To say Walter is impulsive is putting it mildly. It takes him no time at all to make the deal of the century or better yet...the deal of many centuries to come.

But it's two things for me that particularly stick out when it comes to Walter's stupidity. For one, suppose he did indeed get the death penalty at his trial for the presumed murder of his wife? Because he is now immortal, the chair burns up and he emerges unscathed. But exactly what did Walter think the authorities were going to do after they realized he could not be executed? Let him walk away a free man? Come on Walter...think man...you're going to get life in prison one way or the other. If we can't kill you...we'll just put you away and throw away the key.

And then at the very end, before he's done any time at all, Walter uses the escape clause. Why so soon? How about waiting a little time to see how things turn out? After all, Walter has just cheated death in numerous ways. He's going to end up the most famous prisoner in history. He can write his own story. If not, people will beat a path to his door to get his story, write a book or make a movie of his life. Scientists will want to study him to see how he became immortal and how we can copy it. This doesn't sound too boring to me.

If Walter was bored to death because none of his death defying feats turned out to be as thrilling as he figured they would be, then he should turn to the next best thing. Find out how thrilling it will be to the rest of the world.

I rather like this episode. It is different in many ways and manages to pack a lot into less than 30 minutes including some humor in a very dark subject.

My rating on a scale of 0 to 5
4 ~~ Excellent

Review by Linn

I actually enjoyed Escape Clause, but I also found it to be one of the dumbest TZ episodes.

Walter Bedeker can't be killed no matter what, but he also can't escape prison. Did he think that would happen? A death sentence and a prison sentence are two different things. The fact is, he didn't even think he would have to consider that choice. He made a deal with the devil for immortality and quickly became bored with the mundaneness of his life. He tried to kill himself several times by jumping in front of speeding trains and buses just for the hell of it. He even drinks a glass of ammonia. He knew, however, that these attempts were pointless other than allowing him to collect loads of money from the insurance companies.

He had an obvious disdain for his wife who tried her best to be understanding and comforting to Walter, but he was unaffected by her efforts to be a supportive wife. When she ends up accidentally falling from the rooftop of their building while trying to keep Walter from jumping, he shows no shock or remorse. He simply calls the police to say he murdered his wife and relishes the thought of surprising everyone by surviving the electric chair. Well, guess what? Due to fine legal representation, he gets life in prison instead of the chair.

So being in prison and having no life of his own left him with the only real option he had. The Escape Clause. The devil appears in his cell and reminds him of this, Walter agrees to avail himself of the clause and suffers a fatal heart attack. The fat, jolly devil laughs his hearty laugh and Walter goes to Hell.

I liked this episode and rated it as Good. I did find it dumb, though, that a man who is the ultimate hypochondriac and then makes a deal with the devil for immortality cannot enjoy that either. One would think he'd go out and have the time of his life with all of that insurance money, and even more so after inadvertently causing his wife's death. I guess Walter Bedeker is proof that you just can't make some people happy no matter what you do.

Review by Ken

One word sums up this bizarre story. WEIRD!!! Bedeker is bored with life... He makes a deal with the Devil to receive immortality. My first question is why?? He get's his wish. Nothing harms him. He can't die. The scene where the wife falls to her death was depressing. At this moment I was completely disgusted with Bedeker.

Again Serling depicts death as ordinary and routine. In ep.2 (Angels) the Reaper was well dressed. Here in 'Escape Clause' the character of the Devil is a jolly fat man who seems pleasant.

The story has the intrigue and appeal. But again I have to ask the question. What is the point? Don't make deals with the Devil? Oh really. Give up my soul for the pleasures of life? No thanks.

The closing narration by Serling was clear. The Devil won. He beat Bedeker who will end up in the wrong place.

David Wayne was miscast. His acting was flat. However Thomas Gomez was convincing and persuasive. No desire to watch this episode ever again.

My rating-2 Average

"The Twilight Zone" Episode 7: "The Lonely"

Original Air Date- November 13, 1959
Guest Star- Jack Warden
Written by Rod Serling
Directed by Jack Smight

Review by Kitty

This latest episode is called The Lonely. It stars Jack Warden in a most unusual role.

We start out seeing a barren desert and are told that it is a prison to one man in solitary confinement. It's for a man by the name of James Corry who is serving a fifty year sentence for murder and he has been condemned to live on an asteroid.

He has just finished putting together a car that doesn't work. He writes in his journal that it's the fifteenth day of the six month of the fourth year that he's been imprisoned on the rock. He's lonely and there is a supply ship that's due any time. He hopes that it will have Allenby on it. He's the one person who treats him like a human being. He brings him supplies and other things to keep his mind occupied.

The supply ship arrives and Allenby is on it. Corry begs him to stay awhile and play a game of cards or checkers with him. Allenby tells him he can't due to the rotation of things his window of time only gives him twenty minutes. Another man Adams complains about having to come here four times a year. The man Adams is played by a very young Ted Knight who will later be seen as Ted Baxter on the Mary Tyler Moore show.

Adams tells Corry to ask Allenby about the pardon. Corry asks and Allenby tells him it's still a no go. For what it's worth there are many people on earth who don't like these kinds of prison sentences. Allenby tells Adams and the other man to go out and get the other crate that he brought for Corry.

Corry is discouraged as he admits he killed a man but that it was in self defense. Allenby tells him that he believes him and so do other people as well but they can't change the rules right now.

He tells Corry that his superiors don't know that he brought this for him so don't open it until he and his crew are out of sight. Allenby leaves and Adams asks him what's in the crate and Allenby replies he's not sure but perhaps it's salvation.

Corry opens the crate and is shocked by what he sees. We then see him reading the instructions telling him that he is now the owner of a woman robot. He looks over at the woman and she looks up at him and tells him her name is Alicia what's his? Alicia is played by a very pretty actress named Jean Marsh.

Corry is initially very angry that Allenby would leave a fake woman here with him. Alicia tries to be to kind to Corry and she only gets yelled at and is told that she's mocking him by making him believe that she is real when she's not real.

She responds by crying. Corry then realizes that Alicia does feel and he begins to like her. We then see the two of them playing checkers together and watching the stars together.

Corry writes in his journal that Alicia has now been with him for eleven months and she has been his salvation and that he loves her.

The next morning after they look at the stars, Allenby and Adams come back and Allenby tells Corry that he's been granted a pardon and they are doing away with this kind of punishment.

He tells Corry that he can only take fifteen pounds with him on the ship as they've already picked up seven other guys. Corry is elated and tells him he only has his journal and Alicia.

Allenby gets a worried look on his face and he realizes he forgot all about Alicia. Adams asks who's Alicia. He then realizes what was in the crate. Allenby tells him that he can't bring Alicia and to remember that she's not real, she's a robot.

Corry gets livid and insists that no, Alicia is very real and they can't leave her and besides he loves her. He runs off to find her. Allenby and Adams follow and they do find Alicia.

Alicia looks puzzled by what is happening and Allenby resorts to the only thing he can do. He takes out his gun and he shoots Alicia in the face thus exposing all the wiring. We hear her say Corry about four times before she completely dies.

Allenby tells Corry that all he's leaving behind is loneliness and Corry replies that he'll have to remember that.

This episode was filmed on location in Death Valley which according to Marc Scott Zicree's book The Twilight Zone Companion was a tough shoot as they were filming in 130 to 140 degree heat. Several members of the cast and crew got ill from the heat during the shoot. All of the people involved in making this episode deserve a big thumbs up for persevering in that June heat.

As for the story itself, let's see sending criminals to asteroids to be in solitary confinement, I have to admit I like that idea especially for the sex perverts of the world. I think Rod Serling was on to something. It's a pity that can't come to pass.

As to the acting, I think it's well done. Jack Warden deserves a nod for making me feel a bit sorry for him when in actuality we know nothing of his case. He claims it was self defense but what evidence did the prosecution actually have?

I enjoyed seeing the Alicia character. Jean Marsh played it with the right amount of child like Pinocchio essence to make her character believable. I have to admit that in spite of the fact that she was a machine, she did make Corry happy for a brief time and it was a shame that she gets her face blown off as a reward for that. However, on the other hand she did serve her purpose well.

One thing that Rod Serling didn't address in this story was whether or not Corry and Alicia had sex. It was hard to tell there. I couldn't really say one way or the other. I suspect that's what Rod Serling had in mind.

I did enjoy the episode and I will give it a three for good. It's worth watching and it puts a question to mind that if one were stranded and lonely what lengths would you go to for companionship? We all saw in the movie Cast Away that Tom Hanks in desperation for companionship talked to a volleyball on a daily basis.

Being given a robot for companionship would probably be just fine for many in a similar situation.

Review by Ken

After a string of five grill cheese and chips episodes, we finally get a story with steak and vegetables that has that eerie

Twilight Zone feeling with 'The Lonely.' A man is serving a prison sentence on an asteroid 9 million miles from earth. The setting in Death Valley really looks like it.... At first I thought Serling was borrowing a theme he used in ep.1 where a man is lonely and has nothing to do. But this story changes with the arrival of a female robot named Alicia.

As the story progressed Corry changes his feelings and not only has a companion but a love interest. A little soapy for me. But I was happy that Corry is not so miserable now. At the end Allenby and his crew return and let Corry know he is a free man. Time to return to earth again. Bad news.... Alicia can't come. Corry is depressed and pleads for mercy. Allenby shoots Alicia in the face and we all are stunned that the pretty face is a robot.

The casting of Jack Warden in the lead role was excellent. His many expressions from gloom to joy reveals his fine acting ability. Jean Marsh was miscast. She was way too young looking to be a love interest for an older looking Jack Warden. I am not a matchmaker but I kept thinking they do not look like a couple. Jack Dehner as the Captain was good as the stern leader.

A few problems I have with the story. Nine million miles away from earth?? Let's see. If a spaceship travels at 1000 miles an hour it would take three months to reach the asteroid. A little extreme don't you think. Condemn a man this far away. What was the crime? Maybe he forgot to pay his taxes.

Casting lead roles is key for me. Alicia should have been a little older. Maybe Agnes Moorhead could have played the part. In the end I would have felt more heart broken.

Depressing end to the story. Seems Serling wanted to go for the shock and awe ending with the destruction of Alicia. Instead I would have had a different conclusion. When Corry finds out he can't take Alicia on the ship he should have knocked the Captain and his crew out and leave them behind. He takes Alicia and get's on the ship heading home for earth. Happy ending and Serling closes the narration-"Only in The Twilight Zone."

All in all I loved the episode. It belongs in Twilight Zone lore.
My rating-5 Classic.

Review by Linn

The Lonely was a classic episode, in my opinion. It stars two wonderful actors, Jack Warden and Jean Marsh, in very intriguing roles.

Jack Warden plays a man named James Corry who has been sentenced to serve the next50 years of his life in solitude on an asteroid. His crime - murder. His reason - self-defense. That is all we are given as far as the background of his crime and sentence. This is, of course, supposed to be the future and we are led to believe that the most hardened and dangerous criminals serve their time in space rather than in a cell on Earth. I also feel that Rod Serling purposely left out details of Corry's crime so that we would feel more compassion for him.

James Corry is given some basic comforts such as books, records, a record player, games and even the parts to rebuild an old car. However, as Rod Serling states in his opening narration, James Corry is dying of loneliness. More than his loss of freedom, it's the loss of companionship that cuts the deepest.

Captain Allenby, the commander of a rocket ship that delivers his supplies every three months, seems to believe in Corry's innocence to the point where he shows enough compassion to bring Corry a special gift during the ship's latest visit. The two other astronauts on the ship are not quite as compassionate. One of them is played by the late actor, Ted Knight, who is very unsympathetic and obnoxious towards Corry. Allenby purposely does not reveal to them what he has brought for Corry in a large wooden crate.

When Corry opens the crate, he finds a beautiful woman at the bottom of it. The woman, Alicia, is not real, though. She's a robot. Corry will not accept her at first, but when she seems to have the ability to show feelings, including love, Corry soon has a change of heart. In a short time, he falls very much in love with Alicia. They spend almost every moment together, playing board games and gazing at the stars. The only thing they probably could not share is a sexual relationship, and I don't know how Corry planned to deal with that over time. Then again, he didn't get the chance to find out.

The supply ship returned early with Allenby giving Corry the wonderful news that he had been cleared of all charges, was a free man and would be returning to earth. The only problem is that they could only bring Corry and 15 pounds of possessions. Corry had little to bring back with him, but he wanted Alicia to go with them. Sorry. She weighs more than 15 pounds. Corry will not hear of leaving without her and runs off to find her. Allenby runs after him and when they find Alicia, Allenby has no choice but to shoot her which he does -- IN THE FACE!

This jolts Corry to reality when he sees her wiring exposed and her voice fading out as she calls his name. He sadly had to accept Alicia's demise, and he and the crew then head back to Earth.

I found this to be one of the more poignant and imaginative Twilight Zone episodes and for that reason I gave it a Classic rating.

Review by Bobbynear

I wish that I could agree with Ken and say that this episode works for me but it does not and that is not the fault of the actors.

The problem is that it's too short. I never did like the season that the Twilight Zone went to an hour but this would have been the perfect story for it.

In order for me to have any empathy for this man I need to know something about him and I don't. It's the future and apparently his crime is bad enough for him to not only be convicted of murder, but to serve out his sentence on a distant asteroid.

Well OK...I can think of lots of real life prisoners right now who should face that kind of future. Charles Manson is still in prison decades after the death penalty was overturned by the courts. He's been allowed to sit in jail surrounded by people when he should have been underground long ago.

The fact that Corry says it was self defense means nothing to me. Every prisoner says either that or that he didn't do it. With no background, I'm not about to swallow that so I don't feel all that bad for the man. Besides, is this really any worse than being placed in solitary confinement right on this planet and allowed only a few minutes a day to go outside and exercise? I would say that Walter from the previous episode would be in a lot more trouble were he facing this.

If you have any doubts about being lonely in prison on Earth... go out and rent the dvd of the feature film, "The Birdman Of Alcatraz" with Burt Lancaster. A real life story on this planet a lot like this that also ends with the man's only feathered companions being stripped from him.

There is a lot to tell here in less than twenty five minutes and it just does not happen. That also goes for the relationship between Alicia and Corry. Other than sitting under the stars, we don't get a feel for how close they do become. Does she really have human emotions? Can she show them? She's pretty alright and she certainly can fulfill a basic male need for a woman by his side, but that's not the whole story. I wish I knew the rest.

As for the age thing that Ken mentioned....well check out IMDB Ken... Jack Warden was only 39 years old when they filmed that episode....and Jean Marsh was 26 years old... not that much of a difference by today's standards.

Agnes Moorhead?? Oh really? She was nearly 60 years old when they filmed that episode. A little long in the tooth for Corry. Besides... she's still got some space aliens to do battle with. She hasn't got time for this.

I don't mind this episode but I can't rate it too high since there is so much unanswered. I want and need to feel more sorry for Corry than I do. Maybe just maybe he deserves this. It does look bad but you don't necessarily need to be left on an asteroid to feel lonely. You can ask a lot of people right here right now about that. Sometimes you can be surrounded by people and still feel lonely.

We do know one thing though... Corry and Alicia never had sex.... If they had Corry probably would have been electrocuted... although....if you must face the death penalty... what a way to go... My rating on a scale of 0 to 5

3 ~~ GOOD

"The Twilight Zone" Episode 8 "Time Enough At Last"

Original Air Date-November 20, 1959
Guest Star- Burgess Meredith
Written by Rod Serling
Directed by John Brahm

Review by Kitty

This latest episode is called Time Enough At Last and stars Burgess Meredith in what would be his first of four appearances on The Twilight Zone.

We start off by seeing a very friendly man by the name of Henry Bemis working behind the counter in a bank as a teller. He seems amiable enough but the woman he is giving money to is not very appreciative of his small talk. He is telling her about the book David Copperfield.

As Henry is telling her the main part of the plot, she interrupts him by telling him that he's short changed her by one dollar. He apologizes and immediately gives her the dollar. He continues to tell her about the book only to look up and find her gone.

He shrugs his shoulders and puts up the sign that says Next Window Please and he continues with his book. The bank president taps him on his shoulder and wants to see him in his office. He tells Henry that he needs to stop reading and put his full attention on his job or he won't have a job much longer. He also knows that he sneaks down to the vault during his lunch hour to read and that has to stop as well.

Henry apologizes and tells him that the reason he reads at work is because his wife won't let him read at home. He tries to read a newspaper and she snatches it out of his hands. Whenever he tries to read anything, she takes it away from him.

The president tells him that he thinks his wife is a brilliant woman. Back at home, Henry is reading the newspaper and his wife Helen comes in and takes it away from him. She tells him that no husband of hers is going to read and not engage in the art of conversation. She tells him to get ready as they are going to some friends house to play cards with them.

Henry tells Helen that he'll be ready. She walks out of the room and he reaches under the chair and finds a book of poetry. He puts it in his inside pocket of his jacket. Helen then comes out and demands the book. He asks what book and she reaches in to his pocket and she finds it.

She tells him that she wants him to read her some of the poetry. Henry is delighted. He sits down and when he goes to read he discovers that Helen has very maliciously scribbled out all of the poetry in the book. He's devastated and Helen adds insult to injury by grabbing the book and ripping the pages out. Henry is practically crying as he picks up the pages of the torn book.

The next day we see Henry in the bank and it's his lunch hour so he once again sneaks off to the vault to read. He finishes reading his book and picks up a newspaper. He sees the headline stating that the H-bomb is capable of total destruction. The next thing we see is his watch breaking and the room shaking and we hear a big explosion.

Henry tentatively walks out of the vault and sees nothing but devastation.... He wanders in to the presidents office and hears a tape recorder going of his voice and sees his dead hand.

He walks outside and realizes that he's the only one alive but then he wonders if he really wants to be alive. He walks past his house where he used to live and calls out Helen's name and gets not response. He finds a store with all kinds of food so he won't go hungry any time soon.

He falls asleep on a couch and wakes up the next day and proceeds to look for other people. When he doesn't find anyone, he finds a gun and decides to end it all. He truly believes that he'll be forgiven for doing it.

However, just as he's about to pull the trigger he sees the Public Library. He walks over to it and he sees all of the books and is absolutely overjoyed to see them and realizes that he's got time enough at last to read everything this heart desires to read. He has even put them all in to stacks so he can read them by month.

Let's not forget though that this is the Twilight Zone. Poor Henry's glasses slip off of him and fall on the cement as he's reaching for another book and they completely shatter. Henry is blind as a bat without them and he tearfully wonders why that had to happen when he had time enough at last.

When I think of episodes from the Twilight Zone that stick out in my mind, this one is definitely one of them. Interestingly enough, there is a special feature on the episode that has an interview with Burgess Meredith from 1978 and he tells the interviewer that of all of the TV work he did in his career he said that this episode is the one thing that fans comment about to him the most.

I can understand that because Burgess Meredith portrayed a very likable everyday kind of man who just wants to be able to sit down, relax, and enjoy a good book, quite probably because he's got a pretty mundane life and the stories are certainly ways to take one away from the problems of reality especially if you're married to a nagging wife.

It never seemed to occur to the wife that perhaps the reason Henry doesn't want to talk to her is because she's not a nice person to talk to. I wouldn't want to talk to her either. She's quite the bitch. Henry should have gone looking for a good divorce lawyer. After she scribbled his book up and then ripped it up, I think he's definitely got grounds for mental cruelty.

I don't feel that sorry for him at the office though. Let's face it, you work the front line in a bank, you're expected to pay attention to your customers and give them the proper service that they need so I think the bank president was justified in talking to him.

As to the rest of it after the bomb goes off, I found Henry's reactions to be quite normal initially. We have the survivor's guilt initially and Henry wonders if he wants to keep going. He finds all of the food, so there is nourishment out there. So far we have reviewed seven other episodes and I think what sets this one apart is the sheer sadness that we see at the end.

There truly is no hope for this sweet, harmless, likable man. Now, back in1959, many people did believe that people could survive a nuclear bomb blast like that. We have since come to learn that Henry doesn't really need to feel that sad because it's only a matter of time before he starts to suffer from radiation sickness which will most likely kill him.

However, why can't poor Henry be allowed some happiness before he dies? There lies the real sadness and tragedy of it all. I will definitely rate this episode a five for being a classic as I can't really find much to complain about. Burgess Meredith is almost a one man show here and he delivers on every emotional level there is to the story.

Review by Bobbynear

As much as I love this episode, given that it is tied with another from season five, at the top of my list for best of the entire series, I still dread writing about it. The program is so brilliant in so many ways that nobody can truly do justice to it. But I'll try.

People who have the book, "The Twilight Zone Companion," would do well to read about the filming of this episode. For those that do not, the short version is that it is based on a short story written by a woman who, according to book author, Mark Scott Zicree, that was "bland" and "forgettable...." That is hard to believe given what Rod Serling and others producing the show did with it. Serling was already well known on tv as a brilliant writer, but this took him to a new level he would never leave.

The production design for this tv episode is also a remarkable story. Some feature films haven't gone to this much trouble to be realistic. According to the TZ Companion book... the scene where Bemis is in the bank vault when the bomb goes off and everything starts shaking... isn't just the cameraman shaking the camera... they built the entire set on springs so that everything would shake including Burgess Meredith and be as realistic as possible.

Everything in the episode, from the remarkable painted backdrops of a devastated world and menacing sky to the incredible staircase at the end which has been used in countless feature films, proves that they meant business when they filmed this. Television in 1960 was still just a little past its infancy and this was virtually unheard of especially from a series with less than ten episodes under its belt.

That also extends to the late Burgess Meredith who turns in one of the best performances of his storied career. The two time Oscar nominee is quoted in Zicree's book as saying that of all the films he did, and all of television, including three more Twilight

Zone episodes, this is the one he heard about the most, the one people wanted to talk about.

I can personally attest to that. As an early baby boomer who remembers only too well what it was like to be pulled out of class in school from time to time, marched out in the hallway, told to sit down, shut up and duck and cover during air raid drills in the fifties and sixties, this episode didn't just strike a chord with me....it gave me something new to worry about.

As if it wasn't bad enough to consider the very real possibility that the entire world around me might be destroyed in a heartbeat, during a war, or even as an accident, now there was a new level of concern. Burgess Meredith made me realize there was an even worse possibility. That everyone, including my entire family and all of my friends would surely die... but that I might survive and be in his position. Who needed that??? Who ever dreamed that survival might be the real threat?

This story works on every level from the second it begins. Critical to that success is the portrayal of Henry Bemis. We need to like him and we need to like him quickly since the episode is only about twenty five minutes long without commercials. Meredith makes that happen. Bemis does not appear to be the kind of person you would want to spend your life with. After all, he is one dimensional plus he's not doing his job very well. He's a bank teller in the days long before electronic banking and he's reading secretly while giving people back the wrong amount of money. None of that would be appreciated by any of us.

Yet he is in a strange way likeable, probably because he seems so innocent and demands so little. He just wants to be left alone to read. Everybody should be so accommodating and quiet. No demands from Henry. Just hand him a book and he goes off into his own world.

Then there are the people around him. His expected to be, very annoyed and demanding boss and his disturbingly shrewish wife who cruelly draws lines through his favorite book and then hands it to him. That truly is a new level of cruelty, the kind of thing that Henry would never dream of doing to anyone else. By this time we can hardly be expected to have anything but sympathy for Henry.

When we see him finally find some solace in the bank vault curled up with one of his books that doesn't have lines drawn through it, we feel satisfied that maybe life isn't so bad for Bemis after all. But you can only get away from the real world so far by simply getting involved in a novel.... Real life intrudes and poor Henry finds himself in the most fascinating story of them all... the real world and the dangers in it.

Moving from inside the vault to a bleak and devastated world outside also is unforgettable. The production design is spectacular especially for a tv episode. It looks real, it feels real and I can only imagine myself wandering around like Henry wondering why I was picked to still be alive to see all of this.

Of course, there still are a few very unrealistic items that never get resolved... Such as the idea that Henry is doomed to a lifetime of loneliness... Wandering around in a world full of radiation, eating food and drinking water so contaminated you might die just by getting near it, means Henry will be lucky, if you can use that word here, to survive a couple of days. He will be gone quickly.

Also the very idea that a library full of books made of paper would survive a nuclear holocaust is just preposterous. That's the first thing that will go in the kind of massive fireball that occurred while Henry was tucked inside that vault.

But who cares? This isn't really about science fiction. Let the scientists worry about that. For viewers it's about an unthinkable scenario that finds you in a position you might have earlier actually wished for. To be left alone... really... truly alone... For good... forever.

And then there is that remarkable ending. Not only poignant and disturbing at the same time, but it literally flies in the face of what has always been true about tv drama. As long as there has been free television there have been commercials and sponsors behind them who pay the freight. And they are quite committed to making sure that their audience is not just entertained but happy with the way things turn out.

Oh sure, there are plenty of tragedies, but usually the audience, especially back in tv's early days, was always left with something... anything... to feel good about. For a second we do. Henry will surely die on those library steps... but at least he will have one of his beloved classic novels in his hands and a smile on his face.

That is until Rod Serling pulls out the rug from under him and has his glasses break. It is appalling and you can almost hear the gasps from tv audiences watching at home. It can't be. Nobody would dare to leave this poor man in this untenable situation. Not only is it not fair, it's downright cruel.

And that's where the sponsors come in. Most of them then... and to some degree even now, do not wish to make waves with the home audience they need to keep them in business. Nobody wants to think of people going to the store, picking up their product that was advertised on this show... and then shuddering and leaving it on the shelf because it brings back bad memories. Probably audiences are too sophisticated now with pay cable tv... For that, but remember this is 1959 and tv is just getting started....It was a lot different then.

So it is cruel, there is no other word for it, to have poor Henry's glasses break at a time when it's the only hope he has. Of course, perhaps he should go stumbling around. He might find an optical store that sold glasses or even a magnifying glass... I mean if all of those books could survive nuclear war... maybe glass could to. It's no more preposterous than that....

This unforgettable episode, coming as it does just eight stories into the series, virtually insures it will never be forgotten. Had The Twilight Zone ended after just thirteen episodes, this story would still be talked about. Rod Serling was pure genius. He had his finger in the air before most other people did. He saw which way the wind was blowing and that it was fear of nuclear annilation. He will return to that theme many more times in this series but it will never again look quite like this.

The time between 1959 when this series began and 1964 when it ended, included a lot of worldwide tension over nuclear war and that very much includes the 1962Cuban missile crisis when we all almost actually ended up like Henry Bemis.

This is one of those classic tv episodes that almost everyone knows whether they were alive yet or not when it originally aired. In fact, you don't even need the title. Just say it's the one with the funny little guy who just wants to read and all of a sudden there's a nuclear war and he survives and finds a library full of books at the end, only to trip and fall and have his thick reading glasses break leaving him alone and with nothing. Chances are they will tell you immediately they know exactly what you are talking about.

At the moment I am corresponding with a long time member of another Yahoo group concerning tv's other great classic series, "The Fugitive" This person lives in England and knew little or nothing about The Twilight Zone. She did not indicate at that time any desire to join this group, but I did write and tell her about this classic episode and that it was one that appears online. She watched it and surprise surprise was very impressed. She even went on to watch another classic that is coming up soon and might even visit this group at some point. Nearly fifty years later....it still works.

Incredibly, on November 20 of this year, it will be the 50th anniversary of the first showing of this episode. Though there had already been many classic tv programs at that point during television's glory days, some of them even written by Rod Serling himself, nothing has lasted like this has.

I have some advice for CBS, the network where this story originally appeared five decades ago. When we get to that date in a little over six months... get rid of all that wretched reality and crime programming you keep spewing out for just one night.

Create a special just to show and discuss this episode as an example for people who were not even born yet, just what tv sometimes actually looked like. I guarantee that from baby boomers alone, the ratings will go through the roof.

Even someone as well read as Henry Bemis would have to admit that as a written story, adapted for tv by Rod Serling, only two words can describe, "Time Enough At Last"

Absolutely brilliant.

My rating -- 5 + (Plus) Classic and then some.

Review by Ken

Whenever I talk to people about the Twilight Zone episodes of the past, ep.8 'Time Enough at Last' is almost always talked about. Everybody who has seen this series remembers the story about Henry Bemis a short, quirky man who loves to read books.

Excellent casting of Burgess Meredith to play the lead role. His wide glasses added to his demeanor and behavior. He uses his work time to talk to bank customers about books he has read.

Great scene at home between Bemis and his wife. Notice she looks the opposite of him by being tall and stern faced. Surely an odd couple for the ages. When Bemis sees his book of poetry lined out by his wife I thought he was going to hit her. She deserved it.

Back at the bank and Bemis hides in vault on lunch hour to read the newspaper. Nice headline. H-Bomb can hit at any minute. What do you know a nuclear bomb destroys everything but Bemis. Commercial break increases the tension of the story.

Memo to Rod Serling. Okay this is the third time out of eight episodes you have used the theme of loneliness. Ep.1,7, and now here. Hey Rod are you trying to tell us something??

The second half of the story was terrific with scenes of destruction of the bank, stores, and cars. Bemis wanders around and oddly calls out for his wife. He still cared for the old nag. He lies down and takes a nap with a smoke in his hand. Not a good idea.

He wakes up and decides to end his life with a gun but is saved at the last moment. The library has tons of books on the ground. Bemis is joyful and can spend his life in joy reading for years to come. We all feel glad that Bemis is happy again.

Classic Twilight Zone does not allow it. Bemis breaks his glasses and he is hopeless now. I know the feeling. I need my reading glasses to read the newspaper everyday. Without my glasses I am lost.

Best line of the entire series spoken by Bemis. "It's not fair. Not fair at all."

Only problem I have with the episode is when Serling adds narration right in the middle of the story. Not needed Rod. Let the story play out for the audience. Your closing lines are good enough.

Nice flow to the story and is surely one of the best episodes produced in Twilight Zone lore. It is in my top ten favorites and enjoy watching again from time to time.

My rating-5 Classic. That makes two episodes in a row I have rated as classics. Way to go Rod.

Review by Linn

Time Enough at Last is my all-time favorite Twilight Zone episode. I have to review this episode from beginning to end. I have to mention one thing right off the bat, though. I have watched this episode close to fifty times and never once have I failed to cry at the end. Silly and sentimental? Maybe. But this show has one of the saddest endings of all of Rod Serling's stories.

It starts out with a very sweet, likable, quirky and friendly man named Henry Bemis played by the incomparable Burgess Meredith. Rod's Serling's opening narration describes him as a "bookish little man whose passion is the printed page". I may not have typed that verbatim, but it was close. The episode starts out with him sitting behind his teller's cage at the bank he works for, and is reading while performing his work. I have to agree with Kitty's review that his reading should not be done while performing his job, though. He was shortchanging customers and most likely keeping other customers waiting while talking about the book David Copperfield with the current customer at his booth. He finds that in the middle of his description of the story that the customer has walked out.

His boss calls him into his office him and tells Henry that he is "a reader of books", and if he doesn't pay more attention to his job, he will lose it. Justified enough. However, Henry tries to explain to his boss that his miserable wife won't allow him to read at home. Yet, his boss has no compassion which makes his boss a creep as well. Henry even says he was so desperate to read that he found himself reading the backs of the condiment bottles on the dinner table. His boss tells him that he sides with Henry's wife and also knows that he's been going to the bank vault during his breaks to read. So what? It's his lunch break and he should be able to go wherever he wants and do whatever he wants during his lunch breaks as long as he has legitimate access to the areas.

He goes down to the vault on that particular afternoon to find solace and be left alone to pursue his reading passion. He puts down his book and picks up a newspaper with the headline telling of a bomb that could destroy the world. Next thing we know, his book cover flies open, his watch crystal cracks and the whole building, including Henry shakes. The amazing thing to me is while his watch crystal cracked, his glasses didn't, but that was most likely because they were so thick and the vault protected them. With his glasses hanging half off of his face, he gets to his feet and departs the vault only to find that the bank is destroyed. As he walks through the shambles of the bank, he suddenly hears a tape recorder with the voice of his former boss giving instructions to his secretary which suddenly cuts off.

He then walks outside of the bank to find a vast wasteland of nothing but rubble and destruction. He tries to find his house, but only finds that it has also been destroyed. He calls for his wife (Why, I don't know because I would think he'd be glad to be rid of the bitch), but he gets no answers or sounds from anyone or anything. He sees a car and tries to start it, but that of course was a waste of time.

He finally starts walking around and finds that food has been spared from the explosion. He feels that he won't starve and has plenty of food to last for a few years. Yet, the radiation would most likely kill him before the food supply ran out. Of course, did not know or realize this. He falls asleep that night on a couch he happened to come across. The next morning, he wakes up to the exact same scenario as the day before. No life, no people, no way to pass the time other than eating, smoking and sleeping.

At first, Henry feels that this is nirvana. Solitude. No nagging wife or hounding boss. But it only took the second or third day for him to realize that the loneliness was getting intolerable. As he said, "If only it weren't for the loneliness, the sameness." Finally he comes across a sporting goods store and sees guns in the display case. He makes the decision that he can no longer live as the only man alive in a world of nothingness. He says "I'm sure I'll be forgiven for this" as he puts the gun to his head. Then, ALAS, he sees before him the pillar which reads "Public Library".

Now I agree and disagree with the fact that books and papers would be one of the first things to be destroyed in a nuclear holocaust, but how can we be certain that this is true? I think it's possible that not all papers and documents would be destroyed in a blast. Some could survive.

In the case of the library that Henry Bemis found, it might be somewhat unlikely that all of those books were in pretty good condition, although they all seemed to be, but I feel that it's unlikely that just about all of them were. However, this had had to be the most logical ending to this episode. Books were Henry's truest passion. He found a haven. He found a Utopia in a world of desolation. He could not have been happier. No miserable wife to pull the books out of his hands and scribble out the words, no miserable boss to tell him he was foolish to love reading so much and no job to interrupt his passion. It was a job he clearly hated and was very bored with as well.

He took much effort to put the books into categories to read month by month. He was in heaven. He spoke those infamous words "There's time now. All the time I need. Time enough at last." And in a split second, his Utopia was taken away because he reached for a book, slipped a bit on the step and his glasses fell from his face only to be broken to pieces. The saddest part is that he was so blind without them that he couldn't even walk around to find an optometry shop to see if there were at least some type of glasses that survived the explosion tore place them. It's unlikely if he did find an optometrist's shop that any of the glasses would be unbroken or if he could even find something comparable to those Coke bottle lenses, but who knows. We'll never know because he could barely see his hand in front of his face without his glasses.

Now I can see him wanting to kill himself. He finally had absolutely nothing left. The only problem is - how will he ever find the gun again? He set it down somewhere and would probably kill himself falling down the library steps trying to go find it. One way or another, he was going to die. He most likely couldn't even find his food again. Poor, poor Henry.

One of the saddest Twilight Zones ever with one of the most shocking endings. I give it a Classic, Classic rating.

"The Twilight Zone" Episode 9 "Perchance To Dream"

Original Air Date- November 27,1959
Guest Star- Richard Conte
Written by Charles Beaumont
Directed by Robert Florey

Review by Kitty

This latest episode is called Perchance to Dream. It holds the distinction of being the first script that we've seen that has not been written by Rod Serling.

We start off by seeing a man approaching a building during lunch hour. The camera work in this episode is particularly impressive I think. We see the man watching the people walking through the revolving door. It's quick shots between the people and the man.

We find out the man's name is Edward Hall. He leans against the building and a man asks him if he's ill. Edward simply ignores him and goes in to the building. He arrives at a Dr. Rathman's office. Dr. Rathman is a psychiatrist. He walks in and we see the back of a woman's head tell Edward that the doctor has been expecting him.

He walks in to the office and Dr. Rathman asks him if he's all right. Edward tells Rathman that he's just tired. Rathman tells him he can lie down on his couch. He does. We see Edward close his eyes and a dark shadow falls over him much like what we saw in One for the Angels on that little girl.

Edward then jumps up from the couch and lights a cigarette. He tells Rathman that he hasn't slept in over eighty hours. He asks what his doctor told him. Rathman replies only that his doctor referred him because he had problems sleeping. He has a rheumatic heart condition, he's thirty five and single.

Edward continues to puff away on the cigarette and surveys the room. He walks over to the window and opens it. He looks down. We also get to look down and see that it's a significant drop. Once again the camera work is interesting.

Rathman walks over and closes the window. Edward simply says he wanted some air. Rathman turns on the air conditioner. Edward is convinced that Rathman can't help him and starts to walk out. Rathman tells him that while sometimes you can run away, other times you can't.

Edward turns around and tells him that if he tells him what's been happening to him, will he promise not to have him taken off in a straight jacket. Rathman tells him there are no promises on anything.

Edward looks at the picture in his office of a boat. He asks Rathman if the boat has ever moved. Rathman tells him not that he's aware of it moving. Edward tells him that when he was a kid, they had a picture like it in his house and his mother told him that if he looked at it long enough it would move. So one night he looked at it for over and hour and it did move.

Rathman told him it was an optical illusion. He agreed but then it wouldn't stop moving.

He then explains that about two years ago a woman was killed in her car driving on Canyon Road because someone was hiding in her back seat when she didn't realize it. He tells him that one night, he was driving home on that very same road and while he knew he was alone in the car, he had a feeling that someone was watching him from the back. He kept looking at the rear view mirror when all of a sudden he saw a pair of woman's eyes looking at him.

Of course he knew it wasn't real but that didn't stop him from getting in to a severe accident. His doctor told him that his heart could not take another severe stress like that.

He then proceeds to tell Rathman about how he's now having a terrible dream. He dreams he's at an amusement park. Again we see the amusement park but the way it's filmed with the camera angles is very impressive. It's very surreal looking.

We first see Edward walking up to a shooting range where he pays to be able to shoot a gun at a moving target which is rather strange looking. He then hears another barker shouting that they have beautiful girls there.

He walks over and sees a woman on stage, dressed almost catlike. Her name is Maya and she does a very exotic dance to

Edward. For being 1959, this is a rather suggestive dance that she's doing.

He runs away. He ends up by a fun house and he lights up a cigarette. Maya approaches him and asks him why he ran away. He asks her why she's not working. She tells him she has the rest of the night off. She wants to go in to the funhouse and she wants him to take her. He takes her in.

They are surrounded by all kinds of strange faces and animals. Maya asks Edward to kiss her. He complies and she laughs. Everything starts to zoom in on him.

He runs away. He's back in Rathman's office and tells him that Maya is chasing him in his dreams and that's why he can't go to sleep.

He tells him he knows this because the next night he dreamed about her again in the amusement park and she convinces him to go on a roller coaster with her. She's laughing all the way but Edward is telling her that his heart can't take it and he's got to get off. She tells him it's too late. She continues to laugh.

He then tells Rathman that there's nothing he can do to help him, and he walks out. He then gets out to the reception area and he sees Maya sitting at the desk typing. He then runs back in to Rathman's office and tells him that his receptionist is Maya. Rathman tells him that his receptionist's name is not Maya.

Edward gets a wild look in his eyes and he runs for the window and jumps out. We then see Rathman sitting at his desk. He calls his secretary Miss Thomas into the office. They walk to Edward lying there on the couch and they conclude that he's died.

Miss Thomas tells him that he seemed fine a minute ago when he walked in to the office. Rathman tells her that he just seemed tired and he told him he could lie down.

And so ends the insomnia for Edward. He dreamed his final dream with Rathman and Miss Thomas in it.

Overall, I liked this episode. This episode is probably one of the creepier episodes in that it delves in to the private horror that people can create for themselves in their mind. I thought the camera work was great giving the surreal effects that you needed especially in the dream sequences. That funhouse would certainly creep me out. The roller coaster was no picnic either.

I found the irony of all though that here was Edward suffering from a heart condition and yet it didn't occur to him to quit smoking. The smoking is probably what did his heart in, not any kind of dream.

However, I think the acting on the part of all of the actors, Robert Conti, John Larch and Suzanne Lloyd was well done. I especially liked the transformation from Suzanne Lloyd from femme fatale to unassuming receptionist. I got the impression from watching her that she enjoyed playing Maya. As I said, in 1959,there probably weren't too many TV shows that could give an actress a part like that.

Robert Conti was good as well. The only problem that I might have with the story itself might be that we're really not sure what killed Edward in the end. Was he really having bad dreams and unable to sleep or was he actually just incorporating what he saw in to his last dream and he died simply from his condition?

I guess that's what makes the show worth watching is that is makes you question things from time to time.

I will rate this a 4 rating....excellent

Review by Linn

Perchance To Dream was a very creepy and bizarre episode. I would say it was good, but nowhere near classic. I just felt that it had too many flaws to be rated any higher. Actor John Larch does a fine job as the psychiatrist who tries to help Edward Hall, but Suzanne Lloyd who plays Maya, the seductress, is totally overacting. The main character, Edward Hall, is played by Richard Conte who also doesn't do a bad job, but I felt there was a bit of overacting on his part as well.

The whole premise was rather unbelievable. Hall tells the psychiatrist that he's been awake for 87 hours because he's afraid that if he falls asleep, he won't wakeup. He also says that if he stays awake much longer, he'll die of a heart attack. Sounds like a lose-lose situation, especially since he's taking pills to stay awake. He's basically putting himself in the grave. He's seduced in his dream by a very beautiful and sexy woman who does cause him some stress by making him ride a roller coaster, but if he has to die of either a heart attack from being awake for days or from dreaming about this woman seducing him, you would think he'd go for the more pleasant demise, stressful or not.

The final scene when Edward jumps out the window to his death was a great ending even though it didn't really happen. We find out at the end that he died within seconds of lying down on the psychiatrist's couch. Very creative camera work in this episode for many of the scenes.

Bobby is absolutely correct that weird and strange are trademarks of The Twilight Zone so this one does fit into that category. Not one of the best, but not one of the worst. I give this one a rating of Good.

Review by Ken

Talk about mood swings. I was on a high mountain with the last two episodes-'The Lonely and Time Enough at Last.'

Now all of the sudden comes episode #9 'Perchance to Dream.' Suddenly I feel like I have fallen off a cliff and descended into a low valley. What was that?? What a mess of a script. Wretched, pitiful, pathetic, and despairing story. This episode will be in my bottom ten worst of the entire series. We will see later if it is my no. 1 clunker of all time.

Let's see. A man with a heart problem comes in to see a psychiatrist and complains that he is afraid to fall asleep. He dreams of a nightmare at a carnival where a sexy lady lures him into a funhouse. He is haunted with scary images. He is afraid of the roller coaster and fears for his life. Therefore he takes pills to keep him awake.

The first segment of this episode was boring. Richard Conte's acting here was awful. The creepy look on his face was annoying.

Suzanne Lloyd was even worse. Talk about overacting and idiotic she takes the cake. She reminded me of a nightmare Richard Kimble had about Marcie King.

The chilling music and dark images did not work for me. Even as I kid I could see through all the fake props.

The end scene of this story was absurd and preposterous. Edward Hall sees Miss Thomas the receptionist and goes crazy. He runs toward the window and jumps to his death. But is he dreaming again? The final scene shows him not sleeping but dead. So what happened?? Which scene was real or not? I am in a maze. Why bother? Throw this script in the trash can.

My rating - 0 Lousy

Review by Bobbynear

A truly different and bizarre episode that surely does not look like most of the others. While nowhere near a classic, certainly it doesn't deserve the blasting it took from Ken. There are a few good things to say about it.

Boring it's not. Very fast paced, perhaps too much so, it puts viewers right in the middle of the main character's nightmare. He has no idea what is going on and neither do we. Maybe the whole thing is being imagined, maybe not. The Twilight Zone is legendary for its trick endings. This is just one big trick from start to finish.

Ken is right about the acting. It isn't much but then it's not about acting. It's about images, nothing else. When you actually have a nightmare and wake up, all you remember is the images, not the acting in this story your own mind made up. So it is here and that doesn't bother me.

I think this is one of those rare episodes that actually would have benefited from being a little longer. It's hard to feel anything for a character that just shows up, and then less than a half hour later jumps out a window, or so it appears. We know nothing about this man, other than that he seems terrified.

If nothing else, this episode did make me wonder if any of this is possible. If a man with a heart condition could really scare himself to death if his dreams were too vivid. Normally when you have a really bad nightmare, and find yourself in jeopardy, you conveniently wake up just before finding out if you made it or not. This poor man didn't have that luxury.

I disagree with Ken that the end was absurd. We certainly do know what happened. The Doctor makes it clear that this man came in his office and laid down on the couch and fell asleep. Nobody ever jumped out a window except in his imagination. He did scare himself to death right there. End of story.

Being weird, strange, different is actually a trademark of this series so I think it fits in well. Kitty gave it a four and Ken a zero. I think I'll land somewhere in the middle and give it a 3 rating....good.

"The Twilight Zone" Episode 10 "Judgment Night"

Original Air Date- December 4, 1959
Guest Star- Nehemiah Persoff
Written by Rod Serling
Directed by John Brahm

Review by Kitty

This next episode is called Judgment Night and basically appeals to the idea that what you don't pay for in this life you pay for all the more in the next one.

We start by seeing a man on a passenger ship by the name of the SS Queen of Glasgow carrying cargo from England to New York in 1942. It's a rather eerie night with fog all around. A purser comes out from the dining area to tell him that he should come in and get something to eat.

He walks in and it's clearly obvious that he's agitated about something. He sits at a table with other passengers and orders coffee. He picks up a doll for a little girl who dropped it. The captain of the ship comes in and visits with the passengers. He asks the various passengers where they are from. There is a man from Chicago who is definitely looking forward to going home.

There is a British officer Major Devereaux and his secretary Miss Stanley.... The captain asks the man who clearly has a German accent where he's from. He tells them that he was born in Frankfurt. This seems a little upsetting to the passenger but not as much as you might expect. Nobody is accusing him of being a spy even though this is a British ship and this is World War II.

The man's name is Carl Lanser but that's all he can remember about himself. He does however, remember something about what u-boats do when they attack. In fact, he's very knowledgeable. The captain asks him if he's ever served on au-boat. Lanser tells him no as he spills coffee on himself. He apologizes and asks Miss Stanley if any got on her. She tells him no but he got himself pretty good. The purser tries to help him and he pushes him away.

Lanser then tells everybody that he's not feeling well and will retire for the evening. Later, Miss Stanley is walking back to her room and Lanser approaches her and asks her if they've ever met before. She tells him no. He tells her he can't remember anything about himself other than his name and where he was born but he feels sure that he's been on this ship before and that he knows everybody on board. She tells him he should get some rest.

At that moment, the first officer approaches him and tells him that the captain would like to see him. Lanser goes to the bridge and the captain tells him that they don't have his passport number on file and one is supposed to do that when they board. Lanser explains he doesn't have it with him and he really is not sure how he got on the ship. The captain tells him to get rest and to just bring it by in the next day or two. Lanser leaves and the captain tells his first officer to keep an eye on him.

In Lanser's room, a steward is helping him look for his passport and they haven't found it and the steward offers to put things away for him. He takes out a hat that is clearly a hat that shows command and it shows the Nazi symbol on it. The steward asks him if he's been a German commander.... Lanser grabs the hat and tells him to not concern himself with it. He looks inside and he sees the name Lt. Commander Carl Lanser. The steward leaves and it is odd here that the steward does not even flinch at the fact that he sees a Nazi symbol on his hat.

Lanser panics and goes back to the salon where the bartender is and he starts to drink. The engines have also stopped. Lanser asks the bartender what's up with that and he tells him it happens a lot but they'll get them up and running. Lanser tells him that it makes them sitting ducks for a u-boat.

The first officer comes in and Lanser asks why everybody is so calm when there are u-boats out there. The first officer replies it would do no good to panic. Lanser looks at the clock and sees that it's five minutes after midnight. He tells the first officer and the bartender that something is going to happen atone fifteen. He's not sure what but something terrible will happen.

One fifteen arrives and Lanser realizes that a u-boat is going to sink the ship. He starts to run on deck to tell people and he grabs binoculars and sees the u-boat and the commander of that u-boat he realizes is himself. He starts running all over the ship screaming that everybody needs to get in to the lifeboats because the ship will be sunk. Nobody appears to be hearing him because nobody at first appears to be on the ship.

He runs in to the passenger quarters and he yells to the passengers who don't look the slightest bit concerned at what he's screaming about. He looks to them again and they are not there.

All of a sudden the bullets and the bombs start to hit the ship. One by one, we see the various passengers that he's encountered die before him and he can't do anything to stop it. We see the man in the engine room frantically trying to get out. We see Miss Stanley in her room with fire all around and she's screaming for help. We see two others try in vain to get to the lifeboats but they are killed as they get to them. We see the captain on the bridge with fire all around him as the ship is about to be sunk. Lanser is the last one to fall dead on the deck and we see the boat sink.

Back on the u-boat, Commander Lanser is pleased with what he has done. His young officer Lt. Mueller comes to him and tells him that he's not sure they did the right thing. He tells them that it had passengers on the ship and they didn't give fair warning. Lanser asks him why he would do that when they could radio for help ahead of time.

Mueller can't shake the feeling that they are damned for what they did. He wonders if that will follow them in to the next life. Those people on the ship could only die once but maybe they'll die on that boat every night for all eternity because of what they did.

Lanser dismisses his worries. We then see Lanser again on the deck of the SS Queen of Glasgow being told that dinner is almost over and he should come in to the dining area. He starts to walk in as he did the night before.

I think this episode was well done. I think Nehemiah Persoff and all of the supporting cast did an excellent job. We even got to see a couple of stars before they were stars. Patrick MacNee who would become famous as Steed on The Avengers played the first officer to he captain and James Franciscus played Lanser's first officer however, it was evident that he was not able to cop a German accent as he sounded like a guy from Malibu on that German u-boat but that's OK. It was still an enjoyable episode.

It did seem a little odd initially that the people on that ship weren't more concerned about German u-boats in the area although after you realize that these people are only phantoms of what was and the real person of emotion is Lanser, it makes sense.

I think the idea that Serling was coming up with here was that in reality back in 1942, it is quite plausible that all of those people on that ship were having anxious feelings but the emotions have all been transferred to Lanser. He now has to feel their anxiety and he's forced to watch them die and can do nothing about it before he himself perishes over and over.

It kind of plays in to the story of A Christmas Carol by Charles Dickens where Marley shows Scrooge the dead people who were greedy tyrants in life and never did anything for anyone else unless it benefited them and now they are forced to watch the suffering of the world and realize that for all eternity they must watch and can do nothing to intervene and help which is what ultimately happened with Lanser. He realized too late that the ship was going to get destroyed and he could do nothing to save anyone on board who he came to know, respect and like and like the others he is condemned to die by his own hand.

However, unlike the others on board, he will have to replay this over and over again for all eternity and suffer every night as those people suffered.

Overall, I liked this episode. I think it had a strong theme to it, the acting was good and this is actually an episode that I had not seen before so it was an extra special treat to watch it. I will rate this one a 4 rating for excellent.

Review by Bobbynear

Judgment Night turns out to be a rather nifty little thriller that not only transfers the fear and dread of its main character very effectively to the audience, but also tackles the sensitive issue of just what punishment is appropriate when a massive crime against humanity is committed.

Although it is well done, there is nothing terribly original about this story. Very loosely based on the real life sinking of the liner the Lusitania in 1915 off the coast of Ireland by a Nazi U boat in which over 1,000 passengers perished. Quite controversial at the time, since that ship carried not only passengers but also tons of munitions that were being hidden on it as the world prepared for war. Of course we have no way of knowing if the commander of that U-boat had any remorse afterwards, voluntary or enforced, but that seems unlikely.

In this case, a man named Lanser seems more remorseful that he got caught than over what he did. Now finding himself on the very ship he ordered to be sunk in to the ocean, he gets to see how the other half lived, and died. Most of the suspense in this short story comes early on as viewers try to figure out just what is bothering him so much. At first it seems as though he's on a fictional version of The Titanic and has a premonition of some sort of disaster.

As it turns out, he's the originator of the disaster and the story is pretty much given away when a Nazi officer's hat with his name on it is found. After that, its all about his efforts in vain as it turns out, to warn people about what is coming their way.

Nice special effects with the dark and the fog providing a very eerie and threatening feeling. Good acting by Nehemiah Persoff who is pretty much required to carry the entire story on his shoulders since only he knows the truth.

Good casting since Persoff, who is still alive according to IMDB and will turn90 in August of 2009, was born in Jerusalem Palestine (now Israel). He's still married to his one and only wife Thia, who is also still living. They will celebrate their 58th anniversary in August of this year.

This is what IMDB had to say about Persoff in his biography: "Short, dark, chunky-framed and with a distinct talent for dialects, Persoff became known primarily for his ethnic villainy, usually playing authoritative Eastern Europeans, in a formidable career that had him portraying everything from cab drivers to Joseph Stalin. He was a durable performer during TV's "Golden Age" ("Gunsmoke" (1955), "The Twilight Zone" (1959)) and well beyond("Chicago Hope" (1994), "Law & Order" (1990)), playing hundreds of intense, volatile and dominating characters."

Obviously an excellent choice for this particular kind of story and he makes the most of it.

I do like this episode for those reasons and beyond. It also makes a person wonder just what an appropriate punishment would be for someone responsible for the deaths of hundreds of innocent civilians, especially in wartime, or if there should even be one. Lanser certainly finds out the hard way.

It also has to make you wonder if a real life personality like Adolph Hitler suffered the same kind of fate after committing suicide. Was he also damned to an eternal life of burning in the fires of hell like millions of his innocent concentration camp victims? One can only hope.

My rating on a scale of 0 to 5
4 ~~ Excellent

Review by Linn

Judgment Night is a very creepy and eerie episode, but not terribly original. It seems that this plotline had been touched upon before in earlier movies of that time period as well as being redone with interesting variations by Rod Serling himself in previous and subsequent Twilight Zone episodes.

It's 1942. A man named Carl Lanser is very distraught, and with good reason. You see, he was once a German U-boat commander. He is sitting on a ship called the SS Queen of Glasgow -- the very ship that Lanser gave the order to attack at 1:15 a.m. the very next morning. So how can he be sitting there? He's paying for his crime against humanity by having to relive that night and morning every day for the rest of his life.

The creepiness in this episode surfaces when Lanser first starts encountering the other passengers on the ship. He can't remember anything about himself other than his name and place of birth. However, he knows quite a bit about German U-boats which makes the other passengers of this British ocean liner somewhat uneasy. After all, Lanser is German. He also comes across to the others as rather uncomfortable and nervous.

The ship's captain requests to see his passport, and while searching for it in his cabin along with a steward, the steward comes across a German commander's cap in Lanser's closet with Nazi symbol in it. Lanser seems quite irritated by this and grabs it from the steward, quickly dismissing it.

Finally, he gets the overwhelming feeling that something terrible is going to happen at 1:15 a.m... He believes the ship is going to come under attack from U-boats.

Back on deck, Lanser grabs a pair of binoculars and sees a U-boat in the distance. He's shocked when he sees that the U-boat commander is none other than himself. He tries to warn the other passengers and crew, but they disappear before his eyes. Of course. They are mere phantoms. Suddenly at the specified time, the ship is being attacked. The passengers and crew are dying in front of him. Lanser is the last to die. One particularly chilling scene came when Lanser looks out at the ocean and sees a doll floating in the water - the very doll that a little girl had dropped on the floor in the dining room earlier in the day which Lanser picked up for her.

Lanser was very proud of himself after attacking the SS Queen of Glasgow, but now he is doomed, just as he was warned by his young lieutenant played by a yet unknown James Franciscus. He will suffer this same fate day after day and night after night for all eternity.

The eeriness in this episode comes from the great setting that depicts a very dark and foggy night. A perfect backdrop for an ominous story. Nehemiah Persoff was stellar in his role. The story dragged a bit at the very beginning but then picked up nicely. I give this episode an Excellent rating.

Review by Ken

I always look for the main theme with each story. Clearly deja vu is the main premise. A dejected passenger on a ship is confused, bewildered, baffled, and puzzled with his situation. How did he get on the ship?

Opening narration by Serling is one of the best to date. Ship strolling along in a creepy, foggy night. Question? What is up with opening scenes with a character having a ghost look on his face? Borrowed idea from previous stories we have seen before.

The first half of story dragged along with Carl Lanser talking with passengers. He thinks he is having a nightmare. Mmmm....

where have we seen that story before. Oh yeah-Last episode. Could it be amnesia? Key point of story. At 1:15 something bad is going to happen.

The second half picked up at a better pace. We the audience now know that the ship is going down. Pirates? Bomb? Iceberg? Lanser goes crazy and tries to warn everybody on board. At this point my interest got stirred. Abandon ship. Full scale attack is happening. Stunts were good and the music is chilling. Poor lady in distress cannot be saved. Baby doll floating in water.

Scene fades to a different looking Lanser who looks like a Kapitan Leutenant. He ordered the attack. His crewman feels guilty for attacking and killing people. Damnation is in order? Is there a Judgment?

Lanser scoffs but there is Karma. Repeated dream of people being killed for eternity is his punishment.

All in all a good Twilight Zone feel. Best to watch this story on a cold foggy morning. A little disappointed with some borrowed themes from earlier episodes such as nightmare and perplexion. However the story is worth watching. Good casting of Nehemiah Persoff in the lead role. Nobody else stands out at all.

My rating -4 Excellent

"The Twilight Zone" Episode 11 "And When the Sky Was Opened"

Original Air Date- December 11, 1959
Guest Star- Rod Taylor
Written by Rod Serling
Directed by Douglas Heyes

Review by Kitty

This latest episode is called And When the Sky was Opened. This episode for me epitomizes what one means when they say they've entered the Twilight Zone. This is truly one of the creepier episodes that takes three very ordinary guys and plops them down in to very extraordinary circumstances.

This episode once again looks at the space program. We start by seeing a spaceship, nothing like what our astronauts eventually flew in but this is fantasy after all. It's in the hanger and has returned from space and interestingly enough, we never actually get to see the space craft. It's under wraps, but it's clearly nothing from the Mercury program.

We then see an astronaut by the name of Col. Forbes played by Rod Taylor in a hospital corridor. A nurse, played by Leave it Beaver teacher Miss Landers, ala Sue Randall walks by him and says hello and tells him she hasn't seen him since he left the hospital yesterday. He asks her if she remembers him leaving the hospital and she says yes.

He then goes in to see his friend, Maj. Gart who is still in the hospital with a broken leg. Gart is thrilled to see Forbes and asks what it's like outside. Forbes grabs the newspaper and asks Gart what he sees and Gart tells him he sees a picture of the both of them saying they returned to earth.

He asks Gart what he remembers about the flight. He tells him that they took off from earth, after four hours they all blacked out and then they crash landed in the desert twenty four hours later. Gart tells him that Forbes was discharged the day before.

Forbes tells Gart that he didn't leave the hospital alone. He left with the third astronaut, Col Ed Harrington. He tells him that there were three beds in this room originally. There were three of them on that flight...... Gart tells him he doesn't know what he's talking about as he doesn't know an Ed Harrington. Forbes insists that he has known Ed for fifteen years and that Gart has known him for five years. Gart still doesn't know what he's talking about and wants to call for help for Forbes.

Forbes stops him and proceeds to tell him what happened in the past twenty four hours. We then see a flashback to the day before. Harrington and Forbes are there laughing and joking with Gart. They look at the newspaper and see a picture of the three astronauts.

Forbes and Harrington leave and they go to a bar. They order beer and start to talk to a lady at the bar. The bartender gives them beer on the house. Everything appears to be normal and then Harrington looks straight ahead and gets a worried look on his face. Forbes turns to him and wants to toast to happy landings and when Harrington picks up the beer he drops it on the floor.

The bartender happily gives him another beer. They toast and Forbes asks Harrington if he's all right. He tells him he's fine but the wants to call his parents in Iowa. He goes to the phone booth and makes the phone call.

We then see Harrington call Forbes over to the phone booth and he tells him that he just phoned his parents and both his father and mother told him they didn't have a son named Ed Harrington. Forbes tells him that it must be some kind of gag. Harrington tells him that he was thinking while he was sitting at the bar that he got a feeling like they weren't supposed to be there. He tells Forbes that he thinks that whatever grabbed them for twenty four hours let them go by mistake.

Forbes tells him he's going to get him another drink. Forbes walks to the bar and sees Harrington's beer gone. He asks the bartender where his friend's drink is and the bartender asks him what friend. Forbes tells him that it's the friend he came in with who dropped his drink. He looks at the floor and there is no spilled drink on the floor.

The bartender tells him that he came in alone. Forbes runs back to the phone booth and sees Harrington gone. He asks what's going on. The people in the bar have no idea what he's talking about. Forbes then looks at the newspaper and sees only himself and Gart in the picture. He then yells to everybody that they are crazy and he runs out.

The scene switches to a hotel room and Forbes is trying to get in touch with the general at the air force base that he and Harrington trained at. He's told he'll call him back. There is then a knock at the door and it's Forbes's girlfriend Amy. Amy is very angry at him. She tells him that he sent her a telegram saying that he'd meet her at the bus station at midnight and she was there and waited. One o'clock came along and she was still waiting so she then checked every bar and hotel in town until she found him here.

Forbes then realizes that he told her in the telegram that both he and Harrington would meet her at the bus station. She has no idea who Ed Harrington is. Forbes looks for his copy of the telegram and to his shock he sees no mention of Ed Harrington. He tells her that he put his name there.

Amy tells him she doesn't know who he's referring to. Forbes tells her that they've had dinner with him and have attended dances with him many times. Amy tells him she still doesn't know who he's referring to.

The phone then rings and it's his general from the base and he asks him about Ed Harrington and the general whom they both trained under for twenty months has no idea who he is talking about.

Forbes hangs up and literally goes off the deep end. He's screaming that everybody is in on this prank aren't they? He knows that Ed Harrington is back at the bar. He runs back to the bar which is now closed and breaks in to it and calls for Ed and begs him to please come back as he breaks down and cries in the phone booth.

The scene switches back to the present in Gart's hospital room and he tells him that he's sorry but he still can't remember Ed Harrington and thinks that Forbes is delusional. Forbes then looks at himself in the mirror and sees no image of himself. He then realizes that they are coming to get him. He screams no he doesn't want to leave.

He runs out of the room and Gart hobbles out of bed and calls for help. The nurse comes in and tells him he needs to get back in bed. Gart tells her that Col Forbes needs help. She asks who that is and he tells her that was the man who just ran down the hallway. She tells him that nobody ran down the hallway. Gart tells her he was sharing the room with him just yesterday and was in that bed over there.

He looks and sees no bed. The nurse tells him that he's the only person who's been in this room. She's going to go get the doctor. As the she walks out, he sees the newspaper and the newspaper now shows only him on the front page as the lone astronaut who has come back from space.

He then gets a very worried look on his face and the camera pans upward. The last scene we see in the hospital is the same nurse talking to a doctor who is asking her if there are any empty rooms. She tells yes, the room at the end of the hallway is open. They walk in and there are no beds in there. He tells her they'll put the malaria patients in there.

We then see where the aircraft was and it's gone. The wrap that was covering lays nicely folded in the middle of the area where it once sat.

I thought this episode was excellent. The acting by Rod Taylor is superb as a guy who remembers things that nobody else does. His final breakdown in the phone booth in the bar is excellent. How would any of us react to something like that? In fact, I remember Star Trek, The Next Generation did a similar story to this one where Dr. Crusher noticed people disappearing from the ship and only she had memories of them. She had inadvertently walked in to a different dimension of time.

As I watch this episode I am inclined to think that these three gentleman came back to simply the wrong earth. When I think about the ending, I'd like to think that the someone or something sent them back to the right earth. Rod Serling in this case lets you make up your own mind where you think they went. The reason I hypothesize that is simply because at the end nobody remembers them or the space craft which tells me this earth never had a space craft like that and these three gentleman did not exist in this earth.

Then again, you can go with the more sinister aspect of it where it's diabolical space aliens who want our technology and therefore, used major mind control to wipe the memories of everybody on earth. Again Rod Serling let's you decide in this case.

Overall, I think this episode delivers on what the Twilight Zone is all about. It's about ordinary people getting wrapped up in extraordinary circumstances that nobody can explain and the end leaves you with a big question mark of where did those three astronauts go?

It's exciting, confusing and creepy all in one. I will rank this one a four for excellent. It's not quite a classic but it comes very close.

Review by Ken

My fellow T.Z reviewers. What was that?? Three men recover from a crash-landing. Slowly one disappears. Then another is gone. Then the third one is missing. Three empty beds. And the spacecraft has vanished. Whoopee!!!!

Another ghostly look on a man's face opening. Rod Taylor in the lead role was wasted here. Lovely girl at the bar contributed nothing. Beer falling on floor shocks the audience. What in the world is going on here. Awful story is too nice of a word here. Dud and flop are better words. Terrible, dreadful, deplorable, and appalling episode.

I just wasted 30 minutes of my time watching a story that went nowhere and ended flat as a pancake. Producers what point are you trying to make? Doctor and nurse discover nobody is around. Back to work guys.

I promise everyone ep. 11 will be in my bottom ten worst of the entire series.

Hey Rod! Please come up with better ideas. You can do it.

My rating - 0 Lousy

Review by Bobbynear

This story brings to mind that old adage, "It's better to have loved and lost than never to have loved at all." Perhaps that might be true here. That it's better to have a creepy and disturbing story like this even without an ending, than to never have seen it at all. I wish I could say I felt that way, but I don't.

An interesting premise, done well with good actors turning in uniformly excellent performances ultimately leads nowhere and that is the problem. For awhile there I thought I was watching the series debut episode, "Where Is Everybody?" all over again. Another character finds himself suddenly the only person left in a very unusual setting, only this time it's working in the opposite direction, with lots of people around who are slowly disappearing one by one.

One of the things The Twilight Zone does best is to force you to consider what you would do if some of these things were happening to you. What to worry about most, the fact that your friends are disappearing right in front of your eyes, or that you may be the next to disappear.

For most of the thirty minutes, this premise is enough to keep it interesting. But in the end, there is no end, no explanation, no reason to wait for an ending. It comes to nothing.

In Mark Scott Zicree's book, The Twilight Zone Companion, the author calls this a good but flawed episode. Rod Serling, who adapted Richard Matheson's short story for the small screen is quoted as saying that what happened during the story was so "bizarre" that it "out-shadowed" any need for an ending.

As much as I admire Serling, I'm afraid I have to disagree here. I need an ending. I need a reason to sit through this and I didn't get it. It's a little like sitting down to a four course gourmet meal for dinner, where the main dish is sensational, but there is still something missing, like appetizers, salad and dessert. It just doesn't come together the way it should.

In her review, Kitty seems not to be bothered by the fact that Serling left it up to viewer's imaginations to come up with a suitable ending. In fact, she comes up with several that would have been very interesting to see play out on the screen. Well I don't mind doing a little work myself while I'm being entertained, but in the end I want the writer to finish the job, even if he makes a fool out of me by taking it in a direction I don't agree with.

Maybe Rod Serling should have written a story where a writer comes up with some great ideas, but along the way, things start disappearing until there is nothing left at the end....including an ending. That might have been even more disturbing than what happens in this episode. In fact, it was....

I'm afraid I'm a real stickler for this kind of thing. I was always taught that you need a beginning, a middle and an end. So now I expect it. I don't just watch a tv drama to see if I can kill thirty minutes and stay awake. I need an ending.

In my world, the only thing worse than a bad ending, is no ending at all. It almost always costs you serious rating points, as it does here.

My rating on a scale of 0 to 5
2 1/2 - Fair (Slightly Above Average)

Review by Linn

I've seen And When the Sky was Opened a few times over the years, but since I do not care for it, I usually either doze off or leave the room when it comes on now during marathons or other times. However, before reviewing it, I watched it one more time. I mean, I really watched it to get a better and final perspective of it. I agree with Kitty that Rod Taylor was very good in his role, but after viewing it over again, I do believe that the story should have had some sort of closure as Ken and Bobby pointed out.

Every time I watch this episode, I find myself scratching my head and wondering what really happened to them. It just seemed so bizarre that each man was not only disappearing one at a time from the newspaper story and photo about their return to earth, but also that no one could remember Ed Harrington, including his own parents. Each man was disappearing one by one with no apparent explanation and then the aircraft is gone.

Why were they there in the first place and where did they go? And what do we make of the newspaper article? Whose idea was it to cast that terrible actor James Hutton in the episode? Yes, this was a very open-ended story. While I cannot agree with Ken that it deserves a lousy rating, I also cannot agree with Kitty that it was excellent. I have to go with my instincts and rate it as Average.

"The Twilight Zone" Episode 12 "What You Need"

Original Air Date- December 25, 1959
Guest Star Steve Cochran
Written by Rod Serling
Directed by Alvin Ganzer

Review by Kitty

This latest episode is called What You Need. We start the episode out with a scene in a bar that looks very similar to the bar in the last episode but that's OK, they're on a budget.

A man is sitting at the end of the bar and the bartender who is not thrilled with him there walks up to him and asks him if he can get him another and the man replies no. The bartender tells him that they sell booze there not rent space. The man is not happy to hear this and asks him if he'd like him to rearrange his face and the bartender walks away in disgust saying that they get all types in there.

We get a very interesting narrative from Rod Serling. He tells us that we are looking at Mr. Fred Renard who is a sour man, a friendless man, a lonely man, a grasping, compulsive, nervous man. My first thought was this man is pretty bleak and he's only 36 to boot. Why would a man be so sour in the prime of his life?

Serling goes on to say that he's lived 36 undistinguished, meaningless, pointless, face-laden years who at this moment looks for escape. Enter a little old man who is a peddler selling little items. He's a very kind and unassuming man.

He approaches a young woman in the bar and asks her if she needs anything and she tells him matches and then he all of a sudden tells her that she doesn't need matches but cleaning solution instead. She takes the bottle free of charge with a puzzled look on her face.

He then approaches a man by the name of Lefty who we find out is at the bar every night drinking his sorrows away. The man asks him what he needs and Lefty tells him he doesn't have what he needs which is a new left arm because he injured it playing for the

Cubs. The man then produces a bus ticket to Scranton PA for him. Lefty asks him why he needs a bus ticket and what's in Scranton. The man replies, you never know.

The bartender laughs and tells him it's just coal mines there. The phone in the bar rings and it's for Lefty. Lefty takes the call and it's his former coach who wants him to come and coach the minor league team in Scranton. Lefty is thrilled as he realizes the man gave him the bus ticket that he needed to get there. Lefty then wishes that he could clean the stain off of his suit jacket and the woman in the bar comes forward and tells him she has something that may help.

As this is all unfolding, the man looks at Renard and gets a foreboding look on his face and quickly leaves. Renard follows him and demands to know what he needs. The man gives him scissors. Renard takes the scissors and leaves. When he gets back to his hotel that he's staying at, his scarf gets caught in the elevator and begins to choke him. He grabs the scissors and cuts himself free.

He then shows up at the little old man's apartment whom we find out is named Pedott. Renard tells him that he wants to be his partner because he has a gift. Pedott explains that he uses it sparingly. Renard won't hear of it, he wants to know what he needs tomorrow. Pedott gives him a fountain pen and a leaky one at that but it leaks on the races for the next day.

Renard bets on the horse that the pen dripped on and he wins $240. He wants more but the pen doesn't work the next day. He goes back to Pedott and he demands to know what he needs and Pedott tells him he doesn't need anything that he can give him because what he needs is peace, serenity and kindness in his life and those are things that have to come from within.

Renard won't hear of it and demands he give him what he needs or he'll kill him. He gives Renard a pair of shoes. Renard puts them on thinking that he needs to walk somewhere in them. He finds they are too small and they slip when he walks in them. He gets angry and wants to kill Pedott right there and as he walks across the street to get him he slips and is hit by a car going by. He is killed.

Pedott then explains that he saw Renard kill him in the bar and the shoes were what Pedott needed not Renard.

The police are there cleaning up and a couple comes out of their apartment asking Pedott what happened and he explains it was a hit and run. Pedott then offers the man a comb because it's what he needs. The man takes it but he thinks Pedott is crazy until a reporter shows up to take pictures and the man quickly takes the comb out of his pocket and combs his hair for a picture and the last thing we see are the shoes on the street.

Overall, I like this episode. I initially thought this might have a happy ending as it seemed initially that maybe Pedott was there to give Renard some kind of compass on where to take his life as he was for Lefty.

However, we soon realize that Renard is exactly what Rod Serling said at the beginning and he was a lost cause or more likely a lost soul. The moral being that happiness has to start from within. If you can't find a new lease on life from freeing yourself from being strangled by your scarf in an elevator or winning at the races, you're not going to take joy in anything which explains why Renard was what Serling described him as at the beginning.

While Steve Cochran gets top billing in this story as Renard and he certainly plays this shallow person whom nobody will feel any pity for perfectly, I think the person who steals the show is Ernest Truex who plays Pedott.

He truly is a sweet old man who simply wants to bring some joy to people by simple means. He recognizes his gift as one that should not be exploited by anyone. In the end he reacted the only way he could. It was clearly self defense in setting Renard up to be killed in a traffic accident. The real tragedy is we don't feel anything for Renard in the end because of his shallowness.

How many Renards are there in this world and how many people would mourn them if they suddenly died? It's an interesting and sad question to ponder.

This is one of the rare episodes that I have never seen before and as I said I enjoyed it. I don't know that it's necessarily excellent but I do think it's a very good episode so I will rate it as a three.

Review by Linn

I thought this was absolutely one of the best Twilight Zones ever. This, like Time Enough At Last, is an episode I'll never tire of watching. Both Ernest Truex and Steve Cochran were perfect in their roles. I felt so sorry for Pedott because he definitely feared Renard. I have to agree with Bobby that I also could not understand why he didn't leave the area as quickly as possible after leaving the bar since he knew that Renard was a menacing character. However, Renard did come out of the bar after Pedott pretty quickly. I think Renard would have caught up to him pretty hastily.

This was definitely a very dark and creepy episode. Ken is right. Nobody would want to meet up with Renard in a dark alley. Also, Bobby brought up another good point. Since Pedott knew in his heart or within whatever powers he had that Renard would be his worst nightmare, he should have let him strangle himself in that elevator, but if that happened, it would have been the end of the show so Renard had to live. He didn't appreciate that Pedott had saved his life or gave him the pen that brought about his windfall at the track. He wanted more and more and more. He intimidated and tormented that sweet old man.

Also, it had one of the best endings in Zone history. When the frightened old man gave the thug those shoes causing him to slip and be killed by a hit and run driver, I wanted a applaud as loudly as possible, especially when the old man looked at Renard's dead body and muttered "They were not what you needed, butt hey were what I needed." He knew that Renard intended to kill him.

Absolutely and undeniably a Classic.

Review by Bobbynear

This episode reminded me immediately of the second story of the series, with another street peddler finding himself in considerable trouble not necessarily of his own making.

The difference between the two is immediately obvious though. This is far more creepy and dangerous Trying to outwit Mr.

Death seems almost easy in comparison to trying to escape the street hoodlum in this story.

The plot here is a familiar one except there is a new twist to it. We've seen countless stories in other tv series, about people who can either go back in time to try and reverse events or people who somehow know what is coming and are able to put out warnings. This is different though. Pedott, unlike other fictional characters who go backward or forward and never seem to succeed in changing anything, can actually change one's life with trinkets that seem meaningless at first sight.

Pedott like the main character in Time Enough At Last, is instantly likeable and seems only to want to be left alone. So it surprised me when he kept making eye contact with the bad guy in the bar and then although he left, he went just outside to continue his peddling. For a man who can predict the future, I would expect him to beat a hasty retreat.

I agree with Ken's review re the perfect casting. Especially of long time screen gangster Steve Cochran. IMDB has this to say about him, "Appeared opposite Virginia Mayo in six films, both of them often playing scheming, unsavory types. "Unsavory indeed, this guy's got a chip on his shoulder big enough for everyone in that bar. And the look of fear on Pedott's face when he sees him out the corner of his eye, shows he's on to him immediately.

Like a lot of characters in these short Twilight Zone stories, I was left wanting to know more about Pedott. Where did he get these powers? Was he born with them? Why does he feel compelled to live such a sparse existence himself while helping so many strangers? I also wondered why Pedott gives the bad guy that pair of scissors to save his own neck. Why not just let him strangle in the elevator if you have any inkling that he eventually will come back to kill you?

All in all, a very disturbing episode and that includes the unusual music in the background. Pretty good right up to and including the end where an innocent bystander gets some help from Pedott in the form of a comb so he can make his debut on television. Shows that even after his unfortunate run in with that street thug, Pedott has not lost his touch for helping others in very quiet ways. It also shows that early in the series, Rod Serling's sense of irony is as strong as it ever was.

I watch The Twilight Zone to see surprise endings and to be creeped out and this story gave me both. It scared the hell out of me, especially when I first saw it at the impressionable age of 12. I was originally going to give it a 4,excellent rating but upon further reflection, I have no reason not to push it the rest of the way. It worked for me, then and now.

My rating on a scale of 0 to 5

5 ~~ CLASSIC

Review by Ken

Alright. This is what I needed. No pun intended. A story that keeps me wondering from start to finish.

Great opening scenes introduces many characters that set up the story. Old man Pedott walks into a bar peddling his stuff to interested customers. Girl gladly accepts a gift. Washed up former pitcher gets a bus ticket.

Creepy guy is watching in background. He follows Pedott outside and forces him to give what he needs. Turns out scissors saves him in elevator. Leaky pen leads to money.

Steve Cochran was a perfect choice to play the part of a thug. Who would want to be alone with him in a dark alley. At any moment he may take your head off. He forces old man Pedott again and again. He is not content until he get's everything. Hmmm.... Is Rod Serling trying to teach all of us a lesson in life.

We all know the closing scenes are going to result in a weird and freakish way. But how? The tension builds and the music sets the tone.

Great casting Ernest Truex in the lead role as the gentle but nervous old man helping people in need. He senses danger and his own life and give Renard slippery shoes which leads to his death. I did not see that coming.

Excellent closing line. Pedott slowly says to Renard-"That is what I need...."

I glad we got a significant and meaningful ending to this story unlike the previous dreadful episode. The purpose of story telling is to entertain, enthrall, charm, or intrigue your viewing audience. Bottom line... Keep us interested so we don't turn the channel.

All in all a true T.Z. feel and startling ending. Fade into the night as Serling says 'only in The Twilight Zone.'

My rating - 5 Classic

"The Twilight Zone" Episode 13 "The Four Of Us Are Dying"

Original Air Date- January 1, 1960
Guest Star- Harry Townes
Written by Rod Serling
Directed by John Brahm

Review by Kitty

This latest episode is called The Four of Us are Dying. This episode I think starts out very well with a man walking in to a hotel. The camera work is great here as it's filmed in obscure angles.

However, we find out the man's name is Arch Hammer. He's the best confidence man in the business as we see that he's a different person in the mirror. He changes his image twice before changing back to himself. He's a chameleon who can make himself look like anyone he wants if he simply concentrates.

He finishes shaving and we see him pick up some newspaper clippings that are obituaries of men who have died.

The first man is someone by the name of Mickey Foster. He goes to a bar where a very pretty woman by the name of Maggie is there. He transforms himself in to Mickey and we discover that Maggie was Foster's girlfriend.

Maggie is shocked but very happy to see that Mickey is alive. She asks him why he's alive and he tells her that it was his car that was hit by the train but he wasn't in it, just a guy who looked like him.

Maggie is deliriously happy and Mickey tells her he wants to run away with her to Chicago after she finishes work tonight. She tells him yes and they agree to meet at the train station at 12:06 AM.

Foster/Hammer walks out and as he walks out the band member recognizes him and chases him outside and when he approaches him, Hammer walks out of the shadows and the man realizes it's not Foster. Hammer tells him sorry he's not the guy he's looking for but he'll still accept a light from him as the man was offering to help him light a cigarette.

The man walks back inside and Hammer looks back and hears Maggie singing a happy song in the bar. He says out lout that nobody ever loved him that much so why not run away with Maggie.

He then takes out another newspaper clipping and sees the face of a dead mobster by the name of Sterig. He goes to see the man who took out Sterig whose name is Penell. Penell is shocked that Sterig is alive.

Sterig demands his share of the money from the job he did and doesn't appreciate getting thrown in the river with three bullets in him. Penell tells him his cut in the top drawer of the desk. Sterig takes it and tells him he'll charge interest and take the whole thing since he was shot and thrown in the river.

As he leaves, two thugs come in and he runs for his life. They chase him down the street and he runs in to a dead end. He sees a picture of a boxer on the wall in the alley and assumes his face. The two thugs show up and are stunned to see someone else. They walk away wondering what happened to the other guy.

As he walks away, he passes a newsstand. The old man comes up to him and tells him his name is Andy Marshak. Marshak tells him that he doesn't remember him. The tells him that he's Andy's father. He then tells him that he was his father before Andy left and broke his mother's heart and the heart of a very nice young woman as well.

Marshak pushes the father away and runs back to his hotel. He's in the hotel packing when he hears someone coming in. It's a detective with a warrant for Hammer's arrest as he's wanted by the law for his con antics. Hammer gets his coat and they start to walk out of the hotel.

As they walk through the revolving door, Hammer changes his face back to Marshak and the detective who's very puzzled runs back in to the hotel to look for Hammer. Marshak walks around the corner only to be confronted by his "father".

Pop Marshak takes out a gun and tells him that it's time Andy paid for his crimes. Marshak tells him that this is a mistake that he's not who he thinks he is. He tells him he's only got to concentrate but it's too late. Pop fires the gun and mortally wounds Hammer.

As Hammer lay there dying, he changes faces several times before his face finally becomes his own at the moment of death. Pop Marshak just stands there with the gun in his hand and that is the end of the episode.

This is one of the episodes that falls in to the category of Almost and Not Quite. I think it had a good premise but Beverly Garland as Maggie was completely underused in this episode.

I also felt that if Hammer was destined to get shot at the end, I would have preferred that he be shot by Maggie or one of Penell's thugs. To have Andy Marshak's father blow him away, I think was a little extreme.

For a parent to have that kind of reaction to their child, I would have liked to have known just what did Andy do to be not only disowned but to be killed by his own father. Whatever it was, I can see the disowning but the killing I don't see.

It would have made more sense to have Hammer killed by one of Penell's thugs for obvious reasons as they thought he was Sterig and the mob doesn't need too much of a reason to want someone dead, particularly since they already thought they had truly killed Sterig.

The other possibility is Maggie. Beverly Garland is a beautiful and talented actress and I truly felt her pain when she expressed her grief to Hammer/Foster. What if Maggie had realized that Foster was indeed an impostor and figured it out after he didn't show up. Perhaps she could have thought that he was simply trying to get money out of her as what does happen to unsuspecting women sometimes in real life.

She could have been the one to show up and pull the trigger and I would have bought it.

Over all the acting is good, I just would have liked to have known more about what motivated Pop Marshak so much to want to kill who he thought was his son.

Overall, I will give this a two rating for average.

Review by Linn

I have to agree with Bobby, Kitty and Ken. The Four Of Us Are Dying is also not one of my favorite episodes and I don't care if I ever watch it again. There were way too many loose ends in this one. A man named Arch Hammer can change his face to look like anyone else's face simply by concentrating on it. Yeah, so? Besides this story being way out there even for the Twilight Zone, the choices he makes are pretty crazy.

Hammer turns his face into that of a deceased musician named Mickey Foster and decides to reunite himself with Foster's grieving girlfriend Maggie, played by the lovely and talented Beverly Garland. Maggie is thrilled to see Mickey and can't believe he's still alive. Foster tells her to meet him at a train station the next day. What became of that? They never show her arriving only to find him not there. Beverly Garland's talents were wasted in this episode.

Hammer then assumed the face of a mobster named Sterig and tracks down the man who had him murdered after doing a con job for him. The man is shocked to see that Sterig is alive. Sterig demands his cut of the money from the job he pulled and then ends up running out of the apartment with the whole take. I suppose he planned to use the money to run off with Maggie. However, two of the man's goons chase Sterig down until he reaches a dead end in an alley and in a panic decides to change his face into that of Andy Marshak, a boxer whose face is on a flyer hanging on the alley wall. The goons approach Marshak and can't understand how Sterig got away. They leave Marshak alone and depart.

Still looking like Marshak, he has the misfortune of running into Pop Marshak, his father. Pop Marshak looks at him, tells him he's his father and begins to let him have it for breaking his mother's heart and also for hurting a sweet, young girl. Marshak takes off. He runs into his father again after almost being arrested and his father shoots him dead while Andy tries to convince him that he's not really Andy Marshak. It was never revealed what he did that was so horrible to make his own father want him dead.

Well, so much for this clunker of a story. Way too many loose ends in this one. Absolutely one of the more disappointing Zones. It was nearly impossible to feel sorry for any of the characters other than Maggie. The guy can turn his face into anybody's face he chooses and he picks three losers.

This episode gets a Lousy rating from me.

Review by Bobbynear

What a strange story. I'm afraid it didn't do much for me on any level. For one thing, there is no one to like in this story. A bunch of lowlifes and I couldn't care less what happens to any of them.

The biggest problem is time. In a less than half hour program, after commercials, it's a miracle to find out anything about the lead character, much less this many. There must be, as Kitty pointed out, quite a story behind a father shooting his own son, but don't look here for the details.

Another problem I have with this is how illogical it all is. Ken was right in his review. Why, if you can so easily turn into anyone, waste time on these thugs? Pick out someone famous and make a killing there. I don't know about Romeo... but surely there were some well known and wealthy personalities back in '59 when this story was written, worth emulating right down to looking like them.

All in all, two dark, too bizarre and too unpleasant. When I go searching for Twilight Zone episodes to watch... this is one I would just as soon skip over.

My rating on a scale of 1 to 5
1 ~~ POOR

Review by Ken

Well The Twilight Zone get's more creepy with a story fit to be titled 'The X-Files' in 1960. A man has the talent or gift to change his face multiple times to escape bad guys chasing him. However karma catches up to him and he dies with his real face in the end.

The story was absurd and did not work for me. I know this show is about the unusual and strange. But this story was a mess from the start. Extra-ordinary powers does not fit here in the first season. The stories we have been getting deal with the bizarre turn of events in people's lives.

The failure of ep. 13 is the supernatural went to another level. Arch Hammer could study any face he wants. Why not change into Romeo and sweep every girl off her feet.

I did like Beverly Garland and would have enjoyed more scenes with her. In fact she is the first member in my T.Z. Hall of Fame. Many more members will be added as the show develops. These are talented actresses that have a significant impact on the show.

Casting four lead actors confused the heck out of me. Harry Townes has that T.Z. look on his face. Walking down a dark street with him will give you the creeps.

We now have back to back episodes ending with the death of the villain. Fred Renard in ep. 12 and now Arch Hammer. Time for a different ending Rod....

My rating - 1 Poor.   No desire to view it again.

"The Twilight Zone" Episode 14 "Third From The Sun"

Original Air Date- January 8, 1960
Guest Star- Fritz Weaver
Written by Rod Serling
Directed by Richard L. Bare

Review by Kitty

This latest episode is called Third from the Sun. It has a very ominous start to it as people are getting off of work at a weapons plant and everybody who comes out works in some sort of bomb making capacity.

We see a man by the name of Sturka who is approached by another man who works there named Carling. Carling is telling him that there isn't much time left. There's forty eight hours left if that.

Sturka says what about the other side, what will they do? Carling replies that they will retaliate but they won't do it as well as we will so our losses will be minimal. Sturka says so we'll only lose thirty five million people as opposed to fifty million people.

Carling tells him he's got a bad attitude and they part company. Sturka goes home and is greeted by his daughter Jody. Jody asks him what's wrong and he tells her he's feeling his age. She wants to dance with him and he tells her another time. Jody tells him that everybody seems to be scared all around them.

Sturka's wife Eve comes in and wants to know what's wrong and he tells her that nothing is wrong but their friends Jerry and Ann Riden are coming over to play cards tonight. Eve thought Jerry was away testing an aircraft and Sturka tells her that he's back. He tells Jody to stay home and she tells him that she can't as she has a date. He orders her to break it....

Sturka goes upstairs and Eve follows wanting to know. He tells her that the end is coming and they are leaving this place to go to another planet.... He doesn't want Jody to know until the last minute. Eve agrees.

Sturka gets called by Jody telling him that Jerry Riden is here. Jody tells Jerry that he better have some good stories to tell as she broke a date to be there tonight. Sturka comes down and asks him if he's not coming over tonight and Jerry replies he will be there. Sturka asks if his watch is giving him problems again and he tells him yes. Sturka takes him in to a workshop area and he turns on a machine to create noise.

They speak softly to each other. Jerry tells him that the guard he paid to let them in to the ship got his shift switched and therefore he gets off at 11:00 PM instead of 1:00 AM. Sturka tells him they have to simply leave earlier. Jerry tells him more people will be there earlier but Sturka insists they have no choice.

As they leave the shop, a face appears in the window and it's Carling. Later that night, all four of the adults are playing cards and Eve and Ann get up to get cake and lemonade.

Jody goes with them to the kitchen. Jerry shows Sturka a diagram of where they are headed. He says there is no guaranty that they will get out of the atmosphere or that it will make it eleven million miles to the planet they are going to but Sturka insists that it's a chance they'll have to take.

At that moment the doorbell rings and Eve tells Sturka that Carling is there. Carling is there and wondering what they are doing. Sturka tells him they are just playing cards. He tells him this is the kind of evening to be out on the front porch or sleeping but not staying inside as it's so hot. He tries to pickup the paper that Jerry has the diagram on but Jerry has turned it over and is calculating what Sturka owes them since he lost at card playing.

Carling does pick it up and sees what he lost but never turns it over as it's obvious he's reading through the light what's on the other side. He tells Sturka he lost a bit. Jerry tells him that he won't collect tonight. They'll get together next week and he can try to win it back. Carling tells him he certainly thinks positively.

He drinks some lemonade after noticing Eve is very nervous as she pours it and he makes his exit.

They all decide it's time to go now. Sturka explains to Jody that they are leaving because this world is about to blow itself up. The phone rings and Sturka answers it. He tells them he was in bed and then he says OK....

He tells everybody that they need him at the plant and they are sending a car for him. They have to go now. Eve starts to put the lemonade up and realizes that's silly because they're not coming back.

They are in the car and they arrive in the gated area where the spaceship is. Sturka and Jerry get out of the car and they see a flashing light and they tell Eve to flash the lights once. The light moves closer to them and it's Carling with a gun.

He tells the ladies to get out of the car because he needs to turn these men over to the authorities. Jody sees that his hand with the gun is right next to the door so she opens the door and knocks the gun out of Carling's hand and Sturka and Jerry knock him out.

They get in to the car and they race to the spaceship and run inside. Jerry and Sturka knock out the guards that try to stop them. They take off and Sturka asks Jerry what he knows about the new planet. He tells him that they have people like them on it and they speak their language as well.

He tells him that it's the third one from the sun. It's called Earth! I have always enjoyed this episode as from the very beginning you think you're watching a story about our own planet. Nuclear war was certainly a fear back then as it still is to this day but I think it was a little more scary back then as the technology was so new and the Soviet Union was an ominous presence on the world stage, especially when you have a guy named Kruchev saying that he will bury us.

I bought the emotions of Sturka and Jerry very well. They as scientists know what the repercussions will be and they are terrified by the short sightedness of people running things. Carling clearly represents the other side which is of the person who doesn't care what happens just as long as we fire first and we get to kill more people in the process.

I found Carling to be a scary guy. We're not really sure what he does at that plant but clearly he's got a one track mind and doesn't care what happens in the aftermath. The fact that he doesn't seem to care that he may die in the retaliation doesn't seem to bother him.

As I said from the beginning you think this is a story about Earth and then at the very end you get that little twist telling us that they are escaping to Earth to live. My only question given human nature as it is, if they were to arrive on Earth and they are detected as beings from another planet what would the reaction of Earth be? Would they want to dissect them and study them or put them on display in a zoo?

I sometimes wonder if when they get here they might wonder if it wouldn't have been better to stay where they were.

Overall I like it. I liked Fritz Weaver very much in this. He really is the one who carries the story. I also recognized his daughter played by Denise Alexander. She would later go on to have a long term role on the soap opera General Hospital. I will give this one a four for excellent.

Review by Ken

Back again to a story dealing with the mystery of space. Two families plan to steal a spaceship and head to another planet to begin a new life. Their planet will be destroyed by a nuclear blast.

C'mon executive producers. This story reminded me of a turtle race. Slow, slower, slowest scenes I have ever watched. Finally at the end some action with the families boarding a flying saucer and off they go. But a twist conclusion. They are heading to earth which is the third planet from the sun. What a dud!!! Where is the beef, chicken, and pork??

This episode began with the talk of a coming event or occurrence of a major calamity. The audience is fearful of what may happen. But when the writers, producers, and directors put together a toy story that could be written in 29 minutes then I have a problem. Their weekly board meeting was very short on this one. Ep.14 ending was a twist. Anyone watching the first time will surely be surprised. But a thud could be heard in my household.

A third grader could have written a more compelling story. How about showing the so-called nuclear blast. The ship escapes just in the nick of time. How about showing the two families arriving at their destination? Would they be welcomed with open arms or hostility? What would their reaction be to the people of the new world?

Cast actors added little drama as they stroll around the house playing cards. Daughter should have gone on that date with her boyfriend. The wives should have gone shopping to pass the time away.

The lemonade and cake was about all I was interested in. I fell asleep watching this clutter.

My rating - 0 Lousy

Review by Linn

Well, I have to say that Third From The Sun episode was the second disappointing episode in a row for me. I thought "The Four Of Us Are Dying" was pretty bad, but I think this one is just as bad, if not worse.

I was not very impressed at all with the acting. Four people are aware that life as they know it will possibly end within 48 hours. The whole planet is going to be eliminated. It seems that for three months, two men named Sturka and Riden are planning a "not so elaborate" scheme, in my opinion, to flee the planet before its destruction in a spaceship sitting dormant in a gated and guarded area. I can't comprehend how such a seemingly quick and easy plan took these two supposedly brilliant scientists three months to work out. I guess they had to figure out the workings of the spacecraft. I don't know.

There is another gentleman named Carling who is beginning to sense their little plot of escape. He peeks in Sturka's basement window to find Sturka and Riden conversing. Carling prefers to remain on the planet and fight back against whatever force is going to destroy it. Sturka and Riden have planned to make their escape at 1:00 a.m. in the morning, but plans are changed when Riden tells Sturka that the lookout guard he hired to get them safely to the ship will be leaving his post at 11:00 p.m. which means they have to leave earlier. Their wives have been made aware of the situation, but Sturka's teenage daughter has not. She was asked by her father to break a date and stay home that night because Riden and his wife are coming over to play cards. She reluctantly agrees to remain at home.

The whole time the four adults are playing cards, they are acting extremely nervous. Then suddenly Carling shows up for a surprise visit. Considering that these were four people trying to keep their plan private, their anxious and unsettled behavior in front of Carling was a pure giveaway that something was brewing and Carling was not about to let them follow through. Sturka's wife was shaking like a leaf while pouring lemonade for everyone which Carling commented on immediately.

Carling notices a paper on the table on which Riden drew a diagram of their flight that looked like a five year old drew it. Riden turns it over before Carling gets to the table. Why didn't he simply stuff it back in his pocket? He then proceeds to write down made-up card winnings on the back of it. Carling picks it up anyway. As Kitty mentioned in her review, he surely saw a diagram on the back from the light shining through. Carling was an unsettling man who also seemed very sneaky and conniving. He comments on the amount of money lost in the game and again, the nervousness they all exhibited. When Riden says they'll even the score when they play again next week, it was another tip off to Carling of their plans and even tells Riden that he certainly thinks positively. Carling then leaves but not before making comments to Sturka at the door about the stars and whether he's ever thought of living on one of them. Sturka then gives the dumb answer that it's crossed his mind. I wanted to scream at the television "ARE YOU ALWAYS THIS STUPID, STURKA?!"

Once Carling leaves, Sturka tells his daughter what is happening and they all dash around wildly to get out of the house quickly to make their escape. Not just poor acting, in my opinion, but a lot of overacting. They pile into the car and head for the ship only to find that instead of the lookout guard, it is Carling waiting for them in the darkness giving the "all is clear" flashlight signal. He appears out of the darkness holding a gun and comments that the men are a long way from home. He then goes up to the car and asks the women to get out. The daughter shoves open the car door knocking the gun out of his hand. The two men then knock him unconscious. They start to drive towards the ship. A warning blares out over the P.A. system that there is an unauthorized vehicle on the property. They manage to get the door of the craft open, but in the process they also manage to knock out the two large guards trying to stop them. I don't think I'd want these guards watching over any of my stuff. Also, it seems that the guards were armed so why didn't they just pullout their guns?

Bobby made the funny comment in his review that it seems tougher to steal a car than a spaceship. The surprise ending which revealed that the planet they are heading for is Earth was indeed a surprise because it seemed that the whole story was taking place on Earth, but that ending did not make up for how incredibly boring the rest of the show was.

Ken is right about this one being a snoozer and way too slow-moving. There was just not enough substance in this story to reel me in. Every time I watch it, I start to fall asleep. It was slow and badly written. I also wonder, as did the other reviewers, how the people of earth were going to react to these invaders arriving in their spaceship and how the characters would react to Earth. That definitely would have been more interesting. My last comment is in agreement with Bobby's assessment that the set, props and just about everything else were very cheap looking. The spaceship looked like an enlarged version of a kid's toy from a dollar store.

I give this episode the same rating as the last episode - Lousy.

Review by Bobbynear

If the prior episode contained too much to put in one half hour, then this one contains not enough to fill a half hour. Or at least not enough of the right story. By that I mean that the focus is on the wrong story.

So two families have inside information that a final destructive war is about to break out. There is no escape except to another world. And what do you know, there just happens to be a space ship ready to take them away. How convenient.

Strangely enough, only one person suspects what they are about to do and even though he is determined to stop them, it turns out he is easily dispatched. The two families get to the space ship, which incredibly is in the middle of a field surrounded by a fence easily broken into and two armed guards who virtually crumble when they are touched. Good grief, it turns out that it's tougher to steal a car than it is to steal a spaceship.

OK OK....I get it....a little suspension of disbelief is in order. Forget all of that. There is a bigger problem here. The best part of the story comes after it's over. I can just see it now, a group of earthlings or a group of aliens comes to Earth or wherever and lands...where? In the middle of Times Square or Red Square? Matters not. They are going to be just thrilled when they see the panic they have touched off.

The problem with this story is that the focus is on the twist surprise ending and nothing else. It doesn't matter what happens leading up to it as long as we get there and fool everyone. Great... I love twist surprise endings, especially in The Twilight Zone. It almost always works. It certainly worked to perfection in the first TZ nuclear paranoia story, Time Enough At Last. But there we actually got to see what happened and it was unexpected, ironic and heartbreaking. Here it's just a device to end the story....and say..."ha... I gotcha!!"

A much better ending might have been if the two families had gotten to this other place... Earth as it turns out, landed and found out the hard way that not only are they not at all welcome but that they have arrived in a place just as bad if not much worse than the one they came from. That's a far cry from one of the characters simply telling us they are headed for Earth. Ken was right in his review. Where indeed is the beef??

Beyond all of that is another problem. The whole episode looks incredibly cheap. Quirky and unusual camera angles are used to try to fool us into thinking this is sometime in the future, but still on this planet. Nice idea, but the whole thing still looks like it was filmed in Rod Serling's basement. And that very much includes that toy spaceship that looks like it just took off alright... Right out of a 1959 cereal box. Yes it's true that the series had to operate on a tiny budget compared to today... and it appears they blew the entire thing on Time Enough At Last, which easily convinced me that the world had indeed been incinerated.

The lesson to be learned here is obvious. Don't get so enthralled with your surprise ending, that you forget to put anything in front of it to hold our attention. Don't start from the end and work backwards. It just doesn't work.

My rating on a scale of 0 to 5
0 - Lousy

"The Twilight Zone" Episode 15 "I Shot An Arrow Into The Air"

Original Air Date- January 15, 1960
Guest Star- Dewey Martin
Written by Rod Serling
Directed by Stuart Rosenberg

Review by Kitty

This latest episode is called "I Shot an Arrow in the Air." We start off by seeing a rocket ship taking off. It is called the Arrow I. It has a crew of eight men on board. That's pretty amazing considering that when we finally got the Apollo rockets, the most they carried was three men but we will suspend our imagination for our purposes here.

All of a sudden the rocket ship disappears off the radar screen and nobody knows where they are. The flight commander says "I shot an arrow in the air and where it landed no one knows where."

He then says, where ever they are God help them. We then see the commander Donlin making notes as to what their situation is. He is saying that four of the crew died on impact and one other is critically injured, which leaves three of them, himself, Corey and Pierson.

They believe they have crash landed on an asteroid that has a similar atmosphere to earth. Corey is wanting more water and he doesn't want the injured man to have any since he's going to die anyway. Donlin tells him that until he dies they will take care of him.

They dig graves for the four who are dead and when they come back the remaining man is barely alive. Donlin goes to give him water and Corey takes it away from him and they fight. Pierson then announces that the other man is dead.

It is agreed that they will go search after dark to see if there is any place that can give them a better chance at survival. Corey returns and tells Donlin that they split up.

Donlin realizes that Corey has Pierson's canteen of water and demands to know what happened to Pierson. He admits that he found Pierson and he was dead so he took the canteen of water. Donlin asks him if he actually checked to see if he was really dead or did he just take the canteen and run with it. Corey swears that Pierson was dead. Donlin isn't buying it and forces Corey to walk at gun point to where Pierson was. They come to the area and Pierson isn't there. They realize he dragged himself away. Donlin finds Pierson and Pierson can't talk. He draws something for Donlin indicating what he saw. Pierson then dies.

Donlin decides he's going to go up the mountains to where Pierson pointed to find out what he saw. As he starts to walk away, Corey grabs the gun and shoots Donlin dead as he believes that he can survive longer by himself.

Corey walks the path that Pierson pointed to and in the end he sees what Pierson drew. He drew telephone wires. He sees a road with a truck driving and he sees a sign that says Reno ninety-seven miles.

Corey then realizes that they never left the atmosphere and that's why they couldn't track them. He begins to cry and tells Pierson and Donlin that he's sorry.

This was an interesting episode but one really has to suspend their disbelief to enjoy it. The astronauts don't realize that they are in the desert in Nevada? That seems a little hard to believe. It also seems more difficult to believe that the radar tracking could not pinpoint where they lost contact and hence send search airplanes out to that general area to look for them.

The episode plays in to the survival instinct and basically shows how desperate people will become when faced with certain death. This is not the only time we'll see an episode with this theme but I think other episodes with this theme illustrate it better.

I give this one a two rating for average.

Review by Ken

Say it ain't so-Rod.' Another space story. We just left two families flying in a saucer escaping their planet and heading to earth. Now we have a crew of eight take off in a rocket and crash land on a so-called asteroid...... Four survivors and one by one they battle the elements. A thirsty guy can't live without water and decides to kill the others in order to survive. Big twist at the end and he finds out that he is in Reno, Nevada. Any casinos near by?

I have to admit that I pictured myself in this situation. Would I go batty and take out my fellow crew members. I hope not. I would think I need help from my friends to live and survive this ordeal.

The story kept my interest but was predictable. The musical score was excellent and the desert landscape gave the T.Z. feeling.

Edward Binns was convincing. Poor acting by Dewey Martin. He is the bad guy but I would not be afraid of him. Casting a meaner looking guy would have worked better for me.

The end scene was flat and a letdown. For once play out the scene further...... He runs down the mountain yelling out at the bus driving by. But the bus runs him over. Bus driver gets out and grabs canteen of water. He is thirsty.

Again Rod Serling came on in the second act and started his closing narration too early. This annoys me. Let the story play out and then come on at the end.

So far a certain theme seems to attract and intrigue the producers. Ep.1,7,11,13,14 all deal with the mystery of space. I don't mind but please give me a quality story.

Mixed feelings on this one.

My rating 2 Average

Review by Linn

Oh geez. Three duds in a row. I don't have much good to say about I Shot an Arrow into the Air. This was a terrible episode, in my opinion. Extremely boring, bad performances, and I suppose the ONLY good thing I can say about this episode is that Edward Binns as Colonel Donlin was not so bad in his role. Other than that, there is nothing else good to say about this one.

The unbelievable lack of concern and urgency on the part of the mission control center in taking major action to find and recover EIGHT men whom they sent into space was not only disturbing and careless, it was outrageous. It was also unconscionable, to say the least.

I also have to ask the same question that Bobby asked. When has a space mission ever consisted of eight men? I believe there is a weight limit on these rockets, but I'm certainly no expert in this area. I know the Space Shuttles have sent 6 to 7 people into space, but this episode was long before that type of space technology existed. They never even mentioned what the destination of this mission was supposed to be.

The Corey character was an ass, and all of this walking around trying to find other forms of life or other means of survival should have been obvious to all of them that it was futile. All Corey wanted was everybody's water. What an intriguing episode. A man who kills everyone in his presence for water rather than trying to figure out how to make it out of there. Bobby made a great joke that I'm still laughing at when he said something about them looking for someone to hand them a cold six pack of Coke. I was thinking that maybe they were looking for two little alien kids running some kind of make-shift lemonade stand. Ha! In any case, there was nothing to be found.

Most of the performances were poor and I was amazed that with the sun beating down on them so strongly, they weren't brought to the brink more quickly.

In any case, Donlin was writing in his journal instead of trying to fix the ship. But that doesn't matter. If you send a rocket into space and it crashes back onto the Earth, how is it that Mission Control couldn't find them, and also, how is it that nobody in Nevada heard or saw this rocket crash only a few miles from them? I would think somebody out there in the general area would have heard noticed this. They were in a rural or city area for God's Sake. Also, I agree with Ken that this story was fairly predictable.

How could it take them so long to realize where they were? Dumb, idiotic episode.

When Corey realized at the end that they had never left the Earth, his tearful remorse over killing everyone on the crew, including wishing the ones at the beginning would die, did not make an impact on me at all. Oh, one last point, before he killed Colonel Donlin, he said to him "Two men can live here for five days, but one man can live here for ten days." Then he shot Donlin.

Ten days? Have a happy life for ten days, numb nuts. Another snoozer for me.

I mean, come on, if it walks like a duck and quacks like a duck it's most likely a duck. If it looks like Earth and feels like Earth and you are breathing outside of your spacesuits, it's most likely Earth! I rate this as a Poor episode. I didn't rate it as lousy because Edward Binns was good in his role.

Review by Bobbynear

So, let me get this straight. Man finally ventures out into deep space and the very first time, sends eight men out there. Wow, that's pretty daring... And stupid. Maybe they should have renamed this episode, "We Shot A Condo Into The Air...."

I sure was hardly impressed with the attitude back in mission control or whatever it was supposed to be called. Nobody seems too excited that eight astronauts are missing. All you do is go over to a window and wax rhapsodic about shooting something out there and not knowing where it is now. This isn't exactly Apollo 13, is it? How about launching an immediate massive rescue effort, instead of just acting like,, "oh well, you win some, you lose some."

This whole idiotic story is predicated on the fact that a spacecraft has crash landed on what the commander calls an uncharted asteroid. Really? I'll say it's uncharted alright. Who could imagine that something is actually floating out there where human beings can get out and walk around outside their spacesuits and still be able to breathe normally?

Oh sure... there is some sort of blather about how the atmosphere is clear and the sun looks about the same as on Earth. Hello? Anybody home? Get a clue guys... If it looks like Earth... maybe, just maybe it is. Other problems for me? Well... for a thirsty group about to kill each other for water, nobody seems to look terribly warm or thirsty. They do a lot of drinking, but can we just see somebody, anybody sweat just a little in that hot sun, so I can feel some of their pain and get into this thing?

And why oh why are they expending what energy they have left, with dwindling water supplies yet, to keep trekking across this mountainous landscape? If they think they are on an uncharted asteroid, what are they looking for? What do they expect to find? An alien civilization that will sell them a six pack of Coke?

How about spending what little time you have left trying to reach mission control somehow in the slim hope of being rescued? I think this endless walking is going nowhere. Over the mountains, figures to be, well... more mountains.

There is as usual, an interesting surprise payoff at the end, but the story ahead of it is so poor and undeveloped, there just is no connection. Ken suggested that they get down to the road in Reno and be run over by the bus. I have a better suggestion.

Given that this story follows that Third From The Sun nonsense, they should have combined both into one hour long episode. The poor aliens from that doomed planet in the last story, should have been allowed to reach Earth, only to find that something far worse has happened to them than nuclear war.

They're stuck in Reno for the weekend with no money to gamble.

My rating on a scale of 0 to 5
1 ~ Poor

"The Twilight Zone" Episode 16 "The Hitch-Hiker"

Original Air Date- January 22, 1960
Guest Star- Inger Stevens
Written by Rod Serling
Directed by Alvin Ganzer

Review by Bobbynear

For only the second time in sixteen episodes, and not since the brilliant, "Time Enough At Last", the Twilight Zone is on steroids again as everything comes together at the right time and the right place in a story so quietly terrifying that it crawls up out of the darkness and attaches itself to viewers, for only the next fifty years.

What is truly remarkable about "The Hitch-Hiker" is how scary it all is when nothing particularly scary is actually happening. It all begins rather innocently with a pretty young woman driving alone across the country, an act in itself fraught with dangers.... An auto mechanic is rendering aid to her at the side of the road while commenting on how lucky she is to be alive when speeding while having a tire blow out. Not too smart, but none too unusual either. Who among us has not tempted fate by driving too fast, or not making a full stop at a stop sign, or crossing railroad tracks because a train is nowhere in sight even though the signal is going off? Sometimes it's better to be lucky than smart.

Somewhere along the line, Nan Adams must have been warned by her parents, or at least her mother, when she started driving, not to do two things. Don't drive recklessly and never pick up a hitch-hiker.

After all, once he gets in your car, at your invitation, he's got you and you have no options. Nan has already faced one of them and survived. Now she's about to face the second and this time she does the right thing Upon the appearance of a plain looking little man at the side of the road, with his thumb out, Nan notes his appearance but ignores him and keeps on driving. So far so good. You listened to your mother. Only one problem. Mom never told you what to do if he keeps on showing up repeatedly no matter how far you drive.

From Rod Serling's narration: "But from this moment on, Nan Adams companion on a trip to California, will be terror, her route fear, her destination quite unknown."

From this man? A rather nondescript benign figure on the side of the road that even Nan describes as "drab, a little mousey" Although he keeps getting rather improbably ahead of her, he really makes no threatening moves towards Nan. It's nearly ten minutes into the story before he even speaks and when he does, he simply asks if she's headed west. It's actually her response that is disturbing as she answers very nervously and then speeds off

This is basically a short story and so there is no time to waste if it is going to work. We need to get on Nan's side quickly so we can feel the same fear she does. And director Alvin Ganzer does a great job in making us fearful, by using dark lighting and interesting camera angles throughout this episode. Plus we and Nan are so isolated. There are often few if any cars on the road... nowhere to turn and no one to turn to for help.

Nan is ostensibly driving across the country alone but really she's driving the world's biggest bus and all of us viewers are passengers. Rational thought tells us that Nan is being irrational, perhaps even delusional. Oh sure, seeing the same man over and over and noticing that he particularly wants a ride with you is disturbing, but Nan is quickly coming apart at the seams and now we are all in danger.

By the time Nan pulls up to some railroad tracks just before the end of the first half of this episode, the suspense has already been ratcheted up to an almost unbearable level. It's the old theory of less is more and it's working beautifully. The less the hitch hiker does, the scarier he gets. Now, here is something to really fear. A train bearing down on Nan as she sits nearly paralyzed with fear behind the steering wheel.

Why? Because the hitch hiker is standing just across the tracks, once again with his thumb out. Nan is so hysterical that instead of waiting for the train to goby so she can back up and beat a hasty retreat in the opposite direction while he can't see her, instead she starts across the tracks and stalls on them. Although she does survive, as the train speeds by with a special whizzing sound that indicates just how close this was, Nan is now convinced he is trying to kill her.

She claims in her thoughts to herself that he was daring her in a way to cross the tracks. But I disagree. He was doing nothing new, just standing there as always.

What really was disturbing was that he did nothing... made not a move to try and save a woman who was about to be shredded by a speeding train.

Now halfway through this story I'm more convinced than ever that Nan is the one to fear. Speeding along in a car, barely looking at the road as she watches for the hitch-hiker, she's far more dangerous than he is. But she's also right in her musings to herself. Just what does he want anyway? And why her?

From Nan's narration:" Three days and three nights now of driving. The routine goes on. Now it isn't even a trip, it's flight. Route 80 isn't a highway anymore. It's an escape route. So I keep going, conscious of only one thing....I've got to get where I'm going and I can't let the hitch-hiker close in on me."

It might be fair at this point for viewers to ask..." Just who is doing the chasing?"

At the beginning of this story, Nan does the right thing by not picking up a strange man on the side of the road. Unfortunately it doesn't do her any good. Now as the second half begins, she's about to do the very worst thing and her situation will go from dire to hopeless.

First, Nan pulls off onto a side road so dark and deserted, it's hard to imagine it's even paved. If she was isolated before, now she is totally bereft of any possible help. A bad decision especially when she runs out of gas and gets no help at a service station closed for the night.

And then suddenly out of nowhere, a hand appears out of the darkness and touches her. It's got to be the hitch-hiker. She's trapped now...... But it's not what we think. It turns out to be a hitchhiker alright, but a different one, dressed as a sailor and claming he's on leave and headed back home to San Diego.

Interesting, but I'm no fool. This is the Twilight Zone and the first thing that comes to my mind is that the original hitch-hiker has morphed into a more acceptable look... and when Nan offers him a ride, she's as good as dead... If indeed that is his intent. We still don't really know.

By this point in the story, Nan is so possessed by fear and often so irrational that almost anything is possible. But if I'm in the back seat, and let's face it... we really are, I'm screaming hysterically when Nan offers this total stranger a ride, all the way into San Diego if he wishes!

Excuse me...but is she kidding us? All that fear and terror on the road over one man hitching a ride and now this? The sailor asks her what she's doing out so late. Well I have a better question for him. What the hell is he doing on this totally deserted, black as a coal mine road in the middle of the night hitching a ride? What is he planning to do? Walk all the way to San Diego? Because there surely won't be any cars anytime soon.

The sailor is delighted and before you know it, the two are in the car together. God only knows what will happen now. But for me, if there is anything I treasure in a classic movie or tv episode, it's not just being surprised, but being surprised when conventional wisdom is tossed right out the window and this is perhaps one of the best examples ever.

If there is one sure prescription for disaster from a woman's point of view, it's that she find herself inside her car with a strange man in the middle of a dark and deserted night. This is almost too easy. We can see it coming. Will a ride into San Diego really be enough? And for a few seconds it appears the answer is no, when the sailor tells Nan that nobody will believe he got a ride into town with a woman who looks like a movie star. It's a mild come-on to be sure, but it could be just the beginning.

But for this sailor, opportunity knocking quickly turns into remorse when Nan sees the hitch hiker again and tries to run him over this time, nearly wrecking the car for good. The poor sailor doesn't take long to realize that he's bitten off so much he might be the one eaten. He can't wait to get out of the car.

Well aren't we surprised? When was the last time a story showed this kind of a set up with the man getting scared instead of the woman? However, it's not quite over yet. Nan takes his mild come on and takes it just a little higher with her own...

"I like you I really like you very much... As a matter of fact that's why I picked you up... because I liked you. I thought that we could be friends and I thought that maybe you could take me out."

Take her out? Well if this wasn't such a dark and deadly episode, this might actually be kind of amusing A late fifties version of a serious come on, suitable for family tv audiences. Goodness knows what it would look like were it filmed today.

But that doesn't matter, because nobody is laughing at this point. When the sailor realizes that bad is quickly getting to worse, he runs away and Nan's plaintive cries out the window for him to come back are so gut wrenching it's almost hard to listen to them. The darkness that has been creeping up on her ever since day turned into night, now seems to be threatening to totally envelope and stifle her for good. But the funny thing is... the focus of all of this attention, that hitch-hiker, is nowhere to be seen at this moment when Nan is most vulnerable wonder why.

And now as time begins to run out, the 'fait accompli' of this entire episode is upon us. Having tried everything, Nan is now forced to accept whatever demon it is that has been chasing her across the country.

But first she does something she probably should have done from the start after she had that first close call on the highway. She decides to check in back home with her mother. She goes to a telephone booth and calls her mom, only to be connected to a different female voice she is not familiar with.

It seems that Nan's mother can't come to the phone. She's had a nervous breakdown after hearing that her daughter was killed in a car accident in Pennsylvania while traveling across the country. The first scene in this episode was the end, not the beginning. Mr. Death makes another of his numerous appearances in this series in a variety of configurations. Can we assume that Mr. Serling had something of a fetish over an early death as he scours the world looking for stories to adapt to tv? Something to ponder on this day as I write this, the thirty fourth anniversary of his own death at far too young an age.

Even this early in the series, it is what we have come to expect. The payoff, the surprise, the twist, the unexpected but ultimately expected ending and it does not disappoint. It is a stunning conclusion and the look on Nan's face as she hears the news, says it all. It is a shattering moment, all too reminiscent of the shattering of those glasses at the end of Time Enough At Last.

Listen carefully. You can almost hear Henry Bemis crying in the background...."No, that's not fair. That's not fair at all..." Having watched this moment now, too many times to count over nearly five decades, I'm still shocked and horrified. But there is that 20/20 hindsight gained through years of experience and I can't help now but wonder how incredibly terrifying it might have been, had that final scene been played out just a little differently....with a male voice answering the phone at the other end. As now, we see only the phone, not the person answering it. The scene plays out the same only at the end the camera pans back to reveal that the hitch-hiker is speaking to Nan on the other end....and asks her, "Now, are you going my way?"

Nevertheless, it is still an incredible moment as Nan first stands and looks up at the dark sky in a moment of sweet surrender and then walks almost lifeless as if all the blood has drained from her, back to her car Nothing left now but to have the newly revealed hitch-hiker make his final appearance. There are many possibilities.

He could simply step out of the darkness. He could come up to the window again. Perhaps he could even be sitting behind the steering wheel when Nan returns to her car only to get in the back seat as a passenger this time.

No, that wouldn't be frightening enough. Instead it's time for Nan to meet her adversary up close and personal. She gets in her car and immediately pulls down the front visor and there in the mirror in the back seat is the hitch-hiker who tells her quietly, "I believe you're going....my way."

Nobody will ever know how many people around the country went out to their own cars immediately after this episode was over and removed any mirrors that may have been attached to their visors. Or how many people to this very day get in their cars and check that mirror to see who is in the back seat... just in case. I was lucky. I wasn't driving yet.

But even for a twelve year old kid who had long ago realized that nothing would jump out of the darkness in his bedroom and eat him overnight, the creep factor that this particular story engenders is still as awesome as ever. Watching it now on a computer screen, the stuff of science fiction back in 1959, instead of on a black and white tv, nothing really much has changed in one area. It stills cares the hell out of you.

For all of its compelling fear in story telling and all of its stark images and brilliant direction of a tale that began as a radio presentation and then was adapted brilliantly by Rod Serling for tv, it really is the acting that makes the difference here.

Inger Stevens in a bravura, practically one woman performance most of the time, easily does her best work ever. She would go on to an impressive film and tv career. And yet, unbeknownst to anyone at the time, was how eerily similar this particular episode would turn out to be to her real life in the near future.

An incredibly beautiful and talented natural blonde from Sweden, Inger Stevens had everything to live for, much like Nan Adams. And yet she could never truly find peace and happiness in her life. It was almost as if there was someone standing at the side of the road beckoning her to go forward only to find more unhappiness further down the road of life. even as a star in Hollywood. As we have found out far too many times, including recently, just because you build a place called Neverland, doesn't necessarily mean you will find happiness there.

Her chronic bouts of depression along with her penchant for falling easily in love with her leading men in feature films is the stuff of Hollywood legend. Finally it caught up to her when she shockingly took an overdose of drugs and alcohol on April 30, 1970 and ended her life voluntarily at the appallingly young age of 35.

Although she seemed to be a natural born actress, she also seemed oddly vulnerable onscreen no matter what her role. A foreshadowing of her real disturbing life off-screen perhaps that she just could not shake. Ironically however, it makes her virtually perfect for the part of Nan Adams. To watch this episode now and its almost impossible to avoid foreshadowing of Inger Stevens future, adds yet another eerie touch to this story as once again real life imitates fiction.

As The Hitch-Hiker concludes, Nan Adams sits totally bereft at the wheel of her car staring blankly ahead as Rod Serling puts his usual finishing touch to this most memorable episode...

"Nan Adams, age 27... she was driving to California ...to Los Angeles ...she didn't make it... there was a detour... through the Twilight Zone.

At this moment in time, with almost fifty years between then and now, as well as the knowledge of how the real person ended her life... we might well be tempted to amend those memorable words as art imitates life just a little too close for comfort:

"Inger Stevens, age 35....she was headed back to California, to Hollywood to continue her work as an actress... She didn't make it... There was a detour....Through real life when her own personal hitch-hiker finally caught up to her."

We live in a world and in this internet discussion group of numbers and ratings. It is the only way we have of separating the good from the bad, the excellent from the classic. But sometimes, something comes along that transcends mere numbers and this is one of those times.

Familiar words like brilliant, riveting, unforgettable are appropriate when describing this truly masterful story. The numbers are totally off the charts... sometimes a little bit of evil jumps right off of a tv or movie screen and attaches itself to you. You keep telling yourself that it's only fiction and though entertaining it will fade with time. Sometimes it does.... sometimes it does not... like this time....

My rating on a scale of 0 to 5

5 +++ ...and then some. An all time television classic for the ages.

Review by Linn

SPECIAL GUEST REVIEW OF "THE HITCH-HIKER ~ FROM NAN ADAMS' AND LINN'S PERSPECTIVE

My name is Nan Adams. I'm 27 years old, and I was driving on my way from Manhattan to Los Angeles for a vacation when one of my tires blew out on a Pennsylvania Highway. An unfortunate thing, really, and perhaps a bit reckless. I was driving 65 mph when the tire blew. The mechanic told me that between my speed on that road, the skid marks and soft shoulders on the road, I was on the side of the angels because I should be in a hearse. I laughed it off because at least I survived. I got into my car to follow the mechanic into town to have my tire replaced. Suddenly, before I started my car, I saw a shabby looking man in the distance holding up his thumb to hitch a ride. I ignored him and followed the mechanic. He replaced my tire. I paid him and joked about the cost being cheaper than a funeral. While waiting for him to bring my change, I looked in my vanity case mirror and saw the shabby hitchhiker again standing not far behind me.

I felt a strange and fearful feeling. The mechanic came out with my change and saw the disturbed look on my face. He asked if I was okay. I said yes and that I was only looking at the hitchhiker across the way. He asked "What hitchhiker?" I looked and he was gone. The mechanic agreed with me that he probably got picked up. Again, I tried to laugh it off. I started on my way again. I saw the hitchhiker again 50 miles later and then again on a stretch of road to Virginia. He didn't look terribly menacing – just a mousy, shabby, scarecrow-looking sort of man - just standing there. I should have ignored him, but everywhere I went and everywhere I stopped, I saw him. I couldn't lose him. He always seemed to be ahead of me somehow. Could it just be a coincidence?

Now I'm on the turnpike and I'm extremely frightened. I suppose it's the feeling that something is very wrong and everything seems vague because that hitchhiker is vague. I finally stopped at a diner for a sandwich and asked the waiter if they got many hitchhikers in the area. He told me that anybody would be a fool to try and hitch a ride on the turnpike. He said it's a long stretch of road with practically no speed limit. As I left the diner, I fearfully told the waiter I just wanted to stop driving and hated my car.

Still, I didn't know why I couldn't shake this man who was scaring me to death at this point. How could anyone not be scared, and I was terrified. As I started off again, I was stopped by a road worker who told me I'd have to wait a few minutes before going on due to construction up ahead. It would feel good to get out of that car and stretch my legs. I opened the car door AND THERE HE WAS!! I quickly got back into the car, frightened, trembling and about to scream as he approached my passenger side window and asked "Heading West?" I thought I was going to lose my mind. I panicked and screamed out "NO! I'M NOTHEADING WEST! I'M JUST GOING UP THE ROAD!" I barreled up the road with the road worker yelling for me to stop. I didn't care. My heart was pounding out of my chest at this point.

I came to a railroad crossing and had to stop because the train was coming. I was feeling only slightly calmer....until...there he was again across the tracks! I started my car and tried to make it across the tracks but my car stalled. The train kept coming and the hitchhiker kept standing there with his thumb in the air. I tried and tried and tried to start the car, but nothing. Finally, just before the train smashed into me, I managed to put the car in reverse and get off the tracks. The train passed, and the man was gone again. At that point, I knew the fear was no longer vague or formless. It had a form. He was beckoning me and wanted me to die. I didn't know what to do. Should I turn back or keep going? The terror was engulfing me. I was alone - nightmarishly alone. I knew I'd see him everywhere I went. I just broke down and cried. I decided to continue on. I'd been driving for three days and nights and kept seeing him. I would only stop for food and then drive on. I knew I had to reach my destination before he closed in on me...

I decided to take a side road on the fourth day as night was falling just hoping to lose him, but I ran out of gas. Scared out of my wits, I got out of the car and ran up the road to a gas station. I yelled out for help. The owner of the station opened his window and said he was in bed; the station was closed and would not give me gas till morning no matter how much I pleaded and told him about the man who was stalking me. Suddenly I felt a hand on my shoulder and almost had a heart attack. It turned out to be a sailor on leave heading back to his ship in San Diego. I begged him to ride with me and I would take him to San Diego. He willingly agreed. He made the man at the station give us gasoline. My fear was so great at this point that I welcomed any company in that car with me. I had no fear that he might try to make a pass at me even though he told me I looked like a movie star. He even asked if he could remove his shoes because his feet felt like a couple of hot bricks. Honestly, I didn't even care about the stench of his smelly feet as long as I had company. I even tried to rationalize with him as to whether or not a hitchhiker might be able to out pass me constantly on the road in a faster car. He said possibly. Then I saw the hitchhiker again as we were driving and nearly drove us off the road. The sailor said he saw nobody. A few seconds later, as we were sitting there on the side of the road, I saw him again and this time I tried to hit him and kill him. Again, the sailor saw no one, got scared and assumed I was crazy when I said I wanted to kill that man because he'd been following me. He decided he couldn't stay in the car with me any longer. I even went so far as to tell him I liked him and wanted to go out with him if he would stay. He spent about five seconds considering it and then realized he had to get away from me. He grabbed his shoes and left. At that point, I went to pieces.

I made it to a diner outside of Tucson that had a pay phone so I could call and talk to my mother in NY. I needed to hear a warm, comforting voice. Some reality. I reached my mother's home and a woman I didn't know answered. I asked for my mother. The woman said my mother was in the hospital recovering from a nervous breakdown due to the death of her daughter, Nan, who was killed in a car accident in Pennsylvania when her tire blew out. I dropped the phone and slowly walked out of the phone booth. I was no longer fearful. I was numb. Every emotion seemed to drain out of me. I was a cold shell. I was aware of my surroundings, but it was really nothingness now. I would find out what he wanted, but I think I knew. I got back into my car and looked into my rearview mirror. There he was in the back seat, but I feared him no more even as he said with a slight smile "I believe you're going...my way?" Death was beckoning me home.

I had to give this review from Nan's perspective, but from mine as well, because every time I see this episode, I imagine what she must be going through and how I would most likely be going through the same thing. I don't know if I could have handled such terror. How many women could? That's why I added some of my own thoughts about what she might have been feeling. This is one of the scariest and creepiest Twilight Zones ever made, and Inger Stevens was tremendous in her role as Nan Adams. Leonard Strong was perfect in his role of the somewhat non-menacing, yet still somewhat ominous, Hitchhiker. It was brilliantly directed by Alvin Ganzer whom I was informed just recently died at close to 100 years old. Inger Stevens was a talented and beautiful actress who left us much too early at the age of 35. This episode never fails to give me chills, especially with Inger's wonderfully expressed background narration throughout the show.

Kelly brought up a point in her review that I have also pondered. I wonder if the sailor and all the other people Nan met along the way were real, or were they all part of her death dream. If she was dead, how could they see and talk to her?

Ken was correct in his review that this is exactly what the audience tunes in to see, and also when he mentioned that the final scene is classic for the ages.

Bobby made many excellent points in his review, but he said it best when he wrote that watching it now on a computer screen, the stuff of science fiction back in 1959, instead of on a black and white TV, nothing really much has changed in one area. It still scares the hell out of you. Also Bobby, I never could figure out myself what that sailor was doing wandering around such a deserted area. Nan was so terrified that she didn't wonder about it either. You also mentioned her reckless driving while looking for the hitchhiker. It's amazing she didn't run into a few trees every time she looked away from the road or over her shoulder.

In any case, this is one of the top five classics in my book. Sorry my review was so long, but I had to put a little twist on this one. It was worth it. A DEFINITE SOLID 5 RATING

Review by Kitty

This latest episode is called The Hitchhiker and it's well titled as that is what you see throughout this episode.

The story starts out where we see a woman by the side of the road in Pennsylvania getting her tire changed. Her name is Nan Adams. The man changing her tire asks her how fast she was going and she said about sixty five and he tells her she's lucky. With that speed and the turn she was taking, she should be getting picked up by a hearse not getting her tire changed.

He tells her to follow him in to town and he'll get her fixed up with a new tire. He pulls away and as she pulls away from the side of the road, she sees an odd looking man hitchhiking by the side of the road. She drives on.

When she gets to the gas station, she pays the man his money and she tells him its cheaper than a funeral. He laughs and takes the money in and she realizes the hitchhiker is behind her by the side of the road. The man brings her the change and sees that she appears to be shaken up. He asks her if she's all right and she tells him yes.

She later appears in a diner and she asks the man in the diner if they get many hitchhikers along this stretch of road and he tells her no as it's not that busy of a road and there's very little in between. He asks her if she's seen any and she tells him no. She gets very upset though and she says she all of a sudden doesn't like her car very much.

She then gets in the car and drives. Along the way every few miles, she appears to be seeing this hitchhiker along the side of the road. She realizes she can't shake him and so she is just driving nonstop. Her destination is California.

She is stopped for road construction and while she sits there waiting for the go ahead, the hitchhiker appears to her at her window and asks if she's going out west. She tells him no, she's only going down the road a ways. She starts to drive away before she's told to and she ends up stopping for a train that's coming. She sees the hitchhiker on the other side of the tracks.

She sees the train coming and tries to drive away but the car stalls on the tracks as she sees the train coming. She has to try several times before the car starts and she puts it in reverse and gets off the tracks as the train comes by.

After the train is gone, she sees the hitchhiker is gone but she realizes he'll be back and he'll keep coming back. She continues to drive frantically to California and stops in New Mexico late at night where she realizes she's out of gas. She walks to the nearest town but the man who owns the gas station won't give her any gas because they are closed. She begs and pleads with him and tells her that a strange man is following her but it's no use, he tells her to come back in the morning.

At that moment a hand reaches out to her shoulder and she turns around and sees a Navy man on leave. He tells her that he saw her car outside of town. He's on his way back to San Diego to his ship. She asks him if he'd like a ride from her. He tells her sure. She then informs him that the man won't come out and give her any gas and he bangs on the door demanding the man come out and sell the woman some gas.

They get back to the car and proceed to be on their way. The Navy man can't believe that a pretty woman picked him up and he tells her the guys at the ship will never believe it. She assures him she'll sign an affidavit and they'll get it notarized.

She asks him if he does a lot of hitchhiking and he tells her yes when he's on leave but it's mainly truck drivers that give him rides. Most people in cars won't stop. She then starts to wonder if that man who's been following her is simply getting rides with people who are driving faster than she is.

She then sees the man by the side of the road and she tries to run him down. The Navy man grabs the wheel and asks her what she's trying to do. She asks him if he saw the man and he tells her he didn't see anyone.

She continues driving and she sees him again and tries to do the same thing. The Navy man grabs the wheel again and he puts his foot on the brake...... He tells the woman he's leaving because he thinks she's crazy. She begs him not to leave and that she really will take him to San Diego. She tells him she's been seeing a man by the side of the road since Pennsylvania and she just wanted to run him down. The man still wants to leave.

She then tells him that she likes him and would like to go out with him but he's still not buying it. He leaves and Nan is devastated. She keeps driving and finally arrives at a place where she can make a phone call. She just wants to call her mother and talk to her. However, when she dials the number she doesn't get her mother, she gets a woman named Mrs. Whitney who tells her that Mrs. Adams has suffered a nervous breakdown because six days ago her daughter was killed in a car accident in Pennsylvania.

Nan puts the phone down and realizes why the man is following her. She no longer feels afraid and actually feels very little at this point. She knows she'll see the man again and it doesn't bother her now. She gets in the car and she sees the man in the back seat in her rear view mirror and the man says, "Going my way?"

This is definitely one of the best Twilight Zone episodes we've had so far. Inger Stevens played this part perfectly as the woman who truly doesn't realize that she's died in a car accident. The strange man that she sees is clearly the Grim Reaper or Mr. Death as he was known in episode number two.

Again it's interesting that the hitchhiker really isn't that scary looking but the fact that he just keeps showing up makes him scary. My other question would be the people that Nan encountered on the road, were they real or were they simply figments of her imagination based on the reality that she had created after the car accident.

Anyway you slice it, it's an episode that delivers. I remember the first time I watched it feeling for Nan as she felt that frustration particularly after the train incident where she realized that she was not going to shake that hitchhiker. He was going to keep popping up no matter what she did or where she traveled to.

In the Twilight Zone Companion this teleplay was based on a radio teleplay that was done by Orson Welles originally where Orson Welles played the person being pursued by death. It's said the original writer of this story was not thrilled with the changing of the gender of the main character but I thought it was great and having this happening to a woman driving on a cross country trip makes it all the more ominous as a woman is typically perceived as more vulnerable than a guy traveling by himself.

I will give this one a five as this episode is very much a classic episode for me.

Review by Ken

Whoa!! Way to go Rod. I was starting to get frustrated with the continual domination of lead men stories. Out of the first 15 episodes, only ep.4-'TheSixteen-Millimeter Shrine' focused on a story with a woman in the lead role. Ida Lupino played the part of a lonely lady wanting to go back into time and party with old friends. Sadly the story was a bust.

Maybe someone in the board room shouted out and said 'let's have some stories where the women are the focus.' Result is a masterpiece titled 'The Hitch-Hiker.' Inger Stevens nailed a perfect performance. From the opening scene to the end Stevens facial expressions, demeanor, and mannerism was right on the mark. She is relaxed one minute and scared to death the next moment.

I especially enjoyed the way this story opens up. We are introduced to a stunning and gorgeous Nan Adams who needs assistance for a flat tire. After receiving help she notices a creepy guy on the road hitching a ride. She is a little disturbed but proceeds on her way. However, as she continues driving this mysterious character shows up again and again. He is at the gas station waiting to hitch a ride. By the way did you notice that gas was 32 cents a gallon. He is outside at the coffee shop. Did you notice that a hamburger steak costs 65cents. Better yet a meatball sandwich costs 85 cents.

Fear, panic, dismay, and tension continues to grow. The first act ends with a near accident on the train track. What is Nan Adams going to do?

The second act introduces a friendly calm sailor needing a ride to San Diego. Hoping to escape her fears Nan agrees to give him a ride so that she has company. But her crazy emotions and reckless driving force the sailor to leave her. She is despondent and breaks down.

At this point let me add my two cents about this dumb sailor. Nan offers to ride with him all the way back home. What male species would not accept this offer. Who cares how looney this lady is. Her beauty is enough. Okay sweetheart let travel across the country together.

The final scene is classic for the ages. She calls her mother and discovers the weird news. Nan Adams died in a car wreck six days earlier. She get's back in her car, adjusts the mirror, and there is the hitch-hiker in the back seat. He utters those famous words in Twilight Zone lore. "I believe you are going my way."

Chilling story that easily makes my top ten best of the entire series. This is what the audience tunes in to see. Just imagine you are alone in a motel room in nowhere land, the rain is pouring down with loud thunders, it is midnight and you watch this episode. I bet you get up from the chair and check out the window. Any goons outside staring at you.

I am sure there was a lot of water-cooler talk at the office the next day about this episode when it aired in 1960. Even today a fan of the show would talk with co-workers about this first-rate drama.

By the way Inger Stevens is the second woman inducted into my Twilight Zone hall of fame for a brilliant, dazzling, and sparkling appearance in this series.

Props to Leonard Strong for playing the skulking hitch-hiker. I sure would not give him a ride.

My rating-5 Super Classic.

The Twilight Zone" Episode 17 "The Fever"

Original Air Date- January 29, 1960
Guest Star- Everett Sloane
Written by Rod Serling
Directed by Robert Florey

Review by Kitty

This latest episode is called The Fever. I found the episode to be little more than a headache myself.

As someone who has been to Las Vegas many times, I found the premise of the show interesting at first. We see an older couple by the names of Flora and Franklin. Flora won a trip to Las Vegas and is just delighted to be there.

Her husband Franklin is not the least bit thrilled to be there and is being rude and obnoxious to everybody. He thinks gambling is a waste of money and time. Flora walks to a slot machine and puts in a nickel. Franklin yells at her fordoing it and she tells him she might as well pull the arm as she already put in her nickel. She does and she loses.

Franklin is disgusted and tells her he's going back to the room. As he's walking out a very drunk man grabs him and puts a silver dollar coin in his hand and tells him to play it as his wife is calling him. He forces the coin in Franklin's hand and shoves it in the slot machine.

He walks away and when Franklin pulls the arm, he wins some money. Flora is thrilled. Franklin tells her that unlike everybody else, he'll take the money and stop so he actually comes out ahead.

As they walk away, he hears someone say Franklin. He asks Flora if she said something and she tells him no. Later that night, as he lies there awake he looks at the money and he keeps hearing someone calling his name and he sees the money and it's multiplying.

He gets up and he tells Flora that he doesn't feel right about keeping the money. He's going to feed it back in to the machine. He goes down and Flora eventually follows but finds him cashing checks to get more money to put in the machine.

Flora tells him he should stop, he's losing their money. He screams at her in the casino to stop telling him what to do. He calls her a shrew and tells her she's bringing him bad luck. He tells her that the machine is its own entity and that it's supposed to pay out $10,000 but it teases him, he puts in $5 and it gives him back $4. He wants to beat the machine. He knows that if he stays on just a little bit longer it will pay out....

He stays for hours well in to the next morning and as he puts his last dollar in the machine, it jams. He goes berserk and demands his dollar. He's carried out by security.

Back in the hotel room, he tells Flora that he was cheated. He then starts to hear his name being called again and he opens the door and the machine is there beckoning him to play it. Flora tells him that nothing is there.

Franklin loses it completely and he backs up out of the window and falls to his death. The last thing we see is everybody crouching over him and one man tells another that he's seen people get the fever before but never like that.

They all leave and Franklin's lifeless body is there and a silver dollar rolls up next to him and we see the slot machine.

I really wanted to enjoy this episode because I have been to Las Vegas many times and I have thoroughly enjoyed myself and I have played my share of the slots.

However, the main character in this episode comes across as even more unlikable and unsympathetic as the older actress in the 16 Millimeter Shrine... He's grouchy, completely without joy in anything that he does and in the end very self centered.

OK he doesn't believe in gambling and yet he allows himself to be manipulated by a machine. I also found it distasteful that he's not the slightest bit happy to be on vacation. It's a vacation for free. His wife won it.

When he decides it's not right to keep the money, instead of going out and giving it to a homeless person or putting in a Salvation Army collection bucket, he decides he's going to put it back in the machine, so he puts it back in the machine and then he cashes checks to get more money to put in to a machine that hates doing.

Sorry but usually people who have the fever are having a good time when they do all of that. I don't know that I've ever seen a person so angry sitting at as lot machine.

I realize that Rod Serling was making a social commentary on compulsive gamblers, but he really picked the wrong character for this.

Several years ago I caught an episode of Family Ties where the Meredith Baxter character was in Atlantic City and started winning at craps left and right and she couldn't stop playing because she was winning and having a great time. The next day she came back to her family and told them how much she won and everybody was thrilled except her. She felt awful that she had allowed a craps game to dominate her like that and she gave all of the money to a homeless shelter down the road. A lesson was learned in that little episode.

What was learned here? Flora should have taken a friend to Las Vegas with her instead of her husband. As for Franklin not being in control because of the voices? Well, I thought those voices sounded more like bullfrogs than anything else and if Franklin wanted to win, he wouldn't have kept going back for more.

He was unsympathetic and unlikable and in the end I really didn't care if he was dead. That makes it a very sad episode indeed.

My rating is a one ~ Poor

Review by Ken

One would think that after 16 episodes in this series that the production crew would know the difference between good stories that work and bad stories that flop. Ep.17-'The Fever' is not only a tale that is shallow, frivolous, superficial, petty, and stupid, but frankly embarrassing to watch and review for this group.

An elderly couple win a free trip to Las Vegas. The wife wants to have a goodtime but the grumpy husband complains and grumbles. He finally decides to play a slot machine and wins. He continues to play losing money well into the night. The machine calls out his name and he goes batty. A final showdown occurs in his motel room when the slot machine chases him out the window where he falls to his death. The wife is helpless and does nothing to stop the machine.

I guess the point of this story is not to gamble yourself to death. Really!! Yes people lose money in Vegas all the time. Even gambling addiction can cause you to lose your mind.

But ep.17 was way too extreme even for The Twilight Zone. The problem I have is the one-sided message throughout the story. Not all people who go to Vegas to gamble have a terrible time. Reasonable people know when to control how much money to spend. It seems Serling wants to convey the message than gambling will destroy your life. Not true. Ask the millions of people who gamble throughout the years. In my case I have won more than I have lost.

The casting of Everett Sloane and Vivi Janiss as the elderly couple was miscast again. I could not relate to them and had no sympathy at all. And what is up with the slot machine of that day. It looked like something made in 100 B.C.

Again the death scene at the end was bizarre. How about the people who gathered around to view the body. They stand there and do nothing. Then they all leave him there and walk away. The scene fades into black.

After being on a high mountain with ep.16-'The Hitch-Hiker,' we are brought down to the gutter with this mess of a script. Toss this one in the trash can.

Will this series please stick to The Twilight Zone formula with scripts that work. I need that 'nostalgia' feeling so to speak. I want to watch something that I have not seen before. Wise up producers.

My rating ~ 0 Lousy

Review by Bobbynear

While I would never come close to attaching the word "classic" to this episode, neither do I see any reason for the level of vitriol hurled at it by my two co-reviewers. The story, written this time entirely by Serling, is the kind of cautionary tale about the danger of letting anything become obsessive, be it, gambling, drinking, sex, or even overeating, that we have seen many times. Millions of American citizens can relate to at least one of those.

I'm not going to rehash the plot line here. Kitty and Ken have done a great job with that. Instead I intend to take on a few comments that seem out of line to me.

Kitty seems to be turned off by Franklin being a cantankerous old goat who can't even enjoy a free vacation. But I think that adds to the story. His poor wife continues to suffer even when away from home. The story needs to convince us that Franklin has a wretched personality no matter what he is doing and it wastes no time in doing just that.

I've never been to Vegas, but I did go many times to Atlantic City when I lived on the East Coast. The first time I ever put money in a slot machine, I got nothing in return which did not surprise me. What did surprise me is that I got nothing in return in any other way from doing it. If that's fun, I'll pass on it. And the people I saw sitting or standing there pushing coins in machines looked completely disinterested to me. The little return they got, they simply fed right back into it. I'm afraid I was bored by the whole experience.

But there are plenty of people whose lives have been ruined by addiction to gambling. It is all too real. This cautionary tale should be taken seriously. The only problem I have with it, is that it's not likely a man would become addicted simply from putting a single coin in a slot machine. But Serling, as always is up against the clock and in the twenty five minutes he had, there was little time to watch Franklin slowly dissolve into addiction.

As for the voice in the machine....well Kitty needs to read the Twilight Zone Companion and the story of what they had to do in order to make coins falling sound like a man's name. I thought it was quite creative and didn't sound like bullfrogs to me In fact it creeped the hell out of me.

As for Ken, we can all celebrate his ability to walk away at the right time as well as his winning ways in a casino. But let's get serious here. That is a rare event for most people. I also think Ken missed a vital point when he pointed out the absurdity of a slot machine chasing a man out a window while his wife does nothing to stop it.

Stop what? There is no slot machine chasing Franklin. It's all in his imagination. Nobody could have helped him. And as for that bizarre looking slot machine, well it was quite real. Again in the book The Twilight Zone Companion there is an interesting explanation.

Seems that back in '59 it was illegal for anyone in California to own a slot machine. All that they could find had been impounded by the police. The producers had to go to the police impound lot to find one and when they did, they were required to have a police officer standing with it on the set whenever it was used, almost as if it did have a life of its own like in this story and could have reached out and grabbed some poor victim.

There is no way I would give this a 0 rating like Ken did. At the very least, it is unusual and does not look like any other episode and does not require anymore suspension of disbelief than the average Twilight Zone story.

Ken is correct. This is a very one sided story. But I don't think we would have found it terribly compelling to watch a tale of a man and wife who go to Las Vegas... gamble a little... know when to walk away with their winnings... go have a nice meal and then figure they broke even or even came out ahead in the long run. If so, then somebody would have made a movie by now of Ken's numerous trips to Vegas.

Ken used the words, "shallow, frivolous, superficial, petty, and stupid, and frankly embarrassing to watch," to describe this episode. But some of us might just use the same words to describe people who spend all day mindlessly pushing coins into a machine. No no... not everyone... not even a majority....but at least enough to keep those casino operators in business and to pay for all those fancy hotels.

My rating on a scale of 0 to 5   3 ~~ GOOD

Review by Linn

I enjoyed The Fever and found it to be quite Zone-like. I'm not saying I believe it to be classic or even excellent, but I did find it to be quite good.

You see a couple, Franklin and Flora Gibbs, who have won a free trip to Las Vegas apparently due to Flora winning some sort of contest. Franklin is very much against gambling and is obviously not thrilled to be there at all, but he goes and tolerates the trip because as he tells Flora "It's your vacation. You won it." However, he's dead-set against gambling away any of their money. Although Flora is very happy to be there, he is perfectly happy to spend the entire vacation in his room or dining as long as it's far away from the gambling area.

Flora puts a nickel in a machine and Franklin berates her. He is even more disgruntled when she pulls the handle and loses. His attitude suddenly changes when a drunken man forces a dollar coin into Franklin's hand and makes him put it into a slot machine. After glancing over at Flora a couple of times, who was nodding her head for him to pull the handle, he does just that and he wins about 15 or 20 coins. He tells Flora that he intends to take the winnings to their room to be brought home with them, unlike the other fools who just keep feeding it back into the machines and losing.

As they are departing the gambling area to go back to their room, he hears his name being called. It seems that the clanking chips were clanking out his name. Then for some reason, Franklin is lying in bed that night, fully clothed, which I didn't understand since Flora was asleep and in her nightgown. He starts hearing the coins clanking out his name again, but this time more than once. He was imagining that the slot machine was beckoning him, but it seemed that he was putting these thoughts and delusions in his mind because deep down, he actually was excited about his win and wanted to try and win even more. He gets up and tells Flora that he can't keep tainted money and is going to put it back into the machine, but he knew in his gut that he really wanted to keep gambling – the one thing he claimed to so desperately despise. Ah, that's why he stayed dressed. Flora is surprised but lets him go. She eventually goes after him and realizes that he's cashing check after check after check to try to hit the jackpot. He even makes a scene by screaming at her to leave him alone and stop bringing him bad luck...

After over five or six hours, he's down to a final dollar coin in his hand. He puts it into the machine, and the machine breaks down. The handle won't budge. Franklin gets hysterical and pushes the machine to the ground demanding his dollar back. He is taken back to his room by security. Flora tries to comfort him, but he calls the machine an entity and a monster. He begins to hear his name again in the clanking coins. He becomes totally delusional. He opens the door of the room and believes he sees his slot machine in front of him. He slams the door closed and tells Flora that it's following him. Of course, Flora sees nothing. She tries to calm him down but Franklin completely loses all composure when he thinks he sees the machine coming into the room and toward him, backing him into the window which he falls through and plummets to his death.

Kitty mentioned in her review that Franklin was grouchy and found no joy in anything he did. Yes, he was certainly grouchy and found no joy in any way at the idea of gambling, but that does not necessarily mean that he was a miserable person who found no joy in anything else. He may have been a perfectly pleasant gentleman who enjoyed many things with Flora, but he simply despised gambling.

Believe me, I know other people, including my late father, who shared Franklin's view of gambling. He would have no part of it and would not allow my step-mother to even consider it in any way. Yet, they did many other things together and really enjoyed themselves. Also, like you, I have been to Nevada and I live an hour and a half away from Atlantic City, NJ so I've been to casinos many times and played the slots and blackjack and I usually always enjoyed myself, especially when I sometimes won, but I've seen and also have known people who became so addicted to gambling that they lost everything from their bus fare to get back home to their entire bank accounts to their homes and even their families.

I believe that Rod's whole intent in this episode was to point out that even the staunchest protester of gambling or any other type of addiction can possibly end up getting sucked into that very addiction if they actually get a taste of it. That's what happened to Franklin. I give this episode a Good rating.

"The Twilight Zone" Episode 18 "The Last Flight"

Original Air Date- February 5, 1960
Guest Star- Kenneth Haigh
Written by Richard Matheson
Directed by William Claxton

Review by Kitty

This latest episode is called The Last Flight. Compared to the last episode we were subjected to this was a nice change of pace, of course on a personal note, I've always been one to be partial to time travel stories. This was also a special treat as this is one episode I had not seen before.

This episode starts where we see a WWI flying ace in the sky flying in to a cloud. His name is Lt. William Terrance Decker. He emerges from the clouds and lands on an American air base called the Lafayette Air Base in France.

The MP's immediately tell him to stop his airplane and he's quite surprised to see an American air base in France. He tells the men as he looks at all of the planes that he had no idea that the Americans were so advanced. They begin to usher him in to the building and he's surprised to see a female officer walking out of it.

He's taken to a General Harper and a Major Wilson. Harper asks him why he landed there and Decker tells him that he got lost. Harper asks for his name and he gives it to him and tells him he's part of the Royal Flying Corp. Harper says, You mean the Royal Air Force and Decker looks at him puzzled and tells him, No, it's the Royal Flying Corp.

Harper asks if he was part of an air show and asks why he's wearing that costume. Decker explains that he was not part of any air show and this is not his costume, it's his uniform. He was out flying on patrol when he went in to a strange cloud. When he got in to the cloud he couldn't hear the engine of the plane.

Wilson asks him what today's date is. Decker replies March 5th. Wilson asks him what year. Decker replies 1917. Wilson tells him that it's March 5, 1959. Decker asks him if they're making a joke. They both reply no. Decker wonders how it's possible, he was out on patrol with is partner Lt. Mackaye, he flew in to the cloud and he ended up here. Harper tells him Lt. Mackaye? He tells him that Air Marshall Mackaye is coming here today. Perhaps they'll have him talk to him and maybe they can figure it out.

Decker is shocked. He tells them that it's not possible because Mackaye is dead. Harper asks him what he means by that. Decker explains that the last he saw of him, he was surrounded by seven German planes, he couldn't do anything to help him because he was engaged with three himself. He couldn't have possibly gotten away from those seven planes.

Wilson tells him that apparently he did because he was the most decorated flying ace by Britain in the second World War when he shot down some German planes in a blitz attack and he saved many people as a result.

Decker still doesn't see how it's possible. Decker is taken away to another room and Harper looks at his personal effects taken from the plane and from him. He tells Wilson this is one elaborate hoax. Wilson wonders if it isn't a hoax.

Harper thinks Decker may be wanting to harm Mackaye as he shows him Decker's gun. Wilson wonders why Decker would leave a gun in the plane if he wanted to harm Mackaye. They could easily call Britain and confirm if there was a Lt Decker in the Royal Flying Corp in WWI. Harper tells him it's too much trouble.

Wilson goes in to talk to Decker. Decker can't believe that Mackaye is alive. They've been friends for a long time. He calls him Old Lead bottom... He explains that it was a private joke with them because he got shot in an embarrassing place so when it was just the two of them around he called him Old Lead bottom.

He then explains that when he left Mackaye, he wasn't surrounded by three other Germans. He's really a coward. Usually when he and Mackaye go out on patrol they split up. It's Decker's idea because he can play it safe and not go in places where he's likely to encounter Germans. Mackaye on the other hand enjoys the engagements. He looks forward to it. Decker just pretends that he's brave. He sometimes has shot bullets in the plane just to make it look good.

That's why he believes that Mackaye is dead. He said this one time they were together. When the seven planes came out, he got scared and he flew away in to the cloud that brought him here. Wilson tells him that Mackaye obviously got help. Someone must have shown up. Decker insists that nobody was around for at least fifty miles.

Wilson tells him that Mackaye is very much alive and he'll see him for himself. Decker tells him that no, he can't see him because of his cowardice. It then hits him that if someone else showed up to help Mackaye, perhaps it was him.

Decker realizes he needs to get back to his plane and go back in to the cloud. Wilson tells him no, that Mackaye obviously survived without him because he's on his way there. Decker doesn't believe that. He believes that if he doesn't go back in that plane and fly off then Mackaye won't get there. He hits Wilson and he hits the guard outside the room.

Decker runs out of the building and gets back to his plane. One guy tries to stop him but he hits him. Just as he's about to take off Wilson is there with a gun pointed at his head and tells him to get out of the plane.

Decker tells him no, that he's going to have to shoot him. Decker tells Wilson that this isn't about just him, it's about Mackaye and what about all of those other people he saved later on.

Wilson takes away the gun and Decker flies away. Wilson is getting a stern reprimand from Harper when an elderly Mackaye shows up. Wilson asks Mackaye if he ever knew a Lt William Terrance Decker.

Mackaye says, "Terry Decker? I should hope I do, he saved my life in 1917." Both Harper and Wilson look shocked. Wilson asks him what happened. Mackaye explains that they were on patrol and all of a sudden seven German planes came out of nowhere. He saw Decker go in to the clouds and he thought for sure that Decker had abandoned him but, all of a sudden Decker came swooping out of the clouds and started firing at them.

He took out three of them before they shot him down and he was able to get away. Harper tells him that the Germans would always send back the pilots personal effects. Did they send back Decker's? Mackaye thinks about it and tells them no and then asks what this is all about.

Harper takes out Decker's personal items and Mackaye is shocked and asks how they got these. Wilson tells him he'd better sit down Old Lead bottom. Mackaye looks even more astounded as he asks What did you just call me?

I found this episode enjoyable. I really liked the portrayal of Decker by the actor Kenneth Haigh. I thought he brought the right about of humanity to the part. He was perfect as an officer who on the one hand was trying to do his duty but had a hard time following it, but in the end realizes that if he doesn't do his duty, other people will die who shouldn't die.

It's one of those situations where the needs of the many outweigh the needs of the few or the one.

I also think this is one of those episodes that really is what the Twilight Zone is all about. Decker really did pass over in to the Twilight Zone at least briefly enough to see what the world would be like if did his duty and stopped being afraid.

I also liked the characters of Harper and Wilson. I think Harper's reaction was perfectly normal and Wilson played the part well of the person who steps back from the normal constrains of his duty and thinks outside the box enough to think that maybe there is something to what Decker is saying.

I give this episode a four rating.

Review by Ken

A yawn story about a World War I flyer who travels back into time and lands on U.S. Air Force base. Lt. Decker is a coward when fighting the enemy....... He travels to the future and realizes he can be a hero and get a second chance to save a fellow flyer. The end scene confirms that Air Marshal Mackaye was indeed saved by the heroism of Decker.

The moral of the story is if given a second chance to correct a wrong what would you do? Decker was a coward and deserted a friend by flying into a cloud. He lands in 1959 and realizes if he goes back into time he can save his friend in1917.

Couple of problems I have with this concept of time travel. Every time I watch a time travel story I get frustrated. If a person travels from 1917 to 1959 does he not also age with the time. Decker should be 42 years older. This story would have looked better if Decker looked older with gray hair and wrinkled facial features. He looks at his appearance and is perplexed at his condition. He meets Mackaye and they discuss the events of the past. Then Decker realizes he must go back into time to save his friend. The end scene shows his escape and while flying into the cloud he becomes 42 years younger again. Now that would be The Twilight Zone angle.

The writers deceive the audience and make us assume that anybody can travel into the future without ageing. I don't buy it. Same with traveling into the past. I would think that a 100 year old man going back into time 75 years would like he is 25 again.

Ep.18 'The Last Flight' was too shallow of a story for me. I need more explanation on this theory of time travel and how it works. To pluck somebody down in another time zone without telling us how makes no sense.

If writers would develop their theories on time travel and explain it with something I have never heard about then I will listen. It is easy to write a story about people going back into time. The television series 'The Time Tunnel' flopped after 30 episodes because writers could not come up with enough stories.

People traveling hundreds or thousands of years into the future is also easy to write about. But to explain how it is done is the hard part. Writers can you develop this story?? The movie 'The Time Machine' did not work for me. Rod Taylor travels 800,000 years into the future only to find Morlocks, ape like hairy men. Worst dud ending of all time.

Rambling Ken will stop now. My rating on 'The Last Flight' is 1 Poor. Nothing to get excited about.

Review by Bobbynear

I'm afraid I have to agree with Ken on this one. Not even worth writing about it extensively so I won't.

You have to really try hard to screw up a time travel story but this one manages to get there. Boring and trivial....I couldn't stay awake. I didn't care about any of these characters and I rarely get involved when an entire tv episode is nothing but men talking to each other in a room, unless it's jury deliberations.

I have no feelings one way or the other the way that Ken does... Regarding characters going back in time and looking younger... unless of course... I would look 75 years younger after watching it. Now that would be something worthwhile.

If you required that in time travel stories... that would mean that the guest star would either have to be replaced for most of it, or there would need to be extensive make up work done which is quite expensive.

We recently reviewed "Walking Distance" where guest star Gig Young was transported back to his childhood... but he was still an adult. If they did it Ken's way... Gig Young would have to be replaced by Ron Howard as the focal point of the story. This makes no sense. Time travel is only interesting because the time traveler is still the same... but in a different era.

Ken also mentions the old tv series The Time Tunnel... but there the lost characters sometimes went back thousands of years... do we really want to see them looking that old? Who is going to pay for that? Ken says the show ran out of ideas. Kitty seems to remember that it went off the air because it was too expensive to produce given the ratings it was getting. And that was...without... the characters changing appearance at all.

The Time Machine is one of my favorite movies of all time. Sure would love to know why Ken was so disappointed in the ending with the hairy little morlocks... and how his ending would be more compelling.

Back to this episode... Ken is right... nothing to get excited about... or to stay awake about either... it was even worse for me...

My rating on a scale of 0 to 5

0 - LOUSY

Review by Linn

This will, without a doubt, be one of shortest reviews I'll ever written. The Last Flight sucked royally. I hated it, it was boring and it made me fall asleep. Yeah, Kenneth Haigh was okay in his role, but as far as the rest of the story, where are we going with this? All they did was stand around and go back and forth with each other trying to prove or disprove Decker's reason for being there, who he really was and his mental state.

This episode is a great cure for insomnia. I have only three words to describe it and they are - STINK, STANK, STUNK.
I give it a 0 - Lousy rating.

"The Twilight Zone" Episode 19 "The Purple Testament"

Original Air Date- February 12, 1960
Guest Star- William Reynolds
Written by Rod Serling
Directed by Richard L. Bare

Review by Kitty

This latest episode is called The Purple Testament. This brings us an interesting aspect to war. The idea being if you knew if someone was going to die, could you do anything to prevent it?

We start out seeing a platoon of men getting off a truck in the Philippines in 1945 and a man by the name of Lt Fitzgerald is the commanding officer. He tells his captain by the name of Riker that they lost four men today and have twelve wounded. Riker can see that Fitzgerald is deeply shaken by this and offers him a good bottle of wine and conversation.

Riker asks Fitzgerald why this is bothering him more than usual. They've lost men before and he's never been like this. Fitzgerald gives him a piece of paper and Riker reads the names of the four men and their dates of death. Riker doesn't see the point. Fitzgerald then tells him that he wrote that the day before. He was telling his platoon their mission and when he looked in to the faces of those four men, he saw a light on their faces and he just knew they were going to die.

Riker is skeptical. He asks him is he's sure that he didn't write these names down today after it happened and Fitzgerald insists that he wrote them yesterday.

We then see Riker at the hospital explaining to a Captain Gunther that Fitzgerald maybe needs some observation. Gunther tells him that he's already there visiting the men who came in wounded.

Fitzgerald is talking to a man by the name of Smitty. Smitty doesn't appear to be doing so good and smoking a cigarette doesn't appear to be helping but Fitzgerald tells him not to worry that he'll be going home as soon as he's healed. He then looks in to Smitty's face and sees the light. Fitzgerald is so overcome with emotion at seeing it, he passes out.

He awakens to see that Smitty has died. The doctor explains that sometimes the soldiers go very fast. Fitzgerald walks downstairs and sees Riker and Gunther. Riker tells him that the doctor told him Smitty would be all right and Fitzgerald tells him that no, Smitty is not all right, he just died. Gunther offers to go up and check on him and Fitzgerald asks why he's dead.

Fitzgerald then tells both of them that he saw the light on Smitty's face before he died. He asks Riker how many more need to die before he's believed. He doesn't want anyone to understand him, just believe him.

Riker is then debriefing all of the lieutenants on the current mission. Riker then asks Fitzgerald if he's up to this and Fitzgerald tells him yes but then he sees the light over Riker's face. He tells Riker not to go because he saw the light over his face. Riker gets angry and tells him that he's going to be fine and after they're done with this mission, they'll both be back here and have a drink. Fitzgerald tells Riker he won't be back.

Fitzgerald leaves and Riker takes pictures of his family out of his wallet and removes his wedding ring and leaves them on the table. As they are getting ready to leave, all of the men are badgering Fitzgerald to tell them who will die on this mission. He's looking at them all and there is no light on any of them.

Riker shows up and tells the men that there have been grossly exaggerated rumors about Fitzgerald being able to see who will die. It's all nothing more than a rumor and there's nothing to it. Fitzgerald confirms it.

They go on the mission and when they get back, Fitzgerald walks in to Riker's tent and throws his tag on the table with the pictures and the ring. The colonel comes in and Fitzgerald tells him that they lost Riker. The colonel laments that Riker was a good man.

Later, as Fitzgerald is shaving, he looks in the mirror and sees his own face having the light on it. He bumps the mirror and it falls to the ground. He's then told that he's being recalled to headquarters for a little while. He goes to get in the jeep and he sees the driver get a light on his face.

The driver is then told to be careful because there are road mines out there and they haven't gotten them all yet. The driver tells Fitzgerald to buckle up because it will be a long drive. Fitzgerald tells him that he doesn't think it will be that long.

We then see a very serene scene with the soldiers just hanging out and one of them is even playing a harmonica. The colonel walks by and then all of a sudden, everybody hears a big bang. It gets dismissed as thunder but we all know the jeep has blown up.

I think this is one of those episodes that has a strong premise to start with but falls a little flat at the end.

First, I think the two main characters, Fitzgerald played by William Reynolds and Riker played by Dick York are played out very well. I haven't seen Dick York in too many serious roles so this is a treat to see him here.

However, this is the third episode that we've seen so far where death is at the doorstep of someone and instead of being a grim reaper type of character that's behind it, it's a person who can simply see who is going to die next.

I would have liked to have seen more of the battle to see how Riker got killed. Since Fitzgerald knew that Riker was slated for death, you would have thought that he might have tried to stay closer to him to perhaps protect him in someway or maybe even sacrifice his own life to save Riker. It was established that Riker had a family at home and maybe Fitzgerald would have seen the purpose behind being given this gift.

Instead we don't know how Riker died only that he did die and everybody is bummed about it. At the end when Fitzgerald saw his own impending doom and the doom of his jeep driver, I'm surprised he did nothing to try and stop what was going to happen.

I also found myself wondering if it was really all that realistic to think that they would send two soldiers in a jeep down the road knowing there were possibly mines in it. Now I could see it if it were an emergency situation but this not an emergency and I can only say that if it were me, I'd simply refuse of fake an illness so I wouldn't be able to be in a car. You could worry about court martial's later.

I also found myself wondering that if the soldiers knew that there were mines out there why everybody dismissed that loud bang as thunder when two soldiers just left in a jeep. That just doesn't seem like normal military protocol.

Overall, I think it was a good episode but as I said falls a little short of its purpose and potential in the end. My rating is a three.

Review by Linn

Well, The Purple Testament certainly was a strange episode. I have to agree with Ken that it did drag on at times. I also agree with Bobby that the episode also had some intrigue to it.

Kitty asked a good question. If you knew someone was going to die, would you do something to prevent it? I would certainly try if it were in my power, but the problem with this scenario, Kitty, is that they were at war and because of that, Lieutenant Fitzgerald may have known who was going to die, but he most likely didn't know when the bullet or grenade was going to strike. That's the worst part about war. You never know when you're going to go. Every day, soldiers at war pray that they'll live to see the next day, but they also know as soldiers that any day could be their last.

I was not thrilled with this episode. The acting wasn't bad. We see Barney Phillips as Captain Gunther in one of his numerous appearances in Twilight Zone episodes. This was one of the few times I was able to stomach Dick York. He was fine as Captain Riker, but I just never liked the guy since watching him as a kid playing Elizabeth Montgomery's husband on Bewitched. He always annoyed me.

William Reynolds was good as Lt. Fitzgerald, but there's one thing I really didn't understand, and this relates to Kitty's question even more. At the end, he knew that he was going to die along with the jeep driver in a mine explosion. What baffles me in this case is that he could have prevented his death and the driver's death simply by not going or making some excuse not to go. I'm sure he could have thought of something. Yet, he heard about the mines and let the driver head out with him anyway. This made no sense to me. He could have saved his own skin and the driver's skin in this instance and didn't. The jeep driver, by the way, was played by a young and yet unknown Warren Oates. I loved Warren Oates in the movie "Stripes".

Overall, it was a rather strange ending and not a favorite episode of mine by any means.

I have to give it an Average rating of 2.

Review by Bobbynear

An intriguing episode to put it mildly. This story takes the blood and guts of war and brings it to a new level by giving its main character the ability to know just whose blood and guts are about to be spilled.

In the first paragraph of her review, Kitty asks if you could do anything about it if indeed you knew someone was going to die. Good question. But not answered in this story where Lt. Fitzgerald simply mopes around over his newly found ability to predict the future, without trying to find a way around it.

Even when he himself becomes the final victim, he does nothing to stop it... In fact he almost embraces it. I'm not convinced that you could change history just because you know it is coming but I think it a little unrealistic to think that a person would not at least try.

Actually this eerie episode brings up a much larger question about real life. Which is, that everyone who is born is doomed to die one day. The saving grace is that you don't know when. We know what an average lifespan will be but that's no guarantee it will work that way for you.

What would indeed happen if people knew exactly how long they had to accomplish whatever they set out to do? Would the world be even more frantic than it already is, with people trying to do as much as possible and make as much money as possible with one eye always on the clock? Or would they be more like Lt. Fitzgerald in this story, unable to function on a daily basis at all when the thought of impending doom consumes their every thought.

Of course that would be long term. In this story, in a battlefield setting during a war, every second counts and just living till the next battle is all consuming. The bigger issues of whether or not soldiers are better off not knowing would need to be dealt with in a story much longer than twenty five minutes.

Although there are some quality actors here and they do a convincing job, the story comes up a little short in not really giving us the chance to discover the possibilities of a commanding officer knowing which of his soldiers will live or die. He's lost it just over the fact that he does know.

Another Twilight Zone episode that brings up a lot of questions and then fails to answer any of them. A common occurrence in this series.

My rating on a scale of 0 to 5
2 1/2 - SLIGHTLY ABOVE AVERAGE

Review by Ken

Back to the war trenches with a story that is really bizarre. Who is coming up with these preposterous episodes? A Lieutenant has a sixth sense and can tell who is going to die next by looking into their faces and seeing a glow. One by one men die and the story drags on and on. Eventually, the Lieutenant sees his own glowing face in the mirror and is scared. He rides in a jeep and sees the glow on the driver's face. What happens next? The jeep hits a land mine and boom!!!

I know war is hellish and men will crack under the duress. But what a strange tale even for The Twilight Zone. The problem I have again is shallow writing. I could not engage in the characters because death is coming. The story ended with a dud louder than the land mines. The episode fades into the Twilight Zone sky of stars and I am left hanging on to nothing.

Another wasted television viewing on my part.

My rating-0 Lousy

"The Twilight Zone" Episode 20 "Elegy"

Original Air Date- February 19, 1960
Guest Star- Cecil Kellaway
Written by Charles Beaumont
Directed by Douglas Heyes

Review by Kitty

This latest episode is called Elegy. We start out by seeing three astronauts in a rocket that is hopelessly lost in space. They are running out of fuel and they find an asteroid to land on.

To their surprise, it has the same atmosphere as earth. They get out of the spacecraft and they see it looks like twentieth century earth. It's not their earth though as they look up and see two suns but it's hospitable none the less. There's just one problem. The first creature they see is a dog and the dog is not moving. It's just frozen in time.

They see the farmer and he's frozen. They continue to walk and come across a man fishing and he's frozen in time. They hear a band playing and go to check it out and while there are band members with the instruments as though they are playing them, they are not. The music is being piped in.

They walk inside to see a newly inaugurated mayor. However, everybody is still frozen. One astronaut wonders if these people are simply moving at a slower pace in time and that they are just moving much faster. The other two dismiss the idea.

They agree to split up to check it out. They come across a lobby in a hotel where everybody is frozen, a room in the hotel where a couple is dancing to string players playing for them but they are all frozen.

The last astronaut comes across a beauty pageant where the winner appears to be a very homely looking girl and everybody is frozen. He yells, what is wrong with you people and runs out. At that moment we see an older gentleman turnaround and smile.

The three of them walk along the street and come across an old house and to their surprise the person sitting on the porch puts down his newspaper that he's reading and he talks to them and invites them in to the house. They are skeptical about following him in and he assures them that it's perfectly safe. He introduces himself as Wickwire.

They ask him where they are. He explains that they are in a cemetery. This is the twentieth century earth section. There are many other sections as it all depends on where the people want to be after they are deceased. They are from a cemetery called Happy Glades He asks them where they would like to be most. They all three concur that they would like to be back on the ship heading for home.

He offers them a drink and they all drink together. The captain explains that they are from earth and they are stuck there as they got lost and their ship ran out of fuel. Wickwire asks them if earth ever had that atomic war. They said yes, in 1985 and it's taken them two hundred years to pick up the pieces.

They ask Wickwire when this cemetery came to be and he said Happy Glades opened in 1973. They are shocked they ask how he can be a caretaker who's over two hundred years old. He explains that he's not human, he just assumed this shape for their benefit.

They all three start to fall to the floor gasping for air. They realize they've ingested poison. They ask him why as they meant him no harm. Wickwire tells them that as long as there are men there is always a risk of harm.

The last thing we see are the three astronauts frozen and looking like they are having a good time on their ship. Wickwire is dusting them off.

This was an interesting episode and definitely a different take on the subject of death. I thought we were going to find out that the astronauts had crash landed and were already dead and didn't realize it as we saw in a recent episode but this is quite different.

I found all of the astronauts believable in their disbelief of what was happening to them. This is actually a very sinister episode when you get right down to it because these three unsuspecting guys are murdered by a psychopathic alien who has elected himself judge, jury and executioner on mankind but, Wickwire comes across as such a charming guy, you really can't hate him too much when he gives the three astronauts the poison.

I give all of the extras in this episode credit for being able to hold their poses for the camera when they had to. Marc Zicree's book claims that in some scenes you see the actors sort of moving but I think you really have to be looking. This is another episode that I have never seen before and I didn't notice anyone moving when they shouldn't have been.

All in all, I didn't find it to be an episode that knocked my socks off but I did find it enjoyable to watch. Wickwire, played by Cecil Kellaway really stole the show in my opinion. The only part that I found a little strange on the part of the astronauts was that I don't think astronauts would walk out of their rocket ship into an earth like atmosphere would keep their space suits on. They do have clothes on under them.

I know the rocket at the beginning looked a little cheesy but let's give Rod Serling a break here as CGI had not been invented yet. Overall, I liked it. I'll give it a three rating.

Review by Linn

Oh my. What can I really say about this Elegy other than I don't know what to make of it. Okay, there were three astronauts who had no clue where they were and wanted nothing more than to be back on their ship heading toward home. Not to be. They were stuck in an empty world with non-moving people and animals and nothing other than their own existence. Interesting. How did this come to be?

Finally! They stumble upon a man named Mr. Wickwire who runs this non-existent world they are in. Is he going to send them home? Nope. He's going to make them a part of his non-living museum. As these astronauts search and search for some sort of life form before coming across Mr. Wickwire, who by the way was played wonderfully by Cecil Kellaway and was the one person in this episode who could actually act, they keep coming across lifeless bodies and still don't get it. How many lifeless bodies do you need to knock over before you realize there is no living, breathing life there?

Well, I will say it was a somewhat interesting episode, but it really didn't do a whole lot for me. Sure, I'd watch it again, but it just didn't excite me. I have to mention here that Bobby made a great observation in his review by saying the poor old man has to get up and dust these people every day. Glad all I have to dust are some knick-knacks and my furniture - and that's bad enough!

I'll give it a 3 rating of good only because of Cecil Kellaway. If not for him, this episode would be worthless.

Review by Ken

Space, spacesuits, three lost spacemen, asteroid 655 million miles away from earth, and frozen figures of flesh. Bingo! Time for another weird script with a subtle message. As long as man exists there will never be world peace.

After suffering through glowing faces on the battlefield in the last episode, I tune in to ep.20 and see silly spacemen walking around trying to figure out why people are motionless. Finally Mr. Wickwire breaks the ice and meets the men. He reveals that everybody is in a cemetery. Strange. The goal is to ensure everlasting peace.

The story was unique and kept my interest until the end scene. I already knew the men drank poison. No surprise for me. Funny watching the spacemen frozen in the ship. Wickwire dusts them off. Got me laughing out loud.

If I landed on this asteroid my dream would be slugging a home run in a ballgame. Freeze me swinging the bat.

I like the casting of Cecil Kellaway as Wickwire. The spacemen were a drag. I would have cast Rod Taylor instead. Remember him from the movie 'The Time Machine.' It was watch able but fell flat at the end. Questions: Were the plants, grass, trees, lakes, also frozen in time? Any frozen dogs chasing frozen cats? Any frozen birds in the sky?

My rating 3- Good

Review by Bobbynear

The Twilight Zone began in 1959. Man landed on the moon just ten years later. That really is amazing since Rod Serling and his group of writers, in this case, Charles Beaumont certainly had no confidence that would happen.

Here again we have another story of astronauts crash landing somewhere and being totally clueless of where they are, how they got there and what to do about it. Serling obviously didn't think much of the US space program. Also, it is said several times in this episode that there was an apparently final world war in '85 and that it has taken 200 years for mankind to recover. Really?? We were always told that if there ever is a nuclear war, mankind would be bombed back to the stone age. I feel a lot better now, knowing that we can recover in a mere two centuries.

Beyond that, there really isn't much to this episode, other than watching a platoon of extras trying to stand still for a few seconds. It is eerie at first, finding all of these people frozen in position. But after about ten minutes of this, there is nothing left to do but find more and more and more of them. This really gets kind of tedious after awhile.

Writer Beaumont knew that so he inserted this old man to create some new interest. But the trouble with casting Cecil Kellaway as the old man is that, like in the countless movie and tv parts he had in his career, he seems so benign that he's hard to take seriously. So much for any terror in this story. Slow gets even slower.

Viewers who are still awake will figure out long before the idiot spacemen that this is probably a cemetery of some kind where people are buried above ground. There is nothing left to do now but dispose of them. No problem there. The old coot brings out drinks and they happily consume them as though they had been invited to some outer space cocktail party.

Come on guys... even when you were kids, out trick or treating on Halloween, your mom warned you to bring back candy for her to look over first... before you consumed any of it. Remember?

I'm afraid I don't feel very sorry for them. They were going to be awfully bored so they might as well become part of the furniture. I feel sorry for the old man....who is destined to get up every day it appears and keep things in order. That's the trouble with collecting things. Dusting them off all of the time, is such a royal pain in the ass.

My rating on a scale of 0 to 5

2 1/2 Slightly Above Average

"The Twilight Zone" Episode 21 "Mirror Image"

Original Air Date- February 26, 1960
Guest Star- Vera Miles
Written by Rod Serling
Directed by John Brahm

Review by Ken

To all my fellow Twilight Zone reviewers I wanted to add a special review and comment on this series. Obviously, when we watch any television show or movie we have to suspend our disbelief and take in what we are watching. For a moment I want to do the same thing and write a memo to Rod Serling. I know he has been gone for many years. But I wanted just for fun write him a letter and express my feelings and sensation I have over one particular episode: "Mirror Image."

Dear Mr. Serling,

I wanted to write and congratulate you on producing a fine and distinct television series that has captured millions of fans worldwide. We all are attracted and intrigued by the stories that are created week by week. Whether it be monsters, aliens, ghosts, or just the everyday bizarre turn of events in people's lives, this show continues to stir the imagination and curiosity of all of us.

I wanted to share with you my review of episode 21-'Mirror Image.' I first saw this story way back in the 1960's. I was only 6 years old at the time. All I could remember is asking myself a disturbing question. Do I have twin too? Since then I have seen this episode 4-5 times in various marathons over the years. Just recently I viewed it again with delight.

I love the way the story opens. Lighting, gray sky, pouring rain sets the tone. The musical score provides and adds to the moment. A dark late November night in a lonely bus depot. The scene shifts to an attractive young lady sitting on a bench with her luggage. Her name is Millicent Barnes. By the way what an odd name. Why not Mary or Sally Barnes. Anyway it is 2:05 a.m. She gets up and proceeds to ask the ticket agent when the bus arrives. He is annoyed at her questions. Nice casting of Joe Hamilton. He played the quirkily old grump nobody likes. Miss Barnes is confused and bewildered. Why has this man seen her before? Why is her luggage missing?

Perfect casting of Vera Miles who gives a stellar performance. She doubts her sanity. All the people in bus depot claim to have seen her before. But Miss Barnes has no recollection of past events. She enters ladies room and confronts a station attendant who is cleaning up. Clock shows 2:10 a.m. and a chilling moment. Millicent sees a mirror image of herself sitting on the bench. Shocked, she closes the door in haste. She gathers herself and boldly goes out into the lobby. To her surprise the lady is gone... What just happened?

As Millicent gathers her thoughts on the bench she is approached by a friendly by-stander who comforts her. Clock shows 2:13 a.m. and the two begin to discuss the events of the night. Great casting Martin Milner to play the part of Paul Grinstead, a gentlemen willing to help. Clean-cut suit and tie with overcoat and hat. No need for Millicent to be afraid.

Time to board the bus and the two leave the depot. Casually, Millicent looks up and sees her duplicate is on the bus. Frightened, she panics and runs inside. The person on the bus does not move. She stunningly glares with an odd slither. Her reaction is motionless and downright creepy. The first act fades into commercial.

The second act returns with a distraught Miss Barnes resting on the bench contemplating her plight of the evening. Possibly, a revelation. Are there two planes of existence? Two parallel worlds? Identical twins, duplicates, counterparts, exist side by side? Paul is perplexed and baffled and does not believe. He calls police who take away a dejected Miss Barnes. Clock shows 2:30a.m.

All is calm now until Paul realizes his luggage is missing. Alas, the same fate befalls him. Who is that man running out the door? He chases after him but to no avail. His duplicate outruns him and smirks away into the forbidden night. Paul cries out in vain... "Hey, Where are You?"

Closing narration: "call it parallel planes... insanity... only in the Twilight Zone."

Well, Mr. Serling you have completely shaken me out of my boots. As a small kid this story had an adverse affect on me. You got me wondering about this parallel universe theory of yours. Could it be there is someone out there that looks exactly like me? Is he a good person? Bad person? Will I run into him one day. Will this duplicate treat me the same way as the person running away from Paul Grinstead? Why did the mirror image person on the bus not want to meet Millicent Barnes?? How could you write such a story and leave all of us hanging? A million questions entered my mind. I shouted at the television set. Hey mirror image guy stop running. Talk to Paul. How could it be that you are in the same bus depot in the middle of the night in an isolated town? What in the world is going on???

Frankly, I grew up with a watchful eye that one day I may meet my duplicate in this world. Where is he? What would our encounter be like? Is there a force that prevents our meeting? Year by year goes by with no resolution.

In grade school I kept wondering. Will I see him in high school? Is he around the corner whenever I travel. Is he in one of my college classes? Or is he halfway around the world living the same life as me. Is he at the airport? Bus station? Train station? A cruise ship? Mr. Serling you have stirred my thirst for knowledge on this subject. Don't you realize that people may actually believe what you are writing. Look at what you have done to me. My questing mind cannot shake the possibly that my identical twin is out there. I dream about him. My nightmare is that I won't find him. Someone help me, please.

What am I going to do? As I approach my 55th birthday I keep probing for answers. Seek and you shall find. Knock and it shall be opened. Ask and it shall be given.

Sincerely,
Ken Ardizzone.

Immediately, questions arise from people. Ken, why are you so enthralled by this story? Well consider this. What is it that people are so concerned about day by day? Tell the truth folks.

Every human being on this planet is concerned about one thing and only one thing. It is me, myself, and I. That is all we think about. How do I look? What do people think about me. Am I loved by others. Do people care about me. Am I respected.

Now what would really happen if you saw your mirror image in the same room. How would you react? Would you be shocked and scared like Millicent Barnes? Would you be confused and puzzled like Paul Grinstead. Both Millicent and Paul did not get to meet their mirror image. They were deprived of receiving answers to this mystery. They are left hanging in Twilight Zone lore.

In my case all I want to do is meet my mirror image and learn about myself even more. Hey dude what is up. What's going on man. You look exactly like me. Are you the same height? Do you weigh the same? How much money to do earn? What is your profession? Married? Kids? Belong to any Yahoo groups? What have you learned in life? Any tips on how I can be a better person. Any experiences you have had that will enrich my life. Can we hang out for a couple of days and talk about life's journey. Want to go to a ball game together. How about a round of golf or bowling.

The Twilight Zone series has stirred my interest to no end. Ep.21 'Mirror Image' is compelling in many ways. There are no monsters, aliens, strange creatures, spaceships scaring or a threat to us. All you have is two people who are literally shaken out of their normal lives. They saw something they have never seen before in all the days of their existence. Who??? A splitting mirror image of themselves. WOW! All they wanted was some answers. Who are you? Where did you come from? Can we talk? How are you doing? Sadly, they never got their questions answered. Millicent landed in a police station and treated like a psycho. Paul is running around in circles in the dark night. The mystery remains.

What can be more frustrating than to go on in life with an unsolved mystery. Days turn into weeks, months, years, decades. Thanks-Rod. Because of you Millicent, Paul, and myself cannot get a restful sleep at night.

Side note: Automatic induction of Vera Miles into my Twilight Zone hall of fame. Even on a cold, dark, rainy night, who would not love to sit by her in a lonely bus depot in the middle of nowhere.

By the way my rating for `Mirror Image' 5 - Classic.

Review by Linn

Mirror Image is, without a doubt, a perfect Twilight Zone episode. It is very ominous and creepy.

The first things you see and hear when the story begins are long, crackling lightning bolts and rumbling sounds of thunder. How appropriate to start a story like this. Millicent Barnes, played excellently by the wonderful and beautiful actress Vera Miles, is waiting at a bus depot for her transportation to a new job in New York. The bus is delayed due to the weather so she walks up to the curmudgeonly old man at the ticket counter and asks how much longer he thinks the bus will be delayed. He tells her that this is the third time she's asked and all of her asking won't bring the bus in any sooner. She is stunned as she tells him that this was the first time she's asked. She then notices a luggage bag that looks exactly like hers on the floor behind his counter. She looks back to where she was sitting and sees her own bag sitting next to the bench.

She blows it off and sits down again. Then, her curiosity gets the best of her and she had to ask the counter man about the bag. He tells her that she checked in her bag when she arrived. She says she didn't but when she looks back to where she was sitting, her bag is gone. She walks into the bathroom and the attendant tells her she doesn't look well and was just in there a few minutes ago. She adamantly tells the attendant she was not in there before. She opens the door and sees her own self sitting on the bench. She panics and slams the door shut. When she opens it again, her mirror image is gone.

She believes she may be losing her mind. Her bag keeps disappearing and reappearing. She asks an old couple if they noticed anyone sitting in her place and they said they didn't.

Suddenly, a very young and handsome man arrives at the station. His name is Paul Grinstead played by Martin Milner. This was also an excellent casting choice. After speaking with Millicent about her present experiences, and also after trying to comfort her for as long as possible, he realizes that she needs help or so he thinks. He pretends to call a friend who can give them a ride, but in fact, he has called the police to come and take a screaming Millicent Barnes out of the depot after she gets hysterical when the bus arrives, sees her own self looking out of a bus window at her and runs back inside.

Then Paul experiences exactly what Millicent experienced. He chases himself down the street when his own bag disappears. His mirror image turns to him, grins and takes off. If there was ever a journey into The Twilight Zone, this was it. I think Paul should have gone to the police station and gotten Millicent out of there since he most likely came to the realization that she wasn't imagining anything. This was real......or was it?

On a personal note, this experience happened to me when I was back in my late teen years. My mother worked as a ticket cashier at a movie theater. She told me that a young man walked up to her booth and asked for a ticket to seethe movie. She looked at him and asked "What are you doing here?" She said he looked at her and said "I'm here to see the movie." She said "Well, I didn't expect to see you here." He asked her what the heck she was talking about. She told him to stop being silly. Silly? No. He was just confused because he asked if she knew him and she still continued to say stop being silly.

The guy was an absolute identical twin of my brother, Charles. When he finally made her realize that he was not her son and showed her his ID, she was shocked. She showed him a photo of my brother which shocked him as well. He eventually came to visit her at work once every couple of weeks to say hello, and one day she asked me to show up at her job on a day when he usually stopped by. She wanted me to see him. I damned near fainted. He looked exactly like my brother. If I had seen him on the street before she did, I also would have run up to him and said "Hey, Charles!" I had to share this experience because I've heard many times in the past that everyone of us has a twin somewhere. That was quite an experience. I don't know where that guy is today because he eventually stopped showing up, but all I can say is WOW because you hear about everyone supposedly having a double, but it's weird when you actually experience it first-hand.

I gave this episode a Classic 5 rating.

Review by Bobbynear

Actually, "Much Ado About Nothing" might have been a better title for this story. Because not much of a threatening nature really happens to anyone.

A rather nervous woman, with a theory about "parallel planes" already stuck in her head, sits alone in a bus station in the middle of the night. Along the way, she spots a woman sitting in a seat waiting who just happens to look like her. So?

How about being a little curious and actually trying to find out who she is, instead of immediately panicking and going off the deep end? If it were me, I might wonder... a relative of mine? Do I have a twin I didn't know about? Some sort of joke... what??

Although there were a lot fewer people in the world than there are now (70billion), I think it is the height of arrogance to believe you are one of a kind. There surely must be somebody out there somewhere who looks like you. Granted it's far fetched that this duplicate would be in a lonely bus station the same time you are, but nothing is impossible.

This poor woman, Millicent, actually is having a much harder time with the other people in the bus depot than with her body double. From the cantankerous old goat ticket seller who gets agitated at every inquiry, to a cleaning lady who is immediately suspicious simply because a woman visits the ladies room for the second time. I think I would rather hang around my double. Of course, Millicent does meet a man who looks like he wants to help, but somehow the look on his face seems to indicate he thinks she may be off her rocker as well.

I do have to give credit to Serling for creating a creepy disturbing atmosphere in spite of nothing much happening. The background music goes a long way here in helping to do that. The two duplicates in this story remind me very much of that odd looking man in "The Hitch-Hiker" He didn't do much either except stand there. Maybe Millicent learned the lesson.

While neither Millicent's nor Paul's double do anything threatening, in fact his is actually smiling when he runs away at the end, there is one truly disturbing moment in this story that has not a thing to do with either of them.

Suddenly out of nowhere, a police patrol car pulls up to the front door of the depot, two cops jump out and hustle poor Millicent into the car and speed off into the night, without so much as asking for her id or asking a question or saying a word. When did this begin? I sure do hope that Paul, when he becomes a cop later on himself in Adam 12, remembers to follow the law better than this.

Ken wonders in his review if perhaps there really is a duplicate in the world for each of us. I sure hope so. That way I can blame all the stupid decisions and wrong headed things I did throughout my life that got me in trouble... on him.

As for this episode, my own duplicate who is with me all of the time, wanted me to give this story a 4, because it just doesn't quite live up to Twilight Zone standards.

I told him to get lost... I'm in charge... for now.
My rating on a scale of 0 to 5   5 CLASSIC

Review by Kitty

This next episode is called Mirror Image and that's exactly what you get. We start out seeing a bus station with a very pretty woman sitting in there calmly waiting for a bus. Her name is Millicent Barnes and she's played very well by Vera Miles.

She has her suitcase sitting next to her and she gets up to ask the man behind the counter when the next bus to Cortland is due. He tells her that it's late. It was late thirty minutes ago when she asked and it was late fifteen minutes ago when she asked and it's going to remain that way due to the weather no matter how many times she asks the question.

She's very puzzled because she tells the man this is the first time she's asked him the question and he insists it's her third time. She then notices a suitcase behind the counter and she turns and sees that it looks just like hers that's sitting right by the bench where she was sitting.

She goes to sit down but then gets back up and asks the man about the suitcase behind the counter because it looks like hers and when she turns to look at hers by the bench, she's amazed to see that it's gone. The man very angrily tells her that she checked her bag a few minutes ago and that she needs to go sit down and stop bothering him.

She sits down but then goes in to the ladies room and the attendant looks amazed to see her. Millicent splashes cold water on her face and the attendant asks her if she's all right. She tells her that she's fine and wants to know why she asked. The woman replies because she was just in the ladies room a few minutes ago.

Millicent tells her that isn't possible because she hasn't been in there before. She opens up the door to the lobby and to her horror she sees herself sitting on the bench. She closes the door quickly. The attendant tries to give her a cold cloth for her face and Millicent pushes her away and walks back in to the lobby.

Her other self is gone but her bag is now sitting by the bench where she left it. A man walks in played by a very young Martin Milner and he's soaking wet. He sits next to Millicent and tells her he was supposed to fly to Buffalo but the flight got cancelled due to the weather and so he took a cab there but it broke down outside of town and so he had to walk to the bus station.

His name is Paul Grinstead and he's going to a new job. Millicent tells him she's on her way to a new job as well in Syracuse. He notices that she's upset. She relays all of the strange events that have taken place to him and he tells her that she must have had a delusion. She tells him that she's never had this kind of problem before.

The bus then pulls in and they proceed to go to the bus. As Millicent is about to board the bus, she looks up and gets very scared and runs back in to the bus station. Paul runs after her. The camera pans up to the bus and Millicent's other self is already sitting on the bus. She has a very coy smile on her face.

Millicent is lying on the bench half delirious and Paul tells the bus driver that they'll take the next bus. The ticket agent tells him it won't be until seven o'clock in the morning and he tells him it's fine.

The ladies room attendant tells him that this woman needs a doctor for her head. She leaves and only Paul, Millicent and the ticket agent remain. He goes back to work and Millicent sits up and tells Paul that she read about this somewhere. She said she had read about other planes of existence and that everybody had a twin and that some times they come through and they have to eliminate them. She then goes in to almost a catatonic state.

Paul is convinced that Millicent needs help. He tells her he's going to call a friend who lives nearby and maybe he can give them a ride to where they need to go. He walks up to the agent and he tells him he doesn't have a friend. He thinks Millicent needs help so he calls the police.

He takes Millicent outside to get some fresh air and then the police arrive. They take a screaming Millicent off in the police car. Paul puts his case down on the floor and is going to lay down on the bench and get sleep when he sees that it's gone and the door just flew open.

He starts to chase the elusive person but to his surprise the person turns around and smiles at him and Paul realizes that the face of the person is himself. He stops in stunned silence.

The first time I saw this one a couple of years ago I really liked it a lot and I very much enjoyed it this time as well. Serling definitely wrote a story that delivered. From the start of it to the end you are left wondering just what is going on.

In the beginning, you don't know if Millicent is crazy or is it everybody else. My only question in this is why didn't the bus driver say something odd to Millicent as well since her exact double was already on the bus......

Otherwise I think it was well done. Vera Miles was great as the confused person but knew much more than everybody else did. The ticket agent played by Joe Hamilton was excellent as the old guy who was just trying to do his job and didn't like annoying customers. Martin Milner was fabulous as your typical nice guy, the knight in shining armor that comes in and wants to save a damsel in distress but then turns out to be no such kind of guy because he writes Millicent off as being mentally ill but his reaction at the end was terrific when he sees himself running away from him.

The question remained, what did these exact doubles want? Was their plane of existence collapsing and were they here to invade our plane and replace everybody or was it just Millicent and Paul?

That's one of the many questions in the Twilight Zone. I will give this a five rating because it is one of those episodes that does stay with you......

"The Twilight Zone" Episode 22 "The Monsters Are Due On Maple Street"

Original Air Date- March 4, 1960
Guest Star- Claude Akins
Written by Rod Serling
Directed by Ronal Winston

Review by Linn

Oh my, what a lovely, peaceful Saturday afternoon on Maple Street. Sunshine, children playing, people doing their yard work and everyone going about their business as usual. Until...a flash of light and a loud, roaring sound in the sky changes everything about their peaceful existence.

A meteor? Perhaps. It's anyone's guess. The only thing everyone on Maple Street knows for sure is that their lives are at a standstill. There is no electricity, no phone lines, no running cars, no anything. The only things still operating are the people themselves.

Claude Akins is wonderful in the role of Steve Brand, the voice of reason and a neighbor whom all of the other neighbors seem to like and respect. When he can't start his car, he decides to walk into the next town with his paranoid neighbor, Charlie, played very well by actor Jack Weston. A little boy named Tommy warns them not to go because he believes that what flew overhead was not a meteor, but rather some sort of alien spaceship.

In the meantime, another neighbor named Pete Van Horn says he's going over to the next neighborhood to find out if the power is out on that street as well. The crazy thing is that everyone is starting to become frightened by the kid's story of what he's read in comic books about this sort of thing and how these aliens send a family of people to earth who look exactly like everyone else, but are really aliens. Everyone's face becomes stricken with looks of both worry and skepticism. I mean, who's going to believe some kid and his comic book stories? Hmmm. Yes, just who?

The most reclusive neighbor on Maple Street can't start his car either. Buy wait. He gets out of his car and the car starts on its own…twice. Well, there you go. He's the one, isn't he? He and his family must be the aliens so the other neighbors start throwing their verbal stones at him. He suffers from insomnia and stargazes so that's the proverbial straw that breaks the camel's back according to one woman. The man becomes defensive and tells them they have no idea what they are starting. Still, they keep a vigilant watch on his house and family into the evening hours.

Suddenly out of desperation, they all start finding every little idiosyncrasy they can find in each other that seems out of the ordinary in an attempt to find out who the aliens really are. Absolutely amazing. No one is above suspicion.

Uh oh, wait. Not to worry. Here comes the monster walking down the street toward them in the darkness. SHOOT HIM! SHOOT HIM! Yes, that's just what Charlie does. Except….it was not the monster. It was their neighbor Pete Van Horn. Charlie shoots him dead. He doesn't recognize him in the darkness. The lights and power start to come back on and Charlie's house is first so he's the first one suspected of being the monster. He, in turn, tries to accuse young Tommy of being the alien because he knew too much. As each house regained power, another person was accused and so on and so forth until they were chasing each other allover the place and hurling rocks at one another.

Yes, aliens WERE responsible for this mess. They were on a mission to see how earthlings would react to each other under duress and suspicion.

As Rod Serling said in his closing narration "Prejudice can kill and suspicion can destroy". So true.

My only question throughout this show is why it took Pete Van Horn all night to go over to the next neighborhood to find out if their power was also out.

Nonetheless, this is one of the classic Twilight Zone episodes and gets a 5 rating from me.

Review by Bobbynear

The year is 1959. Beaver has been living on his street in the serene town of Mayfield for two years. Opie will move into Mayberry the following year in 1960.They are the towns we wished we lived in. All is right on tv and not a discouraging word can be heard. And then along comes Rod Serling to remind everyone that it won't take much to turn even these bucolic places into a living hell.

There isn't much I can add to what has already been said. I agree with all of it. However a few things do stand out for me.

I grew up in the 50's, a time when you could actually let your child roam the neighborhood without much fear that he would be molested along the way. And that's exactly what I did... I lived in a big tough city, not a small town. But nevertheless, I went everywhere to neighbor's houses where I was always welcomed and even fed from time to time.

At the end of the day, my mother went out on the porch and called me home for dinner and I always returned unscathed. My only prohibition was to stay on our side of the street... not cross over since there was no traffic signal. So I mostly only knew the people on our side.

In a true story similar to the one Ken relates in his review, less than a year after this episode aired, we had a huge blizzard. It snowed for more than a day and then suddenly we heard a loud pop and crack outside and all the power went off. Bad enough as it was....we looked out the front window and although we were all in the dark... all of the houses on the other side of the street had full power.

Luckily there was so much snow piled up in front of our door and everywhere, we couldn't get out to go across and investigate the chosen people who still had power, much less riot in the street about it. It was only after it was all over that we found out the street was divided in two on two different power lines. Who knew such a thing? It took 4 days for the power to be restored. The people across the street offered us nothing.

I had seen this episode not long before this storm and I never would have imagined long time neighbors turning on each other, but this story came immediately to my 12 year old mind and I began to wonder, so this episode had a profound impact on me. I would continue to roam about but now with this in the back of my mind, I wondered just how little it might take for people to turn on each other and if I might be caught in the middle of it.

Just about everything in this classic episode is brilliant From the dazzling array of familiar character actors who give it their all, to the lighting and camera angles that add so much to this story. It also is amazingly claustrophobic given that it takes place outdoors. As it goes on, the street seems to be getting smaller and smaller pushing people increasingly into each other's faces. By the end of the story when the aliens are revealed as watching from far above, the view below looks like a fishbowl with people scurrying around like scared animals.

I also like the way this story dares to be different from most other conquering alien stories in both feature films and tv. Just about always, the aliens arrived with massive sophisticated weapons before which we are no match. Take a look at War Of The Worlds, impressive indeed with aliens able to zap everything in their way with laser beams. This story is more like Invasion Of The Body Snatchers suggesting that an invasion may be so much through the backdoor, we won't even notice it.

This episode also practically predicts the future. Coming as it does at the very end of the fifties, less than ten years later, there actually would be rioting in city streets, whether due to racial discrimination or protests against the Vietnam War. Luckily for us, if aliens had been watching back then, it must have scared them so much, they decided not to get involved.

The Twilight Zone doesn't get much better than this. In fact, there is almost enough here for a full length feature film. As relevant today as it was 50 years ago, the words of the aliens as they return to their ship promising to go one to the other until we have destroyed ourselves is as chilling today as it was then.

A remarkable piece of writing and filmmaking, there really aren't high enough numbers to describe this one. But for our purposes here, a rating of 5 couldn't be more obvious.

Review by Kitty

This latest episode is called The Monsters are Due on Maple Street. We start out by seeing a very serene summer day on Maple Street in Any Town USA and all appears normal.

We then see that there is a bright light that people see going overhead and people are puzzled as to what it is. Initially it is simply dismissed as a meteor. It doesn't take people long to realize that they've lost their power. Not only have they lost their electricity, they have also lost their phone service and their portable radios do not seem to working either.

A neighbor, Pete Van Horn says he will walk over to the next block to see if they've still got power of any kind and he leaves.

Everybody is a little shaken up and our two main characters Steve and Charlie played very well by Claude Akins and Jack Weston are thinking someone should go in to town to find out what's happening. Steve tries to get in his car to start it but it won't start. He's asked if there is gas in the car and he says yes.

Steve and Charlie agree to walk in to town. Just then, a fourteen year old boy named Tommy comes forward and tells them that they shouldn't go in to town. Steve asks why. Tommy explains that he doesn't think they want him to. Steve asks who are they? Tommy tells him that it's the aliens who landed from outer space. The ones who landed first are probably among them pretending to be them. He tells him this is how all of the science fiction stories start.

Steve is quite skeptical but Charlie is getting very anxious about this. Just then a neighbor, Goodman, tries to start his car and it won't start.... He's quite puzzled by it. When he gets out of his car, it inexplicably starts. Everybody starts to wonder about Goodman. He was the one neighbor who didn't come out of the house when the meteor or whatever it was went overhead.

He tells them that they're crazy. One woman tells everybody that she some times sees him outside at night looking at the sky. He rolls his eyes and tells them that he suffers from insomnia and he likes to go outside.

Later in the evening, everybody is watching Goodman's house. Steve asks Charlie how long he's going to stay out there watching. Charlie says as long as it takes. Steve asks who appointed Charlie judge, jury and executioner.

Goodman then asks Steve about his radio that he keeps in his basement and is wondering who he's talking to. Steve's wife comes forward and tells them that it's just a Hamm radio. They can all go look at it if they like. Steve refuses as he shouldn't have to defend himself to his neighbors....

Just then they hear someone walking towards them. Charlie panics and goes to his house to get his gun. He brings it out and Steve takes it away from him and accuses him of going crazy. The walking gets closer and Charlie grabs the gun and shoots because he's convinced it's a monster.

They all run to the body only to discover that it's Pete Van Horn who had left earlier to see if they were having the same problem on the next street over. Unfortunately, Pete Van Horn is dead.

Charlie feels terrible as he thought he was shooting a monster. Charlie is then accused of being the monster. They all theorize that maybe Charlie knew that Pete knew something and was coming back to tell them. Charlie balks at this but then his lights in his house go on and people start throwing rocks at him.

Charlie screams that he's not the monster but he knows who is. He tells them that it's Tommy. He's the one who started all of this with telling the story about the aliens from outer space. People start to turn toward Tommy but then everybody's lights start to blink on and off and basically all hell breaks loose. People grab guns, rocks and whatever they can find and start to kill each other.

The camera then zooms out to the hill above and we see two aliens and one is explaining to the other one that this is how it basically works. The one in training asks if it always ends this way. The other tells him yes but just with variations but the end is always the same. They will go to all of the streets on this earth and they will get them to destroy each other one by one.

This is by far one of Serling's most brilliant scripts that he ever wrote.... Yes there are aliens in it but the main star of this episode is fear. I have always remembered that one of Franklin Roosevelt's most famous speeches is the one that says, "The only thing we have to fear is fear itself." This is a prime example of it.

I'm not sure if this is what FDR had in mind when he said those words but it fits here never the less.

You have a group of neighbors who have known each other for years. You have what appears to be a simple power outage and phone outage, add on a teenager with an overactive imagination and people go nuts.

Unfortunately, as Serling says at the end of the show that fear and prejudice do not exist only in the Twilight Zone. These are things that can happen anywhere at any time and you don't need aliens to be the instigators. How many of us remember what it was like in New Orleans after Katrina hit, there was anarchy in the streets to put it mildly.

How about on a bigger scale, in Nazi Germany where Jews were rounded up and how was that so successfully done initially? It was fear propaganda by the Nazis to show what a threat they were to everybody else.

This episode illustrates how it really doesn't take that much to throw people into a mob mentality, even with people they've known for years. We can all say that we'd never go off the deep end like that with our neighbors but push the right buttons on some people and I'm not so sure. There were plenty of scares back then. The Red Scare as it was put back then in 1960 was very real just as there are very real threats in today's world as well.

This is by far one of the best stories Serling did. Claude Akins and Jack Weston deliver on the emotions perfectly. This is definitely a classic and I easily give it a five rating.

Review by Ken

What is great about this series is that you never can expect what tale you will get week by week. A whole range of stories will keep you guessing what The Twilight Zone will offer. At times I am frustrated with shallow writing. Case in point "Denton, Millimeter, Purple Testament," etc... Sometimes I am blown away as in the case of "Time Enough at Last," "The Hitch-Hiker," or my personal favorite "Mirror Image." By the way I have increased my search for my double. I am taking a cruise down to Cabo San Lucas, and Matalzan. Maybe, just maybe I will run into him.

Anyway ep.22 'The Monsters are Due on Maple Street' falls into the category of downright creepy. I love the title and the opening scene is typical T.Z. mood and feeling. On Maple Street the power goes out and the town folk start to panic. Along comes Tommy to warn everybody about aliens from outer space. Yikes! Can it really be true that we are being invaded. The cast of characters used here reminded me of my own neighborhood. I live on a street where we all know our neighbors and often say hi to each other...

Eventually, suspicion grows and people start pointing fingers at each other. One person gets shot and the town is in an uproar. A mob starts to form and the town is in a frenzy. I can't imagine what my street would look like if this happened.

The build up of this story is excellent. What is going to happen? Is Tommy's crazy comic book fable true? Great acting by Claude Akins, Ben Erway, and Jack Weston. Maple street scenes, musical score, and the dark forbidding sky add to the drama.

The end scene shocked me. I had no idea aliens were up on the hillside watching all the developments. Their conservation is classic for the ages. Hmmm.... 'Turnoff the power and throw people into turmoil. They will turn on each other and destroy themselves.' God help us all if this is really true. I hope my street does not act this way.

True story. One night during a rainstorm the power went off on my street. It was8:00 p.m. and all the neighbors went outside after the down pour. We talked about having no power and we did not know what to do. We can't watch t.v. or turn on the computer to surf the internet. Our cell phones were off because the towers were damaged. We looked at each other with candles and flashlights and felt helpless. Thankfully, we did not throw stones at each other. Instead we went to sleep in the darkness. Nothing else to do. Power came on in the morning. No aliens up on the hill watching.

What a powerful message and revealing story for this series. When the T.Z marathons come on I tune in to this one every time. Surely it will be in my top ten favorites.

My rating-5 Classic.

"The Twilight Zone" Episode 23 "A World of Difference"

Original Air Date- March 11, 1960
Guest Star- Howard Duff
Written by Richard Matheson
Directed by Ted Post

Review by Kitty

This next episode is called A World of Difference. This is also one episode that I had not seen before. We start out seeing an average business man named Arthur Curtis walking in to his office. He greets his secretary and tells her that his daughter is getting excited about her birthday on Saturday but that he would like her to call the airline and move his and his wife's flight to San Francisco to Saturday night. She agrees to do that.

Arthur walks in to his office. He picks up his phone and can't get a dial tone. He starts to walk out to the outer office to see his secretary Sally and he all of a sudden hears the word Cut! He looks and realizes he's on a movie set. The director by the name of Marty walks up to him and asks him what the problem is. He also address him as Jerry.

Arthur doesn't know what he's talking about. He walks out to where Sally is and she's sitting with her feet up on the desk reading a magazine and she asks Mr. Raigan what the problem is. He goes to make a phone call and he can't get a phone number for his home. The director is telling someone to call his agent Brinkley.

He runs outside and almost gets hit by a car. The woman inside the car, Nora asks "Jerry" if he's been drinking again. She wants her alimony money and she wants it now. Arthur tells her he doesn't know what she's talking about. His name is Arthur Curtis and he needs to get home. She thinks he's crazy.

They drive and Arthur can't find his street Ventner Avenue. He gets out of the car and he thinks he sees his little girl but when he grabs her, it's not his Tina and the little girl starts to scream and run. Nora tells Arthur to get in the car unless he wants to be arrested for assault.

He gets in the car and Nora drives him home. Arthur insists that it isn't his house and Nora tells him it is. They walk in and Jerry's agent Brinkley is in the house. He tells Jerry that he has got to get back to the movie set. If he doesn't finish this picture they're agency is going to drop him. He tells him that he'll call the studio and tell them that he's sick but he's got to go back. Jerry insists that his name is Arthur Curtis.

Nora, meanwhile is searching for a checkbook and demands that Jerry sign the check for her alimony. Jerry/Arthur refuses to sign the name of Gerald Raigan because that is not his name. He tries to call the operator to get a listing for his place of business and he's told that there is no business by that name. He loses it mentally.

The next thing we see is that Arthur is waking up and Brinkley shows him the script and reads the characters. The first character being, Arthur Curtis. Jerry/Arthur doesn't want to hear it because he knows he really is Arthur Curtis. Brinkley tells him that there is no Arthur Curtis because they've cancelled the movie. Brinkley tells him that Arthur Curtis is dead. He throws the script in the trash.

Arthur tells him he needs to get back to his office. Brinkley tells him the prop people are probably tearing the set down right now. Arthur runs out of the house and drives away. We see a frantic driving sequence here to the studio and when Arthur comes running in, he sees things being taken away from his office.

He tells them not to take them but the prop people tell him they are just following orders. Arthur goes back in to what's left of his office and all of a sudden his wife Marian comes in wanting to know where he's been all day. He's relieved to see her.

They walk out to see Sally and she gives him the new tickets and Arthur tells Marian that they should start their vacation right away. He hears the prop people in the background and he insists that they have to leave right now and they do.

Brinkley is back on the set wondering where Jerry is and nobody can find him but nobody saw him leave. He then takes one last look at the script that says The Private World of Arthur Curtis.

We then see a plane taking off for San Francisco.

Overall I liked this episode and since I had never seen it before, I really wasn't sure how it was going to end. As Serling said at the end that some people leave this world in a pine box but others slip through the door to the Twilight Zone.

I liked all of the actors in this. Howard Duff played it just right as a guy who goes to work and all of sudden finds out he's the star of a movie.

I thought the story was creative and while I was expecting to see someone die or be in a coma at the end, I was glad to see that it had a bit of a different ending. Arthur wasn't having a delusion he was just caught up in two worlds and he made his choice in the end. Not a bad choice I would say.

I'm going to give this a three rating for good.

Review by Linn

Oh hell. We go from a classic like "The Monsters are Due on Maple Street" to this piece of crap. Can someone tell me what A World of Difference is all about? Yes, I know. A working man living a normal life who suddenly gets pulled out of it and into a movie set. Why and how? I don't get it. This has to be in my top twenty worst Twilight Zone episodes.

I like Howard Duff, but his talent was wasted in this one. Rod Serling is known for using the same actors over and over again in his episodes, and this was no exception. He used David White as the main character's agent. In fact, Rod has used most of the main characters from the TV sitcom "Bewitched" at one point or another. He used Elizabeth Montgomery, Dick York, Agnes Moorehead and David White, some of them more than once.

Howard Duff plays a man named Arthur Curtis who suddenly becomes a man named Jerry Raigan simply playing a guy named Arthur Curtis in a movie. He's bewildered and can't understand where his previous life has gone. I can't figure out where it went either. I don't get the point of this episode at all, but maybe I'm missing something. This was one of the most boring and senseless Zones ever. Yes, he does get his original life back in the end, but what was all the other crazy stuff about? Even when he goes up to hug his "supposed" daughter during his crazy movie life, she doesn't even know him.

I could find nothing to like about this episode. Even the woman who played his horrendous movie wife in this one was not only a bitch, but over acted beyond belief. Glad he didn't sign over that check to her. Totally bad episode and I will be generous only because I like Howard Duff and give it a 1 - Poor rating. I won't give it a Lousy rating because Duff didn't write the script.

Review by Ken

Memo to producers. Change the title of ep.23 to 'A World of Nonsense. 'The entire cast of writers, producers, stage men, and directors have been working hard lately on this series. As a result nobody had a clue on how to produce the next show so they slopped a script together in 6 minutes and wanted to go home for the weekend. What a shame that the show could put together such nonsense.

A man says he is not an actor on the stage set. He spends all his time trying to figure out what is wrong. He is delusional and runs around in circles. Pretty girl wants his money. His agent wants him to act. Finally the man figures out what to do. Get in a car and drive fast. Return to old set to learn your wife is there. He is happy now. But a problem. He is on another stage set.

Howard Duff acting was awful. David White was a drag. I could not wait for the end credits. I vow never to watch this dreadful story again.

My rating- 0 Lousy.

Review by Bobbynear

Like Mirror Image, another story that suggests that life might not be what we think it is. Perhaps it is nothing more than a game or a story and we are just here for the amusement and entertainment of someone else.

The difference is that Mirror Image had a substantial creepiness factor about it and this has nothing but a bewilderment factor about it. The main character has no idea what is going on and by the end he still doesn't and neither do we.

Had it been fleshed out we might have found out something compelling like whether or not this man is so miserable in his real life, that in his mind he's created a fictional one that he prefers to live in. Instead they take the easy way out by just throwing it onscreen and wishing us luck in figuring it all out. No thanks.

As usual, there just isn't enough time in twenty five minutes to tell a story like this. In order to get anything out of it we would need to know his real background if there is one and who he really is. Instead we get one incident that tells us nothing.

The end result is a big fat zero...

My rating on a scale of 0 to 5.

0 - Lousy

"The Twilight Zone" Episode 24 "Long Live Walter Jameson"

Original Air Date- March 18, 1960
Guest Star- Kevin McCarthy
Written by Charles Beaumont
Directed by Anton M. Leader

Review by Kitty

This latest episode is called Long Live Walter Jameson. It's another episode that I have never seen before so any time that happens I consider it a treat.

This episode stars one actor that I always enjoy seeing, Kevin McCarthy. McCarthy plays Walter Jameson, currently a history professor at a university who's known for his highly interesting lectures on subjects of history. He is currently giving a lecture on the burning of Atlanta by General Sherman.

He tells the students in his class that the men under Sherman didn't want to burn Atlanta and in fact did not like Sherman very much. They felt it wasn't necessary to burn Atlanta because they had secured victory but Sherman told them to burn the city so they had no choice. He reads a passage out of Hugh Skelton's diary to the class about what he thought of General Sherman.

The diary is handwritten. At the end of class, an older professor approaches him. His name is Sam Kittridge. He has sat in the class to hear for himself why people praise Walter Jameson's lectures so much and he was not disappointed. He asks Walter if he can borrow the diary to look at and Walter tells him no.

Sam asks him to come over to dinner and Walter asks if it's him or Susanna asking. He tells him that it's him. He'd like to talk to him about something.

Walter leaves his house that night and walks across the street to Sam's house and as he walks away, we see a very old woman emerge from behind a tree in front of Walter's house.

He arrives for dinner and Sam has cooked. He's asking when he'll get a chance to try Susanna's cooking. Susanna comes down and gives him a big kiss. She tells him that she'll have plenty of time to cook for him after she gets her PHD and they get married. Walter jokes why she needs a PHD when she's going to be a housewife.

Sam takes offense and tells Walter that he can marry his daughter be he can't take away her brain. They eat dinner and Sam orders his daughter to go upstairs and study for her PHD. She reluctantly agrees as she knows she needs to do it.

She walks up the stairs and Walter reminds Sam that his daughter is thirty years old. Sam tells Walter he wanted to speak with him privately. Sam shows Walter his hands and compares them to Walter's.

He tells Walter that he's now seventy years old. He tells him that twelve years ago when Walter arrived at the university he was fifty eight and had all of his teeth and all of his hair that was just graying. Now he's an old man.

He comments that Walter looks the same. Walter says he just lucky. Sam asks Walter how old he is and Walter replies forty-four and Sam reminds him that he told them twelve years ago that he was thirty-nine. Walter admits that he's fifty-one. He wonders if Sam thinks he's too old for Susanna.

Sam tells Walter that he was curious about the soldier he mentioned earlier in the day named Hugh Skelton. He asks Walter if his grandfather served in the Civil War. Walter replies no. Sam then tells him he looked at a book of Civil War pictures by Matthew Brady and he found a picture of Hugh Skelton and it's a dead ringer for Walter.

Walter looks at the picture and tells him it's just a coincidence. Sam tells him that it's not a coincidence that Skelton is wearing the same ring and has the same mole on his face. He asks Walter just how old he really is and Walter looks at a bust of Plato and tells him that he's old enough to have known Plato.

Sam is shocked that he's been alive for over two thousand years. He wants to know the secret because he's afraid of dying. Walter tells him he shouldn't be afraid of dying and tells him that he's not sure what the secret is to his immortality. He wanted to live forever so he could learn and know more. He went to an apothecary and the apothecary demanded a lot of money but Walter paid it. He took the drugs and he ended up in a coma for weeks. When he woke up, the apothecary was gone and he thought he'd been had but then he slowly started to notice the people around him growing older and he wasn't.

Sam asks if he had a wife. He tells him yes, he had a wife and children and he watched them all grow old and die as well as all of his friends. He realized that knowing you're going to die is what makes life worth living. Sam asks if he has had other wives and he admits that he has.

Sam asks him if he ever got sick or hurt. Walter replies that he never got hurt in all of the two thousand years that he's been around. Sam tells him that he can not allow him to marry his daughter knowing that he won't grow old and she will.

Walter tells him that living like this is nightmare. Every night he takes a gun out of his desk and puts it to his head but he can't bring himself to pull the trigger. He tells Sam that he wanted to leave six months ago when he knew that Susanna was interested in him but Sam talked him out of it.

Sam asks him why he let it go on. Walter admits that he loves Susanna and wants to be happy with her. Sam tells him no, he can't marry his daughter and he'll tell her the truth. He tells Sam that she'll never believe him. Susanna comes downstairs and wants to know what's going on.

Walter tells her that her father doesn't want them to get married because he thinks that he's too old for her. She tells him that's ridiculous. Walter agrees and suggests that they get married tonight. He tells her to go upstairs and pack her things and they'll leave tonight. Susanna is thrilled with the idea. She runs out of the room. Walter walks out and back to his house across the street.

Inside the house, he takes the gun out of the desk drawer and tries to pull the trigger and once again can not. He puts the gun on the table and suddenly a voice in the shadows says Hello Tommy. Walter asks who's there. The old woman appears to him and asks him if he recognizes her.

He tells her no, she's got him confused with someone else. She tells him to look closely at her eyes. He once told her she had the most beautiful eyes he had ever seen. She turns on the light and tells him that she knows he's Tom Bowen who is her husband who left her years ago.

She saw his engagement picture in the newspaper and had to see for herself. Walter still denies it until she picks up the gun. She asks him is he's going to eventually leave this one the way he left her? He then calls her by name Laurette and begs her not to shoot him and she says he can not go around hurting people like this and it's got to stop.

The scene switches to Sam's house and he hears a gunshot. He runs outside and sees Laurette standing outside of Walter's house and Sam asks her what happened. She shrugs her shoulders and walks away.

Sam runs in to Walter's study to find him sitting behind the desk visibly shot. Sam wants to call for help but Walter tells him not to. Sam sees Walter's face get progressively older as he dies. Sam runs out and Susanna has come in to the house. She wants to see Walter and Sam tells her she should go home. Susanna won't hear of it and she goes in to the study where they both find Walter's clothes on the floor but all that remains is dust.

Susanna asks Sam where Walter went and Sam simply tells her that he left. She asks what's on the floor and he tells her that it looks like dust. They walkout.

I have to say one thing to start with, the old saying is true, Hell hath no fury like a woman scorned. It's not clear how long ago Walter left Laurette but it's obvious that time did not heal that wound for her. I'm not sure if this was supposed to be a commentary on men leaving wives who get older but this scenario clearly illustrates the idea of a man who sees his wife getting older and decides he wants a younger one.

Good for Laurette that she didn't sit back and take it. Walter was selfish and after he was discovered, he couldn't walk away like he knew he should have. He would have ultimately done the same thing to Susanna that he did to Laurette.

I really liked Kevin McCarthy in this role. He played the part very sincerely as did the other actors and it worked. I had a feeling early on that the old woman was a woman from his past who was going to ultimately do him in but I didn't mind.

I found Walter Jameson interesting and I even sympathized with him to a certain point. Nobody really wants to die after all but to outlive all of your friends and relatives only to acquire new ones and outlive them and have it go on and on forever. However, to leave them with no explanation is also very scoundrel like as well. I'm giving this episode a 4 rating.

Review by Ken

Okay folks I have had it with these male-dominated scripts we have been getting lately. What is going on here. Can't the writers start using females in the lead role. So far in season one we have three episodes devoted to a female in the lead role. Ep.4 'The Sixteen Millimeter Shrine'-a dud of a story. Ep.16 'The Hitch-Hiker'- a true classic. Ep.21 'Mirror Image'-another classic. So out of 24episodes we have reviewed, 21 of them are devoted to males in the lead role. C'mon producers.

For God's sake ep.24 tells another mundane story that got me lost in the forest. Let's see-Walter Jameson is a professor who give details in his lectures about past history. Could it be he is older than he looks. Another professor exposes Walter and he confesses he is 2000 years old. Yikes!!

Questions I would ask is what, where, who, why, and how. Did you see Christ walking on the earth? The Roman empire?

Walter reveals that immortality is a curse. But he wants to marry another pretty girl. She will age in time but Walter remains young. It seems he cannot die. But a huge problem. A former wife who is older is mad at Walter. Out of anger she kills him with a gun. Walter dies and turns to dust. Scene fades to closing narration.

Did I just finish watching a soap opera. Walter wants to get married again. Pretty girl falls for him and asks no questions. Former wife is mad and takes out Walter. End of story. Lesson learned. Be careful of former angry spouses. She just may blow your head off and you will turn to dust. Don't wear a nice suit because it will remain on the floor dirty. I am shaking my head in disbelief. This series is better than this. Sorry guys.

My rating-0 Lousy.

Review by Linn

Well, Hello Modern Day Professor Walter Jameson. Or should we say Hello Civil War Major Hugh Skelton or should we say Hello to Tom Bowen, the estranged husband of a withered old woman he abandoned many, many, many years ago and who is still alive?

In fact, Professor Walter Jameson has been numerous people because he is over2000 years old? How can that be? I suppose it's every simple if you pay an alchemist that many years ago in exchange for immortality. Unfortunately for Walter, Professor Samuel Kittridge, the father of a pretty young girl named Susannato whom Walter is engaged finally becomes overly suspicious of Walter's extensive knowledge of all things and events in the past. Professor Kittridge has worked with Walter Jameson for twelve years. He invites Walter to have dinner with him and his daughter one day after sitting in on one of Walter's history classes. This was a class in which Walter discussed the Civil War and a Major in that war named Hugh Skelton. He talks about the war, the soldiers and this particular Major with a preciseness and insight that could not merely be taken from history books. It was as if he had lived through it.

After dinner, Kittridge sends his daughter out of the parlor to have a talk with Walter and tells him that it is amazing how he has not aged one bit in all of those 12 years while he himself has aged into an old man. How is that possible? Kittridge also brings it to Walter's attention that the age he said he was when they first met does not match up to the age of 44 he says he is now. Walter finally says he's 51, but that's far from the real problem.

Kittridge decided ahead of time to look through a book he owned containing old Civil War photographs and finds one of Major Hugh Skelton taken over 100 years ago. Skelton and Jameson look identical right down to the mole on their chins, and they are both wearing the exact same ring which Kittridge says is a dead giveaway.

Walter finally admits that he is over 2000 years old and even points to a bust of the philosopher Plato and says he knew him personally. Kittridge is stunned by all of this. He tells Kittridge the whole story and how he watched his wives and kids aging and his friends dying while he stayed the same. He says there is no way to change things now and realizes he was wrong. He says he's tired of living but is too much of a coward to kill himself. Kittridge decides he cannot allow him to marry his daughter without her knowing the truth. Susanna agrees to marry him that night without knowing the truth. However, it was not to be.

A withered old women who was a wife had abandoned many years ago, Laurette Bowen, confronts him in his house and tells him she can't allow him to keep on marrying women and hurting them. She picks up Walter's own revolver and shoots him. Kittridge hears the shot and runs over to Walter's house to find him dying and deteriorating right before his eyes until there was nothing but a mass of clothing and dust on the floor. The dust was in the shape of a man's head and two hands. Susanna runs in and can't understand what has happened. It was actually surprising that she did not become more hysterical when she witnessed that sight and Walter was nowhere to be found. His father said he didn't know where Walter went. Then they just walked out.

While I felt that the camera and make-up work at the end of this episode during Walter's deterioration was pretty remarkable, the rest of the show was too far-fetched for me. I found it very hard to believe that it took two thousand years for someone to finally realize that this guy had been around more than a few blocks. Nobody ever recognized him from anywhere else in all of those years, decades and centuries? His former old wife finally did, but he was selfish enough to keep marrying young women who merely grew too old for him, and then he moved on to the next one. I didn't like him and the basic story was lame. I liked the "dust man" on the floor at the end, but that's about it. I know the Twilight Zone is supposed to be far-fetched many times, but this one was too off the wall for me.

My rating is a 1 for Poor and that's being generous for the good deterioration scene.

Review by Bobbynear

There surely is not much I can add here to what everyone else has said. I find myself almost liking this episode just a tiny tiny bit because I don't think I've ever seen a premise quite like this. There have been countless time travel stories since then, but not one where a man doesn't age physically and yet goes from century to century the normal way. At least without the benefit of a time machine.

I have to agree with Ken. A fantastic missed opportunity here to ask this man questions that nobody living will ever be able to answer. He did manage to keep it all a secret though. However, this was filmed back in the late fifties. Today he would be mighty tempted to come out of the closet or out of the vacuum cleaner if somebody sucks those ashes up by mistake... make a fortune by writing a book, appearing on just about every talk show on tv...and just basking in the fame that would come to him.

This story is about as far fetched as you can get. But it is not unwatchable, providing that you can control your laughter that is. I have to agree with Linn. The sight of a man's body still in his suit but turned to ashes is quite unusual. At last the old adage about 'ashes to ashes, dust to dust' is something we can actually see before it happens to us.

My rating......1 - POOR

"The Twilight Zone" Episode 25 "People Are Alike All Over"

Original Air Date- March 25, 1960
Guest Star- Roddy McDowall
Written by Rod Serling
Directed by Mitchell Leisen

Review by Bobbynear

A truly outstanding episode, one of the best of the entire series for a variety of reasons. Not the least of which is the excellent performance by Roddy McDowell who changes attitudes multiple times throughout this story... At first fretting out loud just what he and his astronaut friend, Marcusson just might find when they land on Mars and then later believing he had found paradise. Also let's not leave out the awesomely beautiful Susan Oliver who isn't required to do much here other than just looking gorgeous, and why not? Always do what you are best at.

It has often been speculated by me and my reviewers that it sometimes seems Rod Serling was trying to send a subliminal message to viewers on those stories that he wrote. Was he trying to rail against nuclear war in Time Enough? Was he putting out astern warning about gambling in "The Fever?"

As humans, we seem to have this endless ability to rationalize everything we do. No matter how questionable it might seem, we can always find an excuse to do it. After all, we created nuclear weapons, but we had to in order to end World War II. We routinely slaughter animals, and not always humanely, because after all, we have billions to feed around the world.

As I watched Sam Conrad at the very end of this story, gripping the bars that imprisoned him and bemoaning his fate as a lifetime exhibit for the amusement of Martians in what appears to be a zoo like setting, I was taken back to my childhood and some other disturbing images that bothered me even at a very young age.

I was born in and lived until adulthood in a large metropolitan city. Like most big cities, mine had an extensive zoo and my father often took me there. Like most kids, I enjoyed it very much.

But even at a very young age, I wondered, as I stood there staring at animals from outside the bars, just how they felt behind the bars. This came home to me while I watched the lions and tigers pacing back and forth endlessly right in front of those bars, as if in some sort of trance, completely oblivious to the outside world and probably living only for a chance to escape.

But it was not so much apparent there as it was in another part of the zoo. An exhibit known by most zoo patrons as The Monkey House. An indoor exhibit, where patrons entered one end and walked along a very long walkway holding onto a railing... while watching all species of monkeys play and frolic in cages... but not with bars... actually they were behind glass. I suppose to stop the possibility of one of them reaching through them and grabbing onto one of the many children who walked by.

Frankly it was my favorite place. However, even as a small child of about 6 or 7, even I noticed that the monkeys were not playing and frolicking around as expected. In fact, it was quite the opposite. Almost without exception, you would see them, even when there were several together, sitting off in a corner, looking down at the floor quite forlorn. Tapping on the glass to arouse them did no good. They seemed to be incredibly lethargic and almost in a trace. Even the food they had been given was sitting there uneaten.

At the end of the building was the big attraction, the massive gorillas. Even they were behind glass in cages, and if anything they looked even more miserable. Luckily for everyone, this story has a happy ending. Within a few years, the zoo had torn down the monkey house. In another part of the zoo, instead they built a huge outdoor area for all of the primates. It was surrounded by water and in the middle they had built a large igloo like building, only made out of rocks. Zoo visitors stood somewhat above the structure looking down at the animals, while still holding onto a railing, only this time, there was no glass between animals and humans.

The difference was startling. The very same monkeys that we so unhappy and so lethargic in their former home, were now the complete opposite... They played with and chased each other around and around this huge moat like setting and people were even allowed to toss them things like bananas and peanuts which they endlessly begged for.

That was back in the fifties. Today in more enlightened times, most big city professional zoos have animals in settings that approximate their natural surroundings in the jungle. That includes the city I live in now. A friend of mine recently showed me some home video of her trip to the local zoo and the images I saw of animals in a more natural environment were a world apart from what I saw as a child.

Rod Serling wrote this masterpiece as an adaptation from a short story written by a different author. As with the other former episodes I mentioned earlier in this review, it's hard to tell if there is a hidden message here. After all, as far as I know, Rod Serling was not an animal rights activist.

But then again, neither am I. After all, I am not a vegetarian and I've always enjoyed watching animals in a captive setting. However, being able to rationalize eating them and imprisoning them for our appetites and amusement does not change one basic fact. There is a right way and a wrong way to do things. It's interesting to note that in this story, the Martians are not the superior beings that we might expect, but instead disturbingly, a lot like us.

Back in 1959, the space race was just about to get started. Then, as now, there was always speculation about just what we might find should we ever be able to land on another planet. Even though reaching the moon was thrilling, I think that secretly a few of us were still disappointed that the only thing our astronauts came home with were rocks and not a living, breathing space alien. I always thought it was quite arrogant of us to just assume that another life form would be all that happy to be invaded without any warning. At the very least, they might be openly hostile.

This episode brilliantly turns that on its head as so many Twilight Zone stories do. My late mother used to tell me "You catch more flies with honey than you do with vinegar" as a warning to not be so openly hostile and aggressive yourself if you are trying to get along with others.

Obviously these Martians took that to heart. Plying Conrad with Scotch and cigarettes, those all too familiar staples to guarantee a happy life to Earthlings, as well as dangling a possible beautiful girlfriend in front of his face, they are quite easily able to hide their evil intentions.

With one of the best twist surprise endings of the entire series, "People Are Alike All Over" is endlessly fascinating to watch. I never tire of viewing it. Watching poor Sam Conrad gripping those bars at the end and hearing him tell his late partner, Marcusson, that he was indeed right, brought me right back to those days as a child, watching those monkeys doing pretty much the same thing. Only unlike those animals, there is no hope for a better future for Conrad, he's already in his natural environment.... for good.

One day far in the distant future, Man might just find life on another planet. With any luck...they WON'T be just like us.

While probably more deserving, at least in my mind, of a rating of 50....for our purposes here, on a scale of 0 to 5...my rating....

5 ---- CLASSIC

Review by Linn

The place – Mars. The scene – A colony of Martians going about their daily Martianary business. UNTIL.

They hear a crash. A thunderous crash rumbles the ground beneath them. They all look at each other wondering "What the...? We need to check on this. "They venture out and see a rocket ship in the distance. Again one of them says "What the...?"

Ok, let's start banging on the ship and see if whoever is in there will come out. Bang, Bang. Bang. Bang. Oh, they just won't come out. Keep trying. Bang. Bang. Bang. Oh geez, finally he opened his door. Now we can get somewhere. Who are these strange beings who invaded our planet? Aha! It's a man who thinks we are exactly like him. He didn't question our early Roman Empire fashion trend. He thinks we are just like him. He said he and his friend came here from planet Earth. Oh, this is great. Never thought we'd get a species from another planet to visit us. Ah, but this is bad. His friend Marcusson is dead.

Okay, we'll bury him properly, but this guy named Sam Conrad is still alive. Well, we have to tell him that he is speaking our language and not his own. He's not going to care when there is a gorgeous blonde haired woman standing right in front of him telling him this.

Yes, he wants to know a whole lot of stuff about us, but we'll keep quiet for right now and take him to his new home. He's going to be living here now, so he has to get accustomed to that. Teenya, the gorgeous blonde, is the one to assure him that we mean him no harm. He will believe her. We really don't mean him any harm. We want him to be comfortable here. We're smarter than Earthlings so we can make him believe anything. Nice house, huh? Yeah. Great house full of great Scotch and cigarettes. Uh oh. He can't get out of this beautiful house we've built for him. Well yeah. We sealed it up. Come on. Do you think we were just going to let him leave? Get real. Oh, get a grip, Conrad. At least you have some great Scotch to enjoy while entertaining the crowds in your new "habitat".

This was an outstanding episode. Roddy McDowall and Susan Oliver were phenomenal in their roles. Nobody wants to be caged, even animals, but we do it every day. This episode put the shoe, paw, hoof, etc. on the other foot. I loved this episode and figured I would tell it from the Martians' point of view.

I give it a Classic 5 rating.

Review by Kitty

This episode is called People Are Alike All Over. We start out seeing two astronauts staring at their rocket that will be taking them to Mars in just a few hours. The one astronaut Markusson is the pilot and is very excited to see a new place. The other is Conrad and he's scared to death.

He's a biologist but he's fearful of what the natives of Mars will be like if they actually find people. Markusson assures him that he believes that all people are alike because God must have had a blueprint for people so they must be similar.

We then see them blast off from Earth and they make a crash landing on Mars. Conrad wakes up dazed. The ship is a mess from the crash but Markusson is in bad shape. Conrad gives him a shot of something but he's not going to make it.

Conrad sits by the door and hears noises outside and Markusson wakes up. He wants to go outside. Conrad won't open the door. He's frightened. Markusson tells him that he wants to see what he's going to die for because he knows he's bleeding inside.

Before they can get the door open, Markusson dies. Just after he dies, the door starts to open. Conrad grabs a gun and looks out and to his surprise, he sees people that look just like himself. They are all wearing clothes that look to be about of the Julius Caesar era but they are people none the less.

He walks outside with a gun but it is soon taken away from him and thrown away. He is very excited to see that they are people just like him. He tries to explain where he is from.

One of the Martians looks inside the ship and tells them that the other man is dead. Conrad is astonished to see that they can speak his language.... A beautiful woman named Teenya tells him that actually he's speaking their language through mental telepathy.

Conrad is very excited. He wants to see their cities and meet their people. The one Martian tells him that they can do all of that in good time. Right now, he can rest in his ship and they'll prepare a place where he can stay while they repair his ship. They will take his friend and bury him and they can let him know what kind of marker to put on the grave.

They start to leave and Conrad asks Teenya if she'll be back tomorrow and she tells him yes. She assures him that nobody will harm him.

The next day they all come back to see him and they take him to a surprise. He is surprised when he walks in to a replica of a middle class suburban house. He is amazed and asks them how they did that. They said they built it in the night and they got the images from his mind.

They tell him to stay there for awhile and they'll be back. Conrad offers to show them to the door and as his back is to them, two of the Martians give each other the Martian version of hi-fiving. They walk out and as Teenya walks outs he looks very sad.

Conrad asks her if he'll see her later and when she gives no response, the one Martian tells him of course and they walk out.

Conrad is getting used to his new surroundings and loves the scotch and the cigarettes that they have provided him. He's in the kitchen when he realizes that there are no windows in the kitchen. He tries to open the door in the kitchen and it won't open.

None of the doors open and he starts screaming why they have locked him in. He then grabs the drapes and he tears them down and realizes there are no windows in the living room either.

All of a sudden the panels open and he sees bars outside and a whole lot of people looking at him, including Teenya and the other Martians who befriended him. He asks them why they're doing this to him. He then looks down and sees a sign. He grabs it and it says, Earth Creature in his natural habitat. He then realizes he's in a zoo.

Teenya is very upset at seeing this and she runs away. Conrad looks up and yells, You were right Markusson, people are alike everywhere Poor Conrad he's destined to spend the rest of his life in a Martian zoo.

This is one of my favorite episodes. Roddy McDowell is cast perfectly as Conrad who is scared and then far too trusting of these strangers. I have to admit, the first time I saw this episode, I was taken in by them just as Conrad was. The most human of them was Teenya. She at least saw that what her superiors were doing was just wrong After all, he was hardly a threat to anyone on Mars.

Teenya is also portrayed by the lovely Susan Oliver who once again turns in a stellar performance as she did in all her guest spots on TV back in the 50's and60's.

As for the content of the story, I thought it was very good. As for people being alike everywhere. I don't know, I suspect if a Martian landed on Earth, he'd more likely be taken to Area 51 to have a lobotomy done on him. Putting him in a zoo would be the least of his concerns.

Overall I enjoyed it. It has that nice little twist of an ending that I really wasn't expecting and I am going to rank this one a five for classic.

Review by Ken

Glad to be done with Walter Jameson who for 2000 years has been flirting with who knows how many women and married many of them along the way. But fate caught up to him and a former wife blew him away into dust.

Time to review the next episode in line and blasting off to space we go for the seventh time. I sit in my chair and say here we go again. What will the two space explorers find this time? They are going to the planet Mars. Will they find aliens, monsters, frozen people, or scary creatures.

Excellent casting of Roddy McDowall to play the part of frightened Conrad who does not know what to expect when the spacecraft lands on Mars. His partner Marcusson is injured and dies before they can explore the planet. Conrad is afraid because who is banging on the ship from the outside.

What and who could be outside the ship? Finally the moment has come and Conrad sees human beings who look like him but are wearing clothes from the Roman Empire days. But lo and behold he is comforted by gazing into the eyes of a gorgeous Teenya played by Susan Oliver.

The Martians assure Conrad they mean him no harm. They all bring him to a house and say take it easy and relax. Conrad is no longer afraid but Teenya has a look of sorrow. Just before Teenya leaves the house Conrad asks her if he will see her again. She pauses but must be on her way. Hey Conrad you blew it big time. If I were you I would insist that Teenya stay with you in the house. In fact Conrad should have insisted that he marry Teenya that very day. Invite everybody to an open house party.

But this is The Twilight Zone. Conrad realizes something is wrong with the house. No doors to escape from and no windows to look outside. Final scene reveals Conrad is locked in a cage with bars. People gather around to view this new 'Earth Creature.' Conrad sees Teenya but she turns away and leaves. What is worse for Conrad? Being incarcerated or seeing the love of his life run away?

Again this show delivered a classic. No space monsters or hairy creatures to worry about. Conrad has encountered a society who not only have a bad taste of clothes but are fearful of earth creatures. Lock them up for viewing. Study their habits. Hmmm... Would we earth creatures do the same thing if Martians landed on our planet?

I loved this story and have watched it again on many occasions. There is no way on earth I could have guessed the ending. No big bang scary, terrifying, fearful moment. Just a feeling of frustration, failure, gloom, sadness, and misery. Roddy McDowall nailed the part to perfection. Susan Oliver is always a joy to watch. Just the look on her face requires me to include her in my Twilight Zone hall of fame for women. She joins Inger Stevens, Beverly Garland, and Vera Miles. More women will be included later when we get to their stories.

My rating - 5 Classic.

"The Twilight Zone" Episode 26 "Execution"

Original Air Date- April 1, 1960
Guest Star- Albert Salmi
Written by Rod Serling
Directed by David Orrick McDearmon

Review by Linn

Execution was an interesting and intriguing episode. The year is 1860. The man is Joe Caswell. The place is the scene of a hanging in the Old West. His crime is murder. He shot a man in the back.

The murdered man's father, a reverend and the town judge attend the hanging. It wasn't much of a hanging, though. After a few words are exchanged among the men, including Caswell's declaration that he needs no prayers or soul-saving, they commence with the hanging. There's a noose around his neck supported by a tree branch. there's a horse beneath his rump and Caswell is showing no remorse. The horse is slapped, he bolts and Caswell is sent plunging downward to his neck-breaking death. Time out! Caswell just disappeared into thin air. The noose is left hanging there minus a neck.

The year is 1960. A man is lying on a couch. The man is Joe Caswell. The place is New York. He has been transported to the future by a professor of science named Manion via a time machine. Caswell is the first person to make the journey.

The professor quickly surmises that Caswell is not quite the great find that he expected. It took him little time to realize that this man was dangerous. The professor is a brilliant and seemingly gentle and caring man. The role is played by actor Russell Johnson who went on to play a much similar role, and the one he is best known for, in the TV sitcom classic Gilligan's Island.

Manion spoke these words into a tape recorded assessment of Caswell - "Heaven help whoever gets in his way." He should have taken heed to his own words. Once Caswell decided he wanted to look at this new world full of carriages without horses and other things he couldn't imagine, Manion foolishly tells him that he needs to send him back to his own time and place. Bad idea. Caswell murders Manion. Then Caswell takes in the new world of 20th century New York completely blind to what awaits him. He can't handle the lights, crowds, traffic, loud music, etc. He pushes into crowds, stops traffic and tears up a bar. He finally returns to Manion who, of course, is dead. Caswell is very distraught by what he's experienced.

Finally, a thug with a gun walks into the office and confronts Caswell. They tussle. The thug kills Caswell. The thug accidentally walks into the time machine which closes behind him. No way out except at the end of the noose that Caswell so abruptly abandoned.

Albert Salmi played the role of Caswell and he was perfect for that role.

Three complaints about this one - (1) the professor's stupidity by not somehow tricking Caswell back into the time machine instead of telling him he was going to return him to his death sentence. The professor should have known that Caswell would not go quietly or easily; (2) the bartender at the bar Caswell tore up could have been a little more scared and bit less cordial to a man who was obviously dangerous (you don't offer to put on the TV for him only to have him shoot it out); (3) the thug who killed Caswell was much too small and thin to have taken out someone so much larger and stronger. The thug had a gun but ended up strangling Caswell with a curtain rope - within 5 seconds nonetheless. I do believe it takes more than 5 seconds to strangle the life out of most people.

I liked this episode, though, despite its flaws. Pretty good story and acting.

I rate it as 3 - Good.

Review by Kitty

This latest episode is called Execution. We have yet another time travel episode and I have to admit I found this to be quite a little roller coaster to watch. This is another episode that I had never seen before so it was a treat to watch it.

We start by seeing a "Necktie Party" in 1880. It's a party for a character named Joe Caswell who is played by Albert Salmi. He's being led to a hangman's tree by horseback. He is a very cocky criminal who is being hanged for shooting a man in the back. He isn't interested is praying or really in saying any kind of apology only to promise the man whose son he killed that he'll do a jig just for him and then he asks if they can just get on with it.

As he is being hanged we see his shadow on the ground and all of a sudden we don't. The men presiding over the hanging are completely perplexed as to what could have happened to Caswell as this certainly is not supposed to be what happens to someone when they are hanged.

Caswell wakes up on a bed with a very cerebral looking man by the name of Manion bending over him. Caswell wants to know where he is. Manion explains that he's a long way from where he was. He's in New York City and he is eighty years into the future. Manion explains that Caswell is the first time traveler. He was experimenting with his time machine and he reached back in time and took him out. He wants to know all about where he came from as he's sure Caswell wants to know about the year 1960.

Manion then notices rope marks on Caswell's neck and gets a worried look on his face. We then see Manion talking to his tape recorder saying that Caswell has told him that he was driving cattle in Montana when he blacked out and woke up there. He has no explanation for the rope marks on his neck. Manion then says on a personal note that he fears he may have plucked a primitive in to the twentieth century jungle and he fears for anyone who gets in this man's way.

Caswell then appears at the door and wants to know about the tall buildings and the carriages that require no horses. Manion opens up the drapes and Caswell is shocked by what he sees. Manion tells him that some things change but not right and wrong or justice.

Caswell admits that he killed over twenty men. He's not sure how many because he stopped counting after twenty. He tells Manion that it's very easy for him to talk about justice but try it when you're outside freezing to death and the only thing between you and survival is the coat that someone else is wearing.

Manion concludes he must go back to the past. Caswell isn't interested in going back because he's already been hanged once and doesn't want to do it again. He starts to hit Manion and when Manion goes for a gun, Caswell picks up a lamp and beats him to death with it. He grabs the gun and runs out.

However, Caswell is finding this new world isn't his cup of tea. He puts his hands over his ears because it is so noisy. He nearly gets hit by cars a few times. He finally makes his way in to a bar where a juke box is playing and the music is too much. He picks up a chair and smashes it.

The bartender is angry and demands payment for the juke box. Caswell pulls out a gun and demands booze. He puts the bottle on the table and Caswell proceeds to drink it straight up from the bottle. He looks up at the TV set and he asks what that is. The bartender tells him it's a TV. Caswell tells him it looks like a window.

The bartender turns it on so he can see it and it looks like he just turned on Gunsmoke. A cowboy walks closer and closer to the camera and proceeds to takeout his gun to shoot. Caswell panics thinking it's real and he picks up the gun and shoots the TV set out. The bartender starts yelling for the police and Caswell runs out.

He runs in to the street where he once again almost gets hit by a taxi only this time he shoots the poor taxi driver dead. The sirens are coming for him in the distance. He runs back to the office and realizes he's killed Manion.

At that moment a petty thief comes in with a gun and wants to rob the place. His name is Johnson. Caswell wants no part of this thief and they begin to fight culminating with Johnson strangling Caswell. Johnson starts to look around because he's convinced that Manion had a secret hiding place for valuables. He turns on the time machine and walks in with the door closing behind him.

Johnson then appears in the hangman's noose back in 1880. Now the people at the necktie party are even more perplexed. They are wondering if they executed an innocent man. One ponders if this is the work of the devil and yet the minister tells them that he's not so sure this was the devil's work.

And so ends this episode. I really enjoyed this episode at the beginning especially after Caswell killed Manion because I originally thought that this would be an episode of simple talk but I liked the scenes where Caswell was out and about in 1960 New York. I enjoyed seeing Albert Salmi portraying someone totally confused from another era and it was obvious that he was thinking at the end that he'd be better off at the end of a hangman's noose.

I was disappointed with the ending though, not that I minded having another criminal show up but once Caswell was strangled and taken out of the picture that really took away from the story when they decided to have the other thief take his place at the hangman's noose. While it's intriguing and shocking, it really wasn't necessary.

I was expecting an ending that went something like this. During the fight the window and that high rise was broken and I expected Caswell to be pushed out of it and when he landed he was back in the past only as the doctor would realize when he reappeared that he didn't die because he was hanged, he died because of a fall from a very high place. That I think could have brought the story a little more full circle. Having Johnson go back and trade places with Caswell was not necessary.

I did enjoy the acting in it though. Russell Johnson portrayed Manion and it was apparent why he was picked as the professor on Gilligan's Island because he really did sound and look like a scientist.

Overall I will give this episode a three rating. I think it's a good episode and I did enjoy watching it. I would have given it a four had the ending been a little bit better.

Review by Ken

If I were watching this series in 1960 I would already consider 'The Twilight Zone' as must see T.V. Every week you never know what story you are going to get. What other show can puzzle the mind and keep you hanging on for every scene. What possible bizarre moment will happen next?

A mixture of the Old West and time travel make for an intriguing story with an unnatural ending. Excellent casting of Albert Salmi to play the bad guy who is about to be hanged for gruesome murders. Just before the rope does it's job he is transported to present New York City and meets a professor played by Russell Johnson. Notice the contrast between these two characters. The bad guy is corrupt, gross, heartless, and downright dangerous. The professor(who knew he would repeat the same role on Gilligan's Island) is calm, moral, and peaceful. Disturbing scene when Caswell decides to kill the professor for no reason. Poor judgment on the professor's part trusting Caswell to come to his senses.

Great acting scenes by Salmi as he runs all over town in dismay and terror. He reminded me of that thug(Fred Renard) in ep.12-'What You Need.' Take your pick. Who is more threatening, Caswell or Renard? I would not want to be alone with either one of them.

Surprising twist toward the end of this story. A new character is introduced who happens to be an armed robber. He confronts Caswell and the have a fight scene. Justice for Caswell as he is choked to death. The dumb robber enters the time machine and is transported back to the end of the noose. Justice for him for taking Caswell's life.

Again this series never ceases to amaze me with the stories the writers come up with. Serling drives home the point between right and wrong and Karma wins out in the end.

The only flaw in this episode is the casting of the robber played by Than Wyenn. He was short in stature and did not look that dangerous. Also, how does he overtake Caswell who is huge and aggressive. I would have a cast a more sinister looking character who is even more ominous than Caswell.

I have to go with a 4 rating - Excellent.

I reserve my classic ratings to episodes I watch again and again. This story was great but two or three viewings is enough for me.

Review by Bobbynear

Wow! What a story. The 'Professor" should have stayed where he was and continued to play footsie with Ginger and Mary Ann....Gilligan's Island was never like this.

This is one of my favorites....doing what The Twilight Zone did best....cramming a lot of story and action into less than 30 minutes... it's on a fast track and hardly leaves viewers time to breathe before something else is happening.

A most unusual time travel story, really more about justice served than anything. Albert Salmi with his gruff exterior, the perfect choice to play this role of an unrepentant killer who is dangerous in any era.

The best scenes of course are of Caswell out and about in a world that we are used to but is driving him crazy. Makes you wonder how we put up with it. Classic moments in the bar, played almost for comedy, as Caswell shoots out a cowboy who is advancing on him on a tv screen. It's a good thing the bartender didn't turn on Bonanza. Caswell might have taken out the entire Cartwright family and changed tv history. But this story is deadly serious and one killing seems to follow another.

Yes there are some hard to believe moments such as the strangling and the Professor's bad decisions, but I think basically a lot of suspension of disbelief goes a long way in helping you enjoy this episode.

Watching this one made me think of how nice it would be if we could take a few of our current well known killers, O.J. and Charles Manson come immediately to mind, and transport them back to the old West and a dose of frontier justice at the end of a rope, since we seem unable and unwilling to take them out on our own.

One of my all time favorites, and unlike Ken, I never get tired of watching this one.

My rating on a scale of 0 to 5....

4 ~~ EXCELLENT

"The Twilight Zone" Episode 27 "The Big Tall Wish"

Original Air Date- April 8, 1960
Guest Star- Ivan Dixon
Written by Rod Serling
Directed by Ronald Winston

Review by Kitty

This episode is called The Big Tall Wish. It's a tall tale for sure and one that I found enjoyable to watch as well.

We start out by seeing a man looking in the mirror at the various scars on his face and that man's name is Bolie Jackson. He's played by the very talented actor Ivan Dixon. We find out from the narration that he's an old prize fighter attempting a comeback this evening. Behind him is a wide eyed child named Henry who clearly idolizes him and tells him he knows he's going to win tonight.

Bolie is a bit cynical. We see him tell Henry that you can tell where a fighter's been by just looking at his face. He explains to Henry where all of his various scars have come from.

Henry tells Bolie that he's going to make a big wish for him tonight that he wins and doesn't get hurt. Bolie is clearly flattered by the gesture. He walks down the stairs to see Henry's mother Frances, who's clearly a single mom. She wishes Bolie good luck and she thanks him for all of the time he spends with Henry taking him to the park and to ball games and such.

Henry comes down the stairs and tells Bolie again that he's going to make a big tall wish for him. Henry goes in to his apartment and Bolie dismisses it as a little kid's imagination but Frances tells him that maybe there is something to what Henry says. She explains that last week she was fifteen dollars short on the rent money. Henry made a big tall wish that she'd get the money to pay the rent. The next day she got a check in the mail from a woman whom she had taken care as she's a nurse of some kind and the check was for fifteen dollars.

Bolie still dismisses it as a child's imagination. As he walks out on to the street he's met by the neighbors who all wish him well. At the arena, the man he's hired to be his manager for the evening, Thomas is smoking a cigar and Bolie demands that he put it out as he'd like to breathe before the fight. Thomas obliges but doesn't hold out much hope for Bolie. He tells him that he's a washed up fighter but if he signs with him, he can put him in his ring of fighters and as long as he can guaranty at least two rounds a night, he could make a pretty good living at it...

Bolie doesn't give him an answer one way or the other, he's more interested in this fight. He asks Thomas to tell him about this fighter. Thomas tells him that he's never seen him fight. Bolie knows that he's lying. Bolie knows that he's seen him fight six times in the past year and realizes that he has bet against Bolie.

He goes to hit Thomas but he misses and hits the wall instead. His cut man Mizell tells him that he's got four broken knuckles. It's time to go out. Bolie tells him to put the gloves on but he knows he's going to disappoint Henry.

The next part of the episode is quite interesting. We hear the fight going on but since we all know Bolie has an injured hand, we see the reactions of the crowd with their hands. It's quite fascinating to see with people ringing their hands, clenching their hands, holding their hands over their face and some hands are just shoving popcorn in their mouths.

We then see Bolie get the knock out punch. He falls to the mat and the referee starts to count. We then see Frances and Henry in their living room watching the fight on TV and Henry runs to the TV and starts to yell Bolie's name in to the TV.

We see Bolie on the mat about to be counted out when suddenly everything freeze frames. I have to admit, I was watching this on DVD and I initially thought something was wrong with my DVD player. Before I had a chance to start worrying too much about it, things started to happen and we see the hands of the crowd and then all of a sudden when the referee yells ten, it's not Bolie on the mat, but his opponent who's down and Bolie is declared the winner.

After the fight, Bolie is amazed and realizes that his hand doesn't even hurt and he tells Mizell that he was wrong about his knuckles being broken. Mizell doesn't know what he's talking about.

Bolie goes home and everybody on the street is telling him what a good job he did. He goes to the top of the building where Henry is with his pet rabbits and he tells Henry that he won. Henry tells him he made a wish for him. Bolie tells him that it wasn't the wish but that he really did win. Henry walks away.

Bolie wants to know what happened. Henry explains that he was down and so he wished hard that wasn't down and that it was the other guy and the wish came true.

Bolie refuses to believe it. Henry tells him he has to believe it or it won't be true. Bolie refuses to believe that there is magic and Henry shouldn't believe it either. Henry tells him he must believe it or it won't be true. Bolie tells him he can't believe it.

The next thing we see is Bolie back on the mat and the referee yells ten and the other fighter is the winner. Bolie comes back to the neighborhood and everybody is just looking at him as a total loser.

He goes to see Henry and Frances tells him he's in bed but that he's probably awake waiting for him. Bolie goes in to see Henry and Henry tells him that he wished really hard for him but it wasn't enough. Henry tells him that maybe he's too old to believe in magic and he should stop... Bolie then tells him that maybe magic does exist but there just aren't enough people who actually believe in it. He then tells him that he'll still take him to a hockey game tomorrow and Henry agrees.

The final comment is that Bolie had a chance for a second chance but left it on the mat of the ring because he simply could not believe in a miracle.

I have to admit I found this episode quite charming. I really liked the interaction between Bolie and Henry and even with Frances.

According to The Twilight Zone Companion this was one of the first shows on TV to have almost an entire black cast and there wasn't any kind of racial issue involved in the story. These were just regular people living their lives. The character of Bolie could have just as easily been portrayed by a white actor but I really liked Ivan Dixon in this story and the child actor Steven Perry was a delight to watch as well.

I thought the camera work was great at the fight. I found it very unique that obviously due to time and budget restraints for showing a real fight that you see the fight for the most part through the gestures of people's hands. The stopping of the fight and the change was unexpected.

The ending I thought was well done that Bolie simply lost his shot because he couldn't believe in a miracle. How many people in today's world find miracles hard to believe in?

This was the first time I had ever seen this episode and I could easily watch it again. My vote for this one is a five rating.

Review by Linn

OH NO NO NO. This is not the Hallmark Channel and this is not the Lifetime Channel. This is the Twilight Zone. I have seen the Rocky movies and I loved them, but Rocky is not in the Twilight Zone and neither is The Big Tall Wish.

I want The Twilight Zone. This episode was not even close. We see a boxer who has seen his best years come and go. We see a child who wishes the best for him in a comeback bout. The child wishes as hard as he can for his hero and buddy to win. He does win. Then he doesn't because the boxer (played well by Ivan Dixon) refuses to believe in wishes. He blows off the child's ability to wish things to come true and loses the fight in the end. It's all a fantasy and comes to nothing in the end.

I'm sorry, but this episode fell very short for me as far as a true Twilight Zone story. Nothing stood out for me other than the performances by Ivan Dixon and the child. For that only, I will give this episode an average rating of 2.

Review by Ken

The Twilight Zone enters the boxing ring and presents a story about a boxer who has many scars to show. He is the idol of a little boy who wants him to win. Magic and fate as Henry wishes do come true. The prizefighter wins the match and is puzzled and learns the truth. The boy wished him victory.

I did not like the reaction of Bolie and he started to annoy me. I guess the moral of this story is that Bolie wanted to win the fight fair and square. The boy wanted his hero to succeed. In the end Bolie wonders why the world does not have enough people like the little boy who dreams.

Mixed feelings on this one. I don't know what I wanted when watching the story. How would I give more of a T.Z. feeling that I got with previous stories. Still bothered by male-dominated stories. Rod please start using females in the lead role. There are plenty of stories to tell. My rating-slow, dull ending. 1 - Poor

Review by Bobbynear

During The Big Tall Wish, I found myself having a big tall wish of my own. And that is that this episode have a little fire behind it and be a little more interesting than it is.

Too bad, because the acting is first rate. But the story, really more of a single incident than a full fledged story, is too slow paced to keep any interest in it.

The best reason to watch is to see Ivan Dixon's remarkable performance as a nagging boxer who has been on the mat so many times that he can no longer get up, even when an impressionable and adoring young boy wishes him the chance to change failure into success.

This boxing story, about as far removed as possible from the Hollywood, crowd pleasing ending that the first Rocky movie would provide many years later, is notable for daring to be so sad at the finale. But it's plodding nature makes this one to generally avoid.

My rating on a scale of 0 to 5
2 1/2 Slightly Above Average (FOR THE ACTING)

"The Twilight Zone" Episode 28 "A Nice Place To Visit"

Original Air Date- April 15, 1960
Guest Star- Larry Blyden
Written by Charles Beaumont
Directed by John Brahm

Review by Kitty

This episode is called A Nice Place to Visit. We start out seeing a two bit crook robbing a jewelry store. The man's name is Rocky Valentine who as Rod Serling explains in the beginning never got a break and is doing the only thing he knows how to do which is steal what doesn't belong to him.

The police arrive on the scene and chase Rocky from the store and he drops the jewelry that he stole. As he makes his getaway over a fence and shoots at the police as they in turn shoot him dead.

All of a sudden there are white shoes next to him and a voice is calling his name. Rocky wakes up and wants to know who he is and the man tells him his name is Pip and he's been assigned to take care of his every need. Rocky doesn't buy this jovial white haired man in a white suit wanting to take care of him and he pulls a gun on him.

He demands his wallet and Pip explains he hasn't carried a wallet for many years. Pip tells Rocky that he knows that it's money he really wants. He reaches in to his pocket and gives him $700 and asks Rocky if that's sufficient. Rocky is thrilled. Pip tells him that he needs to follow him. Rocky complies but not without brandishing his gun.

Pip leads him to an amazing suite with every amenity possible. Pip gives him new clothes to wear. Rocky gets in the new clothes and wants to know what the catch is. Pip tells him that there is no catch. This is all for him. Rocky still doesn't believe it and he shoots him and the bullets go through him. Rocky wonders if the gun is real and he shoots out a light.

Pip asks him if it isn't obvious what happened. Rocky realizes that he's dead and he's somehow ended up in Heaven. He doesn't understand how that could have happened and concludes he must have done something really nice along the way to make up for all of the bad things he did in life. Pip tells him it's something like that.

Rocky tells Pip he wants a million dollars and a beautiful woman and both things appear. Rocky and Pip and the woman all go to a gambling casino and Rocky is winning every time he plays roulette. He tries his hand at the slots and he wins there as well.

He's thrilled and they all go back to Rocky's place but not before Rocky can slap around a midget cop. Rocky wants to look up his old friends and Pip tells him that's not possible because this place is for him and only him. Rocky still doesn't understand it so they go to the Hall of Records. It's a very impressive place that has a lot of steps with nothing but file cabinets and open air at the top. Pip pulls Rocky's file and Rocky sees nothing in his file that's good.

Pip tells him that if he needs anything to just call him on the phone by dialing P-I-P. Rocky is then seen sitting in the casino winning again and again and he's bored. He's back in his suite with the three women playing cards and he's consistently beating them.

He then throws them all out. He is dissatisfied and then sees a pool table in his room and when he shoots the first ball, everything goes in the holes. He then dials Pip and Pip appears and Rocky tells him that he doesn't belong there. Pip tells him that's not true. Rocky is very insistent that he doesn't belong here because he's bored and he never loses. Pip tells him that can be arranged and Rocky tells him it wouldn't be the same.

Pip suggests that he rob a bank. Rocky initially likes the idea but then realizes he's a shoe in for getting away. No, he wants no part of it. He tells Pip to send him to the other place. Pip then informs that he is in the other place and laughs as Rocky tries to get out of the room.

Larry Blyden didn't do much for me as Rocky. I had no real sympathy for the man. As the saying goes, sometimes God punishes you and gives you exactly what you want. The real reason to watch this episode is Sebastian Cabot as Pip. He's great playing what appears to be an angel and then turns out to be totally the opposite.

It seems a perfect ending though to Rocky's miserable life. He spends his life trying to achieve things by stealing and when he get everything he dreamed of, he's not happy. It's basically a commentary that people like Rocky are probably incapable of being happy.

This didn't really knock my socks off. I've seen it before and didn't think much of it. I give it a two rating for average.

Review by Linn

I actually had to watch this episode again, probably for the fourth time, to realize that it's not as bad as I thought it was. I don't know. Maybe I just really needed to pay attention to it. First off, I've always loved Sebastion Cabot who played "Pip".Larry Blyden doing his Jimmy Cagney impersonation is probably why I lost interest in this episode. The guy is shot dead while pulling off one of his petty thefts. He ends up, courtesy of Pip, in a place he believes to be heaven. All the money, food and women he could want. The excitement lasts only for so long. As BB King said in his famous song, "The Thrill is Gone".

Rocky Valentine stopped being thrilled very quickly. In fact, the person who gave everything to him was Pip and he couldn't even be nice to him because he kept calling him "Fats". In the end, he finds out he's not in heaven as he thought, but he's in hell.

Well, if that's what hell is like, what's the problem? I'll give this one a 3 rating for Good.

Review by Ken

One thing I dislike with any television series is to repeat a similar storyline used before and rehash it again with another angle. As I recall ep.6 'Escape Clause' used the concept of a fat guide presiding over the fate of a man's destiny. Sadly, that story turned out to be a bust for me.

This concept seems to play out again with ep.27 'A Nice Place to Visit.' A burglar is shot and killed and wakes up to find another overweight figure as his guide now. Notice the contrast of clothes between Mr. Pip(White suit) and Valentine(smug dark clothes). I agree the casting of Sebastian Cabot was perfect to play the role of a nice, jolly guy who provides whatever Valentine wants.

Larry Blyden was a good choice to play the wise guy who never is satisfied. His sneering, mocking, jeering, and insulting demeanor was fit for the story. His every move was annoying. Such a loser he would even resort to kill Pip who was amiable to him.

The story continues as we see Valentine is afforded all his wishes and dreams. Money, success, food, wine, clothes, dwelling, girls, and constant pleasure. However, he gets bored and wants something else. True reflection of society as a whole. Give me more and more and more. What else can I buy. Where else can I go. What else can I have.

Again the Twilight Zone leads the audience to a strange and odd conclusion. Valentine wants out. Pip laughs and tells him he is in the other place. Yikes! Rod Serling fools us again thinking Valentine was in a heaven of pleasure. People think Hell is fire and brimstone. So Serling reverses the concept and makes Hell the lust and greed of pleasure which turns out to torment Valentine.

Interesting concept Rod. But I don't want thugs, murderers, thieves, crooks, cheats, robbers, evil people getting pleasures in Hell. Their punishment should be eternal suffering.

Story kept my interest. The actors played their roles well. The girls were pretty to watch. Falls short of a classic.

My rating - 4 - Excellent

Review by Bobbynear

A rather strange little tale that perhaps did not turn out exactly as Serling had intended. I don't know that for a fact of course, but it seems to me that there is quite a message here for humanity, a sort of, "Be careful what you ask for...you might actually get it...." sort of warning that gets lost since it's hard to take any of this seriously.

Played just a little too broadly as comedy, for my taste, there isn't much here other than the twist ending. But I was just a child when I first saw this and fooling me was pretty easy....just like it was to fool Rocky. I seriously doubt that my middle aged parents watching it with me were fooled for one second. You can easily see it coming after about ten minutes.

Larry Blyden is way over the top which perhaps is a good thing in order to take the edge off what just happens to be a very dangerous and deadly criminal. Sebastian Cabot I agree was the perfect choice for Mr. Pip, although now many years later, it truly is disturbing to see "Mr. French" acting this way.

I liked Linn's comment in her review that if it is hell, as long as you get everything you ever wanted... just sit back and enjoy it. After all, you won't be going anywhere...ever... And that is a good point. Except for one little problem.

As just about everyone finds out late in life, it's all a game... and unfortunately life really isn't about successfully gathering together all the riches and material items you can... it's really about the pursuit of them. Just like Rocky, many famous people from entertainers to sports stars, seem intent upon ruining their cushy lives usually in a haze of scandal, drugs and alcohol. Why? Well probably because there isn't anything left to strive for any longer. In order not to be as bored as Rocky becomes... you need to dismantle your life and start over.

The problem for Rocky is that Mr. Pip is in control, he isn't. Now there is just the endless tedium of winning over and over and over again. Humans, it seems, are never happy.

As Ken rightfully pointed out, this is just another version of the earlier episode, "Escape Clause." The only difference of course being that the hypochondriac in that episode, gets to exercise his way out while Rocky has no such option. People in real life however, get an escape clause they don't want, when they die and leave all of those things that were once so important... To somebody else. Life itself it seems, is "A Nice Place To Visit" after all....you just can't live there forever....And perhaps that's a good thing... Just ask Rocky.

My rating on a scale of 0 to 5

3 - GOOD

"The Twilight Zone" Episode 29 "Nightmare As A Child"

Original Air Date- April 29, 1960
Guest Star- Janice Rule
Written by Rod Serling
Directed by Alvin Ganzer

Review by Kitty

This latest episode is called Nightmare as a Child. We start by seeing a very pretty woman named Helen Foley played by Janice Rule, come home from work to her apartment. She's a school teacher. She's met at her door by a cute little girl sitting on the stairs.

Helen engages her in conversation. Initially she doesn't talk but then starts to talk to Helen as an adult would talk. Helen is quite taken with this young girl and invites her in for hot chocolate. The girl says that she would love to but she knows that Helen doesn't like marshmallows in her hot chocolate. Helen looks at her funny and tells her she's right.

The little girl responds that she doesn't like them either. Helen makes the hot chocolate and the little girl tells her it's very good. It's not too hot because she doesn't like things that are too hot and Helen doesn't like them hot either. Helen asks her how she knows that.

The little girl responds that she knows all about her including how she got the burn on her arm which is why she doesn't like things that are too hot. Helen is taken aback by all of this and wants to know the little girl's name. The little girl responds by saying her nick name is Markie.

She knows that she has forgotten many things including how she got her arm burned. Helen admits that yes, she has forgotten a lot about her childhood.

Markie tells her that she remembers a man though. She saw him today when she left school. He was driving in a car, stopped at a light by her school and she felt afraid when she saw him.

Helen yells at her that she wants to know who she is and why she's saying all of this to her. Just then there is a knock at the door. Markie tells her that is the man and she has to run away from him but she'll be back later.

Markie runs out the back door and Helen asks who is at the door. A man's voice says, that it's Peter Selden. He knew her mother and was passing through town. Helen opens the door and lets the man in. Peter explains that he saw her outside her school and recognized her so he thought he' d stop in and see her.

He asks her if she remembers him. Helen tells him that she's forgotten much about that night. Peter tells her he worked for her mother and did her books for her. He lived down the hallway and he's the one who found her after it happened.

She tells him she really doesn't remember much. She then hears Markie singing Twinkle Twinkle Little Star. She asks him if he hears the little girl singing. She tells him that her name is Markie. She picks up the cup of hot chocolate and sees it hasn't been touched and yet she saw the little girl drink it. He tells her he doesn't hear anything. He shows her a picture of the little girl. She asks him where he got it because that's the child.

Peter tells her the child in the picture is her. He also tells her that she used to be called Markie as a child. Helen gets a very confused look on her face. She is laying down and she remembers the night when her mother was murdered. She sees her mother arguing with a man who chokes her and then hits on the head with a club. Young Helen lets out a blood curdling scream and the man runs away. All of a sudden she's back in the present when she hears Markie singing again. She runs outside to the hallway and she sees Markie again. She demands to know who Markie is.

Markie tells her that it's obvious that she's her. Helen then looks at Markie's arm and sees the same scar from the burn that Helen has. Markie tells her she has to remember or he's going to kill her too.

Helen turns around and sees Peter who confesses everything. He knew he needed to get rid of her as well that night but she screamed so loudly it was out of the question. He did her mother's books and when she caught him skimming money she confronted him and told him he was fired. He got angry and killed her.

He's followed her through the years and knew it was only a matter of time before she would remember and finger him for the murder so he has to get rid of her as well. Helen runs out of the apartment and begins to knock on doors for help. Peter catches up with her and she pushes him down the stairs where he conveniently breaks his neck and dies.

The last thing we see is the doctor and the police officer talking and saying that this woman was lucky as she was almost a homicide victim today.

Helen is lying on her couch and once again hears a little girl singing Twinkle Twinkle Little Star but when she opens the door, it's a different little girl who lives in the building sitting with her doll. Helen tells her she has a beautiful smile.

So, was Markie real or simply figment of Helen's imagination? Probably, the tip off is in the cup of hot chocolate that Helen saw Markie drink but then picked up the cup and saw that it was still full.

It was certainly a good imagination though to not even recognize your younger self. I don't know, I would like to think I've seen enough pictures of myself as a child so that if I did see myself I would certainly do a double take and be suspicious.

However, it makes for good suspense. I predicted the ending. It was obvious that somehow Helen was going to have to kill Peter although I think Peter was sort of a dumb criminal. Helen really didn't know for sure that he was killer until he admitted it to her.

She said that she remembered a man killing her mother but it was clear that it was in the shadows and she never got a good look at the man's face. So, for Peter to just openly admit that he did it was a little premature.

All in all though I did like it. This is one of those episodes that was new for me and I did enjoy it. I will rank this episode a three for good. Even though Markie was really Helen's imagination, who says that can't count for the Twilight Zone? Sometimes imagination is scarier than reality.

The only complaint I'd have is that the little girl played by Terry Burnahm didn't look much like Janice Rule. You'd think since Janice Rule was a brunette, they'd want a little girl who was a brunette. However, Terry Burnahm was a compelling child actress in this episode.

Review by Linn

Well, this episode was pretty lame. First off, they keep saying how beautiful this kid is and as far as I'm concerned, she was not beautiful at all. In fact, she was a dumb looking kid. So sue me. The kid was not beautiful.

Next, Janice Rule is fine in the role, but really. Come on. She doesn't recognize herself? I'm 50 years old and know what I looked like as a child. Then why does this guy come back to kill her when she hasn't said a word about her mother's death or pinpointed him in all this time? Is this episode for real? The guy comes back after she's a grown woman like she's going to turn in a guy she doesn't even remember. So he jars her memory.

Yeah, that makes sense. You've been gone for years so now come back and jar the girl's memory. Are you serious? Tell me why. That's what I want to know.

Yes Ken. You think it's lousy? Me too. 0 for not only lousy but stupid as well.

Review by Ken

Finally the producers have heard the desperate cry of viewers like me and decided to tell a story with a female in the lead role.

The percentage of male-dominated Twilight Zone stories in this first season is staggering to say the least. Out of 29 episodes so far, only three focus on women. Ep.4-'The Sixteen-Millimeter Shrine,' ep.16-'The Hitch-Hiker,' andep.21-'Mirror Image.'

What a relief to tune in and see a fine actress Janice Rule play the part of Helen Foley. She begins to revisit her past and has two visitors to her home to deal with. She welcomes a little girl in for hot chocolate but she never drinks from the cup. No need for marsh mellows. The young girl is a hallucination of her younger self and sings tunes. Miss Foley also welcomes a stranger into her apartment. Not a good idea. What does he want. The strange gentlemen wonders if she will identify him as the murderer of her mother. A struggle between the two occurs and Mr. Seldon falls down the stairs and dies.

Helen is free from her past memories and meets another little girl on the stairway. She sings tunes also and the story ends with a dud.

This script must have been presented to the executive producers from a first grade class. Am I watching Alice in Wonderland?? I am scratching my head as to what sense to make of this mess. However, I will give credit to the stuntman for falling down that stairs. He must have had pads on underneath that suit because that was quite a stunt.

Side note: Janice Rule in the opening scenes gazing into space requires me to include her in my Twilight Zone hall of fame for women. She was gorgeous.

My rating-0 Lousy

Review by Bobbynear

There is a great deal of creepiness about this episode and one or two scenes are disturbing. But like too many Twilight Zone episodes, it's too slow and the payoff is not quite worth the attention from viewers that is required in order to understand any of it.

Like my co-reviewers have pointed out, the story is full of holes. Plus in less than thirty minutes, too much is required and since there is little time to show what happened that created all of this, it's basically all talk, until we get this very short recreation of the murder. It also might have been more effective if the killer had actually been openly stalking Helen for years instead of just watching her from afar like he claims.

Instead this seems to come out of nowhere and I have to agree with the others that Peter has no particular reason to give himself up at this time. He claims that eventually Helen will remember. However, in real life, it's probably morel likely that she will increasingly forget.

There is one glaring mistake however from both Kitty and Linn that I must mention. They complain that it makes no sense that Helen does not recognize herself as a child. But more than halfway through the story, Markie shows her photo to Helen and asks, "Familiar?" Helen responds with "It's supposed to be me, when I was your age. But it's not me Markie, it's a snapshot of you."

Markie goes on to tell her that it's her when she was ten years old and she was called Markie. There is no indication anywhere in the story that Markie is an exact duplicate of Helen at an early age. If they were supposed to look alike in any way, obviously Markie would not have needed to say any of that. You can hang this story for plenty of reasons but not for that.

If you want to clobber this story, you need nothing more than the ending. It is patently absurd. For one thing, the police don't seem to want to investigate why a man is dead at the bottom of the stairs.

There are no witnesses anywhere and no proof that Helen was assaulted by this man. How do the cops know that she didn't throw him down the steps deliberately for any one of an endless number of self serving reasons? She's not even going down to police headquarters to give a statement? This is it? The cop tells the doctor that "It all ties together. "It does???

The next to last scene between the cop and the doctor is almost laughable. Do you mean to tell me that this "doctor" got to the bottom of what had been secretly bothering Helen for years by just talking to her for a short time? That is amazing. Years of psychotherapy in real life has often failed to get to the bottom of anything. This instant analysis to say nothing of any proof that Helen didn't just throw this guy down the steps to get him off her back is ludicrous. This is where the story comes apart at the seams.

Too bad because I basically like the premise and had it been fleshed out over a longer period without so much endless talk and an idiot ending, it might have been an effective and chilling little thriller.

Sorry Rod......Not this time.

My rating on a scale of 0 to 5

0 -- Lousy

"The Twilight Zone" Episode 30 "A Stop At Willoughby"

Original Air Date- May 6, 1960
Guest Star- James Daly
Written by Rod Serling
Directed by Robert Parrish

Review by Ken

Imagination and visualization is good for the soul. Along comes an insightful story in The Twilight Zone that has stirred up my sensitivity. 'A Stop at Willoughby' delivers with a fancy tale of a man who has had it with work, boss, nagging wife, boring train rides, and his general surroundings. How can he escape his doldrums lifestyle? Take a nap on a train for a few moments and then open the window. Listen for the train conductor shouting 'next stop Willoughby, Willoughby.'

Ideal casting of James Daly to play the part of Gart Williams a smirky guy who needs to relax and take a vacation or something. Notice how Rod Serling teases the viewing audience with Gart almost getting off the train to explore Willoughby. But no! He wakes up two different times to find out this is but a dream. Oh how he wishes he can go back and find out what Willoughby is all about.

Peace, rest, comfort, solace; how can Gart get it back for one day let along one precious moment. No support at work or at home. Help! I need escape. What can Gart do? Alas! The secret. Board the train and fall asleep near the window. Hope the snowy winter night will turn to a glorious sunny summer day. Where is that friendly train conductor with a gentle face and demeanor. Yes I will exit the train at Willoughby. I see two little boys with a fishing pole heading to the lake. I want to join them. I see neighborly people strolling along in a sociable and civil town in 1888. No trials, tribulations, loud cars, inconsiderate folk. Just a warm breeze and a benevolent, accommodating atmosphere to enjoy.

For a moment all Twilight Zone fans can identify with Gart Williams. Who among us would not want to get off that train and explore Willoughby. Who knows maybe no income taxes to pay. What is our own Willoughby??? For some people it is the escape into the sports world. For others their Willoughby may be the theater, opera, concerts, symphony, culture, history, geography, geology, music, art, money, drama, travel, etc... We all have day dreams of Willoughby. For me let me get off the train at Cooperstown, New York and let me play sandlot baseball with all my boyhood friends again back in the warm summer of 1962. Forget my business of mowing lawns and grumbling customers. Give me a classic coke and let me have a baseball bat and glove. I will play from morning to night.

The end scene of this episode is classic for the ages. Gart gets off at Willoughby and his face is glowing. But Rod Serling you have let me hanging again. Why are you ending the story and not letting us see all of Willoughby for ourselves. Stop your annoying narration. I want to visit the town and eat the food. I want to meet the lovely ladies. I want to go down to the lake and fish with the boys. I want cotton candy and soda. I want to visit the saloon. I want to take a buggy ride. Visit the hotel, play cards with the guys, enjoy the piano music.

Gamble my money away. Run barefoot in the green grass. Rod you are driving my curiosity crazy. You did the same thing to me with ep.21'Mirror Image.' Millicent and Paul did not catch up with their doubles. Thanks Rod. What did Gart do in Willoughby? Another unsolved mystery in The Twilight Zone.

Anyway my rating for Willoughby is a solid 5-Classic and more.

Review by Bobbynear

JAMES DALY PLAYS AN ABUSED AND OVERWORKED BUSINESS EXECUTIVE NAMED GART WILLIAMS WHO FINDS THE VERY BUSINESS WORLD THAT MADE HIM A SUCCESS IS NOW MAKING HIM A BASKET CASE. HIS OVERBEARING BOSS WITH HIS

RELENTLESS CRIES OF "PUSH PUSH PUSH" AND A DEMANDING WIFE GIVE HIM NO SOLACE WHATSOEVER UNTIL HE MANAGES TO FIND HIS OWN FORM OF ESCAPE.

NOT MUCH HAPPENS IN THIS STORY BUT IT IS SO EERIE AND UNCOMORTABLY CLOSE TO REAL LIFE THAT IT IS DISTURBING NONETHELESS. IT DOESN'T TAKE A GENIUS TO FIGURE OUT THAT WILLIAMS HAS CREATED AN IMAGINERY WORLD FOR HIMSELF, BUT THE ENDING IS SOMETHING OF A SURPRISE. TWO MINOR THINGS THAT DID MAKE ME PAUSE FOR A MOMENT WHILE WATCHING THIS EPISODE WERE WHY IT SEEMED TO ALWAYS BE SNOWING SO HARD WHENEVER WILLIAMS WAS ON THAT TRAIN, AND HOW HE WAS ABLE TO GO INTO THE BATHROOM AND BREAK THAT MIRROR WITH HIS HAND WITHOUT SO MUCH AS SCRATCHING A FINGER.

IT'S ALSO INTERESTING TO NOTE THAT ROD SERLING WROTE THIS STORY. SERLING WAS KNOWN AS SOMETHING OF A WORKAHOLIC IN THE TV INDUSTRY EVEN THOUGH HIS DECLINING HEALTH DICTATED AGAINST IT. SO THIS STORY MAY HAVE MORE THAN A LITTLE OF SERLING'S PERSONAL FEELINGS ABOUT THE PRESSURES OF SUCCESS IN IT. IN FACT, ACORDING TO MARTIN GRAMS' BOOK, "THE TWILIGHT ZONE" THIS TRAIN TRIP IS QUITE CLOSE TO ONE THAT SERLING ACTUALLY TOOK IN HIS EARLIEST DAYS OF SCREENWRITING WHEN HE COMMUTED FROM OHIO TO NEW YORK. THAT TRAIN MADE A STOP IN A PLACE CALLED WILLOUGHBY.

ONE CAN ONLY HOPE THAT IN REAL LIFE, ROD SERLING WHO DIED AT THE ASTONISHINGLY YOUNG AGE OF 51 AND THE STAR OF THIS EPISODE, JAMES DALY WHO PASSED AWAY AT ONLY 60, BOTH MANAGED TO FIND THEIR OWN FORM OF WILLOUGHBY AFTER THEY PASSED FROM THE SCENE.

NOT QUITE A CLASSIC IN MY OPINION BUT STILL AN INTERESTING TAKE ON REAL LIFE AND THE PERILS OF

SUCCESS THAT HITS PERHAPS JUST A LITTLE TOO CLOSE TO HOME FOR SOME PEOPLE.
MY RATING ON A SCALE OF 0 TO 5
4 --- EXCELLENT

Review by Linn

It seems to me that most of the men in Twilight Zone episodes are married to very sweet, loving and understanding women. For instance, take Franklin Gibbs in The Fever. He was married to an angel, but gave her a bad time because she won a vacation to Las Vegas and he hated gambling. Look at Escape Clause. A man named Walter Bedeker was married to an wonderful woman who cared very much about her hypochondriac husband only to end up dying herself trying to save him and he didn't even care.

However, you then have Time Enough At Last where a sweet and lovable little man named Henry Bemis is married to a royal bitch of a woman and thankfully she was blown away in a nuclear explosion. The only problem is that poor Henry was left to roam around in complete solitude and loneliness to the point that he almost wanted her back.

Well, Willoughby is very similar to Time Enough At Last in the fact that you see a very nice man named Gart Williams played very well by actor James Daly who is married to woman who is just as much of a crumb bag as Henry's wife was except that Gart's wife is actually pretty and Henry's wife looks like a beast.

Gart is disgusted with his life, his job and everything surrounding him. The only thing that gives him any pleasure is his idyllic nap on the train ride home from work. He falls asleep each afternoon on his ride home and imagines he's at a stop called Willoughby. Each time, he wants to get off, but he doesn't. At one point, he gets fired from his job for telling off his fat, ignorant creep of a boss. He goes home and looks to his rotten wife for some sympathy and compassion only to find a heartless, unfeeling woman who cares nothing for him . She makes him feel lower than dirt. It turns out that he gets his job back, but he's still miserable and decides to depart the train at Willoughby saying to himself "Next time I'm getting off there". Yes, he did get off there.

He jumped off the train to his death. BUT, he was in a better place. No more rotten boss, rotten wife or horrible job. Yeah, Willoughby was a funeral home. He was dead, but he was in a much, much better place.

My rating for this episode is 4 for excellent.

Review by Kitty

This episode is called A Stop at Willoughby. It's more of a stop in time rather than simply a place. We start by seeing a group of executives sitting around the table in silence. Why, one might wonder. Well, it's called they are waiting for an assistant of Gart Williams to come in with the particulars of an advertising account for automobiles. It's supposed to be a three million dollar account.

They were supposed to be on a conference call and the assistant is a no show. Gart gets on the phone to find out where the assistant is only to get a message from him stating that he spent lunch deciding to go with a new firm and he took the three million dollar automobile account with him.

Gart's boss Mr. Misrell is not a happy camper about this. He publicly reams poor Gart out in front of everybody there for giving the responsibility of an account this important to someone who's just out of college and is so green.

He continues by yelling at Gart and tells him that this is a push, push, push kind of business. Gart is clearly not feeling well as he puts his hand to his stomach and he finally yells at Misrell to shut up, but not before calling him fatboy.

He storms out and is later on the train home to Westport CT. It's dark outside and snowing and it's the middle of November. Gart sits back and falls asleep. He awakens to a much smaller looking train and when he opens up the blinds it's warm and sunny outside and it's the 1880. The conductor comes by and tells him the stop is Willoughby.

Gart asks where is Willoughby and the man tells him right outside. He tells him it's a wonderful place to live a peacefully, slow life. Gart asks how this is possible to have sunshine because it's November. The conductor tells him is summer time and it's July. The train begins to move and Gart wakes up. He asks the current conductor if he's ever heard of a place called Willoughby and he tells him not on this run.

Back at home, Gart fixes himself a drink and is met by a beautiful but very unsympathetic wife. He tells her that he's not the competitive guy she wants him to be. He doesn't like being in a house they can't afford and he doesn't like being at the country club. He wants to be somewhere else. She asks him where. He tells her about Willoughby and she's not impressed. He's a dreamer and she basically has no use for him.

We then see him back on the train and the conductor comes by and says Willoughby. Gart is surprised to hear the conductor say that name. The conductor explains that he checked all of the old maps that he could find and to his knowledge there's never been a stop called Willoughby anywhere on this line.

Gart then falls asleep and once again dreams of Willoughby. He starts to get off but the train starts up too quick because he hesitates by stopping to grab his personal belongings. He wakes up and says next time he's getting off.

At the office, Gart is once again having a terrible day. He's got Misrell on the phone making demands on him and then once he's off the phone, he gets two more phone calls basically telling him of nothing but problems and as he's dealing with the two phone calls his secretary Helen comes in and tells him that Mr. Misrell wants to see him right now.

I must say this is not much of a secretary. Secretaries are supposed look out for their bosses and to come barging in and repeatedly say that Mr. Misrell wants to see him while he's engaged in two other conversations with important clients is unforgivable. I mean really what's the poor man supposed to do, just hang up both phones on clients? Hey that would go over really well with Mr. Misrell......not! This is one secretary that ought to be fired.

Gart puts both phones down and goes in to the bathroom and is so frustrated that he punches the mirror out. He walks out and the worthless secretary is gone. Good riddance to her.

Gart calls his wife and explains over the phone that he just can't take his job anymore and he needs to quit and to please just be there when he gets home. His bitch goddess wife simply hangs up the phone on him. Good riddance to her as well!

On the train, Gart falls asleep and he is once again stopping in Willoughby. This time he exits the train leaving his personal belongings behind. He gets off the train and everybody knows his name and is welcoming him with open arms. Two boys have been fishing and Gart offers to go with them the next day. They say sure. A horse and buggy driver welcomes him. He walks to the gazebo where a band is playing.

The next thing we see is the train stopped in the snow and Gart is lying in the snow dead. The conductor is explaining to the railroad man that he's not sure why he did it. He just jumped from the train screaming Willoughby. The funeral home will take the body in to town for an autopsy.

Gart's body is loaded on a stretcher and put in the back of the hearse. The door closes on the hearse and the words on the door say Willoughby and Son Funeral Home.

Overall, I liked this one. I remember the first time I ever saw this one in my teens and thought it was such a bizarre ending. I was truly not expecting to see the poor man commit suicide.

However, it was a happy ending because it was obvious Willoughby was Gart's version of Heaven and that's what he got in the end.

I thought the acting was well done. James Daly played the part perfectly as a guy who's so burned out on reality that he literally creates another one. Who can really blame him?

What support does he have in his life? He's got a boss who apparently forgot how to be a human being, a secretary who's a ditz brain and a wife who's pretty ungrateful. In spite of it all, she's dressed quite well and they are hardly living in poverty.

However, it appears they are in debt up to their eyeballs and yet all she does is complain as opposed to try and help her husband out.

No, I can't say I blame Gart one bit for exiting to the Twilight Zone. When I think of Twilight Zone, this is definitely one that comes to mind and in fact there is even a place here where I live that whenever I drive through it, I am reminded of Willoughby and for that reason this episode gets a five rating from me. I definitely consider this a classic.

"The Twilight Zone" Episode 31 "The Chaser"

Original Air Date- May 13, 1960
Guest Star- George Grizzard
Written by Robert Presnell
Directed by Douglas Heyes

Review by Kitty

This episode is called The Chaser. We start out seeing a man in a phone booth in a store by the name of Roger and he is frantically making phone calls but keeps getting busy signals. There are three people in line to use the phone and when another shows up desperate to use the phone, he pays the first three people in line for their place. It's amazing what a dollar can buy you in 1960.

The man in the phone booth finally gets through to a beautiful woman named Leila played by Patricia Barry. He tells her he loves her and is simply desperate to see her. She on the other hand wants nothing to do with him and tells him to take a flight to the moon. She hangs up on him

The older man pushes his way in to the phone booth and tells him his time is up and Roger insists that he needs to call her back. The man then gives him a business card for a Professor Daemon and tells him that what he needs is at the professor's house.

Roger goes to the house and finds that when the door opens, it leads down a very dark area of nothing to yet another door. He opens the door and he is greeted by an older man who asks if he's come for a bottle of the glove cleaner for $1,000.

Roger tells him no, he's there because he wants a woman named Leila to love him. The man tries to talk him out of it as he can give him potions for various other things like riches and power but Roger tells him he only wants the love potion. The man sells it to him for $1.

Roger is amazed that it's so cheap so he buys it and goes to Leila's place. He brings Leila flowers and champagne and Leila agrees to have one drink with him. He pours the champagne and puts the love potion in it.

Leila gladly drinks it all and then tell Roger to leave. Roger asks for just one last kiss. Leila gives him a lame kiss but then starts to change and she starts to tell Roger that she loves him and Roger is ecstatically happy as they both kiss each other with much more passion.

We next see that Roger and Leila have been married for awhile and Leila is now driving Roger crazy. She won't stop kneeling at his feet and staring at him. She wants to do everything for him to the point where it's annoying.

Roger can't take it anymore and he tells Leila he has an appointment that he has to get to but he'll be back later.

He goes back to Professor Daemon and he tells him Leila is driving him crazy and he can't take it anymore. He wants the glove cleaner. Daemon tells him that it's guaranteed to work with no trace of any wrongdoing.

Roger reluctantly gives him a check for $1,000 and Daemon tells him to use it immediately because if there's any hesitation it won't work. As Roger leaves, Daemon says it's the same onld thing every time, the love potion followed by the glove cleaner chaser.

Roger comes home with flowers and champagne and Leila is delighted. She tells him that this is just like it was six months ago when she realized that she loved him.

Roger puts the glove cleaner in the champagne and Leila pulls him on the couch and tells him that things have changed since then. She holds up a baby bootie that she's been crocheting and Roger is so shocked that he drops both glasses of champagne.

He gets a look of resignation on his face and says he probably couldn't have done it anyway.

The last thing we see is Daemon on the balcony smoking and blowing a smoke ring in the shape of a heart and Daemon smiles and disappears.

Yes, it's too bad that Roger got exactly what he wanted. This episode is a little reminiscent of Escape Clause as clearly Professor Daemon was not someone out to really help people.

I have to admit I didn't really feel a lot of empathy for Roger. He was in love with a totally conceited woman who was clearly in love with herself first and foremost. He then tried to create true love by manipulation and as everybody knows that's doomed for failure. He found her annoying at the end and I found the episode a bit of an annoyance.

I did like the special effects in this episode though. I liked the darkness effect to Daemon's door and I did like the effect of blowing smoke rings in the shape of hearts at the end. Knowing that they did not have CGI abilities back then, it was a feat to achieve that smoke effect.

This is not an especially inspiring episode. It's one where I don't particularly like any of the characters so I will give it a one rating.

Review by Bobbynear

THE DECISION BY THE PEOPLE BEHIND THE TWILIGHT ZONE TO DO A LIGHT HEARTED ALMOST COMICAL EPISODE IN ITS INAUGURAL SEASON, IS RISKY. THE SERIES HAS SET ITSELF UP AS A SERIOUS LOOK INTO BOTH SCIENCE FICTION AND THE POSSIBILITY OF OTHER WORLDS WE MAY NEVER UNDERSTAND. THERE AREN'T MANY LAUGHS ALONG THE WAY.

NOW ALONG COMES AN EPISODE YOU CAN HARDLY TAKE SERIOUSLY. KITTY MENTIONED IN HER REVIEW THAT THIS IS REMINISCENT OF THE EARLIER SEASON ONE EPISODE, "ESCAPE CLAUSE", WITH THE PROFESSOR BEING ANOTHER CHARACTER OUT MORE FOR HIMSELF THAN FOR THE BENEFIT OF THE PERSON WHO GOES TO HIM FOR HELP. PERSONALLY I FOUND IT WAY TO MUCH LIKE THE VERY RECENT EPISODE, "A NICE PLACE TO VISIT" ANOTHER PERSON WHO GETS WHAT HE ALWAYS DREAMED OF AND LIVES TO REGRET IT.

THE MAIN CHARACTER ALONG WITH THE PEOPLE AROUND HIM ARE JUST NOT LIKEABLE AND CARING ABOUT ANY OF THEM IS ALL BUT IMPOSSIBLE. PLUS ITS PRETTY OBVIOUS HOW IT WILL END UP.

TRYING A LITTLE COMEDY TO LIGHTEN THE ATMOSPHERE MIGHT NOT BE A BAD IDEA, BUT NOT THIS EARLY. NOT IN SEASON ONE. PLUS THIS STORY SETS THE STAGE FOR SOME RATHER ODD SEASON ENDING CHOICES, INCLUDING A MAN NAMED BEVIS AND A BASEBALL PLAYER WHO IS REALLY A ROBOT. JUST WHERE IS THE TWILIGHT ZONE GOING AS IT HEADS INTO ITS SECOND SEASON? YOU HAVE TO WONDER.

A LOT OF PEOPLE MAY BE WONDERING...BUT I'M AFRAID, NOBODY IS LAUGHING... INCLUDING ME.

MY RATING ON A SCALE OF 0 TO 5

0 -- TOTALLY WITHOUT MERIT

Review by Linn

Oh my. How many of us have loved and lusted after someone who was so far from our reach? Someone we could not have.

Roger Shackleforth did just that.......until...... he found a man who was able to give him a love potion to make the object of his desire want him as much as he wanted her. Oh yes, it was wonderful at first.

Then it became a smothering, terrible thing for him. I guess the two expressions "be careful what you wish for" and "too much of a good thing can be too much" are appropriate for this episode.

I can't say much more about this episode because it speaks for itself and I've lived through it as well.

My rating - 2 for average

Review by Ken

'I took my troubles down to Madame Rue.. You know that gypsy with the gold-capped tooth.. She's got a pad down on Thirty-Fourth and Vine.. Sellin' little bottles of Love Potion Number Nine Nine....'

Hey Rod! Are you on vacation. I notice that this episode was written by Robert Presnell. Who? Does he know what the proper formula for writing T.Z. scripts. I feel embarrassed even commenting on this mess of a story. The casting of the main characters turned me off immediately. Not only could you hear loud groans from me over this one, I feel the need to delete even the memory of 'The Chaser' from my brain. I know sometimes producers get off track but this story was a train wreck. I am trying to scratch my head and figure out why the show wanted to get involved in a love potion soap opera. At least cast a beauty to play the part of female who is now in love with a dunce. I can't talk anymore about this catastrophic blunder that is part of this series. No excuses producers. My dog will eat this script.

Guess what my rating is 0-Lousy, horrible, offensive, dreadful, awful, disgusting, repulsive, and terrible.

"The Twilight Zone" Episode 32 "A Passage For Trumpet"

Original Air Date- May 20, 1960
Guest Star- Jack Klugman
Written by Rod Serling
Directed by Don Medford

Review by Kitty

This latest episode is called A Passage for a Trumpet. We start out seeing Jack Klugman playing a man by the name of Joey Crown. Joey is in the back of the club and he's hearing a trumpet player playing. He opens up a trumpet case and he takes out his trumpet. A man comes out named Baron. Joey asks him if he can use a trumpet player that night.

Baron tells him no. Joey insists he's been away from the booze for the past seven months. Baron still tells him he doesn't have anything available. Joey takes his trumpet case and a bottle falls on the floor so Joey hasn't been as sober as he's been implying.

Baron gives Joey money for old times sake. Joey tells him the reason he drank was because he played better when he drank. He goes to the rafters and he tries to play but he's not hitting the notes like he should.

Joey gets disgusted and leaves. He goes to a pawn shop and sells the trumpet for $8.50. Joey takes the money and goes to a bar and drinks it up. He comes out of the bar and he sees his trumpet in the pawn shop window for $25. Joey taps on the glass and the pawnshop dealer tells him that he's got an overhead to think about. He also assures Joey that he'll never get that much for it.

Joey turns around and starts walking to the street. He decides that he has nothing to live for and he steps in front of a truck. We see a pedestrian woman scream and Joey falls to the ground.

We then see Joey wake up later that evening where he sees a policeman and he gets up and tries to talk to the policeman and he simply walks away.

Joey walks to the movie theater and he asks a man if he's got a light and the man ignores him. He tries to talk to the woman in the ticket booth and there's no response from her. He walks to another man and he is lighting his cigarette in the mirror and Joey realizes he's not in the mirror.

He initially thinks someone is simply pulling a gag on him. He walks to another man coming out of the theater and he asks him for a light and while it appears that he's going to light Joey's cigarette, he lights his own cigarette.

Joey tries to talk to the woman in the booth again and she still has no response for him. Joey concludes he's dead and he's now a ghost. He walks to his favorite bar and he doesn't recognize anyone in the bar but nobody says anything to him, not even the bartender who doesn't make any acknowledgment when Joey pours himself a drink.

Joey goes back to the club and is surprised to see a woman there that he doesn't know. He then hears someone playing a trumpet in the rafters. He goes up and sees a man in a tuxedo playing the trumpet.

Joey tells him that he plays beautifully. The man looks at him and thanks him and calls him by name. Joey is stunned that the man can see him and hear him and knows his name. Joey asks him if he's also dead. The man explains that no he's not dead and neither is Joey. The people he's encountering are the ones who are dead, they just don't realize it. He explains that it sometimes happens like that so they put them in a familiar surrounding so they can gradually get used to it and they eventually figure it out.

He tells Joey that he's in between. He could go either way. He asks him if he'd like to play the trumpet and Joey tells him he'd love to. Joey plays perfectly this time. The man asks him if he'd like to return. Joey tells him that originally he wanted to die and that's why he stepped in front of the truck. However, he's started remembering all of the good times that he had. He just forgot about the life he had before he started drinking. He'd like to go back and play his trumpet again.

The man tells him then by all means to go back. He takes the trumpet and starts to walk away. Joey calls out to him and asks what his name is. The man turns around with a light over him much like a halo and he tells him name is Gabe, short for Gabriel. He walks off in the darkness.

Joey runs back to the scene of the accident and sees his trumpet in the window and then he sees himself lying on the sidewalk. The man in the truck gets out and helps Joey get up. He asks him if he's all right. He apologizes and tells him he just didn't see him. Joey tells him he wasn't looking to where he was going.

The man tells him he hasn't had an accident in fourteen years so he'd appreciate it if he just didn't say anything since he's going to be all right. He hands Joey a handful of money. Joey walks in to the pawnshop and he buys his trumpet back.

We then see Joey sitting on top of his apartment building playing his trumpet and playing it well. All of a sudden there's a young woman on the roof telling Joey that he plays beautifully and would he play more for her. Joey tells her that he'll play anything she wants to hear.

The woman tells him her name is Nan and she just moved to New York. Joey tells her she'll love it there and tells her about all of the sites. Nan asks him if he'd show them to her. Joey tells her that he'd love to show all of those places.

So, the episode ends where Joey has a new lease on life and a possible soul mate as well.

Overall, I liked this episode. No, there's nothing really scary that happens but this is a different twist on the idea of death. Joey here has a choice between dying and living. Another twist is that the people Joey are encountering are already dead.

Jack Klugman is a terrific actor and while he is not a trumpet player, according to the companion book, he met with a trumpet player to learn fingering so he could make the scenes of himself playing the trumpet look authentic. He makes Joey believable too.

I found Joey a likable and sympathetic character. Everybody gets down on their luck from time to time and Joey is basically been given a gift, a chance to reflect to see if he wants to go on. In the end it's the right decision. He begins to see the world from a different perspective.

Overall I am going to give this episode a four rating for excellent. We don't see too many really happy ending episodes from the Twilight Zone so to get one every once in awhile, it's kind of treat.

Review by Bobbynear

In some instances, acting trumps the story that surrounds it and that is the case here. There is nothing terribly original about yet another tale of a talented man, this time with a trumpet, finding more solace in a bottle than in his success as a musician.

But Jack Klugman makes this story work. Mainly by making Joey a sympathetic character who can and does change his ways after getting the unusual chance to watch himself die and then thinking it over. Oh sure it's easy to be critical of a man who squanders his talent like this, but Klugman makes believers out of viewers...making them understand that Joey really wants to change and that he can if just given a second chance.

I certainly do agree with Linn that Jack Klugman has been for many decades one of his generation's greatest actors. Klugman always throws himself into a role making you quickly forget he's just acting, whether in straight dramas or as the sloppy half of television's oddest couple. No doubt this is why he appears no less than four times as a guest star during the run of this series.

I also agree with Kitty that this is indeed an unusual change of pace. With all of its legendary twists and surprising outcomes, there isn't much room in The Twilight Zone for happy endings...except here, where an accomplished actor makes you understand that there are many ways to die inside while still being alive on the outside and vice versa, and how to change that around and be alive both ways.

Maybe not all that original, but a quiet and thought provoking value lesson that got through to me.

My rating on a scale of 0 to 5

4 ~~ EXCELLENT

Review by Ken

The Zone decides to enter the world of music and religion. An angel named Gabe makes a strange appearance. I am wondering if the writer borrowed a theme from that classic movie 'It's a Wonderful Life.' A man get's to see life beyond death. Joey gets hit by a car and sees what happens afterward. Everybody ignores him because either he is dead or all the people he sees are dead. No reflection in the mirror. Bizarre.

Enter Gabe who talks about how great life can be. Joey can go back and play his trumpet again. A lovely lady is attracted and Joey can show her the town. Okay. But why take so long to get to this point. Again I want to see the relationship develop between Joey and the lady. I will never know. The Twilight Zone wants you to wonder and guess.

I liked the trumpet playing and the music sounded great. But not much else to get excited about. But I was surprised to see Gabe the angel. First question I would ask. How old are you? Did you come down from heaven? Did you meet Adam and Eve? Noah? Abraham? Slow story. My rating 2-Average

Review by Linn

I have always loved Jack Klugman. I don't think I've ever seen this man in anything that I didn't like. The Odd Couple would never have worked without him. This Twilight Zone episode is no exception. I didn't love this episode, but I did like it.

Jack made it work. It reminded me in some ways of the classic Christmas movie "It's A Wonderful Life" but I had no problem with that. It still worked. I'm not sure if that was Jack actually playing the trumpet or not, but it was a good episode.

Sometimes I wonder what my life would look like if I was no longer around. What would people say about me? Would anyone miss me? Would anyone care? Who knows, but I don't want to know.

Once you die, you will never know, but Joey got to know, so for that reason I will give this episode a 3 for good because I love Jack Klugman and everything he does, he does wonderfully.

"The Twilight Zone" Episode 33 "Mr. Bevis"

Original Air Date- June 3, 1960
Guest Star- Orson Bean
Written by Rod Serling
Directed by William Asher

Review by Kitty

This episode is called Mr. Bevis. I would have to call this a lighter fare type of episode.

Mr. Bevis starts out his morning in an apartment that is in shambles as he frantically runs around the place with a coffee cup in his hand and he is scurrying out the door to get to work.

He puts down the coffee cup and as he walks out, he's greeted by a dog in the hallway. The small dog is friendly to him and he allows him to pick him up and carry him down the stairs.

As he walks down the stairs, he sees the banister just calling to him to slide down it. One boy calls to him to do it. Bevis puts down the dog and slides down the banister and out the door and on to the street. The children of the neighborhood help him up. His landlady is not amused. Before leaving for work, he plays ball a bit with the children on the street.

Bevis goes to his car, a 1924 Rickenbacker and needs the kids help to get it going, so they all give him a push and off he goes. Bevis's office is a typical office with many desks but his looks like a museum as his boss Mr. Peckinpaugh puts it and tells the ladies there to tell Bevis that he wants to see him immediately when he gets there.

Bevis does arrive and goes in to Peckinpau's office and is promptly fired for being late, low production levels, having his desk look like a museum, playing zither music and bringing in Christmas carolers in to sing to the employees during business hours.

Bevis sadly fills a box with his stuff and walks out. As he walks out, another car backs in to his car, locks bumpers and drags it down the street before it breaks loose and falls sideways on the road. Bevis asks a policeman if he's ever had one of those days.

Bevis walks back to his apartment, only to find himself getting evicted for being six weeks late on his rent. This poor man is certainly having a bad day to say the least.

Bevis goes to a bar to drown his sorrows and as he is fully loaded on liquor, he sees a man in the mirror waving to him. He turns around and doesn't see the man. However, when he looks in the mirror, he sees him again. He asks the bartender if he sees the man in the mirror and the bartender doesn't know who he's referring to.

Bevis gets up and goes to the table. The kindly man appears to him and tells him that he's his guardian angel J. Hardy Hempstead. He explains that several hundred years ago, an ancestor of his did something very altruistic and therefore, he's been assigned to one descendants guardian angel in each generation and it's his turn.

Hempstead proposes that he make the day start over again with changes so that his day will go better. Bevis likes the idea. The first thing Hempstead does, is change his clothes. Bevis no longer is going to wear bow ties and checkered jackets. He now looks like an undertaker as Bevis puts it.

Bevis walks out of his apartment and is surprised that the dog doesn't like him this time. He goes to slide down the banister but Hempstead stops him. Bevis walks out to his landlady and she thanks him for giving her the rent three weeks in advance.

He tries to play with the kids but they are ignoring him. He then looks for his car and Hempstead tells him that he doesn't drive a Rickenbacker anymore but a fancy two seater sports car.

Bevis drives it to work and he sees his desk with nothing on it. Peckinpau comes out and tells everybody that he's going to raise Bevis's salary by $10 per week. Bevis is perplexed and asks him about the Christmas carolers and he asks him what Christmas carolers.

Bevis decides he needs to get some air. Bevis tells Hempstead that he's grateful for the raise but he'd just as soon go home and play ball with the kids. Hempstead tells him that the kids won't play with him now. Things are different.

Bevis then decides that if he can't play ball with the kids and listen to zither music and build model ships, then he'd rather go back to being himself. Hempstead tells him that things will be back to the way they were and he said that's fine with him.

Bevis is back in his old suit and he goes in and is promptly fired. He sees his car wrecked again and yet when he's in the bar drowning his sorrows, he's now happy to be himself. He tells the bartender that he lost his job, his car and his place to live but that's OK because it's happened before.

Bevis walks outside and is surprised to see his car there but, it's about to get ticketed because it's in front of a fire hydrant. However, the cop looks again and realizes the fire hydrant is in front of his motorcycle. Bevis shrugs his shoulders and gets in to his car and drives off, smoke and all and very happy indeed.

I wouldn't say I disliked this episode. I had not seen it before so I didn't know what to expect. I found Bevis a likeable enough character. He's your typical eccentric who marches to the beat of his own drum and you have to admire him for that. He truly does care about the people around him. One could make the case that if there were more Bevis's in the world, perhaps the world would be a kinder place.

However, I found the ending a little empty. I would have liked to have known what happened to Bevis. Since Hempstead was still looking out for him, I was expecting Bevis to finally find the right job that would be a perfect fit for him. Right now, he seems a bit like a misfit who's lost. Granted, he's a happy misfit who's lost but it still would have been better to see more resolution to this.

I think Serling here was trying to be kind of cute and funny. I don't know if it really works that well because Bevis is treated so badly by his boss and his landlady that what makes the character endearing is a little bit lost.

Overall though, I would say that I liked it all right. I give it a two rating for average.

Review by Linn

Oh no no no. Really terrible episode. A nerdy, geeky, loser of a guy loves his nerdy, geeky, loser of a life. Okay, that's cool. But then he gets a guardian angel who gives him an incredibly wonderful life and he doesn't want it.

Are you serious? He gets a fantastic car, a great job promotion and all kinds of other things, but he prefers his broken down car, his lousy job and his horrible landlady. Go for it, Bevis, but as they say, don't look a gift horse in the mouth. I hated this episode and give it a lousy zero 0 rating.

Review by Ken

A light heart story about man who meets his guardian angel after having a bad day at the office and a notice that he is being evicted from his home. Orson Bean plays the part of a loser who does not care what people think about him. He likes his clunky car and old antiques. He clothes are an eye sore but that is his nature.

How would you like to be Orson Bean in 1960. The Twilight Zone calls and says can you play the part of clumsy but nice guy. "Sure, why not. I need the money and this will look good on my resume."

Side note. Did not the last episode also deal with an angel. Back to back themes should be avoided.

His guardian angel changes everything without asking and Bevis is a new man. But oddly Bevis prefers his old self. So the story ends with Bevis looking and acting like a loser happy as can be.

Comic relief does not work for me in this series. The Twilight Zone deals with the abnormal and strange. This story veers off into nothing. Even though my interest and curiosity kept me tuned in, I had an empty feeling at the end. One viewing is enough. A few chuckles from me. After wasting 30 minutes of precious time on this earth I feel cheated and disgusted with myself. I could have used the extra time tuning in to Peyton Place. They use pretty girls.

My rating-1 Poor

Review by Bobbynear

What? Another guardian angel story? Say what?? Another lovable loser who gets what he thinks he wants and lives to regret it? What happened to my science fiction series? What happened to my series about weird out of this world events that startle everyone? The Twilight Zone sinks into a morass of sentimental goop that threatens to change history that hasn't even been written yet.

I'm not about to rehash the details that have already been given here. Orson Bean is admittedly, the perfect choice for this part, but watching it once is challenging while watching it again is an endurance test. He only had to act in it...plus he got paid.

Memo to Rod Serling: If this loser, along with that love struck idiot with the "glove cleaner" want to have things a certain way, that's their business....just don't tell me about it.

Hint to Serling: Combine this idiot Bevis with the delusional fool from the previous story...and call it Beavis And Butthead.... Do it now before someone else does and makes millions off of it. My guardian angel loved it...but I didn't.

My rating on a scale of 0 to 5
0 - L-O-U-S-Y

"The Twilight Zone" Episode 34 "The After Hours"

Original Air Date- June 10, 1960
Guest Star- Anne Francis
Written by Rod Serling
Directed by Douglas Heyes

Review by Kitty

This episode is called The After Hours. This episode starts off with a Anne Francis walking in to a department store. Her name is Marcia White. She is looking for a gold thimble for her mother.

She gets on an elevator and the man in the elevator asks her what she's looking for and she tells him a gold thimble. He tells her she needs the ninth floor. As the camera shows the elevator from the outside there is clearly not a ninth floor.

She is taken to the top floor and she walks out and it's dark and barren. She tells him there must be a mistake but the doors close and she's left alone. A woman approaches her from behind a counter and asks if she can help her. She tells her she's looking for a gold thimble as a birthday gift for her mother.

The woman tells her she has one. She takes her to a case with just one thimble in it. Marcia says she'll take it and the woman asks her if she's wants to charge it and Marcia tells her no, she'll pay cash.

She takes the thimble away and the saleswoman calls her by name and asks her if she's happy. Marcia wants to know how she knows her name and the woman tells her she's probably seen her in the store before and Marcia insists that she's never seen her. She also objects to the woman calling her by her first name. The woman apologizes and calls her Miss White.

Marcia runs back in to the elevator and realizes the thimble is scuffed and bent. She wants to make a complaint. The elevator operator takes her to the third floor. The floor manager is telling the store manager that a strange woman is complaining about her thimble that she bought and the manager tells him to take her back to specialty and replace it.

He's telling him that she claims that she bought it on the ninth floor. The store manager says that there is no ninth floor so he goes out to talk to Marcia. He tells Marcia that there is no ninth floor there and asks her if she got a receipt. Marcia tells him no but she sees the saleswoman in the store. She runs up to her only to see that she's a mannequin.

Marcia passes out and wakes up in an office after the store has closed. She finds herself trapped in the store. She walks past all of the mannequins and realizes that one of them looks like the elevator operator from earlier in the day.

All of a sudden, she starts to hear voices calling her name. She looks to all of the mannequins and she runs in the elevator and finds herself back on the ninth floor. When the door opens, it's the mannequin of the woman who sold her the thimble. Marcia crouches to the floor in fear and crying in despair. The woman walks up to her and tells her they'll help her.

As they walk past each mannequin, it comes to life. Marcia then realizes that she's a mannequin. They explain to her that she was due back yesterday and they were starting to get worried. It turns out that mannequins are given a one month vacation each year but they can not overlap each other. The saleswoman is one day late on starting her one month vacation with the real people. She doesn't hold a grudge on Marcia though and out the door she goes.

The man asks her how it was out with the real people. Marcia tells him that it was fun as she takes the stance of a typical mannequin.

The next day Marcia the mannequin is out on the floor and the floor manager walks by her and does a double take.

I did enjoy this episode and it is certainly very creepy. Marc Zicree's book says it's a scary episode and I didn't find it particularly scary but it is creepy and it's got one of the best surprise endings out there. I certainly never thought Marcia was going to turn out to be a mannequin in the end when I saw it for the first time.

Anne Francis and Elizabeth Allen were very good in their parts although I did find the dialog a bit strange between them when Marcia bought the thimble. It was odd to me that she would simply not tell Marcia who she was and that she was honing in on her vacation time.

I am going to give this episode a four rating.

Review by Ken

I first saw this episode way back in the 1960's. Whenever I think about this series and the odd stories this one stays in my memory. Certain T.Z. scripts are really out there and amazing. Who comes up with these zany stories.

Nice casting of Anne Francis to play the role of a woman who is shopping in a store. But why is there no 9th floor and gold thimbles? After Marsha passes out and wakes up the story gives viewers that T.Z feeling. A dark store and nobody around. Anyone can relate to that lonely and scary feeling. Then the climax completely surprised me. The sales lady that helped her earlier is actually a mannequin standing near the elevator. Then a weird thought occurs to me. It is possible that mannequins are really hiding out in the store just waiting for their opportunity to escape into the real world.

The end scene is awesome. Not one or two mannequins but there are ten of them. They all want the chance to live among the human race. Turns out they all take turns. Time for Marsha White to pose frozen for the store again.

Even to this day when I am in the mall I stare at mannequins. Is there life beneath that outward shell. Could it be they know what the store shoppers are doing. I would not mind if some of the Victoria Secret' models would come to life.

Anne Francis joins my T.Z. hall of fame for women.

Nice twist of a story to present in this series. My rating-4 Excellent.

Review by Bobbynear

After so many unfortunate end of season one forays into the world of comedy and fantasy, The Twilight Zone returns at last to its roots. A short trip into a duplicate world that we neither know about or could possibly ever understand even if we did and the effect is positively scintillating.

I first saw this episode when I was thirteen years old and knew better....but much earlier in life when I was a very small child, things were a lot different. My mother and older sister used to drag me along with them every Saturday to various department stores rather than pay a babysitter to watch me.

They would go into dressing rooms and try on clothes, leaving me standing just outside of the rooms usually surrounded by these odd looking plastic and plaster people who never seemed to move. Yes Virginia, there was actually a time in America when you could leave your child alone for five minutes and not worry that his face would end up on a milk carton or on a syndicated tv program searching for child molesters.

But that was no comfort for me. I was convinced, like Ken, that this wasn't what it seemed to be. These people had to be real. Perhaps just salespeople watching for shop lifters, or perhaps something far more sinister. I was determined to get them to give themselves away so I would stare at them endlessly figuring they had to blink or sneeze or cough or go to the bathroom or something eventually.

But I was like that. When I was given my very first wristwatch as a birthday present, I couldn't understand how the time changed but I could never see the "hands" move. So I spent hours staring at that too, until one day things got the better of me and I decided to take it apart to find out, only to have the entire insides fall out into my hands.

That was a rather innocent trip into curiosity compared to the mannequins who really did scare me. It never occurred to me that they might live in their own world. They might decide to make me a part of theirs.

I was afraid that they might kidnap me off the floor and I would end up in the boy's department wearing one of the latest fall coats or lost forever in the pages of the Sears catalog and never get the chance to grow up.

Now, thanks to Rod Serling, I know I had reason to worry.

Creepy, disturbing,, dark and scary, The After Hours is firmly planted in the deepest regions of The Twilight Zone. One of the very best episodes.

My rating on a scale of 0 to 5

5 ~~ CLASSIC

Review by Linn

Oh yes. Now we get to an episode that I absolutely love. This is one of the best that the Twilight Zone has to offer.

Do mannequins really come alive? Wouldn't that be cool? Here's an episode where mannequins get to come alive for one month per year and live their lives as real live people. Marsha comes alive but forgets when her time is up. She tries to buy a golden thimble for her mother from one of the other mannequins. It's the only item in the display case. What baffled me about this one was if they each had to take turns being alive, why was the elevator operator who was also a mannequin alive and why was the woman who sold her the thimble alive?. Didn't they have to take turns? If they were already alive and hanging around, what was the problem? Just go and do your thing. I don't know, but I loved this episode very much so I looked beyond the craziness and just enjoyed it.

My rating for this one - 4 for Excellent

"The Twilight Zone" Episode 35 "The Mighty Casey"

Original Air Date- June 17, 1960
Guest Star- Robert Sorrells
Written by Rod Serling
Directed by Robert Parrish and Alvin Ganzer

Review by Kitty

This episode is called The Mighty Casey and clearly borrows from a prior episode called The Lonely and from The Wizard of Oz.

We start out seeing a very empty baseball stadium and it is explained that it is where a team called the Hoboken Zephyrs once played and what we are about to see is a story from the past where it is try out day and we're about to meet a most unusual player named Casey.

There is the manager of the team, McGarry played by Jack Warden. He is speaking to the general manager of the team Beasley. Beasley is basically telling him that if the team doesn't start to win then he's out of a job. The players are pretty pathetic looking.

All of a sudden they get a phone call telling them that a player is coming in to try out. McGarry thinks it's initially a joke when he sees an older man walk in to the dugout named Dr. Stillman. Stillman assures him that he's not the one who's trying out but another person, Casey.

Casey walks up to McGarry to shake his hand and he nearly takes McGarry's hand off. Casey goes out to the field and starts to throw balls to the catcher Monk. He's throwing everything and they are perfect.

Stillman then admits that Casey is a robot and that he's only three weeks old. He created him. McGarry is thrilled as he starts to imagine winning the pennant. He tells Stillman to just keep it between themselves.

McGarry tells Beasley to sign him up. Casey starts to win games for them and pitches one no hitter after another until one day he gets pummeled with a baseball. He's taken to see the team doctor and he's given a clean bill of health which surprises the doctor since he took such a hard blow to the head.

He then tries to feel Casey's pulse and doesn't feel it. He then tries to hear for a heartbeat but can't hear that. Stillman comes clean and tells the doctor that Casey is a robot. The doctor tells them that he's bound to tell the commissioner. The commissioner comes in and tells them that Casey can not play because he is not human.

Stillman asks him what would make him human. The commissioner concurs that if he had a heart that would make him human. Stillman tells him that he can arrange it and the commissioner tells him he can play if he can.

As they wait for Casey to come in from getting a heart McGarry gives everybody a win one for the Gipper speech. Just then, Casey walks in and for the first time we see Casey doing something he's never done before. He is smiling. Casey puts on his uniform and proceeds to throw every softball in the world to the opponent.

At the end of the first inning, the visiting team is up 14 runs. Back in the locker room, McGarry wants to know what happened. Casey explains that he didn't want to hurt those poor guys feelings or their careers by striking them out. Stillman explains that with the addition of the heart, Casey has emotions and doesn't understand competitiveness yet.

Casey tells him that he wants to go in to social work and help people. Stillman gives McGarry the blueprints for Casey as a parting souvenir. Stillman leaves and McGarry starts to look at the blueprints. He obviously sees something that he likes because he runs after Stillman on the field to ask him questions.

Rod Serling's voice comes on and explains that this was the final season for the Zephyrs but McGarry took the team to the west coast and won several pennants and series. His baseball players never smiled much though.

As I said at the beginning this is part The Lonely and part The Wizard of Oz with a little of the Knute Rockney Story thrown in for free.

I found it very interesting that Jack Warden ended up in two episodes that dealt with robots. This is obviously a more light hearted episode. The heart with the robot is right out of Oz with the Tin Man taking on a different look. McGarry telling everybody to win one for the big guy is from Knute Rockney telling everybody to win one for the Gipper.

I did enjoy Jack Warden's passion for the game in this episode though. I did find it odd that they would allow the team doctor to examine him because it was only obvious that the doctor would figure it out.

Robert Sorrells as Casey played it with just the right deadpan and naiveté to make it work.

It didn't knock my socks off but I will give it a two rating for a fair episode.

Review by Linn

Absolutely one of the worst Twilight Zone episodes ever. I don't know how they could have ever come up with this one, but I'm sorry they did.

You've got some robotic baseball player which is unreal to begin with and then after getting beaned in the head, he finds feelings and can't play normally anymore. He now can't strike anyone out because he gives a crap. He's a robot. He cannot have feelings or care about anyone. This episode was totally stupid and without any merit or sense. I don't know who came up with this idea, but it stinks.

Rating from me - a multiple zero rating 000000

Review by Bobbynear

Let's see now...we're in the ninth inning of season one of The Twilight Zone...and a love struck jackass and a brainless boob who actually enjoys getting stepped on, have been up to the plate and both have gone down swinging...

Two outs...time is running out...what to do? Hey, how about a baseball story....everybody loves baseball....almost anything can happen in the Twilight Zone...

How about updating to the future...Babe Ruth comes back to life and is sensational only nobody believes he could be that good without the use of performance enhancing drugs...plus he makes the mistake of betting on baseball games other than his own team...and he gets kicked out of both baseball and the Hall Of Fame...Nah...nobody would believe it...

How about a losing team creates a star pitcher out of a robot and wins it all...or at least would have if only he had a heartbeat...Hmm...I can think of plenty of ballplayers today who have no heart...and they're still playing.

Hey Rod...want to do a bizarre sports story? Try this...An ultra famous and talented athlete with a drop dead gorgeous wife and enough money and product endorsements to eat for dinner, plus the adoration of millions who don't even know how to play his game....decides to throw it all away for a few moments of pleasure with a variety of expensive whores and cocktail waitresses.... Nah....even in The Twilight Zone that won't fly.

Final Score: Hoboken Zephyrs - 0

Twilight Zone Viewers - 0

Scorecard: No hits No runs Lots of errors

Game called on account of stupidity.

My rating on a scale of 0 to 5

0 -- LOUSY

Review by Ken

Twilight Zone enters the sports world. We saw boxing in ep.27 'The Big Tall Wish.' Now baseball takes center stage. A pitcher has a canny knack for throwing fast-balls and curve-balls by hitters. Robert Sorrells was poorly cast as a the ballplayer who really is a robot with no heart. The scenes on the mound were awful. He winds up to throw the pitch and the camera zooms in on another pitcher who has a nice windup and delivery. I was not fooled at all. C'mon producers at least cast an actor who can throw a baseball over the plate.

The story drags on with the Zephyrs winning their games. Suddenly, the commissioner decides to suspend Casey because he has no pulse and heartbeat. The scientist who created Casey obliges and gives Casey a heart. Now Casey lets everybody hit home runs off him. What a shock. The story comes to a pathetic conclusion with the manager hoping he can use Casey's blueprints and make another robot. Jack Warden is cast as the overweight manager. Again terrible casting. I liked him stranded on that asteroid way back in ep.7 'The Lonely' playing checkers with Alicia. What is up with Warden and robots. I suffered watching this mess.

My rating-0 Lousy.

"The Twilight Zone" Episode 36 "A World Of His Own"

Original Air Date- July 1, 1960
Guest Star- Keenan Wynn
Written by Richard Matheson
Directed by Ralph Nelson

Review by Ken

What a nice, gentle, and crafty way to end season one of a science fiction series but to tell a sweet, kind, tender, soft, considerate, charitable, pleasant, light-hearted, amiable, compassionate, sympathetic, understanding, helpful, obliging, neighborly, accommodating, delicate, easy-going, good-natured, patient, tolerant, mellow, genial, sensitive, courteous, agreeable, thoughtful, and most of all well-disposed story about a playwright who can anytime describe a character in detail and presto that person comes to life before his gleaming and lustful eyes.

Only three people and an elephant are needed to be cast and the set only needs an office with a fireplace in order to produce this episode. Rod Serling himself decides he needs to fulfill his life-long dream of appearing on television. So why not show up at the end only to show the magic of how to appear and disappear on screen. End the season on a comic note and see you next season because he already knows the series has been renewed.

Keenan Wynn is cast to play Gregory West who can talk in a voice that soothes anyone listening. All he cares about is Mary who pours him a drink and rests her head on his shoulder. Mary La Roche plays the part of this man's fantasy and pleads with him please don't send me away again.

The highlight of the story is Gregory's wife who comes home and finds out what her husband has been up too. Phyllis Kirk plays the man's wife and is determined to find out about his infidelity. She threatens to leave him but an elephant will have no part of it. Meanwhile Gregory is confused and learns the lesson about his characters. He needs to fine tune them next time so he will have no problems in the future. So goodbye old wife and hello my new love.

Throw the old tapes in the fireplace because I want to rest up on the couch and snuggle up with Mary. Hey Rod you are history too.

I am embarrassed and abashed to comment on this story. I was hoping this season ending episode would even top 'Mirror Image', 'Time Enough at Last', 'The Hitch-Hiker', 'People are Alike All Over', 'Willoughby', or 'Monsters Due on Maple Street.'

Instead I am reminded that writers, directors, producers can sometimes resort to laziness, sluggishness, apathetic, dallying, loafing, lagging, inattentive, flagging, weariness, careless, lethargic, and most of all asleep on the job.

Sorry guys. My rating for the season monumental climax is 0. Lousy.

Side note: Phyllis Kirk joins my T.Z. Hall of Fame for women. Anyone who puts up with Gregory and an elephant gets sympathy from me. Besides with all that makeup she has on how could I resist.

Review by Linn

In my opinion, this is one of the greatest Twilight Zone episodes ever. First off, Keenan Wynn was great in his role of writer Gregory West. Then he has this absolutely beautiful woman named Mary played by Mary La Roche and then he has this horrible wife (once again we get a horrible wife in an episode) named Victoria. He is able to bring people alive from his stories simply by describing them.

Luckily for him, he brought his horrible wife alive and was able to get rid of her. Then he brought Mary back. Yes, Mary. The sweet woman he should have brought to life in the first place.

The reason why I love this episode so much is because Rod Serling shows up at the end and for the first time in any episode, he becomes a part of it. Gregory gives Rod a bit of a mild brow beating for saying that all of this bringing people to life through a tape recorder is nonsense, so he tells Rod that he's very wrong and takes out the envelope that says "Rod Serling" on it and throws it into the fireplace and eliminates Rod. Oh well.

My rating for this one is a 5 - Classic rating - Rod Serling never showed up as a part of any other episode but this one so this makes it classic to me.

Review by Kitty

We have come to the end of season one and this episode is called A World of His Own.

We start out by seeing an average middle class looking home and inside is a middle aged man by the name of Gregory West. We see Gregory looking very happy as a beautiful woman is handing him a drink. She is clearly his mistress as he refers to her as such.

However, enter the wife looking through the window. She clearly is not a happy camper at what she's seeing. Gregory hears his wife Victoria calling to him as she comes in to the house.

Mary is deeply upset by this and begs Gregory not to do what he's about to do and he tells her he has no choice because that's his wife coming through the door. Victoria is banging on the door to the study and wants to be let in.

Gregory answers the door with his scissors in hand and Victoria storms in and proceeds to start looking for Mary. She can not find her anywhere. She asks Gregory if there are any secret doors in the room and he tells her no.

She demands to know about the woman she saw in the room. Gregory tells her that she must have imagined her. Victoria gives him the full details of the woman and Gregory is impressed that she imagined someone with so much detail. Victoria demands the truth or she's leaving him.

Gregory explains to her that he writes his plays by dictating them in to a tape recorder. He explains that he is able to give so much detail that the characters come to life. He tells her about a character he wrote named Philip Wainwright and that he came to life one day and they had a conversation and that was what Mary was, a character that he described who came to life.

Victoria thinks Gregory is crazy and starts to pick up the phone to call her lawyer to have her committed. Gregory puts the phone down and locks the door and tells her he'll prove it to her. He describes Mary in to the recorder and while he's doing that, Victoria steals the key from his pocket and opens the door but to her astonishment, Mary walks in to the house.

Victoria thinks this is just a trick. Gregory proves to her that it's no trick. He takes the tape that he just recorded of Mary and he throws it in the fire and Mary disappears. Victoria still thinks he's crazy and she proceeds to leave. Gregory tells the tape recorder that there is a giant elephant with red eyes in their hallways and sure enough a big elephant appears to Victoria. She starts to scream and runs back in to the study.

She truly believes Gregory and she tells him she'll stay for the time being but she will eventually leave him. Gregory goes to a safe and he takes out an envelope with Victoria's name on it and he shows her the tape that describes her. He tells her that she is his creation.

Victoria thinks he's just playing with her mind and she grabs the tape and throws it in the fire. She then realizes he was telling the truth as she disappears.

Gregory runs to the tape recorder and starts to recreate Victoria but then stops and realizes he'd prefer to have Mary be his wife instead and Mary appears before him and fixes him a drink.

The final scene is rather cute. Rod Serling appears in front of the camera in an episode for the time and starts to tell us all that what we saw was purely fictitious but Gregory gets up and takes an envelope out of the safe with Rod Serling's name on it and he throws that in the fire and Rod disappears.

All in all, a cute and entertaining episode. I enjoyed the interaction between Keenan Wynn and Phyllis Kirk as Gregory and Victoria. It's also a fun ending to the season to see Rod Serling appear in the actual episode. It's obviously a precursor to what was in store for future episodes.

I will give it a three for good.

Review by Bobbynear

I'm afraid I have little to say about this episode. Not only because it is so awful, but because of where it is located.

It's just flat out incredible that a series like The Twilight Zone would end its first season with a story like this. As if it wasn't bizarre enough to have comical hard to take seriously stories like, "Mr. Bevis" and "The Chaser" and "The Mighty Casey"...along comes one to trump them all.

The story itself may not be as horrible as some we've had to sit through, if that is you like this sort of thing...I don't....but the real problem is that it almost makes a mockery of all that has come before it.

The Twilight Zone is supposed to be dark and forbidding and...well...scary. Had they done say about 75 episodes over more than two years, a little kidding around might have been a release from all the terror. But coming at the end of season one, it's just baffling frankly.

I believe firmly in closing strong....whether it's in a tv season or a sports season. No playoffs in television however. Just a long hot summer in which people need to recall just why they watched the series in the first place. To say nothing of the promises ahead. Just how terrifying will it be in season two?

Apparently not much. So much frivolity recently leads me to believe it's turning into a sitcom with the creator as one of the co-stars. I sure hope not because Rod Serling's talent, if we go by this appearance remains firmly ensconced in writing and not in acting. His appearance at the end of the story didn't make me laugh. Too gimmicky for my taste.

It's interesting to note that in Martin Grams Jr's book on The Twilight Zone, it is written that this story by Richard Matheson was originally done as a serious one but that Serling insisted that it be rewritten in a lighter vein.

Too bad. All of this business with people throwing scripts into that fireplace to make characters disappear might have been put to better use by throwing this script in there first.

Let the summer rerun season begin. At least we'll be able to relive the glory days of "The Hitch Hiker" and "The Monsters Are Due On Maple Street"

I'm afraid I have to agree with Ken....
My rating on a scale of 0 to 5
0 - LOUSY

TWILIGHT HALL OF FAME (SEASON ONE)

The first season of "The Twilight Zone" is known for it's actors and actresses outstanding, momentous, critical, unforgettable, crucial, famous, illustrious, distinguished, great, notable, significant, decisive, enduring, lasting, eventful, interesting, exceptional, unusual, and monumental performances that make this series a grand success. In order to be nominated to the Twilight Zone Hall of Fame the episode the actors starred in needed to receive a majority of classic or excellent ratings from members in the Yahoo group site.

Here is a list of nominees:

Earl Holliman	Ep.1	"Where is Everybody?"
Jack Warden	Ep.7	"The Lonely"
Burgess Meredith	Ep.8	"Time Enough At Last"
Nehemiah Persoff	Ep.10	"Judgment Night"
Steve Cochran	Ep.12	"What You Need"
Ernest Truex	Ep.12	"What You Need"
Inger Stevens	Ep.16	"The Hitch-Hiker"
Vera Miles	Ep.21	"Mirror Image"
Martin Milner	Ep.21	"Mirror Image"
Claude Akins	Ep.22	"The Monsters Are Due On Maple St."
Jack Weston	Ep.22	"The Monsters Are Due On Maple St."
Roddy McDowall	Ep.25	"People Are Alike All Over"
Susan Oliver	Ep.25	"People Are Alike All Over"
Albert Salmi	Ep.26	"Execution"
James Daly	Ep.30	"A Stop At Willoughby"
Jack Klugman	Ep.32	"A Passage For Trumpet"
Anne Francis	Ep.34	"The After Hours"

BEST TO WORST EPISODES (SEASON ONE)

Group members from 'The Twilight Zone Revisited and Reviewed' Yahoo discussion group gave their ratings to each episode. The ratings followed this criteria:

- 5 - CLASSIC - Unforgettable ~ The very best The Twilight Zone has to offer
- 4 - EXCELLENT - Falls just short of classic but still very interesting and memorable
- 3 - GOOD - Very much above average but with too many flaws to be rated higher
- 2 1/2 - FAIR (SLIGHTLY ABOVE AVERAGE) - One or two fairly good points about it make it only slightly above average
- 2 - AVERAGE - Nothing special about it
- 1 - POOR - Barely Watchable but very disappointing and not up to usual Twilight Zone standards
- 0 - (LOUSY) TOTALLY WITHOUT MERIT - Boring, badly paced and poorly acted episode that I completely disliked. Very forgettable, have no desire to see it again.

Below is the following results from Best to Worst Episodes.

	Episode	Rating
1.	Time Enough At Last	Classic
2.	The Hitch-Hiker	Classic
3.	The Monsters Are Due On Maple Street	Classic
4.	People Are Alike All Over	Classic
5.	Mirror Image	Classic
6.	A Stop At Willoughby	Classic
7.	What You Need	Classic
8.	The Lonely	Classic
9.	Where is Everybody	Classic
10.	The After Hours	Excellent
11.	One For The Angels	Excellent
12.	Judgment Night	Excellent

13.	Walking Distance	Excellent
14.	A Passage For Trumpet	Excellent
15.	Execution	Excellent
16.	Elegy	Good
17.	The Fever	Good
18.	Perchance To Dream	Good
19.	The Purple Testament	Good
20.	A Nice Place To Visit	Good
21.	Escape Clause	Good
22.	The Big Tall Wish	Average
23.	And When The Sky Was Opened	Average
24.	The Four Of Us Are Dying	Average
25.	Mr. Denton On Doomsday	Average
26.	I Shot An Arrow Into The Air	Poor
27.	Long Live Walter Jameson	Poor
28.	Mr. Bevis	Poor
29.	Nightmare As A Child	Poor
30.	A World Of Difference	Poor
31.	The Sixteen-Millimeter Shrine	Poor
32.	Third From The Sun	Lousy
33.	The Last Flight	Lousy
34.	A World Of His Own	Lousy
35.	The Mighty Casey	Lousy
36.	The Chaser	Lousy

EPILOGUE

If you would like to become a part of the continuing discussion, you are invited to join our group at-
http://tv.groups.yahoo.com/group/thetwilightzonerevisitedandreviwed/

You can also discuss all aspects of the series, live on the air or via email on Talk Shoe. Visit our Twilight Zone website and click on the links to the show and the archives.

Much has been written about this classic tv series. Now for the first time ever, fans will get a chance to write their own reviews of episodes and even take part in viewer polls.

One strong word of warning. The Twilight Zone is well know for its numerous trick and twist endings and our reviews will be giving them away in order to fully cover each episode. Take this spoiler warning seriously and if you are one of the few people who have not seen these episodes, take the time to view them first. They are all available and are frequently shown on cable's Sci Fi Channel and as a dvd set.

Ken, Kitty, Linn, Bobbynear.

"There is a fifth dimension beyond that which is known to man. It is a dimension as vast as space and as timeless as infinity. It is the middle-ground between light and shadow, between science and superstition, and it lies between the pit of man's fears and the summit of his knowledge. This is the dimension of imagination. It is an area which we call the 'Twilight Zone.'

Rod Serling ~ October 1959

Made in the USA
Middletown, DE
02 April 2023

28076782R00168